"Invisible threads are the strongest ties."

Friedrich Nietzsche

ISABEL...
A stone's throw from Santiago de Compostela's towering cathedral Isabel's marriage hangs by a thread as her husband plots the ultimate betrayal.

ANGELA...
Only silence has kept the blackness at bay since the day the policeman called to say that Daddy was dead. But Angela is about to suffer another loss.

MARK...
In a desperate attempt to shed half his body weight, Mark is walking the Camino de Santiago before his online girlfriend discovers that his social media profile pictures are digitally doctored.

FR DELUCCI...
Just hours behind Mark, the priest has also set out upon the Way. What he experiences in the days ahead will either renew his commitment to the Church or see him abandon it for good.

THE VAGABUNDO...
Meanwhile, on a bridge spanning the mighty River Minho – the natural border separating Portugal from Spain – a tramp is about to make a discovery.

Pins and Needles is a tale of turning points upon Spain's ancient and mystical Camino de Santiago.

THE SOUP OF THE TIRED HORSE: *Cassidy, with some fellow pilgrims that he'd met along the way, at a converted stable on the outskirts of Porriño. Here he discovered "la sopa del caballo cansado" – a Spanish excuse for an early glass of the delicious local Albariño wine. The experience of the character Mark, related on page 103, is directly inspired by this day.*

About the author

Cassidy's journey has taken him from journalism, through film making to creative writing. His shift from fact to fiction came in 2007 when he was commissioned by Amnesty International to make a short drama on human rights. Success followed with his 2008 Irish Film Board funded *Whatever Turns You On* scooping major awards at film festivals around the world. After it's *Best Short Film* win in Aspen, Colorado, USA it qualified for *Academy Award* consideration in 2010.

A move to Hollywood was abandoned at the news that his father, an artist who had been a key inspiration for the film maker, was suffering from terminal cancer. Cassidy's debut novel, *Pins and Needles,* had set out as an idea for a film script. It became a book, instead, developed and written in Ireland with his father over the period leading to and after his death in November 2014.

Cassidy walked the section of the *Camino de Santiago* upon which the book is set over ten times during the writing of the novel.

"I could wallpaper a bedroom with the certificates that they give you for walking *the Camino* at this point," he jokes, "but *The Way* has become incredibly important to me. Each time I've walked it I've had a completely unique experience, with new people to meet and new insights to realise."

Cassidy is currently developing the book's sequel, *Sticks and Stones,* which will see a return of some of the first novel's characters and the introduction of new ones.

"Working in film is very enjoyable with the controlled madness of the set and collaboration with so many talented people," remarks Cassidy. "There's something about writing a book, though, that is truly satisfying. You sit in a coffee shop in some obscure corner of the world and bring all of these characters to life. Then, like a worried parent, you send them out there, hoping that they'll make a few friends and avoid getting bullied."

Declan J Cassidy

To my Dad for leading by example,
for the endless encouragement and
for the great gift of eccentricity.

Thanks to Gillian for the spark of the idea on that sunny day at a family lunch by the sea, to my family for all the love, patience and encouragement, to Ita Kennedy for suggesting that the book should come before the film, to Sean O'Flaherty for the time and advice, to friends who read drafts and made suggestions, to Tanya and Grace for not giving up, to Fiona Ashe for her professionalism and input, to Martha Christie for her unwavering faith, to Martine, Jacinta and Moira for constructive criticism and the female perspective, to my older, wiser brother Chris for the humour, to Bill, Ken, Richie and Darren — my four pillars of friendship, to Carmen for checking the Spanish, to Jason for the long chats, to Sophia for the comma, to the inspirational Dr Susana Bayo Belenguer and her team in the Department of Hispanic Studies in Trinity College Dublin for nurturing my love and understanding of the culture, to Aiden Maher, my old english teacher from Beneavin College who, against all the odds, nurtured my love of the language, to my long–suffering Mum for her unshakeable love and approval and to Philip Land without whose friendship, advice and support my way would doubtlessly have been a lesser way.

COVER ART: *from a painting by my talented sister and good friend Moira Cassidy.*

Many paths, one destination...

Pins and Needles

Declan J Cassidy

ISBN 978-1-9998051-0-4

Author blog at:
www.declancassidy.com

Published by screenpublications.com 2017
Printed in the European Union

mail@screenpublications.com

A division of Timesnap Limited, Ireland

1

Contents

1. James

*"But every man is tempted, when he is drawn away
of his own lust, and enticed."*

SANTIAGO DE COMPOSTELA, SPAIN
– 12 years ago

THE FOUR MEN, *bedecked in their gaudy ceremonial hats, knee
high boots and starched white shirts, laboured gamely under the
weight of the platform. Upon it, its feet obscured by the intricately
woven floral wreaths, the statue of the saint swayed from side to
side like a drunk. Behind them, Don Juan Sebastian Quintana
strode with small, deliberate steps. It was the first year that he had
been granted the honour of walking at the head of the* Procesión
del Patronato del Apóstol Santiago, *and he soaked up the attention of the colourful crowd that lined the narrow streets of the old
town. His short but heavy frame did much to shield the girl from
the crude public gaze, but Anxo saw her at once and their eyes
met. He was slouched nonchalantly against one of the columns of
the long portico that ran down the flagstoned street, holding court
to the inevitable group of giggling girls. Anxo winked and Isabel
flinched, feeling her face redden as she turned her head hurriedly
to focus on the finely tailored seam that ran down the back of her
father's coat. Anxo grinned and the girls who were competing for
his favour turned to see what had captured his attention.*

Quintana's daughter had turned out to be quite a guapa, *the
young man mused, and although she had looked away when he
winked, he had noted her discomfort with a sense of satisfaction.*

3

She would be about 16, he decided. In just a few minutes the procession would be passing by Quintana's stately, historic home close to the heart of the prestigious old city centre. Of course, he had never seen the inside of it but his ripe imagination had no difficulty in conjuring up a vision of solid mahogany furniture, perhaps the armour of a conquistador standing mute guard in the hallway and, in the Don's private study, a generous leather–topped desk. He pictured himself laying Quintana's Catholic–school, virgin daughter across the desk and taking her roughly as she squealed like one of the women from the porn movies in the substantial collection that he kept hidden from his mother under the loose floorboard in his bedroom at home.

"What are you smiling about?" asked a girl whose name he hadn't bothered to remember.

"Nothing."

He watched Señorita Quintana disappear from sight, swallowed up by the body of the procession that followed in the wake of her father. I must find out her name, he thought.

Isabel gave a gasp of relief as the procession finally turned a corner, leaving him and his groupies behind. She had imagined that she could feel his eyes burning into her and hadn't dared to look back. Now, safely out of sight, she felt her breathing beginning to return to normal.

"Anxo."

She whispered the name out loud in the noisy din of the procession and it stirred a delicious flood of conflicting emotions. He had seen her. He knew she existed and, just before she'd had to look away, she was almost sure that he had winked. She became suddenly aware that her secret dream had jumped from the secure world of fantasy into the perilous realm of hope. The realisation both thrilled and frightened her. Raising her eyes to the swaying statue upon the platform, she began an earnest prayer to the saint.

SANTIAGO DE COMPOSTELA – Present

"ARE YOU asleep?" he whispered.

She continued to control her breathing. She knew, only too well, the pattern of a sleeping person's breath. When they were first married she would sometimes lie awake, watching him smile in his dreams and thanking *the saint* for making Anxo hers. She had been young and hopeful.

"Isabel."

His voice was urgent. Impatient. A memory, long misplaced but now as vivid as if it had occurred yesterday, sprang to mind. She was at school. The algebra question from last night's homework was written on the blackboard and the teacher's eyes were scanning the class as he decided who he should call forward to demonstrate the solution. That was when the prayers to *the saint* had begun.

"*San Tiago* is in the church there," her mother had explained, pointing from the window over the red tiled rooftops to where one of the towering Gothic cathedral's three steeples rose to fill a gap in the line of closer buildings. "That makes him our neighbour so our prayers go straight to the top of his list."

That memory, along with precious few others, stood out in her mind like glints of gold in the shifting mud of a river bed. The cancer had taken her mother two days before Isabel's sixth birthday despite the little girl's entreaties to *the saint*. Although her father had explained that it had been her mother's 'time' and that nobody should be blamed, Isabel had suspended any communication with her saintly neighbour until that day in school when desperation found her affording him a second chance. This time the result was satisfactory. *San Tiago*, it seemed, had succeeded in rendering her invisible to Señor Llabata's searching gaze and had continued to do so faithfully each time he was called upon. *The saint's* intervention didn't, however, prevent the knot of panic that would sit like a cannon ball in her stomach for those few second that dragged on indeterminably while the teacher selected his victim. The loss of her mother had proven, after all, that the system was fallible.

The bed creaked and Isabel's thoughts were snapped rudely back to the present. She let her body fall slack, allowing herself to slide forward a little as the mattress dipped under Anxo's weight. She feigned a sleeper's disturbance – a breath that was half a sigh – and then resumed her slow respiratory rhythm. She heard him fumbling, the distinctive noise of a zipper, and then a chaffing sound as the bed start-ing to creak and shake. His breathing fell quiet for a moment. Then it began to come in small pants, making her own care-fully controlled breaths seem ever more false.

"Bela, wake up *nena*, wake up."

His hand gripped her shoulder and she could no longer reasonably pretend. She opened her eyes, acting the part of one suddenly awakened. He towered over her, the combined street and moon light framing his shoulders and throwing strange shadows across his face that cast him as 'the bad guy' in an old Hollywood 'B' movie. He grunted, drawing her for-ward by the shoulder that he still held.

He didn't speak again until afterwards, as he lay, spent, on the bed, giving an occasional shudder like the last, futile efforts of a dying fish in the bottom of an angler's boat.

"*Joder*, baby. That was so good."

Isabel was lying on her side with her back to him. She was gazing at the dark, wet patch that she had left on the white cotton of the pillowcases.

I only put fresh bedding on today.

She slid out of the bed and stood up.

"Bathroom," she said, glancing at him with a plastic smile that switched off as soon as she had turned away from his self–satisfied gaze.

Behind the sanctuary of the bathroom door she turned on the cold tap and, with some difficulty, due to the small size of the hand basin, managed to get her lips under the flow of wa-ter. She let it fill her mouth and overflow. Outside she heard Anxo leave the bedroom and make his way noisily down the stairs. She took a swig of mouthwash, gargled, spit it out and then, stepping back, stared at herself in the mirror. The woman who looked back at her did so with a care–worn and troubled frown, accentuating the fine lines that had begun to radiate from the corners of her eyes and across her forehead. Not for the first time, Isabel was cast back to a sunny day in *Parque Alameda* on the edge of the old town. She was sitting on one of the white wooden benches with her school friends Carmen and Rosa. They were eating slices of takeaway pizza and discussing their inevitably flawless, rosy futures.

"By my thirtieth birthday I'll be married with three kids – two girls and a boy," she'd said when her turn came. It had all seemed so simple and so desirable then. The memory left her with a sudden sense of grief for the ghost of her naive self – long since crushed beneath the burden of time and decisions.

Turning sideways, she consulted the reflection of her profile. She was surprised at how long she had been able to hide it, but she would not be able to do so for much longer. She had always been slim and the swell of her stomach had become very noticeable to her in the past few days. She felt the now familiar pang of anxiety and the internal argument resumed. They had agreed that they wanted children so Anxo should be happy at the news. They had, however, also decided to wait until her father's inheritance came through.

"We want to be able to give the kid the very best start in life," Anxo had said.

Did it really matter at this stage, though? They had only two years to wait. By the time their child needed anything much beyond basic love and care the money would be there to provide it. The argument rang hollow. If it was so straightforward why had she passed on every opportunity to tell her husband that he was to be a father?

Tomorrow. Tomorrow I'll tell him.

When she emerged she could hear Anxo clattering around noisily in the laundry below. The pillows were strewn across the bed, their soiled pillowcases removed.

That's unusually thoughtful.

BOSTON, USA – 36 years ago

THE MAN WALKED past the basketball court, where an impromptu game amongst local kids had drawn a small but vociferous crowd. He barely glanced. As a child growing up in this same neighbourhood, anyone seeking him would have found him in the thick of the game. But his wife and son would not be there. Joe wasn't that kind of boy.

The small church, with its New England Romanesque detail, looked somewhat out of place amid the square, soulless architecture of the tenements. As he entered the porch the noise and bustle

7

of Saturday, Boston suburbia became instantly muted. He pushed open the heavy wooden door, with its stained glass insets, and stepped into the further silence and gloom of the interior.

As soon as he'd received the call to say that the meeting was cancelled he had rushed home to spend a rare weekend with his family. Anxious not to waste a moment, he hadn't bothered to change from his business suit and polished, black leather shoes. The steel tipped heels on the mosaic tiled floor sent staccato stabs into the silence. His eyes, in making the transition from the harsh midday sunlight to the dusky interior, were drawn to the glow from a blaze of candles in an alcove. It softly illuminated a statue of the Madonna and Child. As he looked the draft that had accompanied his entrance reached the dozens of small flames. The statue seemed to come alive as the warm, flickering light danced across its smooth, alabaster surfaces. The figure of the child was reposing in its mother's arms, its face studying hers with an intelligence that belied its newborn state. She, however, was gazing down past her son with a benign look that seemed to fall somewhere between wisdom and boredom. As his eyes adjusted to the semi–darkness the man saw that the statue's gaze appeared to be fixed on the figure of a woman whose attention, in turn, had been captured by something in the deeper recesses of the church.

He recognised the figure of his wife instantly and sought out the object of her interest. It was his son, kneeling before the old statue of St James the Apostle to whom the church was dedicated.

The boy knelt with a rigid, soldierly perfection, his hands joined in prayer before him, as erect as the blade of a sword. He was concentrating on the face of the towering statue but his reverence, it appeared, was lost upon the cold, stone figure. The statue's head was upturned with an obvious disregard for little boys or, indeed, worldly matters in general. Whether by accident or by design, the artist's chisel had shaped a face of suffering, tempered, somewhat, by a look of holy fortitude. The staring, stone eyes were turned in a permanent communion with the heavens above.

BOSTON, USA – Present

THE PASSAGE of several minutes without the confessional booth door creaking open signalled an end to the line of penitents. Yet Fr Joe Delucci remained, unmoving and unmoved, in the dark and silence. He reflected, with the desperate heaviness of heart that had become an almost constant companion lately, on how his role as a conduit for God's forgiveness had ceased to be the powerful source of joy that it used to represent for him. He had always been able to listen to the sins of his flock – both innocent folly and dire deed – with a comfortable detachment made possible by the knowledge that he would soon sweep the stains clear, leaving the sinner, at least temporarily, cleansed again. His father had kept a small fishing boat on the coast. Each April Joe would help him to hoist it ashore and scrape the accumulated barnacles and seaweed from its bottom before applying the messy, toxic anti–fouling paint to its sanded surfaces and returning it to the water. By the end of summer, it was fouled again but for the first few weeks after they launched her the little boat was as good as new. That, he realised, was the gift that he had been able to give to his parishioners. He had *believed* – and that belief had carried a conviction that allowed them to believe and to leave his confessional with a soul as stain–free as the newly anti–fouled boat. Now, however, he was faking it.

"My faith is built upon solid rock," he remembered glibly informing a school friend who had tried to dissuade him from his priestly vocation. Now *the book* had collided with his rock like the misplaced blow of a sculptor's chisel, and it had sent fractures to the very core. To his parishioners the rock might look intact, but Fr Delucci was all too aware that only force of training and habit were holding the myriad pieces together.

The book in question was a paperback by a South American author whose prolific works dominated the 'self–help' or – depending on the varying systems of categorisation – 'spirituality' shelves of large bookstores. It had been left behind by a parishioner after Mass and the cleaners had deposited it into the 'lost and found' box in the sacristy where Fr Delucci, inspired by idle curiosity, had picked it up. His mother had told him, with great frequency, that the devil made work for idle hands. It had become apparent to the priest, however, that he also made words for unwary minds.

The story was set against the backdrop of the *Camino de*

Santiago – an ancient pilgrim trail that started in the French Pyrenees and crossed about 500 miles to the city of Santiago de Compostela in the Spanish province of Galicia. For Fr Delucci, the quasi–mystical spirituality of the tale leapt vividly from the pages in a way that the biblical stories once did for him but had long since ceased to do.

His reverie was disturbed by the sound of slow footsteps approaching outside. The confessional door creaked open. The booth echoed a single footfall on the wooden floor and then all fell silent. The priest slid back the small wooden hatch that separated his section of the booth from that of the penitent. There was neither sound nor movement in the blackness beyond but he was keenly aware of a presence. After a moment a low, aged voice spoke with a kind of universal English that was hard to place.

"Bless me Father for I have sinned. It is… well, many years since my last confession."

"Not to worry, my son. The main thing is that you are here now," said Fr Delucci.

"Thank you," replied the voice.

There was a heavy silence before it spoke again.

"I'm afraid that's the only bit I remember, Father. What do I say next?"

"Just tell me what's on your mind. What brought you here today?" said the priest, in his warm, long–practised tones of assurance.

The man gave a sigh that seemed burdened with the weight of the world.

"I don't remember the prayer but there was a line in it that I haven't been able to get out of my head today," he began. "*'For what I have done and for what I have failed to do.'* It's what I have failed to do that's on my mind, Father."

"That's from the *Confiteor*. It's in the *Penitential Rite*," said the priest. "Tell me. What is it that you have failed to do?"

"A great many things, Father. Do you know that little voice in our heads that we argue with constantly?"

Before the priest had a chance to answer a thought seemed to strike the man.

"Actually, maybe it's only me. I've always presumed that

everyone has it but, now that I think of it, I could just be some sort of freak."

"No, I know exactly what you mean," said Fr Delucci. "That internal argument is what helps us to reach a well thought out conclusion. It's simply a way of weighing up the options in any given situation. When it's informed by our moral compass then it's the thing that we call our conscience."

"I suppose so," said the man. "Well, what I've failed to do is to listen to that part of myself. I've kept that little voice in my head locked up for years."

He paused as if searching for the words to articulate his thoughts.

"Have you ever continued to act in a certain way because the logical part of your brain knows that it's what's expected of you while, deep inside, that voice is crying out that it's all wrong?"

An image of the marble altar in the church exploding, sending shards of rock like shrapnel shooting at his screaming congregation leapt into the priest's mind as the stranger continued to talk.

"I've played the part of the dutiful husband, the loving father, the loyal friend, but all along it's felt like self sacrifice. Have you heard the saying: '*If you love something, let it go. If it returns it's yours. If it doesn't, it never was.*'?

"Yes. Was it from Keats, perhaps?" hazarded the priest.

"I'm not sure. Sorry. I pick up quotes and sayings but never bother finding out who said them," replied the man. "I guess it's not that important. The point is that I realise now that this applies to myself too. If I had listened to that voice in my head, if I had given myself the opportunity to be fulfilled, then there's a good chance I'd have returned to my life and been the very same father, husband and friend. The difference is that it would have been my choice. Instead of resentment I could have had the freedom to really love the people in my life. I wouldn't have spent all these years pretending."

There was silence while the priest juggled a number of possible suitable but meaningless responses. In the end it was a question that emerged.

"Why not give yourself that chance now?"

The man laughed a humourless laugh.

"I have a tumour. They operate next week. They say there's not much chance that I'll make it, though I've no chance at all if they don't try."

"Oh, I'm sorry…" began the priest, but the man cut him off abruptly.

"No, no – it's fine. But being able to put my death down to the date and time on a hospital appointment card has had the effect of focusing my thoughts. It all seems quite clear to me now. I've been mulling it over since I found out, though, and I've realised that I've left it too late. There's no point in rocking the boat now – unless, of course I come through it. Then, maybe I'll have the courage to make a few changes."

Fr Delucci could think of nothing to say, but feeling the need to sympathise, he sighed in what he hoped was a suitably sympathetic manner. The booth creaked as the man stood up and the priest saw a figure in what appeared to be a long overcoat silhouetted against the muted lights of the church interior as the confessional door opened. The figure paused.

"Thank you, Father. It has really helped to get that off my chest."

Before the priest could utter the words of absolution, the door closed, plunging him back into a darkness made greater for the moment of light.

MANCHESTER, ENGLAND – 13 years ago

THE CLASSROOM was unusually silent as Mr Cartwright examined the photograph. It showed the boys from his class, some wearing blue bibs and some red, playing football. The reds were on the attack. On the far wing, the photographer had frozen Bradley in action, unmistakably clear, as he sprinted into space to get on the receiving end of a long pass. The teacher, to his great discomfort, felt himself left with no option other than ignominious retreat.

"Well, Bradley, it seems that you were, indeed, present and that I, consequently, was totally mistaken. I can only offer my apologies for doubting you. Though, in my defence, you must have been incredibly well behaved that day. I certainly don't recall having had

to raise my voice at you, give you detention or make you run laps around the sports field."

"That's all right, Sir. We all make mistakes," said Bradley magnanimously, and stifled giggles broke out here and there around the classroom. Mr Cartwright got the firm impression that he was the victim of a hoax but he couldn't put his finger on the intricacies of it. He was distinctly dissatisfied and hit back with the old, reliable weapon.

"Right gentlemen. Onwards and upwards. You've got fifteen minutes to study your periodic tables. We're going to have a test."

The light–hearted atmosphere dissipated and the giggles of moments before were replaced by groans.

Later, during the morning break, the lock rattled in the door of the computer room. It swung open and a chubby boy entered, followed by Bradley and three of his cronies. Mark booted up one of the computers, typed in a password and double–clicked on one of the icons that subsequently appeared on the desktop. The photograph of the football game loomed large on the screen.

"That's the finished picture," said Mark. "Now for the original. Keep watching his face."

He clicked the mouse, the screen flickered and Bradley's face changed, instantly, to the face of another boy. The transformation drew delighted gasps and chuckles from the group.

"No way! It's Noddles," laughed one of the boys.

"Yeah, how could you think it was me with those bandy legs?" said Bradley.

He slapped Mark on the shoulder.

"You're a fucking genius, Fatso."

MANCHESTER, ENGLAND – Present

MARK STOOD waiting for the tell–tale wisp of smoke and the sizzle of melted cheese that would signal the magical metamorphosis from the mundane ham and cheese sandwich to the universally acclaimed delectable delights of the ham and cheese toastie.

It always takes longer when you watch it.

He glanced at the pile of dishes that, unchecked, had erupted from the sink, spreading like a chain of volcanic islands across the draining board and onto the kitchen counter.

He could use these few minutes to make inroads... But the cold of the room dissuaded him. Although it was late summer, the weather had been unseasonably bad and the old house in which he rented a flat was damp and chilly in the best of weather. He placed his outstretched hands over the sandwich toaster for warmth instead and pondered, for the umpteenth time, on what Adelina's birthday present would be. At Christmas it had been the black bath towel. Having something that she had handled was amazing. For him, possessing a tangible object associated with her had been the key to shifting their relationship from the virtual world into the real one. He had run his hands softly over every piece of it, ensuring that whatever part she had touched he would touch also. Later, though, when he emailed her to express his thanks, her reply proved to be the real gift. The jpeg photo attachment showed the black bath towel he now had in his possession draped around her like a shawl while she smirked into the camera blowing a kiss. He had no way of knowing if she was clothed or naked beneath the towel but he had let his imagination conjure up an image of that perfect body he had grown intimately acquainted with from visually sifting through the hundreds of pictures that lived in the albums of her *Facebook* profile. There were photos of her rock climbing and striking poses on drunken nights with friends. In some she was sight–seeing in Budapest, in others, hiking in the Transylvanian mountains. To him her body looked so perfect that it might well have been doctored with photo–enhancement software. It hadn't, though. He, of all people, would have been able to tell. After all, his own two *Facebook* profile pictures were the result of many hours of expert work that had reduced his obese body to a slim, healthy–looking and totally fictitious version of himself. At first the deceit had troubled him but he took solace in the adage that it was what was on the inside that counted. He now liked to think of himself as a motorist driving a rather battered van. Adelina was in a relationship with the motorist. She was simply under the mistaken belief that he was driving a sports car.

The heat from the sandwich maker began to scorch his hands, snapping him out of his thoughts. He opened the machine's lid and looked at the melted cheese oozing from the bread which had turned an appealing golden brown from its coating of butter. The sooner he got his body into shape the sooner he could arrange the trip to Romania where Adelina and a world of possibilities awaited. He was running out of excuses. The thought struck him that, in fact, he should really toss the sandwich into the bin and have an apple instead. That simple act of will power could herald a new beginning.

Too cold for apples. And they've been there a while, anyway. They probably need chucking out at this stage.

He reached for a plate and tossed the toastie onto it, burning his fingertips in the process. He licked them and the salty, creamy flavour of the butter set his taste buds salivating.

I'll start on Monday.

With the delightful smell of the toasted bread and melted cheese wafting from the plate in his hands, he ran the gauntlet of the draughty hall and into the small room that he used as a home office, closing the door behind him quickly so that what little heat the old walls had managed to trap wouldn't escape. He sat down at the computer, picked up the sandwich and bit into it while flicking the mouse to awaken the monitor from sleep mode. His current graphic design project lay open but, if anything, the thought of working on it was less appealing than when he had abandoned it to foray in the kitchen for some comfort food.

The client doesn't expect it until Friday.

He took another bite from the sandwich and clicked the button onscreen to minimise the window. He double–clicked the small browser icon and his *Facebook* profile opened up before him. A tiny number '1' resting on the *'messages'* icon informed him that he had mail. It could have been from any one of a great number of online friends. He was much more popular in virtual society than in the real world. Somehow he knew, though, that it would be from her. Smiling with anticipation he clicked on the icon. He was right. The message, though – the words punctuated with 'smiley face' emojis and exclamation marks – sent a wave of nausea over him and he dropped the part eaten toasted sandwich onto the plate. Given her financial situation, with her mother and younger sister to support, it must have taken her months to save for the ticket but she'd done it.

I hope you don't mind. You did say I could come to visit and I wanted to surprise you.

The booking confirmation was attached. She was due to arrive on October 14th so they could finally meet face to face – the ultimate birthday present. He clicked open the calendar on his computer and did the maths. He had just over a month to shed almost half his body weight.

DUBLIN, IRELAND – 7 years ago

THERE WAS an almost Beckettesque symmetry about the moment. The two men shared an awkward glance over the stooped figures of their partners. Then the father's attention was drawn, again, to his daughter's tear–streaked face as she hugged her mother goodbye, chin resting on the older woman's shoulder. The younger man breathed an inward sigh of relief as a large woman with two small children and an overloaded trolley of suitcases was brought to a halt, unable to get past. He laid his hand softly on his wife's arm.

"Darling, there's a lady trying to get through."

Reluctantly, the mother and daughter parted, and the conventions of public behaviour reasserted themselves.

"Well, we'd better head through," said the father. "With all the extra security nowadays it can be very slow."

Grace and David remained at the barrier after the older couple had passed through the double doors marked with its "Passengers only beyond this point" sign. The opaque glass slid apart every time another traveller approached and, in this way, Grace followed her parents' slow progress through the security check until, finally, they had reached the far side of the conveyor belts and metal detectors. They paused, standing there, waiting for a final wave. When the doors closed on them David turned to go but Grace caught his arm.

"Wait."

A moment later the doors slid open again to admit another group of travellers. The space where the older couple had stood was empty. Grace drew a deep breath and, to her husband, she appeared suddenly very frail and vulnerable. He wrapped her in what he hoped was a big, protective hug.

"We'll see them next month."

The screen at the gate announced that Flight EI584 to Malaga would be departing on time. On the seating beneath, the woman turned to her husband.

"Are we doing the right thing, Frank?"

"Of course we are, love. It's our dream. We've been planning it for a long, long time and you know we've weighed up all the pros and cons. It's the right thing."

They sat in silence for a while but when he spoke again it was as though the conversation had continued aloud.

"She has David and, anyway, we're only a short flight away. It's tough on us all now but when we're sipping sangria and lying by the pool you'll feel better. And you know she's going to take every opportunity to get away from the rain and visit us."

The woman smiled.

"You're right, of course. I just hate goodbyes."

"Parting is such sweet sorrow," he said, softly.

She turned to him and waited until his eyes met hers.

"I love you Frank Casey."

The age dropped off him like a discarded cloak as his face broke into that great, big smile that had won her heart all those years before.

"And I adore you, Helen Elizabeth Josephine Casey."

DUBLIN, IRELAND – Present

THEY HAD LEFT HER in the care of a nurse and moved to the room next door. But the doctor had one of those important voices that always sounded loud so she could hear him quite well and she could see their shapes, colours blurred, through the window with the glass like at home in the bathroom upstairs.

"You're perfectly right, Grace. It is, undoubtedly, a psychological rather than physical condition," he was explaining. "In fact it's well documented. We call it 'selective mutism'. Normally, we find it with young, shy children and usually it's only in certain situations – school, for example – that they can't or won't talk. In your daughter's case it has obviously been brought on by the trauma of her father's... your husband's..."

You see, she thought, triumphantly. *You didn't even know my Daddy and you can't say it. Dead. Dead. Dead.*

The blackness swelled up so she clenched her eyes tightly, clenched her lips tightly and clenched her hands tightly. It receded to just below the surface again, suppressed for now but ready to erupt at any moment.

When he had asked her to write down what she felt she had simply stared at the page, trying to think how she would describe the blackness. Once Jessica O'Rourke had handed her a bottle of cola. As a joke, though, she'd shaken it first so that when Angela twisted off the cap the fizzy drink had exploded all over her clothes. The blackness was like that bottle of cola. She had to keep the cap tightly in place or it would explode and then she would probably die and, although she'd be with Daddy, that would leave Mammy on her own.

Her mother's murmured response to the doctor was too low to make out but his reply was loud and clear.

"Yes, there's always the chance that she'll simply start speaking again of her own accord but that's by no means certain."

He stopped there and Angela wondered what her mother was thinking. After a moment he spoke again.

"There is a class of drugs known as SSRIs. They're in the family of antidepressants..."

"She's a child," protested her mother, her voice raised, "a little girl. I'm not going to have her on antidepressants."

"I understand your concern, Grace, but these are widely used. They're tried and trusted. And any side effects often diminish substantially after time."

"Side effects? What kind of side effects?"

"Well, sometimes headache. Maybe mild nausea in a percentage of cases... Often there's no discernible effect at all. It depends on the individual."

Angela heard the chair move and, through the frosted glass, she saw the figure of her mother rise. She said something to the doctor as her indistinct outline crossed the room to the door but now she had returned to her usual low murmur and Angela couldn't make it out.

She jumped up and ran out into the hall before the nurse

had time to look up, emerging at the same time as her mother who reached out to take her hand.

"Come on, darling. Let's go home. Granny's coming back to stay with us tomorrow until we go to Australia so maybe you can help me to get the bedroom ready for her."

Angela watched a man carefully cleaning each leaf of a plastic plant in the reception while her mother waited for the woman to print out the bill. It struck her that watering a real plant would surely take a lot less time. She came suddenly out of her thoughts to find that she was staring and that the man was staring back. He kept a serious face for a moment and then he stuck out his tongue. Straight–faced, Angela walked over to her mother and held her coat. Mammy was counting out bank notes. Angela saw two fifties and some others. She'd heard Mammy talking to Uncle Tony on the phone

He let the policy lapse.

She didn't know what it meant but she knew it had something to do with money and that it wasn't good. The blackness rumbled and she held more tightly to her mother's coat.

2. Titus

"Unto the pure all things are pure:
but unto them that are defiled and unbelieving
is nothing pure; but even their mind
and conscience is defiled."

SANTIAGO DE COMPOSTELA, SPAIN

IRONICALLY, it was the washing machine door he'd promised to fix that led to the discovery. It was turning out to be a perfect day for drying with a light breeze and blue skies dotted here and there with ghostly wisps of cloud. All week the weather had rolled in off the Atlantic bringing the kind of persistent, miserable drizzle that kept Galicia's thousand rivers flowing fast and Isabel's laundry pile mounting. With this airy sunshine she hoped that she might clear the backlog before leaving for work. As she divided the colours from the whites her mind was elsewhere. She would visit the doctor that day to register her pregnancy. It made sense to get a check up and make sure that everything was fine before telling Anxo.

Although, maybe I should ask if he'd like to go with me for the first visit.

The washing machine dial hadn't moved off '4' where Anxo had twisted the it the previous night and she knew, immediately, what had happened. A faulty hinge meant that the door didn't close without pushing it in a certain way and if the door wasn't closed the machine wouldn't run. As a rule, Anxo never did the washing so he didn't know to check. In fact, the last time that Anxo had attempted to tackle the laundry had been on her birthday three or four years previously when he had forgotten to buy her a present. With great aplomb, he had promised to take on the domestic chores for the day in reparation for his oversight. The results had been disastrous. He had struggled to accept that one small, red overlooked piece of clothing had been responsible for turning so many white clothes pink.

She was about to set the machine in motion when it occurred to her to check this load for similar oversights. Anxo never learned from his mistakes.

As soon as she opened the door the smell hit her. Vanilla and fruit – young. She dragged the clothes out of the machine and onto the tiled floor. There were three towels, a vest and the pillowcases of last night. She picked up the vest and sniffed it. Stale sweat. Nor was it from the towels – she had put them there. Not the pillowcases...

Then she saw that one of them was bulging. She picked it up and emptied a bundled up shirt from inside it. She immediately recognised the distinct paisley pattern with its flamboyant reds, yellows and oranges. It was the shirt that his workmates had bought him for his birthday. The thought came suddenly, with a conviction that hit her like a punch.

It wasn't given to him by his workmates. That was lie.

A range of complex emotions welled up inside her that she couldn't easily identify, but they caught in her throat, threatening to choke her. She took a deep breath and tried to compose herself.

The scent was stronger and she could see the smears of false tan or foundation without even picking the shirt up. But she picked it up anyway. There was a different scent from under the arms. She recognised it as the spray deodorant he had started using a few weeks before because the roll–on had suddenly begun to cause an allergic reaction.

No, that was a lie too. It was for her – whoever 'she' is.

The emotion began to take on two distinct forms – a deep sense of something akin to grief and a cold, rising anger.

She stormed out of the laundry and returned, some minutes later, with her smartphone. She put the shirt on a hanger and hung it from the indoor drying line. Selecting the camera function on her phone, she carefully and methodically snapped the evidence. Having flicked through the pictures to ensure that they were of a suitable forensic standard, she cast the shirt among the items on the floor and shoved the lot back into the washing machine. It was only a half load, a detached part of her mind noticed, so she added in some tea towels from the kitchen. With a practiced jolt she snapped the door shut and the machine rumbled into action. She stared, hypnotised, as the clothes tumbled around behind the dense glass porthole of the small door, intertwining into a hopeless confusion of colours and textures. Bubbles appeared as the detergent and water flooded the drum, turning the colours darker. Pieces of the damning shirt popped up now and then, pressing against the glass and taunting her with Anxo's infidelity. She was unsure of how long she had stared, transfixed, but when she emerged from her stupor she found that she had formed a resolution.

I'm leaving. It's over.

Upstairs, she had difficulty extracting the suitcase from where it was stored under the bed. It had been a long time since they had travelled anywhere so she had to burrow through boxes of Christmas decorations and bags of winter clothes before she managed to tug it free. She hoisted it onto the bed, threw it open and turned to the wardrobe. Inside, the neat row of her clothes overwhelmed her and she sat back on the bed, staring vacantly.

I was going to tell him today.

Her gaze fell to her stomach and she ran a hand over the swelling.

The cold edge of her anger was gone, leaving her feeling deflated and defeated. She carefully closed the suitcase and returned it to its place under the bed. As she turned to close the wardrobe her eyes rested on the long garment that had hung there, untouched, in its dust cover for years. A defiant spark ignited somewhere inside.

She emptied some shoes from a large, black, plastic bag that lay in the bottom of the wardrobe and removed the garment from the rail. Discarding the dust cover, she took the white silk wedding dress from its hanger, rolled it into a neat ball and stuffed it into the bag. She returned to the laundry where the washing machine lay quiet, its work done.

A couple of hours later Isabel opened a door on the upstairs landing that led to a rickety old balcony above the courtyard where the morning's washing flapped on a line that ran from one end to the other. The balcony gave its usual shift and creak as she stepped out. As she steadied herself her attention was drawn to the steeple of the towering Gothic cathedral.

"San Tiago, please..."

Her words faltered as she realised that she had no idea what she wanted and, therefore, didn't know what to pray for.

"Please help me."

The shirt was dry. Leaving the other items, she took it down to the laundry and spread it onto the ironing board. It had come up like new, she noticed, as she carefully ironed it, folded it and put it on top of the wedding dress in the bag. While handling the offending item made her feel slightly nauseous, she felt that she had to lead by example. She hated when people came into the charity shop with unironed or damaged clothes. As her colleague Paula had once pointed out, it was like slapping the face of the poor and needy.

BOSTON, USA

BISHOP DONOGHUE put the small paperback down slowly, slid it purposefully across the desk and then settled back in the high–backed leather armchair. He regarded the priest thoughtfully. Fr Delucci made no move to pick up the book. He met the bishop's gaze gravely but unflinchingly.

"I've come to believe that if one does not – at some point – face a crisis of faith then one is not giving it all enough thought," said the bishop, finally. Fr Delucci felt that there was more coming so he remained silent.

"So, you mean to walk the *Camino* and visit the venerable bones of the good St James," the bishop said.

"Yes, your Grace" replied the priest. "I don't know why,

exactly, but I feel that this journey will confirm my faith once and for all or..."

Years of conditioning left the blasphemous words unspoken.

"Or you'll leave us," said the Bishop, simply.

The priest looked down miserably at the book.

"I have a friend who has walked the *Camino* several times, you know," said the Bishop with a shift from gravitas to conversational tones. "I presume you are planning to embark upon your quest sooner rather than later."

"Only with your blessing, your Grace"

Bishop Donohue waved a hand as though batting away a troublesome fly.

"You have that, of course, Fr Delucci. Jesus didn't force his disciples to stick with him and neither does his church. No, you'll go if you wish. The reason I ask is that my friend said that summer and autumn are less than ideal on the French route which – probably due to your book there – is by far the most popular. Apparently you can't get a moment to yourself and unless you're up before the lark you are in danger of finding yourself with 'no room at the inn' when you arrive at your destination each night. He recommends the Portuguese way. He says that the pilgrim hostels are very modern and it has the advantage of being, very much, 'the road less travelled'."

"Thank you, your Grace," said Fr Delucci, a great sense of relief surging through him. "I really appreciate your support."

"Light a candle for me when you get there," replied the Bishop, with a flicker of a smile.

MANCHESTER, ENGLAND

IGOTTALOSEMYFATASS.COM was the name of the website.

Tacky, but straight to the point.

It had summed up his situation nicely. Mark's search phrase had been "extreme weight loss techniques fast" and, after the usual sponsored ads, this site had come up at the number one ranked spot on the search engine. He had clicked the link with a healthy degree of scepticism which moderated, somewhat, when he saw that one side of the page was dedicated to client reviews. As far as he could tell they seemed genuine and reading through a few inspired him with enough interest to read on.

The "I–Gotta–Lose–My–Fat–Ass" method appeared to involve some kind of extreme bootcamp that started by having the obese hopefuls put their lives on hold for a week of intense monitored activity before a more orthodox exercise and diet routine kicked in. Mark had clicked on the 'contact us' link and had outlined his case in an email to the guy who ran the show – shay@igottalosemyfatass.com. Now he was trying to make sense of the reply which had come with admirable promptitude.

The first thing that was made clear was that it was going to cost him €2,000. This comprised a €1,000 up-front payment and a further €1,000 if Shay succeeded in getting him down to an acceptable size within a month. The phrase 'acceptable size' was, Mark thought, rather hazy and the fact that the price was in euros rather than US dollars or UK pounds seemed unusual to him. He clicked to check the exchange rate.

Well, I'll probably never have to fork over the second payment.

No sooner had the thought struck him than he admonished himself for his negative attitude. Having battled with his weight for years he had read countless warnings in the diet and psuedo–psychology books that lined his shelves about the self–defeat that resulted from a negative attitude. In fact, he suspected that he could write a credible academic work on what one should be eating, thinking and exactly what exercise one should be doing too. Putting it all into practice was his problem.

After the issue of money the rest was a little vague. It seemed that the activities took place over the course of an enforced march of some sort and that getting to the starting point involved overseas travel – there was definitely a reference to flights and the necessity of having a passport. He'd have to take time away from his business. He considered his current workload. It wasn't particularly heavy. With a bit of effort he could clear his desk and tell his few clients that he was taking a holiday for a week or two. They might be surprised but they couldn't reasonably object. A vacation was something he'd never indulged in since setting up as a freelance graphic designer two years earlier.

He sighed, got up, went down the hallway to the kitchen and flicked the half–full kettle on to boil. He opened the press to take down a cup but there were none. He reluctantly approached the stack of dirty crockery in the sink and poked about to find the least offensive one there. He had to rearrange the dishes in order to make enough room to get the cup under the tap to wash it. He popped in a teabag and went to the fridge to get milk. It was pitifully empty. After Adelina's email, in a passion of good intentions, he'd thrown out anything with a fat content of more than 3%. The lettuce and tomatoes that remained looked unappetising.

It's too cold to eat salads anyway.

The shelf in the door where the milk was kept was empty too. Of course it was. He'd resolved to drink only herbal tea in that same spirit of change. He shut the door.

Bugger.

He opened the cupboard where the herbal teabags were kept and his eye leapt to the tin box which contained the 'biscuits for visitors'. He took the box down and, putting it on the kitchen counter, prised off the tin lid. The biscuits he'd chosen were lavish. After all, who was he to impose the same food restrictions on guests that he imposed upon himself? He did some rapid mental calculations. If he took just two biscuits it would add up to about the same calories as he'd planned to have for lunch. He'd skip lunch, he resolved, and then his calorie count for the day wouldn't go over his allowance.

He made the tea and dipped the second biscuit in. As he went to put the lid back on the tin he found himself reaching for one more biscuit. How could that hurt in the overall scheme of things? He was half way down the hallway with his tea when he stopped with that all too familiar feeling of self disgust. The only way he could stay below his calorie limit now was to reduce his dinner size that evening. He took another step then stopped again and turned around. Back in the kitchen he took the tin box from the cupboard again. Yes, his calculations were right. Five more biscuits meant eight altogether. That was actually fifty calories less than his combined lunch and dinner allowance. Certainly biscuits weren't exactly giving him the nutrients he needed but it was only for today. Tomorrow he'd be back on track.

Twenty minutes later he was feeling both physically and mentally ill. He stared for a moment at the empty biscuit tin and then, picking up the lid, pushed it firmly on. He picked up the box and tucked it under his desk where it was out of sight. In doing so he nudged the edge of the tabletop and the swirling patterns of his computer's screensaver gave way to the still–open inbox of his mail software. There was a new message from shay@igottalosemyfatass.com – subject: "You're wasting precious time!".

SANTIAGO DE COMPOSTELA, SPAIN

SINCE THEY HAD started to keep the shop open through lunchtime it had become their busiest period of the day. Most of the surrounding stores were closed for a few hours and it gave workers, escaping the confines of the office, somewhere to shelter from the rain or sun, depending on the vagaries of the Galician weather, while they perused the eclectic odds and ends that had been donated to raise funds for the *Los Pobres de San Tiago* charity. The extra hours had not seen an increase in the wages of Isabel and Paula but neither of the two women were motivated by the modest salary. Before the change Paula had worked the morning shift until 14.00 while Isabel had covered evenings from 16.30. To cope with the new frantic lunchtime trade Paula had agreed to remain until 4.30 while Isabel came in early at 2pm. The two and a half hours of shared time had brought a new social aspect to the job. In the less busy periods between helping customers, they had begun to cement something akin to a friendship. It fell short, however, of a level that would encourage Isabel to share the inner turmoil she now found herself living through.

She watched from the street outside until Paula had disappeared into the back room to fetch something for a customer before entering with the black plastic bag containing her wedding dress and Anxo's damning paisley shirt. She tossed it among the other bags of donations and followed Paula into the staff area.

"*Hola guapa*," Paula smiled, looking up from where she crouched over a tea set box that she had opened on the floor. "Some old guy's just bought this but there's a cup missing. Don't suppose you know where it is?"

"Sorry. Though we wouldn't have accepted it if there had been pieces missing so it must be somewhere."

Isabel hung up her coat and bag.

"I'm just going to grab a coffee before I start. Want one?"

"Not just now," replied Paula. "I need to find this bloody cup."

Isabel made herself an instant coffee at the small kitchenette that occupied one corner of the room and left Paula rummaging while she returned to the shop floor. The old man was thumbing through a book on gardening.

"I'm sorry, my colleague is just trying to locate one of the cups."

"That's fine," replied the man. "I'm in no hurry."

His face fell, however, when Paula emerged ten minutes later to inform him that the cup was nowhere to be found. She took his number and promised to call him if the errant piece of crockery showed up. Isabel, had been kept busy with a steady stream of customers and a further half hour passed before both women found themselves in a lull.

"I'm going to get that coffee now. Want one?"

"Yeah, that'd be great," said Isabel. "I didn't get a chance to drink the first."

She pushed the cold cup of coffee across the counter.

"*Joder*," said Paula.

"What?"

That's the bloody cup I've just wasted an hour looking for."

She laughed and Isabel was surprised to hear herself join in.

So life can go on.

Paula disappeared into the staff room and Isabel's mental

reprieve gave way to dark thoughts of the impending confrontation with Anxo. A woman entered the shop. Isabel, submerged in her worries, barely noticed. With the upheaval of the morning, she had neglected to make the doctor's appointment. That would have to wait. Confronting Anxo, though, couldn't.

"Are you okay?" asked Paula. She was standing in front of Isabel with two cups of coffee. "You're miles away."

"Sorry. I was just thinking about what I'll make for dinner."

Paula shrugged, unconvinced.

"Well, you do that while I'll sort out some of the donations."

She busied herself with the bags in the corner as the customer approached the till with a number of bright items of clothing which she placed on the counter.

"All of these? asked Isabel, speaking Spanish.

The woman looked apologetic.

"I'm so sorry, do you speak English?"

"Of course," said Isabel, switching.

She began to ring up the prices on the till.

"I really should be ashamed," continued the woman. "I've been in Spain for seven years now but I still haven't managed to learn much more than how to order my tea with cold milk instead of lemon."

Isabel smiled.

"Seven years? Why did you choose Santiago? We get many *peregrinos* visiting but it is usually only the students that stay longer."

"Oh, I'm not living here. I have a place near Malaga. I've just been visiting a Spanish friend who lives in Galicia and Santiago was the nearest airport. I'm flying out this evening."

"You are from England?"

"No, Ireland."

"Ah, sorry," said Isabel. "I always find it difficult to tell the difference in the accent. I've heard that Ireland is a beautiful place but I've never been."

"It is beautiful – not unlike the little I've seen of Galicia, actually," said the woman. "I'm on my way back for a week or so."

"You still have family there?"

"Not for long, unfortunately. My daughter and grand-daughter are about to join my son in Australia. In fact, I'm on my way to help them with the move."

Isabel stopped what she was doing and looked up.

"I know that they say that the world is small," she said, "but Australia is still a long, long way to go."

"Yes," said the woman.

Isabel recommenced packing the purchases. As she wait-ed, the woman's gaze fell on the book of petitions to San Tiago that was kept on the counter.

"I hope you don't mind me asking, she said, "but what's this?"

"This shop is for the charity of *Los Pobres de San Tiago*. The book is for the petitions of our customers. A Mass is offered up each week in the cathedral by the local priest who works with our organisation."

"Oh, how lovely," said the woman, picking up the pen, "May I?"

"Of course."

"It's for my granddaughter. My daughter's husband was killed, you see. A car crash. Angela hasn't spoken since though doctors say it's a psychological problem. Grace – that's my daughter – had to return to work when her hus-band died and she doesn't think it's helping that she's not there for the poor child. She's hoping that Australia will give them a new start. And, of course, she'll have the support of her brother."

The woman began to write in the book. Without being particularly conscious that she was doing so, Isabel watched the sentence appear in firm, neat writing.

For Angela and Grace, that healing will come into their lives.

"What a tragedy for you and your daughter, and especial-ly for the little girl," said Isabel, embarrassed, for some rea-son, to have witnessed the private prayer. "I lost my mother when I was quite young. It has such an effect."

The woman looked up from her writing and 'tutted' sympathetically. Isabel smiled at the acknowledgement.

"It was a long time ago. You never lose the grief but you learn to cope."

"Yes," agreed the woman. "You're never the same. You have good days when you feel that you finally have it under control and then you hear a certain song or walk past a place you used to go to together and it hits you all over again. At least that's the way it is with my husband, Frank. It's almost four years that he's gone now."

She returned to the task of completing the form in the inevitable heavy silence of shared grief that followed. In the column where the petitioners wrote their names, the woman put *Helen Casey*. Isabel rang up the last two items of clothing and bagged the lot.

"That's €22."

"This lot is for little Angela," said Helen, as she fumbled in her bag for her purse. "After her daddy's funeral I stayed in Ireland for a few weeks while my daughter got back on her feet. While she was at work, Angela and I would sit and sew together. She seemed to like that so I'm going to bring these nice fabrics for us to work with. It seems to be much easier to find colorful clothes over here."

Isabel smiled.

"It's great that she has that interest. So many children play only video games."

The woman nodded in agreement. She opened her purse and started counting out money. Isabel looked away and saw that Paula had reached the black plastic bag that she had brought. The paisley shirt was laid in a pile of similar clothing that had come from other bags. Paula was standing in front of a long mirror with Isabel's wedding dress held up in front of herself as, no doubt, she imagined her notional big day.

Isabel stepped briskly to the pile of shirts and selected the offending one. Returning to the counter she pushed it into the bag.

"Here," she said, "Take this also. I'm sure your granddaughter will make something nice from it."

"Oh no. It's practically new and we'll be cutting it up."

"I insist," said Isabel with a smile.

DUBLIN, IRELAND

"EAT UP, it'll go cold," said Mrs Kearney, hovering over Angela to ensure that her instruction was followed. Angela picked up a potato wedge and began to nibble on the end. She was aware that Mrs Kearney was watching her and felt, instinctively, that another 'little talk' was coming. She stared at her plate as Mrs Kearney walked around to the opposite side of the breakfast counter and stood facing her.

"Angela, tomorrow your granny will be here and I probably won't have a chance to talk to you again so it's very important that you listen to what I'm saying, okay?"

Angela didn't take her eyes off the potato wedges. When Mrs Kearney spoke again there was a new edge of hardness in her tone.

"I know you can hear me, Angela."

The moment that followed felt like an eternity to the girl. She could sense the tension mounting until it felt like something she could touch – something suffocating.

"Right. I can't force you to talk but, by God, you're going to listen."

Angela flinched as though she'd been struck as a hand shot across the table. It dragged the plate away and left the girl staring at the empty counter top.

"I know you've been through a lot but you have to start thinking of your poor mother. It's bad enough that she's trying to cope with losing your Daddy but now you have her worried sick about you as well."

She let that hang in the air for a moment before attacking again.

"There's nothing actually wrong with you, Angela. The doctors say so. There's no reason why you couldn't talk if you wanted to. You need to stop thinking about yourself. You have to stop being part of the problem."

Angela flung herself down from the stool, fell, picked herself up and ran from the room. She scrambled up the stairs and into the bathroom where she locked the door and sat, trembling, on the edge of the bath. She listened for Mrs Kearney's footsteps on the stairs. But there was silence. She was upset, but in the blackness she was aware of a glimmer of light that had been present since Mammy had told her.

Granny is coming.

That night – the night when the police man called to say that Daddy was dead – she'd watched Mammy begin to die as well. Before, when she had drawn pictures of her family at school she would draw Daddy on one side, Mammy on the other and her, small and safe, between them. Now Daddy was gone and Mammy was falling. That was when the blackness took over inside. It wasn't until Granny had arrived from Spain that she'd found something to hold onto. Granny hadn't cried. She'd held her and told her it would be okay. She'd talked with Mammy and whatever she had said had given Mammy something to hold onto as well.

In those first days Mammy had slept in Angela's bed with her and Angela had felt her body shake with big, silent sobs when she thought she was asleep. With Granny's help, though, Mammy had slowly started to live again. But something had changed and things would never be the same. Angela knew, now, that Mammy could break.

She hadn't wanted Granny to go back to Spain but she had shown Angela where she lived on the map and explained that it was only four hours away by plane. Soon, though, they'd be living with Uncle Tony in Australia and Angela had checked the map to see how far that was. It was the other side of the world. She couldn't think about that now, though. It disturbed the blackness. She just had to hold on until tomorrow. Tomorrow Granny would be here.

3. Jude

*"Woe unto them! For they have gone in
the way of Cain, and ran greedily after
the error of Balaam for reward."*

BOSTON, USA

"THE BEAUTY of this one," said the youth turning the compass over, "is that it has a space here that will fit a standard "Post–It" pad and this little clamp that you can put a pen in. That's going to be dead handy for keeping notes."

Fr Delucci considered the three models before him and tried to decide if the convenience of being able to take notes outweighed the usefulness of an eco–friendly, wind–up, self–charging torch.

"Of course, the hand–held sat nav would give you everything in the one package but, as you said, you can't be sure about charging it up," observed the shop assistant. "Electricity is different over there."

The priest was suddenly very weary.

"You know, I reckon I'll leave the compass for now and think some more about it," he said. "I mean, from what I've read there are yellow arrows at every turn to tell you which way to go."

"It's totally up to you of course," said the youth, "but I'd hate to think of you stuck on some dirt track somewhere in the dark and getting completely lost 'cos you can't see the arrows."

Fr Delucci pondered that then observed: "If it was that dark I wouldn't be able to see the compass either."

"The one with the torch might be the way to go then," said the shop assistant.

"I'm not sure about that," said the priest. "I had been thinking that there's a bit of a design flaw with that one. The torch is at the front, you see, which means you can't actually point the light at the compass to read it."

"No, I was thinking you could use the light to look for the arrows."

"I'd be better off with a regular torch in that case."

The youth paused before nodding in begrudging assent.

"I've a nice waterproof torch with a rubber casing," he said. "It rains all the time over there."

"I think I'll just take what I've got and get the rest another day," said the priest, firmly. "I'll actually perish before I even start if I don't get a coffee soon."

"Whatever you say," said the shop assistant, making his way back to the counter where an impressive pile of assorted items lay. Fr Delucci looked at the 90 litre backpack, the breathable, waterproof hiking shoes, the aluminum water bottle with an easy–access straw that meant he could drink without having to stop and the various other alien objects. He wondered, not for the first time in recent days, if he was crazy.

MANCHESTER, ENGLAND

THE WALK from the changing room to the swimming pool left Mark shivering in the cold air. He stared, dismayed. An aqua aerobics class was in full swing. A young woman with an Eastern European accent and a boom box was performing jumps to the music and shouting both instructions and encouragement to a crowd of largely overweight women in the pool. Two lanes had been roped off for other gym users but these were occupied by 'real' swimmers who effortlessly glided up and down, tumble turning gracefully at each end. Mark made his way to the jacuzzi and lowered his heavy body gratefully into the warm water. Clasping one of the steps between his feet for leverage, he began to perform sit–ups. This was probably every bit as good as swimming, he reasoned. He had read somewhere that water resistance helped to speed up the toning process. He was on his eight sit–up when he noticed an elderly man approaching from the changing rooms. Mark hurriedly struck a nonchalant pose, hoping that his efforts had not been observed. There was no clear etiquette about exercising in the jacuzzi but Mark suspected that exerting oneself in a place of relaxation was likely to draw disapproval. They exchanged smiles.

"Is it broken?" queried the man

"Oh no, sorry," said Mark, reaching for the button to activate the pumps.

A precursory jet of water disturbed the surface before the machinery rumbled into full swing, filling the tub with a turmoil of bubbles. Mark leaned back heavily and closed his eyes. His own efforts weren't working and it was beginning to look like Shay from *Igottalosemyfatass.com* was a con artist. The money had gone from his account two days ago and he'd heard nothing since.

His misgivings dissipated, however, an hour later when he checked his mail box on the way into his flat and found the brown envelope with its Berlin post mark. He ripped it open eagerly and extracted the three items it contained. There was a folded sheet of paper but he ignored that for now. His eyes were drawn to what was unmistakably an airline ticket. He skimmed the details. The departure airport was Manchester and the destination was Porto.

Where's that?

He whipped the smartphone from his pocket and typed the word into Google. Porto was in Portugal – and quite spectacular, if the search result images were anything to go by. He checked the date on the ticket. The eleventh. God. That was in two days time. He noted that the ticket was one–way. He checked to see if either of the other two document in the envelope was the return. Neither was. One proved to be a bus ticket from Porto to a place called Valença and the folded page was a hand–written note. Sinking into a chair, Mark read.

Pack light. Wear good walking shoes. DO NOT, UNDER ANY

CIRCUMSTANCES bring a smartphone, tablet, computer or any other web–enabled device. Take the flight and the bus, then spend the night at Albergue Santo António in Valença. Leave the following morning at exactly 05.45 and follow the yellow arrows. At the third column of the bridge over the Minho you will find a bag. Further information there. Shay.

It was all a bit vague and mysterious at the very least but Mark realised, with some surprise, that it was the thought of leaving his phone at home that frightened him most.

He got up, walked thoughtfully into his work room and sat at his computer. He opened the web browser and began a series of searches on Porto, Valença and the river Minho. The Minho, he found, separated Portugal from Spain. An image search showed him the bridge. It was a trellised metal structure resting on a number of massive columns. The design, he noted, had been inspired by Eiffel of the tower fame. He thought for a moment. Fuck it. What had he got to lose? He looked up the weather forecast for northern Portugal. He was going to need tee shirts and shorts.

Opening his *Facebook* profile in the browser he wrote a message to Adelina.

"Hey there," he typed. "Hope your day's going well and you managed to get your tennis in. All well this side. Just landed a new client in Portugal of all places. Looks like I'll be heading over there later in the week to iron out the details. It seems that it's in a pretty remote place so if I'm not online as much don't worry…"

Oh what a tangled web we weave when first we practise to deceive.

SANTIAGO DE COMPOSTELA, SPAIN

AS ANXO BROUGHT the sleek, long saloon to rest at the kerbside, he was pleased to see Vicki, behind the huge hairdresser's shop window, pause with the sweeping brush to watch the car. With the black tinted glass she couldn't know that it was him. He took in the vision of her long, slender legs beneath the micro shorts. Like so many 20–year–olds, her face wore the flawless mask of make–up that she'd perfected from studying countless YouTube tutorials. Although they had been seeing each other regularly for weeks, she had never let him see her without her 'face' on, but Anxo suspected that it was superfluous. Her bag of tricks might put the flush in the right place on her cheeks and make her eyebrows appear like uniform arches but her full lips, cute nose and glinting mischievous green eyes were just as nature intended them.

She's hot and she's mine.

The thought thrilled him. He clicked a button and the driver–side window descended smoothly. He saw her eyes widen as she recognised him. She held a slim finger up and mouthed the words '*un momento*' before disappearing into the recesses of the shop interior. He picked up his phone and wrote a two–sentence text message to Isabel explaining that he'd be home late due to a last minute task at work. The door of the hairdresser's opened and Vicki came out, waving goodbye to an unseen figure inside before making her way around to the passenger side of the car. He pressed 'send' and dropped the phone into the pocket in the car's centre console as the door opened and she slid in.

"Are we going out?" she asked.

"I'm afraid not. The *niña* has a show tonight and I wouldn't miss that but I wanted to see you so I thought I'd come to drop you home."

Inventing a daughter had been his master stroke. It was a much less objectionable excuse for staying married to Isabel than the truth. Vicki looked disappointed but didn't object – as he knew she wouldn't. Whatever her true feelings were, she couldn't, in all consciousness, have an issue with a father insisting on being there for his little girl. Her gaze ran over the cream leather interior and dashboard with its lights, buttons and knobs combining to resemble more the cockpit of a fighter plane than a car.

"When did you get this?" she asked. "The other one was nice but this..."

Words failed her.

"I was getting bored with the Beamer," he said, "and I saw this one in a showroom window. Impulsiveness – it's my one fault."

"Well," said Vicki, settling back into the seat. "Your impulsiveness stops you from becoming boring. I get bored easily."

Anxo smiled and pressed the accelerator. The big car slipped into the stream of rush hour traffic that was desperately trying to escape the city centre.

"Speaking of bored, I've changed my foundation. What do you think?"

Anxo glanced as she turned her face first to one side and then the next. Trial and error had equipped him with the answer she was seeking but he paused long enough to give an impression of genuine consideration before he delivered it.

"Flawless. It looks very natural."

She smiled.

"Do you really think so? Great. I wasn't sure but it goes on really smooth and it gives really good coverage. They do a translucent powder too. I might..."

She chatted away happily and Anxo only half listened as he tried to work out why the traffic even heavier than usual.

They made poor progress. They were stuck in a long line of cars on Avenida da Coruña as it turned onto Avenida de Rosalía de Castro. The lights were remaining green long enough, only, to let four or five vehicles through. A constant trickle of backpackers, the tell–tale shells marking them as pilgrims on the *Camino*, were making matters worse. Weary, no doubt, from having walked at least 100 kilometres, and with their destination – the Gothic cathedral of Santiago – now almost in sight, they trudged over the pedestrian crossing, paying scant attention as to whether the little man on the signal was green or red.

"Fucking *peregrinos*," said Anxo, watching the needle on the car's economy gauge sink further into the red zone.

"Don't call them that," said Vicki. "They are better people than you or me."

He looked at her, surprised. She seemed somewhat embarrassed by her words but defiant. A rosy flush was visible through her make up. She looked adorable. Anxo leaned over and kissed her shoulder. She snatched it away but looked pleased, nonetheless.

"I'm sorry, *guapa*," he said. "I'll go to confession."

She looked at him in mock annoyance and he answered with a look of penitence. They both laughed. However, he didn't find her next words amusing at all.

"Will you also tell the priest that you are cheating on your wife?" she asked, abruptly. He felt his annoyance return but he suppressed it and tried to answer with a lightness that he didn't feel.

"It's not cheating if there is no marriage. I told you. As soon as Anna is old enough Isabel and I will get a divorce."

He felt her regarding him thoughtfully so he kept his eyes on the road ahead. Finally she spoke.

"I wonder if your wife would say the same thing."

"She would."

"Then maybe I should ask her."

The traffic had ground to a halt again so he was able to turn and face her.

"Look, Vicki. That's not even funny. It's like I told you. Isabel and I have an understanding but, even so, I'm sure she doesn't want this – us – thrown in her face."

"Oh, so the story's changing now, is it? You told me she doesn't care."

The driver behind beeped and Anxo saw that the traffic ahead had moved on. He hit the accelerator and the car lurched forward angrily.

"You're twisting my words," he said. "Believe what you want."

They broke, suddenly, through the invisible border between traffic chaos and normality. The car moved steadily now, its occupants maintaining an uncomfortable silence until Anxo added:

"Anyway, you can't ask her. You don't know where I live. You'll just have to take my word for it."

"Whatever," said Vicki as if the subject now bored her. "I'm thirsty. I need water."

They were approaching a *Repsol* station. Anxo glanced down at the red light on the petrol gauge and swung into the forecourt. As he pumped a minimal €10 worth of fuel into the tank the fresh air wafted the extremes of his ill humour away. He entered the shop and glanced around. His gaze fell on a rack of cheap soft toys. He selected one – a gorilla with disproportionately long arms. Carrying a bottle of water and holding the gorilla out of sight behind his back, he returned to the car and jumped in. The smile froze on his face and the carefully rehearsed words stuck in his throat. Vicki, with a humourless grin, waved his smartphone at him.

"I have your wife's number now."

"Give me that," he said, a sense of quiet panic hitting him.

She tossed the phone at him and opened the door.

"I'll walk from here," she said, slipping out.

"Vicki!"

Smirking, she blew him an exaggerated kiss, turned on her heel and strode jauntily, but briskly, away. He dropped the soft toy, flung the water onto the passenger seat and started the engine. The tyres squealed as the car shot forward then jerked to a halt as another car blocked the way. The driver waved apologetically. Anxo heard a loud wolf–whistle and looked to where Vicki was crossing the road, the traffic parting for her like the Red Sea before Moses. He hit the horn and the driver of the other car, seeing his urgency, moved deftly out of his way. Anxo gunned the accelerator but his foot encountered a resistance. Slamming on the brakes he reached down and pulled the gorilla from where it had become wedged under the pedal. Flinging it to one side, he looked desperately towards the road. The traffic had resumed its flow. There was no sign of the girl.

"*Joder!*" he cursed, savagely.

When he pulled into the car rental yard Señor Cardosa was leaning against the wall of the Portacabin that served as an office, ritualistically rolling another link in his chain smoking habit. Aghast, his mind racing, Anxo parked the car carefully in a vacant spot beneath the weather canopy where the more expensive models were kept.

What the fuck? Cardosa is always gone golfing by this time on a Thursday. He never comes back after lunch.

He pulled the bonnet release catch and the hood popped up. Taking a deep breath he bounced out of the car, looking, he hoped, carefree, confident and competent. He was prodding a pipe that came from what he suspected was the fuel pump when he felt Cardosa looming beside him. Anxo pretended not to notice. His boss simply stood, watching. At length, the situation grew ridiculous so Anxo stood up and lowered the hood.

"Señor Cardosa," he said, seeing the pretence through with a feigned start of surprise.

His boss said nothing but regarded him coldly.

"It seems okay now," said Anxo, wiping his hands and nodding to the car. "The customer who dropped it back complained that she was running rough. So I took her out for a spin to check it out."

"Well. This is fabulous news," said Cardosa with an elaborate charade of joy. "We've had you cleaning the cars for the past few years and all the time you're a natural–born engineer. Fantastic. We'll sack the mechanics and you can do their job too."

"I just thought..." said Anxo, but a warning glint in his boss's eye stopped him from finishing the sentence. He changed tack.

"Actually, Señor, the truth is that there was a personal emergency. I can't say more than that because I would be betraying a confidence but I have absolutely no doubt that you would understand if you knew."

Cardosa's look didn't waver and Anxo was struck with the sudden intuition that his job was in the balance. The older man nodded a confirmation as he saw the realisation dawn.

"You are well aware that I only tolerate you because you're married to my Goddaughter but even my loyalty to her late father has its limits. At the end of the day I have a business to run."

He watched Anxo closely, gauging the impact of his words. Then he continued.

"I haven't discussed this because it is a subject about which I am far from comfortable but, as the executor of her father's will I am aware that you and Isabel have been married for eight of the ten years that he stipulated must pass before she comes into her inheritance – before you, in other words, get your hands on his money."

Anxo started to protest but Cardosa silenced him with a look as he continued to speak.

"He chose me as executor because he knew that I would have no hesitation in warning Isabel to get rid of you if I thought you were messing her around."

Again he paused, observing the younger man. Anxo, his heart pounding, said nothing.

"For reasons I don't understand, my Goddaughter remains smitten by you, but as far as I'm concerned, the jury's still out. You are on your last warning, Anxo. Do you understand me?"

"Yes, Señor. Thank you. It won't happen again."

Cardosa, dismissed him with a nod. Anxo could feel him watching so he controlled the rage until he had driven Isabel's yellow, battered Citroen out of the yard and into the traffic. Then he yelled, a pure animal howl of frustration, anger and resentment.

Fuck Isabel and her father.

An image of the old man laughing at his own cleverness popped into his mind as it did every time Anxo had to swallow another insult to his pride at the hands of his stuck-up wife or her smug Godfather.

By the time he reached home Anxo had worked himself into a palette of emotions with which he was totally unfamiliar. He pulled the little Citroen into the garage, unclipped his seat belt and sat there, staring through the windscreen at the blank wall ahead. It was only when he found himself coughing that he snapped out of his reverie and realised that he had left the engine running. He must have been there for a while as the air in the garage had grown polluted with exhaust fumes. He switched off the ignition, climbed out of the car and hurried out into the fresh air.

Now that would have been a stupid way to go.

He conjured up an image of Isabel standing with a tear-streaked face by his graveside. Cardosa would be there for her sake but he wouldn't shed a tear. They'd think he'd killed himself, of course. What about Vicki? He could imagine her watching from a distance, sorry that she'd been such a bitch to him but fighting hard not to cry in case her make-up ran.

He wondered if, as Isabel's husband, he'd be put in the ancient Quintana family crypt. No. The Don wouldn't want his blue blood tainted with the rotting corpse of a commoner. Isabel would be accorded that honour but not her husband. With that thought a new scenario leapt to mind. He pictured himself standing by the crypt, looking dashing in his black mourning suit, as Isabel was laid to rest with her father – the last of the Quintanas. The thought struck him like a revelation.

If Isabel dies, everything will be mine. There'll be no waiting, no Cardosa and no more problems with Vicki.

The thought of Vicki reminded him of her threat to call Isabel and shook him from his fantasy. Taking a deep breath, he strode towards the door which led into the house.

As soon as he entered the kitchen a sense of foreboding crept over him. Isabel always cooked an evening meal on the occasions that he 'worked late'. She also made a habit of waiting to eat with him. The room was cold and clinically tidy. No food had been prepared there today. He entered the living room. His wife was sitting by the window gazing out. She didn't turn but spoke calmly and coldly.

"Who is she?"

Now that his fears had been realised he felt an unexpected sense of release. His eyes surveyed the abundance of heavy objects that lay around the room. He could pick up any one of them and bring it crashing on the back of her head.

I wouldn't even have to look at her face when I did it.

The thought passed through his mind with a complete sense of detachment. He teased the idea out.

It would be pretty hard to explain that away, though. No. If I kill her I'll have to be a lot more clever than that.

When Anxo remained silent Isabel felt her anger, barely controlled, begin to boil. She turned, the words "I'm having your child" on her lips, but they froze there. Whatever it was that she expected to see, she was unprepared for the callous, calculating look with which her husband was regarding her. For a moment Isabel felt, suddenly, afraid. And then Anxo blinked and the moment passed.

"Don't believe a word out of that little witch's mouth," he said. Then, as an afterthought: "What did she tell you?"

For the second time in as many minutes Isabel was caught unprepared. She had expected denials. She faltered. Anxo saw her confusion.

"Vicki called you, right?"

"Nobody called."

It was Anxo's turn to look baffled.

"There was makeup on that shirt that you tried to wash, Anxo – the shirt that you said you got from the guys at work."

As she spoke the steady course of her anger re–emerged. The 'Anxo' shot out like a bullet and found its mark. She could almost see the wheels turning in her husband's head as he wrestled with the realisation that he had needlessly given himself away. He crossed the room and sat near her.

"Vicki is a girl who has a crush on me," he said, holding her gaze in an attempt to impress her with his sincerity. "I didn't want to say anything because I didn't want to upset you but when I rejected her she said she was going to call you and tell you I'd been sleeping with her. She's crazy. She must have put lipstick or whatever it was on my shirt to frame me."

Isabel regarded him disdainfully.

"You expect me to believe that this girl managed to put makeup on your shirt while you were wearing it and you didn't notice? And what about these late nights, Anxo. What if I asked my Godfather about all this overtime you say you've been doing?"

"Cardosa hates me. He'd be just too happy for the chance to wreck our marriage. Today I took out a car to check on a customer complaint. I was doing him a favour and he nearly took my head off."

Isabel stared at him. He held her gaze defiantly. It was Isabel who looked away.

"When I went to work today," she said, after a while. "I wrapped up my wedding dress and that stupid shirt and I donated both of them."

"You *what*?"

"You never answered me. How did this girl that you say

has a crush on you get makeup onto your shirt while you were wearing it, Anxo?"

"I have no idea, Isabel, but you could have waited to talk to me before you started throwing our bloody clothes away. I mean, your wedding dress, for fuck's sake. What happened to 'innocent until proven guilty'?"

"I'm talking to you now and you're saying nothing to convince me."

Anxo stood up slowly, stared at his wife for a moment and then walked, purposefully, to the door where he paused and looked back.

"It's obvious that nothing I say is going to convince you. All I've ever done is to try and be the husband you want me to be, that your father wanted me to be, that bloody Cardosa wants me to be. I've worked like a *peón* in that job to prove myself to you all but none of it's good enough. I don't know what more I can do."

He appeared to be on the verge of tears and turned quickly as if to prevent Isabel from seeing him break down – not before, though, he'd seen the doubt in her eyes. She looked as though she wanted to say more but he didn't give her the opportunity. As he stormed out of the house he was thinking very calmly. Things were bad but he reckoned he'd bought himself time. This was a job for Helio. His old friend was ruthless and had a habit to feed. He'd have the balls to take care of Isabel for him. All he had to do was hold his marriage together for a while longer and make sure that nothing could be brought back to him.

Minutes later the Citroen was leaving the narrow streets of Santiago's historic centre. The old buildings gave way to the modern apartment blocks that housed many of the city's 40,000 students who came to attend what was one of the oldest universities in the world. These, in turn, gave way to the featureless concrete of the neighbourhood where Anxo had grown up, stark against the mountainous landscape behind. He parked the Citroen a block away from the bar. Wearing a baseball cap and sunglasses, he climbed out, locked the car and took a couple of steps before stopping.

I've been too long living in the nice part of town.

He unlocked the car again, took a gym bag from the back seat and transferred it to the boot, out of sight. The crime rate in Santiago was relatively low but, like anywhere else in the western world, it had its share of desperate junkies who would smash a window to explore the contents of the bag in the hope of finding something they could sell for a few euro and this *barrio* was exactly where one was likely to find them. In fact, that's what he was counting on.

The bar was on a corner, its entrance on the main road. He approached it from the side street, slipping through a gate into the back yard. It had been three or four years but he was confident that all would be the same. This had been his haunt from his mid teens until he'd moved uptown with Isabel and nothing had changed in all the years he'd frequented it. Sure enough, the same ill–fitting drapes were drawn across the window. He could hear laughter as he approached and gazed, through a gap, into the room beyond. Helio was standing exactly where he had been standing the last time Anxo had seen him – slouched against the wall with a pool cue in one hand. The other was toying nervously with an unlit cigarette. He was closely watching his opponent who was crouched low to the table, lining up a shot. Anxo made his way back to the car, started the engine and drove to a point along the main road from which he could see the entrance of the bar.

More than an hour had passed and the sun was sinking low before Helio's stooped, gaunt frame emerged. To Anxo's satisfaction, he was alone. He waited until Helio had passed and turned the corner before following in the little Citroen. Helio remained alone on the street. Anxo pulled up ahead of him and threw open the passenger door.

"*Cabron*, get in," he called. The latter's hand went into his pocket as he stared suspiciously. Anxo leaned over and removed the sunglasses.

"Fuck me. The dead arose and appeared to many," said Helio, climbing into the passenger seat. Anxo pulled away as the other watched him appraisingly.

"I guess that rich bitch must have finally got sense and

fucked you out if you're slumming it around here again, *hombre*."

Anxo laughed, humourlessly.

"You're not a million miles off the mark, my friend. Actually, that's exactly why I'm here. I need the old Helio magic touch to make my problems go away."

"Am I getting this straight. The rich bitch has become a problem and you need her to disappear?"

Anxo nodded slowly.

"It's worth five 'k'. You up for it?"

Helio stared at him for a moment before speaking.

"How do you want it done?"

"It'll be a break in," said Anxo. "If my dear wife wasn't such a *coño* I'd be in the bedroom to protect her but, because she'll be expecting me to slum it on the sofa until she makes up her mind if she's dumping me or not, I'm going to be sleeping like a baby downstairs while you stick her like a pig."

"When."

"It's got to be in the next few days. She has made up her mind that I'm having an *aventura* with another woman. I've managed to stall her for now but she's like a dog with a bone. She's not going to let go until she gets to the bottom of it and I can't let it get that far or I lose everything."

"And, of course, she's right. You're fucking around, yeah?"

"Sweet little 19 year old. A real *guapa*."

Helio tilted his head back and closed his eyes.

"I got to get me one of them."

He paused, savouring the thought, before speaking again.

"Half now and it's a deal."

"*Vete a tomar por culo!*" laughed Anxo. "Because you're a mate I just might be persuaded to drive you to a *cajero* and sort out a few hundred so you know I mean business. Any more than that and you'll be too busy shooting shit into your arm to even remember me or my problems."

Helio grinned.

"Worth a try. I want the rest of the cash as soon as she's done, though."

DUBLIN, IRELAND

ALTHOUGH SHE HAD BEEN WAITING for it, when the plane landed it took Angela by surprise. One minute the screen said that flight EI743 from Santiago de Compostela was expected in three minutes and then, the next time the information updated, it had changed to a single word – "Landed". She felt a surge of excitement well up in her stomach, completely replacing, for the first time, the darkness that lived there. Turning to find her mother looking at her, she pointed to the screen. Mammy's face lit up with a smile that Angela remembered well but hadn't seen in a long time.

"It'll still take her a while to come through," said Mammy. "It'll be ten minutes before she's off the plane, then she has to wait for her bags and get through customs and passport control. I'd say it could be half an hour."

In the end it was 33 minutes before the glass doors slid apart and Granny appeared. She was wheeling a small suitcase and carrying a bulging plastic bag. Angela slipped under the metal rail that held back the awaiting crowd and ran to her. Granny let go of the suitcase, dropped the bag and Angela felt herself buried in a warm, safe hug with that special smell that only Granny had.

"I missed you, darling," whispered Granny and Angela squeezed her in reply.

"Come on you two. Let's get home," came Mammy's voice. Granny returned the squeeze, released Angela and stood up. She looked Mammy up and down and smiled.

"It's so good to see you, love," she said, but Angela had noticed a worried look before the smile.

As the two women hugged Angela looked at Mammy to see what Granny had seen. She was skinnier. A lot skinnier. How had Angela not noticed before? As the two women finally broke apart she could see that Mammy was as excited as she was.

"It's unlike you to pack your things in something as tasteless as a plastic bag, Mam," said her mother, laughing as she picked up the bag that Granny had dropped.

"Old clothes. I got them in Santiago," said Granny. "Angela and I are going to have a lot of fun making some lovely things from them."

She winked at Angela and it sent a delightful thrill of happiness through her.

"Well, seeing as this is for you, you might as well carry it, Angie," said Mammy, passing her the bag.

Angela took it and glanced inside. On top was a shirt with a wonderful bright pattern of rich red, warm orange and deep yellow. The design was like a series of commas or of strange little fish. She reached in and felt the material. This was going to make something very nice, she thought. An idea came to her. She'd use it to make a special present for Granny.

4. Romans

"And even as they did not like to retain God in their knowledge, God gave them over to a reprobate mind, to do those things which are not convenient."

BOSTON, USA

FR DELUCCI'S FLIGHT was not until 9.10am but he booked the white cab to pick him up at 5.30. Part of this was due to his natural tendency of erring on the side of caution but, mainly, it was to minimise the chance of being seen by his parishioners. After long discussion, it had been decided that Fr Berry would simply announce to them that he was standing in for their parish priest while he was overseas on a sabbatical. Fr Delucci had not, Fr Berry would explain, wanted any fuss.

The first indication that he had over–packed came as he struggled with his backpack down the short driveway to the waiting car. The second followed shortly afterwards with the grunt of the driver has he hoisted the 90 litre monster into the trunk.

"Unusual suitcase for a padre, Padre," he said.

"I'm going on a walking trip in Europe."

"Well, with the weight of that thing, I hope you've been eating your spinach."

At the airport he was glad that he'd arrived early when the young woman at check–in eyed up his backpack disapprovingly.

"You'll need to leave that at the oversized baggage station," she said. "The straps get caught on the conveyor belt."

"Oh," said Fr Delucci, looking around him at the hectic activity in the huge departure hall. "Which way is that?"

"Let's get your boarding pass sorted first."

She began to type, eyes fixed on the monitor before her.

"Window seat or aisle?"

Fr Delucci was unprepared for the question. It would be nice to look out of the window. Maybe he'd get a view of the city from the air as they landed. On the other hand he could end up with somebody falling asleep on the seat beside him and trapping him in. He wouldn't be able to get to the toilet if he needed it.

The young woman looked up impatiently from the screen.

"I'm sorry," said the priest. "I haven't flown overseas before. What do you recommend?"

Her face softened at this consultation of her professional opinion. She glanced at the monitor.

"The flight's not very full today. Why don't I put you in a row on your own. That way you'll be able to lie out and snooze if you want."

Fr Delucci thanked her warmly and was rewarded with careful instructions on how to locate the oversized baggage station. As he picked his way through the crowded building the enormity of the project he was undertaking dawned on him. Throughout all of his adult life, decisions had been made for him on a daily basis. Now something as simple as choosing a seat was proving to be a challenge. Anything outside his realm of understanding had fallen neatly into the category of 'leave it to the will of God'. With that blind faith taken out of the equation a world of insecurity was opening up.

At the oversized baggage station his backpack was subjected to careful scrutiny on grounds of security. The man prodded around for a while before withdrawing the leather satchel containing his bible and breviary along with his clerical collar.

"Fancy dress?"

"No, I actually *am* a priest."

The man looked doubtful. He held up the bible.

"Anything hidden in here?"

"No, of course not," replied the priest.

"Well that's a first," smirked the man. "Our parish priest is always trying to convince me of the opposite."

Ignoring the priest's flush of embarrassment, he held up the collar.

"And you don't need this with you?"

"Well yes. I suppose I'd better. Thank you," said Fr Delucci, taking the white band and putting it into his jacket pocket. "Though we do travel *incognito* sometimes."

"Smart. Why make yourself a target?"

The comment left the priest feeling distinctly dissatisfied – as if a charge of cowardice had been laid against him in such a way that he had no recourse to a defence. Somewhat discombobulated, he joined the throng of people filtering slowly through security. When his turn finally came, he unlatched the gold cross and chain from around his neck. The links of the chain sent a shiver through him as they slid across his skin. A gift from his mother, he had not removed the crucifix since she latched it onto him on the day of his ordination many years before. Almost reverently, he placed the cross and chain in the plastic tray along with his loose change, belt and wallet.

"Shoes and jacket too," said the security guard.

He passed through the metal detector, stripped of all but a few items of clothing. On the far side he slowly put on his shoes and belt. It was too warm in the airport to wear his jacket so he carried it over one arm as he crossed to a monitor and sought out details of his flight to Lisbon, Portugal. Beside him was a trash can. On an impulse, he discreetly took the clerical collar from his jacket pocket and slipped it into the bin. For the first time in many years he felt like plain old 'Joe' Delucci. It was liberating. It was also frightening.

The departure gate proved to be a nightmarish experience. Because he was so early the monitor at Gate 147 read "London" instead of "Lisbon" when he finally found it. A kindly staff member put his mind at rest that the Lisbon flight would arrive there in due course so he settled down to wait with a book about walking the *Camino* that he had bought but had not found time to read. He discovered, to his great annoyance, that it largely ignored the Portuguese route that he was to walk and concentrated, instead, on the vastly more popular French way. He browsed for sections that focused on general tips or information on walking the *Camino*, regardless of the chosen route, but found that he couldn't concentrate. He abandoned the attempt. Instead, he watched the passengers board the London flight until he was alone in the seating area apart from a young woman who was stretched out, fast asleep, on a row of chairs, her handbag serving for a pillow. A thought struck him that left him suddenly perturbed. What if she was supposed to be on the London flight and had slept through the boarding calls? He leapt up and looked anxiously around. The airline staff had vacated the boarding gate desk but the plane was still on the tarmac outside, attached to the umbilical cord of the boarding tunnel. He crossed quickly over to where the sleeping girl lay, her mouth slightly open, her chest rising and falling in a gentle rhythm. There he stopped, assailed by sudden doubt. What if she had simply chosen those seats to lie down on and was totally unconcerned with the London flight? Then again, she would hardly have picked a row of seats in the middle of a plane load of passengers. He bent to shake her then paused again. She could have lain down before the crowd arrived and had slept through the subsequent bustle? He retreated a few steps, stopped, looked back at her, moved towards her again, stopped and finally, in a misery of indecision, made his way back to his seat.

Shortly afterwards, the monitor flickered and "Lisbon" appeared in comforting bold letters. People began to arrive and fill the plastic seats around him. He tried to read once more but soon gave up. He amused himself, instead, by trying to guess which of his fellow passengers were Portuguese and which were American. He was straining to hear the conversation between two young girls who he had guessed were European by their elegant but simple fashion when a commotion drew his attention. The sleeping girl was sleeping no longer.

"... but Gate 147 is supposed to be London," she was saying to a blue–shirted airport staff member who was examining her boarding pass with courtesy but little apparent concern.

DUBLIN, IRELAND

AS HER FINGERS worked the needle in a steady rhythm Angela's thoughts were elsewhere. She was trying to decide what to make for Granny from the lovely shirt with the bright patterns. Whatever she decided upon, she wanted it to be the best piece of work she had ever done. She wanted Granny to think of her every time she saw it. Granny wasn't coming to Australia.

Angela had seen the disappointment in Mammy's face as Granny explained that she was only staying with them as long as it took to help them pack up the house and leave for Australia.

"Spain was our dream," she had said. "Those last months there with your dad left me with so many lovely memories. I couldn't bear to think of leaving him buried out there alone with no family to visit his grave. Anyway, it's like home there now. I have my friends and I have my routine. I drop in to the graveyard every day and tell him all the latest news then I still feel him near me. I'm too old at this stage in life to move to the other side of the world."

"But your family will all be there – Tony, Angela and me – we'll all be there. If we're on opposite sides of the world we'll be lucky if we ever see each other again."

Granny had looked troubled but remained silent. Mammy had stared for a moment and then shrugged. She walked over to the kitchen counter, picked up the kettle and began to fill it at the sink.

"Tea?" she asked, as if the conversation hadn't taken place.

"Thanks, love," Granny had said, and Angela felt as though she'd missed something.

Now Mammy was in the room that used to be Daddy's little office typing on the computer to find the cheapest company to ship their things to Australia. Mammy seemed to always be busy with 'the move' these days but Angela had Granny. These evenings had become even more special to Angela because she knew she didn't have many of them left. At that moment the sun dipped below the level of the house across the street, throwing the room into shadow. Granny reached over and switched on the table lamp. This had come to signal the end of their work for the day. Angela could feel Granny watching her as she brought a line of neat, tiny stitches to an end and, with her tongue protruding from one corner of her mouth, knotted it off.

"You've gotten so good at that," Granny said as Angela handed her the work for approval. Granny turned the small cloth purse in her hands for a moment and Angela watched anxiously.

"How absolutely beautiful," she smiled and Angela felt her face flush.

"Now, you put these bits and bobs away while I start the dinner. I'm sure your mum will be finished soon and if I don't cook she forgets to eat."

Angela waited until her grandmother had left the room before starting her routine. First the big things – such as scissors and knitting needles – went into the wooden box. Next came the spools of thread. She made sure, first, that any stray strands were rewound and then she arranged the spools in order from light shades to dark in their groups of colours. Finally she took the dirty, worn pin cushion – vaguely recognisable as the stuffed–cloth hedgehog it had begun its life as – and carefully began replacing the pins and needles into its back. She was struck with a sudden idea. Granny's gift would be a brand new pin cushion. Smiling, she reached into her own sewing bag and pulled out the special colourful, patterned shirt. She spread it wide on the floor and considered it for a moment. The patterns were all wrong for another hedgehog so it would need to be something different. With a pen, she began tracing an outline. As usual, she started with no fixed idea. Granny had told her that the pattern was called 'paisley'. She let the pen find its way, concentrating on making smooth lines and curves. When the end of the line joined the start she sat back and looked at what she had drawn. It was the figure of a little man. Taking the scissors she began to cut out the shape.

LISBON, PORTUGAL

A DISEMBODIED but friendly voice called for the window blinds to be opened, seat belts fastened, tray tables stowed and seats to be returned to the upright position. The priest strained to make out features from the patchwork of lights below as the plane descended smoothly from inky–blue, cloudless skies to touch down in *Lisbon Portela Airport.* He found himself joining in with the burst of applause that followed the jolt of the wheels making initial contact with *terra firma.* The common euphoria was soon converted into impatience, however, when a late departing plane occupying their allotted gate found them sitting, motionless, on the tarmac for an additional ten minutes. When they did finally move, the plane, a creature of the skies removed from its natural environment, seemed to take an eternity to trundle its way to the terminal building.

The ensuing pushing and jostling to get out of the aircraft was repeated in a jockeying for position at the baggage reclaim area as suitcases and bags of every shape, size and colour spilled onto the conveyor belt. When his backpack tumbled out Fr Delucci noted that it was, undeniably, quite a bit larger than the average piece of baggage. He wrestled it onto a luggage cart before making his way through passport control and into the arrivals hall.

It soon began to dawn on the priest that Portugal might well prove somewhat of a culture shock. Like most North Americans he was quite used to the Central and South Americans talking amongst themselves in Spanish but in his world those who couldn't also speak a good level of English tended to be seen as disadvantaged. English was the verbal currency that made everything go around. Here, however, the tables were turned. His journey from the airport to Santarém by train was fraught with anxiety. The man in the ticket office spoke no English, the signs were all in Portuguese – as was the robotic voice on the train's intercom that announced the next stop. He spent the one–hour train journey from *Lisboa*

Oriente peering into the gloom at each station in an attempt to catch name signs, in a permanent state of semi–panic in case he missed his stop. Eventually, though, he found himself standing with his backpack on the platform of an old country train station. Apart from a few buildings, leaking light from shuttered windows, it seemed like a desolate spot. He checked the sign again. It was definitely Santarém. Outside the station three taxis stood in a line, their drivers leaning on the middle vehicle in animated conversation. The priest approached the first car in line and one of the men hurried over, helping him out of the backpack straps. Fr Delucci showed the taxi driver the address he had printed out. The man nodded and hoisted the backpack, with great difficulty, into the trunk. Soon after pulling away the car began to ascend and before long it was winding its way through the narrow streets of the city. The priest gazed with a mixture of anxiety and interest at the unfamiliar writing on the shop signs and at the crowds sitting outside restaurants, looking so un–American. At first he couldn't put his finger on the difference and then it came to him. The clothing colours were muted and there were little or no brash brand names printed on them. Another thought struck him and his hand dropped, unconsciously, to his stomach. The Portuguese, he had to admit, seemed generally more trim than North Americans.

The taxi moved, now, out of the business area and along a road with little to attract the priest's attention. A wave of tiredness began to wash over him. He was just feeling his eyelids grow heavy as the drone of the car's engine lulled him towards sleep, when they reached his destination. The *Santuário de Nossa Senhora da Paz* was one of the many Gothic–Romanesque buildings that gave a sense of historic importance to the city. The taxi had pulled up at an entrance on a quiet, tree–lined street and Fr Delucci, wide awake again, was plunged into further difficulties as he tried to make sense of the Euro notes that now filled his wallet. Finally, against his better judgment, he fanned out a handful of them and let the taxi driver take his pick. The little man then bounced out of the vehicle, popped the trunk and hauled the priest's oversized backpack onto the cobbled pavement.

"*Gracias,*" said Fr Delucci, realising, even as he said it, that this was a Spanish word.

"You're welcome," replied the man.

The ancient wooden door with its black iron fittings failed to give under the priest's shove. There was a bell to one side with a rope dangling from the clapper. The priest checked his watch. It was approaching 2am. He left his backpack propped up against the doorframe and wandered around the building. It was surrounded by a high, stone wall. At the back there was a wrought iron gate but this was padlocked. He peered through and saw that some of the upper windows of the building showed light. After ten minutes or so he arrived back at the main door determined to ring the bell, now that he had evidence that people were awake inside. He paused with a hand on the rope and listened. All was deathly quiet. Fr Delucci released his grip. With a sigh, he unclipped the mummy sleeping bag from under his backpack, took it from its protective cover and began rolling it out on the ground.

The priest soon realised that sleep would be impossible on the hard cobblestones. Experimentation finally resulted in him adopting a half–sitting position, supported by the backpack, that was somewhat less agonising than lying down. Before his personal crisis he would have offered any such discomfort up for the release of the Holy Souls in purgatory but, suspended as he was between faith and disbelief, it seemed hypocritical. He was, it dawned on him, in a purgatory of his own construction.

He was discovered shortly before 5am by Frade Chico who was on an early morning mission to a local bakery to get the monks' ritual tray of *pastel de nata* – a sweet confectionery that they treated themselves to each Sunday morning.

"Ah, you must be the American. We were expecting you yesterday," said Frade Benedito, the abbot, clasping both of Fr Delucci's arms and, to the latter's great discomfort, planting a kiss on each cheek.

The *pastel de nata*, Fr Delucci decided, were worth getting up at 5am for. As he munched his way through a second, washed down with strong, sweet coffee, Frade Benedito discussed his impending journey.

"How far do you intend to walk?"

The priest blinked.

"Well... to Santiago."

The abbot smiled.

"Of course, but from which point will you begin?"

"Oh. I hadn't really thought about it. When I was planning the trip it was suggested that the first thing I should do was to come here and I presumed that this was the start."

The abbot smiled again.

"The Portuguese way begins much further south but there is no necessity to start there. Many people who are not..."

The priest couldn't help noticing the abbot's appraising look which left him feeling that he had been measured and found wanting.

"... used to walking long distances begin at Valença on the border and walk the rest of the way from there."

"Is that not... well, cheating?" asked the priest.

"Oh no. To receive your certificate you need to walk at least 100 kilometres. From Valença to Santiago is somewhat more than that."

Since arriving in Portugal Fr Delucci had been sinking under the ominous feeling that he had plunged in out of his depth. Suddenly, he felt lighter.

"How long does it take from there?"

The abbot considered.

"There are fast walkers who can cover it in three days. For you, especially with that great, big bag of yours, I would allow five or six days."

"I'd planned on spending more time then that away before returning to Boston," said the priest, doubtfully.

"Of course. You'll want to spend some time in Santiago when you get there. It is a wonderful city. And why don't you spend a few days here with us before you start? Frade Chico will be delighted to show you around. There are many curiosities. For example, in medieval times there was a Christian knight who died and was buried in one of the city's churches. His Muslim lady visited his tomb every day for the rest of her life. When she passed away they could not bury her in the church with him as she was not a Christian but, because of her dedication, they made her tomb on the outside wall of the Church beside his so that, although he lay inside the Church and she outside, beneath the ground they lay together. It is worth seeing. There is a great view from the park there of the surrounding countryside and quite a nice restaurant. Also we have wonderful underground passages beneath the city. And, of course, there is the Portuguese food. You must spend some time sampling our cuisine. Then, when you are ready to start your walk, we can drive you to the border and see you safely on your way. It is not so far by motorway. In this way, at least, you will have seen something of Portugal and our culture because, after Valença you will be in the Spanish province of Galicia."

"Well," said Fr Delucci," if you're sure that it wouldn't be too much trouble, that really sounds delightful."

SANTIAGO DE COMPOSTELA, SPAIN

ISABEL PASSED BY the open living room door on her way upstairs with the laundry basket. Anxo scowled. On Saturdays he would usually pretend that he had to work overtime so that he could meet up with Vicki during her lunch break. Two things prevented him from doing that now. Although he didn't think that Isabel's pride would allow her to check with Cardosa, he couldn't be sure and, with his wife's murder imminent, he needed to keep his bib clean. Getting caught with Vicki now would be disastrous. He rolled off the sofa, and grimaced. The makeshift bed was causing havoc with his lower back. He crossed to the french doors and stepped out to smoke.

When Isabel is gone I can smoke where I like.

The thought gave him a burst of exhilaration but it was short–lived. As he flicked at the almost–spent lighter in an attempt to tease a flame from it, the nagging doubt that had been lingering at the back of his mind refused to be subdued any longer. Helio had let him down. Perhaps he'd chickened out or maybe he'd been content to take the free €500 that Anxo had given him as an advance and shoot it into his veins without bothering to go through the effort of earning the rest of the money that fell due on Isabel's death. Whatever the case, it had become obvious to Anxo that Helio wasn't going to kill his wife. Too many nights had passed.

A noise above snapped him out of his thoughts. Glancing up he saw a line of washing fluttering in the breeze on the old wrought iron balcony at the end of the second floor corridor. The door had swung open and Anxo slinked back into the shadow of the house as Isabel stepped out. As the balcony took her weight Anxo was surprised to see it come away from the wall by at least a centimetre or so. The balcony had always been a source of discontent for Anxo. Throughout Santiago balconies inevitably consisted of a solid stone slab protruding from the old building wall with a wrought iron railing running around the outer edge. At some stage of the Quintana family home's history an accident must have befallen this balcony. The mark where a stone floor had once been was clearly visible on the wall but it had been replaced by an iron balcony that included an iron floor. Anxo had always felt that it cheapened the house. Now, however, his misgivings melted as he realised that he was being presented with an enormous piece of potential luck. In the gap that had appeared between the metal balcony and the wall the four bolts that were holding the structure in place were clearly visible at its four corners. Unaware that she was being observed, Isabel steadied herself, unconcerned. She cast a glance across the rooftops, lost in thought for a moment and then he saw her cross herself before she began to take down the washing and fold it into the wicker laundry basket.

As soon as Isabel had left for work at the charity shop Anxo wasted no time in putting his plan into action. Using electrical tape, he first covered the nuts so that the wrench wouldn't leave fresh marks on the rusted metal. For good measure he dowsed them with water when he had finished so that any unintentional scrapes would quickly rust over. Despite refusing to acknowledge his presence, while she didn't have indisputable proof of his infidelity Isabel had continued to cook his meals and wash his clothes. All Anxo had to do was hope that the next washing day came before the next strong wind because, after his careful handiwork which had left the nuts barely clinging to the ends of the bolts, he felt sure that a stiff breeze was all it would take to bring the balcony crashing down.

DUBLIN, IRELAND

GRANNY had decided not to come to the airport.

"I hate airport goodbyes," she'd said, "and I'd have to make my way home alone."

Mammy nodded and Angela thought she looked relieved.

"Now, you've got everything – passports, tickets and bank cards?" asked Granny. "They're the essentials. You can replace anything else."

"Yes Mum," said Mammy. "I'm not bothered about forgetting anything. I'm more worried about you alone here after we're gone."

"It's only for a few days until the transport company clears out the house then I'll be back to my sunny Spain," said Granny.

"Look Mum, are you sure you won't change your mind? Just think of it – me, Angela and Tony. You'd have the family around you again."

Angela glanced hopefully at Granny but her heart sank at the torn look she saw there. Mammy saw it too and began lifting suitcases into the hallway.

"The taxi should be here any minute."

"I'm sorry, love," said Granny.

Angela felt that the time was right. From her little pink travel bag she took out the gift. Granny was staring out the window miserably. Angela tugged her skirt. When she looked down Angela held out the little man. She was pleased with the way the pin cushion had turned out. The yellows, oranges and reds of the paisley pattern were broken by tiny neat writing, carefully sewn in black thread. She had used different beads for the eyes, nose and coat buttons. The mouth was a piece of red material cut in a moon shape. With a marker she had put lots of little black dots where his beard would be. Angela thought that he looked like a little Mexican bandit.

"For me?" Granny asked, her eyes suddenly watery.

She nodded and Granny took the figure. Angela watched

as she turned the little man around and around in her hands, her face breaking into a big smile and her mouth opening with delight. She saw Granny read where she had sewn the words 'Pin Cushion' in black thread so that she'd know what the little man was for.

All of a sudden Angela found herself wrapped in a huge, warm hug, filled with the lovely, familiar smell of Granny.

"Oh love, thank you. It's absolutely incredible. It's the best you've ever made."

Granny stood up again and re–examined the little–man pin cushion.

"You should really keep this to show everybody how clever you are."

Angela frowned and shook her head.

"I'll tell you what, then," said Granny. "I'll hold onto it but only to mind it for you. I'll bring him back to you. I promise, okay."

If Granny promises to bring him back then she'll have to come to see us.

Angela smiled and nodded vigorously.

"He needs a name," said Granny.

She examined the little man again.

"Pablo," she pronounced. "How about Pablo?"

Angela grinned and nodded again.

5. Peter

*"But these, as natural brute beasts, made to be
taken and destroyed, speak evil of the things that they
understand not; and shall utterly perish
in their own corruption."*

SANTIAGO DE COMPOSTELA, SPAIN

THE WOODEN BLOCK was located just inside the window so that passersby could watch the butcher demonstrate his skill in carving up the cuts of fresh meat. At precisely five minutes to one he fastidiously cleaned and resharpened the blade before slipping it into its leather pouch. He hung the bloodied apron on its hook, washed his hands methodically and was walking towards the door, buttoning his jacket, when the church clock struck the hour. The boy, left alone behind the counter to face the onslaught of lunchtime customers, was soon too busy to notice the man in the hoodie slip in, lean across the low counter to the block and slip out. It all happened in less than a minute.

Helio was late in fulfilling the contract but Anxo's €500 downpayment had resulted in several days of blissful contentment where one fix followed the next without any need to come down. Now he felt sharp, confident and focussed. His back sported a new tattoo: *"No te fies de nadie"*. It was while Helio was having the tattoo done, in an effort to distract himself from the drone of the machine and the relentless pinching sensation of the needle, that he had devised his plan for killing Isabel. The tattooist had given him a book of tattoo art to browse through as he sat, slumped forward onto the armrests of the leather chair. It was a picture of *el ángel de la muerte* that had given him the idea. The tattoo was done simply in black ink. The hooded figure of *the grim reaper* covered the entire back of the person in the photograph. From its clasped hands the handle of the sickle rose on one side. The metal blade of the death symbol disappeared over the shoulder and a second photograph showed how it reappeared on the front of the body, angling down the person's chest where the point fell just above the nipple. Helio had carefully memorised the image. After he slit her throat he would create his own masterpiece as a bonus for Anxo. Isabel's naked body would be his canvas, a blade would be his needle and her blood would provide his ink.

His mother was out when he arrived home. He went into the kitchen and took the *jamón serrano* that hung on a butcher's hook. He put the huge ham on a large plate and placed it on the table. Sitting, he removed the butcher's knife, wrapped in newspaper, from the deep inside pocket of his jacket. Unfolding the paper, he examined the blade. He drew the point across a page of the newspaper and grunted with satisfaction at the clean cut it made. He rotated the plate until the yellow–pinkish pork rind was facing him. Then, frowning with concentration, he used the tip of the knife to carve a row of neat letters.

Soy el ángel de la muerte.

ISABEL SHIVERED as the opening and closing of the door admitted a cold blast of air. From where she was crouched, sorting shoes from a box onto a lower shelf, she couldn't see who had entered but she became aware that Paula, behind the counter, was facing the newcomer with a smile while frantically signalling for Isabel's attention with a hand that remained below the level of the counter and, therefore, out of sight of whoever had entered.

The *buenos días* came in a masculine voice that she recognised and, without thinking, she turned to the mirror for people trying on footwear and adjusted her hair.

"*Buenos días, subinspector*. What a lot of stuff you've brought us," she heard Paula reply.

"There's more in the car. We had staff outing at the station and I thought it would be a good opportunity to organise a collection. The response was really good."

"That's so good of you. I can't leave the till but I'm sure Isabel will give you a hand."

She turned to where Isabel was scowling at her and called, rather theatrically.

"Isabel, it's Subinspector Pedrosa with some bags of donations. I wonder if you could give him a hand?"

Isabel shook a fist, glanced once more in the mirror, fixed a smile on her face and popped up from behind the shelves in time to catch the policeman's flustered expression. They exchanged '*hola*'s before Pedrosa hastened to assure them that he could manage the bags unaided.

"I'm sure you can, *Subinspector*, but we want you back on the street fighting bad guys as soon as possible," said Paula. "In fact, speaking of which, we've had a couple of dodgy looking characters loitering around for the past few days. We were wondering whether we should call the station or not although I suppose they haven't actually done anything. It's just a bit unnerving, isn't it Isabel."

"Yes, a bit," said Isabel turning to Paula in such a way that her back was to Pedrosa and giving her a look of exaggerated bewilderment.

"If you've any suspicions you should definitely give us a call," the policeman answered. "It's always better to be safe than sorry. In the meantime I'll make sure a car swings by from time to time."

Paula smiled innocently and continued.

"That's so good of you. So if they do show up again, which is the best number to call?"

Isabel was caught between indignation and humour at Paula's slyness as Pedrosa fumbled in his pocket for a business card.

"It has my direct line in the office and if you have a pen I'll put my mobile on there too."

"You're a star," gushed Paula, handing a pen to the subinspector. "Is that an eight or a three?"

"An eight. Sorry, my writing is awful."

"Not at all," replied Paula, taking the card. "Here Isabel. I'll give this to you as you're on in the afternoons and that's when they usually show up. Now I'll hold the fort if you want to give the subinspector a hand with those bags."

"What do you think you're up to?" demanded Isabel as they watched Subinspector Pedrosa's car merge with the traffic and disappear up the street.

"He's mad about you and I've seen the way you blush when he comes in – which, incidentally, is becoming ridiculously frequent."

"I'm a married woman," laughed Isabel, flushing.

Paula smiled and then the smile faded and she looked earnestly at Isabel.

"I know it's none of my business and maybe I'm wrong but you don't seem happy, Isa, and it seems very like the kind of unhappiness I had before I had the good sense to get out of my useless marriage."

Isabel stared blankly at her. She found herself biting her lower lip to stop it trembling and Paula realised that she had hit the mark.

"Like I said, it's none of my business but if you want to talk about it..."

For a moment Isabel was tempted to unload her suspicions of Anxo's infidelity upon her colleague but the weakness passed and, instead, she formed the words to politely but firmly retreat behind her wall of privacy. She was just as surprised as Paula, therefore, to hear what came out.

"I'm pregnant."

VALENÇA, PORTUGAL

THE AUTNA BUS drew into Valença station in a sweeping arc and came to a stop with a hiss of hydraulics. Mark climbed down clumsily and stood blinking in the hot September sun, trying to get his bearings. He fumbled in his inner pocket and withdrew the print–out of the email from shay@igottalosemyfatass.com.

"Albergue Santo António..."

Mark had been feeling like a digital castaway since arriving in Porto without the familiar rectangular bulge of his smartphone in his pocket. He was amazed to realise how many times he reached for it – while sitting on the bus to the airport, while waiting at the boarding gate, on the plane, while waiting for the bus in Porto and on the coach that had brought him to Valença. Without a screen to keep him occupied he had looked around at his fellow travellers and found that they were inevitably buried in their smart devices. At the departure gate in Manchester he caught the eye of one elderly man who was regarding him with a benevolence born, no doubt, from Mark's tech–free stance. Mark had felt like he'd cheated in an exam.

Nobody looks at each other anymore.

Now, in Valença, deprived of *Google Maps*, he had decided that he would show the print–out of the address to a local in the hope that he would be pointed in the right direction. He followed the last of the few other passengers who had dismounted with him to the shade of the station building where a noisy farmers' market occupied much of the forecourt. Live chickens squawked from crude cages. Vegetables caked in dried mud – far removed from the pristine and perfectly shaped carrots and onions of the supermarkets at home – lay in boxes on the ground. There were some that he didn't even recognise. Wrinkled women of indeterminate age, and dressed, invariably, in black, presided over them. They haggled with potential customers or, if not, stared jealously at those stall holders who were fortunate enough to be so engaged. A chicken flapped its wings in a futile attempt at escape as a black clad vendor, the bird's legs trapped expertly in one hand, turned it this way and that to show its virtues to a young woman with a little boy holding her hand. Both the boy and Mark stared with equal fascination as the deal was agreed and the older woman tucked the chicken between her knees and, with a deft twist of her hands upon its neck, dispatched it to oblivion. Mark resolved to find his own way into town. He looked all around for clues to the direction he should take. A busy, raised motorway filled the skyline in one direction. He could clearly make out the writing on one of the large, overhead traffic signs – "Espanha"

That has to mean Spain.

Using the motorway direction as a guide, he set off, sweating heavily in the unforgiving sunshine and weighed down by the unfamiliar burden of his backpack. Looking over the buildings in front of him, he saw a large sign which read, simply; "Hotel". Figuring that this building was likely to be in the centre, he began to take any turn in the road that seemed to bring him closer to it. The surroundings were starting to look more commercial when his attention was captured by footsteps approaching from behind. They were accompanied by a rhythmic tapping sound. He turned as two young women, wearing shorts, vest tops, hats, boots and carrying backpacks, overtook him. The tapping sound was made by a branch that one was using as a crude walking stick. In unison they smiled at him and said: "*Buen Camino*", before marching on. Their clunky boots looked out of place with their light, summer clothes, and from each of their backpacks swung a shell. The shells were decorated with little hand–painted red crosses.

The pair had not disappeared from sight when they stopped to consult a map and Mark gained on them. Apparently reaching a decision, they turned to the left. One of them, wearing glasses and with her hair tied up with a red scarf, glanced back and spotted Mark. She pointed at the road they were taking.

"*Esta aqui*," she called with a smile.

"Sorry?" shouted Mark.

"It's just up here," she replied, switching to accented English. "Nearly there."

Mark nodded a somewhat bewildered thanks and followed them. Sure enough, he watched them arrive at a white, red–roofed building that, when he got there, panting and sweating, proved to be the place at which he'd been instructed to stay. A large stone slab outside served as a sign. Beside the name, "*Albergue S. Teotónio*", was the symbol of a shell. He entered the building and the coolness of the shade greeted him like a caress. Stifling a groan, he slid his backpack to the floor and took stock of his surroundings. At a reception counter the two young women were checking in. The conversation was in rapid Spanish so he watched carefully to ascertain what the procedure was. Documents were shown, money was exchanged and the pair were given what appeared to be bed linen in a small transparent plastic bag. Mark waited until they had finished and moved away from the counter before he approached the receptionist – a middle aged man who was writing an entry into a book. He completed his task and looked up expectantly.

"Just one night, please," said Mark.

The man held out his hand.

"*Credencial*?"

"I'm sorry," said Mark. "Do you speak English?"

"I am speaking English. I am asking for your *credencial*."

"I'm sorry. I don't know what that is."

The man smiled, patiently.

"Where have you come from?"

"England," said Mark. "Do you mean my passport?"

"Ah. This is your first night," said the man. "To stay in the *albergues* you must have a *credencial*. It's a type of pilgrim passport that you will also use to record your journey by collecting stamps in it wherever you stop along the way. I have them here. They are three euro."

"Oh, sorry. I didn't know."

Mark zipped open his money belt.

"I'm afraid you'll have to wait until 8pm to see if there is a bed," said the man. "Preference is given to those who have completed a day's walking."

"Oh."

The man relented somewhat at Mark's alarmed expression.

"It's quite late and we still have several beds so you should be okay. If you want, you can leave your bag here and take a walk around the town. It is quite pretty."

"Thank you," said Mark. "Maybe you could recommend somewhere inexpensive to eat?"

When Mark returned at eight he had used the time to find

an internet café. Adelina had written wishing him well with his business trip, her message full of excitement about their approaching time together in England. Next he had read up on the *Camino de Santiago* and had discovered that it was a network of pilgrim trails from all over Europe that led to the tomb of St James the disciple – or *San Tiago*, as he was known in Spanish – in Santiago de Compostela. Pilgrims, or *peregrinos* followed crudely painted yellow arrows that marked the route and stayed at the *albergues* along the way. These, it was now obvious, were the yellow arrows referred to in shay@ Igottalosemyfatass.com's message. His bootcamp, therefore, he reasoned, involved walking at least part of the *Camino*.

The man at the reception in the *albergue* smiled.

"There is a bed," he said. "It's €3 for your *credencial* and €6 for the night."

Mark raised his eyebrows as he passed over the money.

At least this trip will be cheap.

The man reached into a drawer and took out a small booklet, about the size of a standard passport. It opened into one long sheet divided into simple blank boxes on one side and bearing images and writing on the other. He picked up a rubber stamp and stamped the hostel's symbol onto the first box.

"You must remember to get at least two stamps along the way each day so that you can prove that you've walked the *Camino* when you go to collect your certificate in Santiago," he explained, " and fill in your name, *et cetera* when you get a chance."

"Where do I get these stamps?"

"Well, at the *albergues*, of course, but also at pretty much any bar or restaurant and in the churches along the way."

He handed Mark a small plastic bag which, he discovered, contained covers for the mattress and pillow.

"Curfew is at 10pm. After that the *albergue* is locked and you will not be admitted. You must leave in the morning by eight."

"That's okay. I'm on the road at 5.45 so it's an early night for me," said Mark.

The man smiled.

"The dormitory is that way."

The dormitory proved to be a unisex one. It was filled with several rows of bunk beds, many of which were already occupied. Here and there figures lay in sleeping bags. On other beds people sat reading, writing or sorting through their belongings. The two young women who had passed him on the road were busily stretching the mattress covers onto their beds. One of them glanced up and smiled as he walked past. All of the lower bunks were occupied. Mark found a vacant upper one in a corner and hoisted his backpack onto it. He stretched the thin cover over the mattress and succeeded in ripping it in several places. He had better luck with the pillow cover. Finally he spread out his sleeping bag and, with great difficulty, clambered up the small metal ladder. He reached for his phone to set the alarm for 5.00am then realised, once more, that he didn't have it. He dwelt, for a moment, on what he could do as an alternative and then decided that he was too weary to care. He'd just have to hope that he'd wake on time. Turning his back on the room, he closed his eyes. As he listened to the various noises in the dormitory the bizarre nature of his situation struck him. He was a reclusive graphic designer who had never travelled abroad. Now he was in a place he'd never heard of until a couple of days before among a room full of strangers who didn't speak his language and about to embark upon a journey dictated by a stranger he had never met. This was the type of thing that Adelina would probably get up to, he decided. His thoughts dwelled on her. What if this worked? What if he really could get slimmer and fitter? They could go on walking holidays together – perhaps even sun holidays on the beach. Images began to play in his mind like so many home movies – Adelina, bikini clad, squealing with laughter as he chased her through the surf, his bronzed body toned; Gazing out over a valley from a high mountain trail with Adelina by his side dressed like one of the two young women who were somewhere in the dormitory at that moment; Standing at a roulette table in a classy casino sporting a tailored, white dinner jacket with Adelina smiling beside him in a long, shimmering evening dress while he explained to the waiter that he had asked for his Martini to be shaken rather than stirred…

The sounds of the dormitory became the sounds of the casino. He could hear the gasps of the admiring crowd as he put an outrageous sum of money on black. He could hear the roulette wheel spin and the metal ball bounce from number to number. Then, through the myriad sounds one emerged above the rest. It was the rhythmic sound of snoring. A part of his brain recognised that he was the source of the sound, but that part of his brain was disconnected from any desire to act upon the knowledge.

BENDIGO, AUSTRALIA

ANGELA'S DREAM of monkeys blended into a chattering sound that came from outside the open flyscreen–covered window of her bright, cheerful bedroom.

> *"Kookaburra sits on electric wire,*
> *jumping up and down with its pants on fire…"*

According to Uncle Tony they weren't the real words of the song but all the kids in Australia preferred this cheeky version. On the first morning the noise had alarmed her and she'd run into Mammy's bedroom only to find it empty. Before she'd had a chance to panic, though, she'd heard laughter from the kitchen. It was a long time since she'd heard Mammy laugh.

Now she lay with her eyes closed, savouring the comfort of her bed and the last, lovely moments of a good night's rest. The kookaburra made its distinctive call again but a sound within the room stole her attention. She sat up and stared in disbelief. Despite all of Uncle Tony's efforts, the puppy had managed to force her bedroom door open wide enough to wriggle through. He was sat on the cream carpet with his back to the bed, happily making a soggy, torn mess of her pink slipper. Sensing the movement the puppy turned and, with a mouthful of fabric and rubber, stared at her for a moment with his big, brown doggy eyes. Then his body trembled with excitement and his tail began to wag furiously. He ran to the bed, stood up on his little back legs and whined pleadingly. Angela patted the duvet encouragingly.

Throwing caution to the wind, the puppy launched himself upwards. He fell short but Angela was prepared and caught him before he tumbled back. He had been a wonderful surprise from Uncle Tony. When she held the puppy tight she could feel his little heartbeat against her chest and when that happened the blackness couldn't escape.

She lay back and let the puppy sit on her, licking her face. He was so careful to make sure he covered every part.

I can't keep calling him puppy. I need a name – something that says who he is.

Images of chewed footwear, chewed electric cables and Mammy's chewed handbag came to mind. The puppy might be tiny but he had a heart as brave as a lion and teeth that were ready to clamp upon anything he could fit into his mouth.

Chewy. I'll call you Chewy.

Contented, she pushed the puppy off her legs and crossed the room to the wardrobe. Chewy remained on the bed watching her. Uncle Tony had taken her shopping for new clothes just a few days ago. It was a lot hotter in Australia and she'd needed lots of shorts, skirts, sandals and little tops. Mammy had told Uncle Tony not to spend money on them but he had told her not to be silly. He didn't have any problems with money because he had his own business in the city. At first Angela had thought that Uncle Tony was a farmer because he had sheep and chickens.

"This is just a hobby farm," he'd explained. "My real job is quite boring but they pay me lots of money to do it and that means that I can have lots of pets."

Angela loved the smell of newness that hit her when she opened the wardrobe door. The clothes were arranged neatly in order of colour and type, just like the spools of thread in Granny's sewing box. She selected a pair of dungarees and a light, long–sleeved top so that she'd be covered from the sun. The sun was very dangerous in Australia. Uncle Tony told her she had to *slip, slop, slap* every time she went outdoors. "Slip" was for *slip on a shirt*, "slop" was for *slop on sunscreen* and "slap" was for *slap on a hat*. Uncle Tony was taking her gold prospecting today. The best gold in the world had been found in these parts, he'd told her. He had shown her little nuggets of real gold that he'd found with his metal detector.

"We'll go out with the detector and a couple of shovels and I'll be surprised if you don't find your very own gold nugget. Then we can put it on a chain and make a necklace for you."

She chose a blue baseball cap to match her dungarees then, closing the wardrobe door, she looked at herself in the full length mirror. It struck her, suddenly, that she liked the girl who looked back at her. From the corner of her eye she saw Chewy watching her from the bed. She turned, smiling, and knelt beside him. His tail leapt into motion and he ran his little tongue across the tip of her nose. Throwing her arms around him she tried to whisper her good news in his ear, but the words didn't come.

SANTIAGO DE COMPOSTELA, SPAIN

THE CRASHING SOUND wrenched him from a deep sleep. He was on his feet instantly, trying to determine where the noise had come from. Upstairs he heard cautious footsteps, and then the night was pierced by a cry – something short of a scream. He bounded across the darkened living room, banging his leg against the coffee table but immune to the pain in his adrenaline–heightened state. The sight that greeted him when he reached the top of the stairs was unexpected. At the far end of the landing Isabel stood with one hand on the frame of the open balcony door. She seemed frozen, silhouetted against the orange glow of the streetlights. As he approached, trying to make sense of what he saw, he noticed a large, cruel–looking knife lying on the wooden floor at the balcony's edge. Then he realised that the balcony was no longer there. Isabel was staring down, transfixed, into a void where it had been. When he appeared beside her she jumped with a squeal then, recognising him, she buried her head in his chest and gripped chunks of his tee shirt tightly with both hands. Peering over the edge Anxo saw the wrought iron balcony dangling, sideways, from one stubborn bolt. His eyes were drawn, though, to the crumpled body in the court-yard beneath. One leg lay twisted at an unnatural angle that was sickening to see. Helio was beyond pain, however. His unseeing eyes stared, frozen in that moment of shock. From his head a pool of blood was spreading, forming tributaries between the cobblestones and regrouping to flow in a steady stream towards the flower bed of red and white roses.

The thought was instant and brilliant. A sharp push and Isabel's blood would join Helio's on the cobbles below.

No officer, I've no idea. They must have been on the balcony together and it gave way. Perhaps he was a burglar, perhaps her lover, perhaps he was kidnapping her – I don't know. I was sleeping on the sofa downstairs...

He needed to make her loosen her grip on his tee shirt. He didn't want her to drag him with her when she fell.

"Isabel," he said softly. "Isabel. Let go. Look at me."

Although Isabel's eyes were shut tightly she could not erase the image of that twisted body and those staring eyes. She gasped in the familiar scent of her husband. She was not even aware that she was clinging to him until his voice penetrated the madness in her head, and then it all came flooding back.

Everything has changed.

She slowly released her grip on his clothing. She felt his hands clasp her firmly on each arm and the night breeze blew cold on her face as he stepped back. She looked up. Their eyes met and she shuddered involuntarily. There it was again. That look.

DUBLIN, IRELAND

IT HAD BECOME obvious that tonight would be yet another with little or no sleep. She was unused to the soft mattress on Grace's bed and she suspected that her body had not adjusted from the routine it was used to at home in Spain. The removal company was due in two days time, though, and then it was just a matter of cleaning up after them and letting the estate agent take over. After that she'd be back to her life in Spain.

Her thoughts had drifted to Grace and little Angela, settling in with Tony on the other side of the world. It would be daytime there. She had thought about trying to reach them on Skype but dismissed the idea. The last time she had done so Grace had admonished her for still being awake at such an hour. Her daughter had seemed much better. Her face had lost that strained look. With Angela it was harder to tell because she didn't speak.

The thought of Angela had prompted the woman to abandon her attempts at sleeping. Now she was sitting in her accustomed place in the living room where she and Angela had spent so many companionable evenings in silent enjoyment of each other's company. Her sewing box was open but she had removed just two items – the old hedgehog pin cushion and the new, colourful one that Angela had made for her.

Pablo. They had christened it Pablo.

She turned the little man once more in her hands, marvelling again at the perfectly neat lines of stitches, and then, with a wistful smile, she began the task. Selecting, first, a long pin with a round, bright red head from the hedgehog, she plunged it into the soft belly of the figure.

SANTIAGO DE COMPOSTELA, SPAIN

IN AN INSTANT the look was replaced by a grimace of astonished pain, and, with a cry Anxo collapsed on the ground in front of Isabel, knees snapping up to a foetal position. Moments later, though, he twisted and writhed as a new pain seemed to strike elsewhere.

"Anxo, what is it?" gasped Isabel, dropping to her knees beside her husband.

"*Joder...* Pain."

He struggled to get the words out.

"Everywhere, pain."

"Will I get an ambulance?"

A fresh attack cut off any reply that Anxo might have made as his body went into spasm. Isabel scrambled to her feet and ran to the bedroom where her mobile phone was charging on the locker at her bedside. As she snatched it up a small triangle of white card was protruding from one of the pockets in the phone's leather cover.

Pedrosa.

6. Timothy

*"Drink no longer water,
but use a little wine for thy stomach's sake
and thine often infirmities."*

VALENÇA, PORTUGAL

AS IT WORKED OUT, Mark need not have worried about his lack of an alarm. It seemed to him that he had only fallen asleep when he was awakened by the early morning *peregrinos* noisily readying their backpacks.

"Sorry, did I wake you?" whispered the man who had slept in the bunk below him as he rolled his sleeping bag into a tight, neat ball.

"No, that's fine," said Mark, glancing at his watch and finding that he had ten minutes to get himself up and out if he was to obey Shay's instructions. "How come everyone's up so early?"

"You must be new on the *Camino*, then," stated the man, strapping the sleeping bag under his backpack. "You want to get as much of your walking done as possible before the sun comes up. As well as that you don't want to arrive after everybody else and find the beds all gone in the next place."

"Oh," said Mark. "That makes sense."

The man hoisted his bag onto his shoulders and turned to leave.

"Are you going to Porriño today or on as far as Redondela."

"I'm not actually sure," replied Mark.

"Smart move. See how the feet hold out first," said the man. "Well, you can't go wrong. Just follow the arrows."

He headed for the door.

"*Buen Camino.*"

"Right. Thanks. *Buen Camino*," replied Mark, feeling somewhat out of his depth.

It was 5.45am, as instructed, when he left the *albergue,* still yawning, but feeling a growing sense of excitement at the prospect of the adventure ahead. It was dark, apart from the patches of orange glow around the street lights, and a ghostly silver hue from the full moon when flitting clouds didn't obscure it. It was, therefore, with some difficulty that he located the first of the yellow arrows that marked 'the way'. It led him across the road and into a field where a well trodden dirt track took him up a slope and into what appeared to be a medieval walled village fortress. He might easily have got hopeless lost at that point but for the presence of other *peregrinos* who, well accustomed to locating the yellow arrows that marked the way, found them by using their mobile phones or small pocket torches to shed light. Mark exchanged some pleasantries with the others but they seemed anxious to press on and he soon found himself left behind. He trudged through a village of old but well preserved shops and houses, all contained within the fortress walls. Nothing was open and the thought of breakfast preoccupied him. On the far side of the village he bemoaned the lack of a torch or the glow from a mobile phone when the uneven path ran through a twisting, long, pitch black tunnel in the old walls. Finally he emerged from the fortress and descended some broad steps towards the roadway, his backpack jerking uncomfortably on his shoulders at every downward step. A short walk brought him to the metalwork bridge stretching over the mighty River Minho. A brief flash split the darkness ahead. It was caused by a cyclist who had stopped to take a photograph of a large sign that faced away from Mark as he approached. It proved to contain one word; "Portugal". Beyond this point, then, he was entering Spain. Having walked for all of twenty minutes he knew it was vaguely ridiculous but he couldn't help feeling a sense of accomplishment. He decided to take a rare 'selfie' with the sign but remembered his lack of a phone and cursed to himself instead.

He examined the bridge. Pedestrian walkways lay to either side and the road for vehicular traffic ran through the centre. He had a moment of difficulty deciding which of the two footpaths to take as, in the gloom, he couldn't locate any markers to tell him. However, the sky seemed a little less black to what he gauged was the east so he tentatively chose that side. He was rewarded immediately with a yellow arrow, bright against the lifeless cold, grey metalwork. He knew the instructions by heart:

... At the third column of the bridge over the Minho you will find a bag. Further information there...

Peering over the railing of the bridge he could see the huge columns upon which the structure rested. The third one was approximately at the middle point of the river – a vast expanse of water shimmering grey in the pre–dawn light. At the midway section Mark was delighted to see a symbol on the ground before him. It showed a line with a footprint painted with the Portuguese flag colours on one side and a similar footprint branded with the Spanish colours on the other. This, then, was the border.

When he reached the spot where the third column rose, Mark glanced back along the walkway to ensure that he was alone and then peered, once more, over the railing. A small crescent shaped edge of the supporting column protruded below him but there was no sign of a bag. Turning Mark noticed that huge steel girders shot upwards from the column to support the trellised structure above. He examined the base of this superstructure and saw, immediately, a gap between it and the platform upon which he was standing. Checking, again, that he was alone, he took off his backpack, knelt and examined his find. There were, in fact, three holes of varying size created by the shapes of the metal girders. He reached into the first and groped about. Nothing. In the second, however, his hand encountered a plastic bag and his heart jumped with a sudden childish excitement. Retrieving it, he examined the contents. There was a note, a packet of blue chalk and a cheap, old fashioned mobile phone, complete with charger. He examined it doubtfully for a moment. It would manage little more than text messages and phone calls, although it did, he noted, have an alarm function. He turned his attention to the note, recognising the handwriting from the letter he had received back in England. It read:

Your overall mission is to walk the Camino to the Cathedral in Santiago de Compostela. Now buy bread for breakfast in the small panadería at the bottom of the hill on the road past the Cathedral in Tui but don't eat it. Carry it with you as you walk on to the next stop, Porriño, where you will stay, tonight, in the albergue. You will receive further instructions by text on the phone provided as you walk so keep it charged up. Each time you complete a task write your name and the exact time with the chalk so I can check your progress. You will never know when I am nearby watching. Well done. You've completed your first task so start by writing your name and the exact time now. Shay.

To Mark it all seemed rather elaborate. He was also more than a little dismayed about the idea of buying bread and carrying it along without breakfasting on it. He had come this far, though, he reflected, so he owed it to himself to give it a try. Taking a stick of blue chalk from the packet he consulted the phone for the correct time and verified it with his wristwatch. There was a discrepancy of a few minutes. Reasoning that the phone was taking its time from the cellular network, he decided to go with that. He wrote it down, beside his name, on the upright metal girder at the base of which the package had been concealed. He was just putting the chalk back into the packet when two figures appeared on the bridge behind him. He slipped the phone and chalk into the leg pocket of his combat shorts and stuffed the empty bag and rope into one of his backpack's outer pockets as he discreetly observed the new arrivals. It was a young couple, their backpacks marking them as *peregrinos*. It struck Mark that he could now apply that label to himself. The young man was several strides ahead of the young woman. He was wearing a vest top that revealed the type of shoulders and chest that are the result of long hours in the gym. When he saw Mark he slowed down and let his companion catch up.

Despite the tied back hair, hat and hiking clothes it was obvious that she was stunningly beautiful. As the young man drew close, Mark felt himself the subject of an appraising scrutiny. Mark recognised the familiar look of disgust as he was dismissed as posing no threat. The man picked up his pace again so the young woman was alone once more as she passed. His position, kneeling beside his backpack, seemed appropriate to Mark in the presence of such aesthetic royalty and he looked down, abashed, watching her feet as she drew level. The feet slowed.

"*Buen Camino.*"

Mark looked up and found himself faced with a warm smile.

"*Buen Camino,*" he returned, flushing red with embarrassment.

She walked on in the wake of her boyfriend. Mark got clumsily to his feet and hoisted his backpack into place. As he set off after the couple he wondered, not for the first time, why lovely women always seemed to choose assholes.

At first he laboured gamely after the pair but they soon reached the far side of the bridge and disappeared around the corner. When he finally stepped off the bridge and onto the footpath they were nowhere in sight. A similar sign to the one on the Portuguese side of the river told him he was now in Spain. Another blue and yellow sign proclaimed, in bold letters: "Camino de Santiago". Above the writing was the now familiar symbol of the shell.

Some time later, Mark was walking along the street, faithfully following the arrows, when a thought struck him. Here in Spain the clocks went forward an hour. Should he, then, have written Spanish time on his blue–chalked message? He had, after all, passed the graphic on the ground that signified his crossing from one country into the next.

Stopping to look back to where the bridge was already quite a distance behind he made up his mind. The sign could stay written on Portuguese time. There was no way he was walking all the way back to change it now.

He came to a petrol station on a corner and the arrows indicated that he should turn right. This led him to a path that, once more, ran close to the river. As he reached the water, the sun suddenly broke out from behind a hill on the far bank, greeted by a bewildering chorus of birds and flooding the landscape with a golden glow. He stopped, enthralled by the view for a moment, but the weight of his backpack and the thought of food soon drove him on. Although his route seemed to skirt the main road he could hear the town beginning to waken. Carefully following the frequent yellow arrows, he eventually came to the foot of the hill that had been visible since the bridge and began the gruelling, winding ascent along the narrow streets to the cathedral. Despite frequent stops he was almost physically ill when finally he staggered into the square in front of the huge, old church. There he saw the couple from the bridge. The young man had taken his top off and was rubbing sun cream over his torso. The young woman was taking photographs of the cathedral. Mark, soaked in sweat and panting, hurried, unnoticed, past the square and around the first corner until he found himself out of sight. For a while he lost track of the yellow arrows and was afraid he'd have to retrace his steps but then, as he descended a street past an elaborate church building he found himself back on the marked way.

He was agonising over the possibility that he had passed the *panadería* while he was momentarily lost and that he would have to climb back up the hill when he came across it. The aroma of freshly baked bread forewarned him before the shop itself came into sight and set his mouth watering. He put down his backpack and entered. There were two elderly women in the shop, sporadically visible in a back room as they busily laid bread onto battered but sturdy metal racks that looked as ancient as themselves. Eventually one caught sight of him and came out to the shop counter. There were three types of loaf on offer and she smiled, patiently, as he tried to tell her which one he wanted by speaking slowly in simple English and pointing vigorously.

The woman set him on his way with his carefully wrapped parcel and a *buen Camino*. He marched on, sweating under the increasing heat of the day. After a while he left the buildings behind and found himself walking on a level track through farmland. Away from the town a welcome breeze made the sun more bearable, and he became aware of a chorus of birds chirping merrily in the undergrowth. Mark was distracted, however. The paper packaging around the parcel in his hand failed, miserably, to mask the aroma of soft, fresh bread. When he came to a man–made pool of water at the side of the track – he guessed that it was a place where local women had come to wash clothes in the days before launderettes and washing machines – he stopped to put the bread into his backpack and out of temptation. He screwed the cap off a plastic bottle of water he had brought with him from the *albergue* and took a long, welcome swig. With the bread packed away and refreshed by the water, he looked around him in a more appreciative frame of mind. With the smell of the bread replaced by the fresh scent of flowers and foliage he was suddenly struck with a great sense of wellbeing. For the first time that he could remember he felt at harmony with nature and completely detached from the addiction of the world wide web. In fact, he thought, it was quite possible that mobile phones would struggle to find a signal in this remote spot. That thought prompted him to check the phone that had come in the package on the bridge. Two words were written on the small screen.

Message received.

He fumbled with the unfamiliar, archaic keypad for a few moments before figuring out how to open the text message.

After Tui, in the forest after the long stretch of main road, you will find the cross where San Telmo fell with fever.

There you will leave the bread and walk on. It is an important test of your will power.

Remember to leave your name and the time you've completed this task.

Shay

Mark felt like crying.

Bastard.

There was a flutter of wings and a magpie landed at the edge of the pond. It regarded him for a while with its beady, yellow eyes. Then it opened its beak and started cackling at him.

What was that old childrens' rhyme about magpies? One for sorrow, two for joy…

Mark looked around to see if there was a second magpie anywhere in sight. There wasn't.

"Fuck off," he yelled, vehemently, and it did, squawking mockingly as it fled over the fields. Mark watched until it was a small, black dot in the now blue sky but his thoughts were elsewhere. Who was he fooling? Adelina would arrive in a few weeks time and, even if he followed the whims of this Shay lunatic, the best that he could realistically hope for was to be "extremely fat" instead of "obese" by then. There was no way he was going to resemble the athletic fiction of himself in his doctored *Facebook* profile picture. There was nothing sustainable nor healthy about starving himself. He began to open the backpack to remove the bread but his fingers trembled as he wrestled with the strap.

Less haste, more speed.

He paused and drew a deep breath. The strap clicked open easily at his next attempt but the moment had passed. He refastened the buckle slowly and hoisted the backpack into place. He'd hold out until this San Telmo cross place ahead and then he'd eat.

He had four identical light sports shirts for the walk. Each had a pocket to one side of the chest and into this he put the mobile phone. Now, at least, he'd have a chance of hearing the next text message. He sighed and pushed on.

FRADE CHICO embraced the priest and planted the customary double kiss on his cheeks.

"We will miss you, Fr Delucci," he said with genuine warmth.

"Thank you so much for a wonderful week," said the latter. They beamed at each other for a moment then the *frade* sighed.

"You have some walking to do."

He went to the back of the car, opened the trunk and hoisted the priest's backpack out.

"Let me help you to get this on," he said.

Fr Delucci stood waving as the monk pulled away with

a honk of the horn and a squeal of tyres then, staggering slightly under the unaccustomed weight of his bag, he made his way ponderously to the bridge. The sun was beginning its climb on the right hand side and, across the great stretch of water he could see a hilltop town, crowned with what looked like a castle. There were pedestrian walkways on either side of the bridge. He chose the side with the view and set off across the river that separated him from Spain and his one–week hike to Santiago. It was then that he saw his first yellow arrow, crudely painted on the metalwork. His heart gave a little skip of excitement. After all the preparation and travelling he was now officially on the *Camino de Santiago*. He glanced at his watch. It wasn't yet eight o'clock. They had been on the road since the early hours so that he would not be too late upon the way. The abbot had calculated that it would take him four hours to walk the 16km to the first pilgrim hostel at Porriño and had warned him that late comers could not be sure of a bed. He decided to adopt a firm stride. It lasted for twenty yards or so before he had to stop to readjust his footwear. His brand new hi–tech waterproof, breathable hiking shoes were rubbing at the back of each foot. He tried taking the pressure off by walking on the soles of his feet but about half way over the bridge he knew he was in trouble. The weight of his backpack was aggravating the situation. He was sweating profusely.

With some difficulty, he slid the backpack to the ground against a section of the bridge where the diamond shaped metal trellis gave way to a solid column and he stooped to take off his shoes. It came to him, with absolute certainty, that he was not even going to make the first day's walk in that footwear and bearing such a ponderous weight. He opened the bag and pulled out a pair of old, comfortable sandals that he had worn while exploring Santarém with Frade Chico. The relief, as he slipped his feet into them, was instant. Next he addressed the problem of his backpack. Emptying everything onto the ground, he began to make two piles – one of essentials that he would take with him and the other of superfluous items that he could leave behind. There was a liberating feeling associated with the task and the reject pile grew as he became evermore ruthless. The gimmicky items from the hiking shop – the subject of so much agonising deliberation – were dispatched to the reject pile without a second thought. Suddenly he was brought up, however, in an agony of indecision. He held, in both hands, the heavy leather satchel that contained his bible and breviary. An internal argument began to rage. If he had truly suspended his faith then these books had no place on the journey. On the other hand, to leave them would be sacrilegious – especially if the sign he sought came and his faith was restored. From a practical point of view the weight of the books would mean a lot of additional hardship. Indeed, it could put his quest at risk.

He looked up for inspiration and was fixated by what he saw. There, in clear blue writing on the iron supporting column of the bridge – just inches away – he read: "Mark 06.08."

His heart pounded and he found himself in so much agitation that he struggled to open the satchel's buckled fastener. When he did, finally, prise the leather strap free, he removed the bible and breathlessly flicked through the pages to locate the passage.

He charged them to take nothing for their journey except a staff; no bread, no bag, no money in their belts.

The priest knelt staring at the page for a moment and then, in a daze, he carefully placed the bible back into the satchel. His hands were steady, now, as he secured the strap. Next, he swept the two piles of his belongings into one heap and stuffed the lot back into the backpack. From the inner pocket he removed his passport and a notepad with a pen tucked into the spiral binding. He quickly scribbled a note and trapped it under a strap on top of the backpack in such a way that it would be clearly seen. Then, with a lightened back and a lightened heart he strode onwards, carrying nothing but the heavy leather satchel, slung securely over one shoulder.

He smiled at a sparrow that was eying his approach nervously from its perch upon the handrail ahead.

"Hello friend bird. Any idea where I get myself a staff?"

The sparrow flung itself off the bridge, dropped towards the water to gather speed and then rose, shooting like a bullet to the far bank of the river where it disappeared from sight into the foliage of a tree.

The Lord is my shepherd, I lack nothing. He makes me lie down in green pastures, he leads me beside quiet waters, he refreshes my soul.

THE *VAGABUNDO* knew, from a wisdom born of long, hard experience, that the old square in front of the *Catedral* in Tui was his best bet for begging a few coins. Therefore, he wasted no time in Valença. If he got to Tui early enough there was a high probability that he'd find some *guiris* still loitering around, taking photographs of the old building and readjusting their backpacks before tackling the next leg of the *Camino*. The sun was growing in power as it rose ever higher in a cloudless, azure sky and he rearranged his ragged shirt to protect his shoulders from its glare. His progress was slow. Yesterday the sole of his left shoe had finally reached a stage where no amount of ingenuity would hold it in place so the *vagabundo* was forced to walk with a semi shuffle. As he approached the bridge over the Minho it dawned on him that there was a distinct lack of *peregrinos* ahead or behind. At this time of year that was unusual.

He saw it as soon as he had mounted the bridge. At first he thought it was another tramp using the place as a begging point. He, himself, often adapted the strategy of occupying confined areas. It was surprising how many people would go to the trouble of crossing the road to avoid a beggar, but passersby on the narrow walkway would have no choice but to run the gauntlet. As he drew nearer, however, he recognised the backpack for what it was. He was mystified. On the long narrow pedestrian path over the bridge there was nowhere a person could be hidden from view. When he came to a halt in front of the backpack he eyed it appraisingly. It was huge. It also seemed brand new and expensive. It was then that he noticed the note on top. He plucked it carefully from under the strap and unfolded it. His mother tongue was Spanish and he knew enough Portuguese to figure out most writing in that language. This, however, he recognised as English – a language in which he could command little more than the few words necessary to beg a coin from a tourist. Tucking the note back into its place, he peered through diagonal lattice of metalwork that separated the pedestrian walkway from the main bridge where a few cars were trundling across. There was nobody on foot – not that he had expected to see anyone. The gaps in the ironwork were large enough to climb through and he did so, crossing the road and climbing through the trellis on the far side onto the matching walkway there. Still, there was nobody in sight. Returning to the abandoned back-pack, he stepped to the bridge's safety rail and stared down into the river below. The water was running fast, swirling around one of the structure's massive supporting columns directly beneath him, as it flowed steadily towards the sea. Making his way, once more, to the walkway on the far side of the bridge, the *vagabundo*'s gaze swept over the vast expanse of water and along the river banks on both sides but there was no sign of a body. Caught in the main current it could be carried for miles, he reasoned. Returning, once more, to the backpack, he carefully removed the note again and studied it, saying the foreign words out loud as if hearing them might prise open their meaning. As it happened, two words did leap out.

"...kaayyp eeeet."

No. In English, he recalled, the 'e' was pronounced like the Spanish 'i' and the 'i' more like the Spanish 'e'.

"...keep it"

This was a phrase that he was familiar with. Recently, when he had offered to return a coin that had fallen by accident beside the smaller coin a *guiri* had meant to give him, the man had been too embarrassed to take it in front of the girl he was trying to impress with his display of charity.

"Keep it," the man had said, repeating the phrase several times and making the meaning clear with a shake of his head and an upheld hand.

The *vagabundo*'s first instinct was to open the bag there and then to see what riches it might hold. However, he knew that he could be mistaken in his English translation and, even if not, his claim could be usurped by someone else happening upon the scene. The rights of tramps were, experience had taught him, easily trampled upon.

With some effort, he hoisted the backpack onto his shoulders and took a step forward before an idea struck him. He returned to the rail and looked down into the water again. Crossing himself, he muttered what he hoped was an appropriate prayer for the poor soul who had seen fit to shed the backpack and his mortal coil.

"Whatever were your troubles, may you be at peace now," he concluded.

Then, turning towards Spain on the opposite side of the river, he limped onwards, trying to look like a *peregrino* worthy of such a bag. Ahead to the right he kept his eyes fixed on the steep hill of Tui with its cathedral on top and began to say a prayer of thanks to San Tiago.

GALICIA, SPAIN

SAN TELMO'S MEMORIAL was in a forest clearing by a stream that chuckled along as though excited at the thought of its rendezvous with the sea. The area was small enough, however, to be largely sheltered from the increasingly harsh sun by the surrounding trees. With a sense of relief, Mark lowered his backpack to the ground and glanced around the site. A stone slab with Latin looking letters etched into its face rose to the left hand side and, a few feet away, a stone cross kept it company. Both were weathered and moss–stained. Between them, on the ground, was a small enclosure that had a metal–grilled front, giving it the appearance of a letterbox or birdcage. Small pieces of paper of various sizes and colours lay inside the cage and littered the ground around it. A quick examination revealed that each one was a hand written note. All of those that he could see were in foreign languages. He was puzzled for a moment and then the likely answer dawned on him.

Petitions from pilgrims.

On the stone slab sat a mound of pebbles, also placed there, he presumed, by passing pilgrims in some sort of religious habit or ritual. Some of the larger stones, he discovered, also had messages written upon them. He picked up his backpack, leaned it against the stone column and took out the paper–wrapped packet. The bread was somewhat squashed and misshapen but its smell had lost little of its magic. Mark unwrapped the paper, broke a corner of the crust off, held it up and looked at it. A movement in the corner of his eye–line distracted him. A magpie was staring at him from the branch of a nearby tree.

Hardly the same little bastard, he thought, but its staring eyes unnerved him and something akin to superstition stirred in his mind.

"Fuck off," he yelled, but, this time, the cry seemed muted in the heaviness of the forest and the magpie didn't move. Its yellow eyes were fixed on the bread in his hand.

He wants the bloody bread.

It was a relief to think that it was the bird's hunger that emboldened it rather than some strange supernatural manifestation.

He turned his back on the magpie to avoid its longing gaze but something had changed. With a sigh, he put the piece back into the paper bag with the rest of the bread. Opening the little cage he stuffed the package in and closed the grated door.

"If I'm not getting it you certainly aren't," he said to the bird. "See who's laughing now."

He attempted a magpie–like cackle but the bird seemed unaffected and he sounded somewhat unhinged so he stopped. He was half way across a wooden bridge that spanned the stream when he realised that he'd forgotten to sign his name and the time at this, the completion of his second task. Retracing his steps to the stone slab he paused with the blue chalk and checked the time. It was just after eight. Loathed to deface the natural weathered surface, he wrote in small, neat letters at the very base of the slab. Shay would find the message because he would be looking for it, he reasoned. There was a hungry void in his stomach as he struck out once more on the way but he was aware of something else: a rare, pleasant feeling of achievement.

BEHIND A HEDGE by the river the *vagabundo* held his

breath as he pushed his foot into the expensive, brand new walking shoe. He had reasoned that the number "12" on the sole must be a foreign shoe size. He was praying that it was his size. He experienced a Cinderella–like moment when his foot slipped easily in.

"*Gracias a Dios*," he murmured as he wiggled his toes to test the fit.

He put on the other shoe and walked happily around the contents of the backpack that lay piled in a heap on the outstretched mummy sleeping bag. The shoes were probably one size too big but he could fill the gap by putting on a couple of the twenty or so pairs of black socks that were in the heap, each pair held neatly together with a brown rubber band. The preponderance of black clothing amongst those in the backpack had done much to confirm the *vagabundo*'s belief that its owner had suffered from depression and had taken the decision to end his own life. Unfortunately, the unknown man had been quite a bit larger than the tramp so, aside from the socks, the sombre clothing was going to be far from an ideal fit. Nevertheless he took what looked like the smallest pair of trousers and the tightest shirt from among them and added both to his own possessions.

The *vagabundo* opened the brown leather wallet that he had found in one of the bag's many zipped pockets and gazed again at the photograph on the identity card. "Delucci" sounded like an Italian name but one of the words on the card was "Boston" and the credit card was from an American bank. He wondered whether the American had sent word to his people to tell them what he had intended to do or if his family would never know what had happened to him. If his body ever did wash up somewhere in these parts the police would hardly figure out that the dead man was from the United States. The face in the picture had dark features that could easily pass for Spanish or Portuguese.

He crossed himself and returned his attention to the more practical matter of the pile of goodies at his feet. He had already made up his mind to abandon the backpack. After careful consideration he had come to the conclusion that it was too big and too new for somebody like him to have in his possession without raising suspicion. He had been terrified as he passed the rows of police vehicles on the Spanish side of the bridge but nothing had been stirring at that early hour and he had slipped by unmolested. His fears behind him, he had enjoyed the task of selecting which items to leave and which ones to transfer into his own battered backpack. It struck him that, in particular, the mummy sleeping bag would be a really useful acquisition. The *vagabundo* gave a little chuckle of contentment when he managed to stuff it in on top of his other possessions and close the strap to secure it.

He returned the remaining items to the stranger's big backpack until only the brown leather wallet remained. He had already pocketed the seventy five euro that, to his great delight, it had contained. Now he removed the credit card and stared at it. He'd never had a credit card. He tilted it and the small security hologram shimmered hypnotically. He ran a fingertip over the raised plastic letters and numbers, paused and then slipped the card into his pocket. Deftly, he returned the wallet to the zipped compartment in which he had found it. Hefting both the oversized backpack and his own modest one back to the main roadway, he checked to see that nobody was observing him before emerging onto the footpath. He propped the large bag against a lamp post and carefully attached the original note onto the top, exactly as he'd found it on the bridge. If it was, as he suspected, a suicide note, it would make little or no difference whether the police thought "J. Delucci" had entered the river here instead of the bridge. While the *vagabundo* was painfully aware that, by leaving the note behind, he was abandoning the only proof he had that his new possessions were not stolen, he balked at the thought of removing information that could help the authorities to contact the dead man's family in America.

With a firm stride, made possible by his new shoes, he set off for Tui, his mind occupied with the pleasant quandary of whether he should stick to his usual cheap *cartones* of red wine or treat himself to a half–decent bottle of *Rioja*.

FINDING A STAFF proved to be a more difficult task than Fr Delucci had imagined. Filled with a sense of holy purpose, he had made up his mind to use only wood that had already fallen from the tree rather than causing damage to one of God's creations. However, Spain was full, as it turned out, of annoyingly health plant life. After scouting along the river-bank and achieving nothing more than getting scratched and dirty, the priest decided to abandon his search for the present and to forge ahead on the trail. He reasoned that if the Lord had truly given him a biblical message then he would pro-vide the staff when he saw fit to do so.

After a weary walk to the old town on the hilltop, Fr De-lucci found himself at the doorway to the cathedral. With its crenelated towers piercing the clear, blue sky it appeared more like a fortress to the priest than a place of worship. He climbed the steps to the massive porch under the unblinking gaze of its life–sized raised statues – four on either side. The door was open and he stepped, gratefully, into the cool inte-rior of the building.

As his eyes adjusted, he became aware of a man seated at a table upon which lay a variety of pamphlets and book-lets. A standard business letter sized printout, taped to the front, read: "*Credenciales*". Fr Delucci stepped forward with the intention of buying one then remembered, with a shock of reality, that he no longer had any money. In fact, leaving his wallet, complete with his credit card, seemed, suddenly, less like a leap of faith and more like an act of lunacy.

I'll have to phone and cancel the card.

As the priest wondered about the logistics of making a phone call with no phone and no money, he became aware that the man was watching him expectantly, so he picked up one of the pamphlets and pretended that he was considering buying it. To his chagrin, the pamphlet was in German. He replaced it, exchanged nods and smiles with the man and hurried further into the building. There were quite a few tourists around the cathedral so he made his way along the centre aisle to the middle where he reckoned that he had the least chance of being distracted or disturbed. Unstrapping his leather satchel, he removed his breviary and, for the first time in many days, began to fulfill his priestly obligation to pray the *Liturgy of the Hours.*

Almost two hours had passed when Fr Delucci left the cathedral. He felt more grounded after the comforting, familiar ritual but the consequences of his leap of faith were continuing to become apparent. He was powerfully thirsty with no way to buy a bottle of water. He passed the holy water font in the doorway and paused. It was early morning and it was quite full. If this parish was anything like his own in Boston, there was every likelihood that it had been newly refilled. He scooped a palmful of the water and put it tentatively to his lips. To his limited knowledge it tasted fresh. He twisted himself into the awkward position necessary to get his mouth to the surface and drank deeply. A loud cough caused him to jerk upright and bang his head painfully on the font's stone overhang. The man from the table of pamphlets was eyeing him disapprovingly. The priest wiped his mouth with a finger and used it to bless himself reverently. Then, with an embarrassed nod at the stony faced man, he set out on the *Camino* again.

The yellow arrows guided him to the outskirts of town, through some farmland, along a road, past a little church – the name of which he deciphered as *Virgin of the Way* – along a main road and, then, into a forest. By this stage the euphoria of his 'sign from God' had dulled somewhat. A horrible doubt was tapping at the edges of his thoughts. What if the biblical reference in blue chalk on the bridge wasn't meant for him at all? What if it was a mere coincidence? He had abandoned his clothes, his money and even his credit card. He was no better off than a homeless person. In fact, he realised, he was worse off. He was in a country where he didn't speak the language and he didn't even have a ticket to get home. Uncertain of when he would return, he hadn't bothered to book a return flight. What's more, he was finding it increasingly difficult to ignore the returning thirst and the rumblings in his stomach. With his life as a respected priest in an affluent parish, it was a great many years since Fr Delucci had experienced anything approaching hunger.

Keeping an eye on either side of the track in a half–hearted hope that a suitable staff would present itself, he did the one thing that he could do. He marched on. Because it was his first day of walking, he had no idea if Frade Benedito's estimate of four hours to reach the *albergue* in Porriño was accurate or not. His heart sank further when another thought struck him. He hadn't even got the money necessary to pay for his night's accommodation in the hostel when he got there.

At that moment the track opened out into a small clearing with a stream flowing merrily by one side. On the other side of the clearing rose a stone slab, standing about five feet from the ground and, a short distance away, a stone cross of about the same size. On the flat top of the slab rose a hill of small stones. The ones at its point were clean, the ones on the bottom looked as weathered as the structure on which they were sitting. They must, he decided, have been piled up one by one by passing pilgrims over many years – each one representing a hope, a wish, a prayer. On a whim, the priest bent down and selected a smooth, almost round stone from the ground. Standing before the tall slab he spoke aloud.

"Dear Saint James. My soul is willing but my body is weak. I have had a sign but… well I could do with another sign to show me that the first one really was a sign."

He was distinctly dissatisfied with the way that sounded.

"I am sorry. I am worse than Doubting Thomas. He needed only one sign… I'm sorry. Amen."

He blessed himself with the hand that held the stone and then, with a sense of ceremony, he placed it on top of the pile. With a gasp, he recoiled in horror as the entire heap collapsed and tumbled to the ground, littering the grass around the stone slab for several feet. As he stood, transfixed by the mayhem he had unwittingly caused, the blasphemous words of John Paul Sartre sprang to mind, mocking him.

L'homme est une passion inutile.

An 'unnecessary passion' was exactly how he felt as he weighed up his options.

I could retrace my steps to the bridge and maybe the backpack…

He didn't bother to complete the thought. The backpack was long gone. He could return to the cathedral in Tui and make himself known as a fellow clergyman to the priests there, but he choked on the hypocrisy of seeking help from a church he was quite possibly in the process of abandoning and the disapproving face of the man with the pamphlets rose in his mind as a further discouragement. Instead, he knelt slowly, placed the leather satchel on the ground and began to gather the fallen stones.

He had replaced, in a growing pile on top, all of those that had landed in front of the slab and crawled, on his hands and knees, to the back when he froze, his heart leaping at the sight of small writing, in blue chalk, at the base of the stone.

Mark 08.03

Removing his bible from the satchel and thumbing rapidly through the pages, he located the reference.

"...and if I send them away hungry to their homes, they will faint on the way; and some of them have come a long way"

It was as he sat still, considering the words that the faint whiff of bread set his nostrils twitching. He wasn't long finding its source. He had seen the little metal box but it was only from his present position, close to the ground, that it became obvious that there was something contained within. He opened the paper bag and stared with a wondrous reverence at the soft, fresh loaf inside. He noted that somebody had broken the bread and that phrase triggered something in his mind.

He broke the bread, gave it to his disciples and said: 'Do this in memory of me'...

In gratitude for this miraculous sign he would bear his hunger a while longer – long enough to celebrate a thanksgiving Mass. His jubilation was instantly dampened, however, at the realisation that he didn't have the essential items. He had bread, the nearby stream would provide water but it was impossible to say Mass without the third ingredient – wine. He turned, disappointed, to find a man approaching slowly from the trail behind. The man was somewhat dishevelled but sported clean, walking shoes that the priest identified as expensive – they were similar to the ones that had been foisted upon him by the hiking shop salesman – and a battered backpack that marked him as a fellow *per-*

egrino. The man pulled up sharply, staring as if he'd seen a ghost. Fr Delucci didn't notice the look. He was too busy staring in joyous disbelief at the open bottle of red wine in the other's hand.

The *vagabundo* was experiencing a range of conflicting emotions. He was in no doubt that the man standing before him was the same American from the card in the wallet – the same American who he had presumed was floating, face down in the Miño, on the way to the sea. Over the past number of hours he had grown to like the stranger. The amicable feeling had begun when the shoes had restored his ability to walk properly. It had increased with his acquirement of the various goodies that now rested snuggly in his bag and had finally risen to the level of extreme gratitude as he left the supermarket in Tui with a very decent bottle of 2008 *Rioja Crianza*. He had been blissfully swigging upon it as he made his way along the track through the woods. On seeing the American, his first, panicked thought was of the note that he had left behind – the note proving that he had taken the items with the permission of the owner. His next thought was that he was wearing the man's clean, new shoes. They stood out in such contrast to the rest of his clothing that nobody could fail to notice them. It was then he realised that the American was staring at the wine. Anxious to start off on the right foot, he held out the bottle.

"*Quiere usted?*"

It was a fine bottle of wine but even a connoisseur like the *vagabundo* felt that the American's response was excessively exuberant.

"Oh yes! *Sí, sí, sí!*"

He took the offered bottle almost reverently and held it up beside a printed paper bag that he had been carrying in the other hand. The tramp recognised it as coming from the bakery in Tui. With a beaming smile the man then began trying to communicate, using exaggerated gestures and a mixture of languages with, here and there, a word or phrase in Spanish.

"Me. Priest. *Padre. P–aaaa–dre.* You *capito*? You have *vino*. Me have *breado*. We make Holy Mass. Okay?"

"Ah, *padre*," said the *vagabundo*, latching onto the one part he understood. "You *padre*."

"*Sí, sí* and I make Mass."

The tramp smiled encouragingly. He had no idea what the American was getting at but it seemed that he wasn't in trouble, and the black clothing in the backpack was beginning to make sense. Why this Delucci had abandoned it was still a mystery but people had spiritual experiences and did crazy things on the *Camino*. The priest was looking enquiringly at him now.

"You help with Mass?"

The tramp grimaced and shrugged to show that he didn't understand.

"You help. You my assistant."

The tramp shrugged.

"*Lo siento. No entiendo.*"

The priest searched for alternative words.

"Assistant. Helper – like the sign: 'help wanted', you know, 'staff wanted'. "

Whatever the meaning of the what he had just said, it seemed to the tramp that the *padre* had stumbled upon something that struck a sudden chord with him. He grew even more excited.

"Me *Padre* Delucci," he said, eagerly. "You?"

He accompanied the sentence by pointing first to himself and then to the tramp, much like Columbus might have done in his first encounter with native Americans. The *vagabundo*, recognising "Delucci" as the name on the cards in the wallet, had no difficulty understanding that the priest wanted to exchange names. He pointed to himself.

"*Soy Rodrigo,*" he said. "*Pero 'Rod' esta bien.* 'Rod'. 'Rod' okay."

The priest's mouth dropped open. He stared for a moment and then, raising his eyes to the sky, he solemnly quoted.

I will fear no evil: for thou art with me; thy Rod *and thy* Staff *they comfort me…*

He looked earnestly, wide eyed, at the puzzled *vagabundo*.

"It's a sign. You are my Rod and my staff."

7. Hebrews

*"For in that he himself hath suffered being tempted,
he is able to succour them that are tempted."*

MARK WAS HUNGRY, worried and weary. He was neither used to going for long periods without food, nor was he used to walking long distances. For the first time that he could remember, he was experiencing very real hunger.

No pain no gain.

He corrected the thought.

No pain no weight loss.

He tried to distract himself from the gnawing hunger pangs and increasingly weary legs by concentrating on his other concern – the fear of finding himself with nowhere to sleep in this foreign country. Several *peregrinos* had passed him on the road and, although he had exchanged cheery '*buen Camino*'s with them, he couldn't help seeing each one as a competitor who was overtaking him in the race for a bunk. He had no idea how big or small the town ahead was, and he feared that the hostel might prove to be the only place to sleep.

After walking along a dirt track through the forest from St Telmo's memorial where he had so reluctantly abandoned the bread, his pace grew worryingly slow. The surface underfoot changed according to the terrain, but much of the time he was walking on dirt tracks where he had to pay close attention to avoid twisting an ankle. At one point he crossed a bridge over a main road that shot in a direct line northwards. As Mark gazed at the grey, man–made surface that slashed like a scar across the greens and browns of the autumn landscape, a bright red Mercedes roared past. It grew rapidly smaller until it disappeared around a distant bend in the road. An annoying thought struck him.

That guy will probably be in Santiago in less than an hour.

Somewhere in a quiet wood he was startled by a digital sound that seemed totally out of place in the natural surroundings. Then he realised that it was coming from the pocket at the front of his shirt. It was a text from Shay.

Congratulations on overcoming temptation. Take lunch when you want now. Reaching the albergue in Porriño is your next task. Remember to sign your name and the exact time when you get there. Shay.

It was all very well to tell him that he could eat, but it was easier said than done. He was in the middle of nowhere with neither a café nor shop in sight. Nevertheless, the promise of food drove him on with a quickened step.

He had left the wooded area and had come upon a modern, rather soulless rural village when he saw three figures stopped at the roadside ahead. They were female. One was sitting on a low wall examining her foot, one was crouched, rummaging in her haversack and the other was observing the proceedings. It was this third *peregrina* who looked back along the way and saw Mark approaching. She gave a little wave and, recognising her as one of the young women who had shown him the way to the hostel on the previous evening, he returned it. Her companions looked up to see who she was waving at. With a supreme effort, Mark picked up his pace, trying desperately to look less weary than he was.

"Blister problems," said the friendly Spaniard as he drew near.

Indeed, the young woman who was sitting down – a tall attractive blonde with the elf–like features of a Scandinavian – had removed one shoe and sock and was nursing an angry–looking blister. He thought of the blister plasters that sat in one of the outer pockets of his backpack.

"I have some of those special plasters if it's any help," he offered.

"Really?" said the injured woman. "That would be so great."

Ten minutes later the four were walking on together. The third young woman turned out to be Johanna from Finland. The other two introduced themselves as Maria and Berta from somewhere in southern Spain that Mark had never heard of. When he told them so, they explained that it was near somewhere else that he was obviously expected to know. He didn't, but not wanting to appear ill educated, he pretended. They chatted amicably as they walked – their pace dictated by the struggling Finn. As they passed a farm Mark pointed to a small rectangular stone building on concrete legs with a tiled roof and a crucifix on top at one end. The sides contained regular slits which looked like they acted as air vents. The structure was about a metre wide and just over two metres long.

"What's that for?" Mark enquired of the Spaniards.

"It's typical of this region," replied Berta. "You'll see lots of them. The name is *hórreo*. It's for storing the corn in a way that small animals can't get to it."

"Oh," said Mark, relieved. "I thought it might be some sort of tomb with a dead body."

They all laughed and Mark realised that he was relaxed and enjoying their company.

After a short time they came upon a modest building that sported a sign made from horse shoes. A chirpy, dapper man appeared at the doorway. He held up a large unlabeled bottle of white wine and said something in rapid Spanish

Berta responded in tones that sounded, to Mark's chagrin, negative. The man seemed unabashed and spoke animatedly for a moment. The two Spaniards laughed.

"We told him that it is a bit early for drinking wine," explained Berta. "But he says that it's okay in this part of the country. He told us that in the old days they kept horses to work in the fields. They would start very early in the morning and by eleven o'clock the poor animals would be tired so the farmers would get big pieces of bread, dip them into the wine and feed them to the horses. Then they'd be as good as new and ready to work hard again. They called it '*la sopa del caballo cansado*' which means 'the soup of the tired horse'."

Mark laughed.

"Well I'm probably about the same size as a horse and I'm definitely tired so I guess I qualify."

The wine was delightful and, to Mark's relief, their host kept returning to their table with various edible offerings.

"*Mi esposa la cocinó*," he beamed, as he lay down a slice of what proved to be a thick potato omelette before each of them.

"We call it *tortilla español*," expained Maria. "He said that his wife cooked it."

Another offering turned out to be the largest tomato that Mark had ever seen, cut into slices, sprinkled with salt and drizzled with olive oil.

"Oh my God. So this is what a tomato is supposed to taste like," he enthused.

"*Yo, lo cultive en mi huerto*," said the man, who had been loitering to see their reaction.

"He says he grew it in his own garden," explained Berta as Maria addressed the man in, what was obviously, very complimentary Spanish as it caused him to flush with pleasure.

They chatted on and Mark was delighted to find himself fitting in to the mixed company so it was with disappointment that he heard Berta say what they were all thinking.

"I suppose we should be going."

"How far is it to the hostel?" asked Mark as they began to hoist their backpacks into place again.

I think we still have about ten kilometres more."

Mark's heart sank.

"But I thought we had to be close to Porriño by now," he said.

"We're not stopping in Porriño," said Berta. "There's another small place called Mos about five kilometres further on, according to our guidebook. We prefer to stay in the country places instead of the big towns."

Mark, bound by his instructions from Shay, felt a pang of disappointment.

"I've to stay in Porriño," he said.

With a new *sello* stamped into each of their *credenciales* and and having paid a remarkably cheap price for their feast, the four struck off at a steady pace, reinvigorated by the food and the *soup of the tired horse*.

The *albergue* at Porriño was located at the end of a long trail that ran beside a pleasant, meandering stream. It was a modern building and a group of pilgrims was sitting on the grass verge between it and the water, chatting and drinking bottles of beer or glasses of wine. While Mark was glad to complete his first day on the *Camino,* he was disappointed that at least two of his new–found friends would be walking on and leaving him in Porriño. For the rest of the trip, he re-alised, they would always be at least one day's walk ahead. While they queued at the reception – Mark to check in and the girls to have their *credenciales* stamped before walking on to Mos – a thought struck him.

"Are you guys going to hang around for a few days once you get to Santiago?"

"We plan to spend three days there," said Maria.

"Great. Maybe we can all meet up for a celebratory drink or something, then."

"Sure. Let's exchange phone numbers and *Facebook* ad-dresses so we can stay in touch."

Having said goodbye to the Spaniards, Mark and Johan-na took the mattress and pillow covers they had been given and made their way upstairs to the dormitories.

"Do you want to meet for dinner later – say eight o'clock?" asked Johanna.

"Sure. Perfect," replied Mark, delighted.

The sound of snoring greeted them as they entered the room. Mark quickly located the source – a large, middle aged man, lying on his back upon an upper bunk. Two youths were quietly playing cards by the window while another was sitting on his bed, writing in what seemed to be a diary. Smiles and nods were exchanged as Mark made his way to a corner where he found an unoccupied lower bunk. Johanna choose a place at the opposite end of the room and began to busy herself with the contents of her backpack. Mark deposited his onto his bunk with a sigh, sat down and slowly removed his footwear. Much of the discussion that he'd overheard among the *peregrinos* in the *albergue* had focussed on the subject of blisters. Indeed, Johanna was living proof of the havoc they could cause. Maria and Berta had spent a long time reading pilgrim forums online ahead of their journey and, as they walked, had shared the fruits of their research with Mark and the limping Finn. There were the advocates of wearing two pairs of socks so that any friction would occur between the socks instead of between the material and the foot, they explained. Other people swore by Marino wool while socks made from bamboo fibre were, apparently, growing in popularity due to their softness and natural antibacterial properties. Mark was pleased, therefore, to find that – while a little swollen and red – his feet had stood up to the duress of his first day quite admirably. He picked up a sock. It was damp with perspiration. He held it gingerly to his nose and grimaced.

Maybe I'll get myself some of those bamboo ones.

SANTIAGO DE COMPOSTELA, SPAIN

SOMEWHAT IRONICALLY, Anxo's mysterious affliction had the effect of releasing some of Isabel's inheritance. As soon as she contacted her godfather, Cardosa had told her of a codicil to the will that her father had inserted at the suggestion of his lawyer. Should his daughter or her husband suffer any serious illness, whatever funds were necessary to treat it were to be put at their disposal. Those funds had seen Anxo attended to by a bewildering array of specialists at the *Hospital Privado Virgen del Cielo,* and subjected to every type of scan and test that they felt might get to the bottom of his semi–paralysis and terrible pain. He was in a drug–induced stupor now as Doctor Velasco, an eminent neurologist, gave Isabel the sum of their combined wisdom.

"Your husband was brought to me because none of the tests showed any physical source of his illness. The widespread nature and sudden onset of his pain would seem to point to a neurological attack of some kind."

He searched Isabel's drawn, sleep–deprived face to ensure that she was taking in what he had to say. She took the pause as a precursor to bad news.

"Is it a brain tumour?"

"No, no," he replied, promptly. "The scans are coming back clear. This, actually, is one of the problems. Neurological attacks can cause, or be the result of, lesions – such as in the case of multiple sclerosis. In the case of fibromyalgia, on the other hand, there is generally unusual brain activity. We have ways of locating such anomalies. However, while your husband is displaying symptoms, every scan and every test is telling us that there's nothing wrong."

"Are you suggesting that my husband is making it all up?" snapped Isabel.

"Of course not. He's clearly in real pain and very deep distress. What I'm saying is that we're dealing with something that, so far, we don't understand. There are some more tests we can carry out but at this point all we can do is try to manage his pain and hope that he improves. Despite all our medical advances, the human body's ability to heal itself is still the most powerful tool that we have in our toolkit."

Left alone at Anxo's bedside, Isabel stared into the tormented face of her husband. Her dark thoughts were broken by the faintest flutter in her stomach. She held her breath and waited, her hand on the spot. It came again and this time she felt it on her palm also. She had prayed to *the saint* to help her. Was the answer to that prayer about to leave her child with an invalid for a father – or worse? Her grandmother's words came back to her again.

Be careful what you pray for. You might get it.

GALICIA, SPAIN

SHOWERED AND CHANGED into clean clothes, Mark was leaving the *albergue* to explore Porriño when he stopped with a jolt. He had completely forgotten to leave the chalked message for Shay saying that he had arrived. Cursing himself, he went back to the dormitory, pocketed a stick of blue chalk, left the building and walked to the back where nobody was in sight. For a while, he tried to figure out the time that they had arrived but, after some consideration, changed his mind and wrote down the current time instead. The longer that Shay thought it had taken him to complete the first day's walk, he reasoned, the less time pressure he would be under in the days to follow.

Crossing the river, Mark made his way over the level crossing at a railway line and onto a pedestrian street that extended to the right. There were several cafés on either side, each one with people sitting outside, enjoying the warmth of the sun as it began to cool into evening. It was several hours since the *sopa del caballo cansado* and eight o'clock seemed like a long time away.

If the soup of the tired horse was breakfast and I'm going to be eating dinner with Johanna then I should have something now for lunch.

His mind made up, he began looking for the best place to eat. One café seemed particularly popular and, on a blackboard outside, it had a sign saying '*Menu Peregrino* – €7.95'. It went on to explain that *Menu Peregrino* consisted of *sopa del día*, *lasaña* and *postres*. Mark was pretty sure that this was soup and *lasagna*. The *postres* was a mystery but, overall, it seemed like a good deal. Mind made up, Mark turned to find a seat and, suddenly, had a feeling that he was being watched.

The fat guy salivating over the menu.

Avoiding eye contact with the café's clients, he found himself a vacant table in the corner. He was about to sit when a voice, its accent distinctly North American, stopped him.

"I wouldn't, man. They're a bit flimsy."

Mortified, Mark turned to find the couple from that morning upon the Minho bridge seated two tables away. The young man, looking like an advertisement for some rugged designer clothing brand, was regarding him coolly. His girlfriend, her hair luxuriant, her face a picture of beauty and the pastel tones of her summer dress setting off her golden tan, sat beside him, but her face was turned away and, in the moment that Mark had the courage to glance at her, she seemed uncomfortable.

"Sorry, man. I'm presuming you speak English?"

Mark realised that he was staring.

"Oh yeah, I do," he mumbled.

The young man bounced to his feet, took his own chair and dragged it across to Mark's table.

"Here. This one's a little more robust," he gushed, swapping the chairs.

He put out his hand and beamed a toothpaste advertisement smile.

"Brad," he said and Mark hated him, even as he extended his own hand.

"Mark."

"You were that guy crawling over the bridge, weren't you," laughed Brad. "Extreme way to do the walk, man. "

"I was fixing my bag," said Mark.

"I'm just kidding."

He turned.

"I'll leave you to get some grub. *Buen Camino.*"

"Oh, thanks for the chair," said Mark to his back and sat, miserably down, angling himself so that he wouldn't have to face anybody – especially the beautiful young woman that Brad hadn't bothered to introduce.

HER NAME WAS TANYA and her own troubles were set aside, for a moment, while her thoughts were filled with empathy for the poor guy who Brad had just embarrassed. He was sitting with his back to the rest of the diners, pretending to read the menu so it could act as a shield in front of his face while he gathered himself after Brad's onslaught. Tanya knew this intuitively. She had hidden behind menus more than once in the past before she'd been '*Bradified*' with her boyfriend's self confidence techniques. As Brad settled himself, smiling, into the lighter chair he had carried over from the heavy guy's table, she wondered how someone so immersed in psychology could be so clueless – or possibly, she reluctantly acknowledged, so cleverly cruel. As she played with the thought she became convinced that the latter was the case. Under the guise of clumsy concern, Brad had humiliated an obviously vulnerable stranger. Her thoughts went back to that first day in the gym.

"That's the thing about you English girls. Even when you're fat there's something hot about you."

She was so weary of the patronising comments from friends about how slimming a particular size 18 dress looked on her, or about how she looked as if she'd lost weight when the scales that morning had set a new personal record of excess, that his blunt honesty was refreshing. She was too full of self–disgust to be insulted, so she clung to the compliment that had followed the insult. She blushed as this Adonis of a man looked her up and down with the professional eye of the personal trainer that he was.

"You know, you can work your ass off in here and you won't," he said. *"Work your ass off, that is."*

He grinned a disarming grin.

"We can get the toning right in the gym, but a six pack is fuck– all use if it's hidden under kilos of fat. You'll have to get it right in the kitchen and you'll have to get it right in here."

He tapped the side of her head and she winced. He noticed the reaction.

"Sound like too much hard work? If it does you may as well get back into your…"

He looked her up and down.

"… size 18 clothes and head home."

She stood, transfixed and he continued.

"But if you'll work with me – and I mean mind, body and soul – then we can get rid of this cocoon of yours and let the butterfly out."

"What?"

Brad was regarding her with a bemused look.

"Oh, I was just trying to decide if you were being helpful or horrible."

He laughed.

"I was being horribly helpful. Sometimes people need a kick up the ass – though I doubt that guy would feel it."

"It's not funny. That he looks like he wishes the ground would open up and swallow him."

"It'd want to be a big fucking hole."

"You can be such a creep, Brad. You've no idea what it feels like to be in a constant struggle with your weight."

Brad leaned back dismissively.

"And you do? You had a few extra pounds, babe, but you were never fat like that and, more importantly, you had the balls to do something about it."

"He's obviously walking on the *Camino*," snapped Tanya. "So what do you think he's trying to do?"

Brad turned slowly around to where Mark was now in conversation with the waitress.

"At the moment, I'd say he's ordering the *lasagna* and chips. How much do you want to bet?"

"You know what I mean. He's making an effort and what you did was..."

She searched for the appropriate word and failed to find one that expressed the depth of her disapproval. She had to make do.

"...cruel."

Brad tilted himself back in the chair and put his hands behind his head in the superior, steepling gesture that Tanya found so very irritating.

"I don't have to tell you how useless exercise is if you eat like a pig."

A number of possible responses came to Tanya's mind but the immediacy of the conversation melted into the bigger problem that had been subconsciously growing behind her thoughts for quite a while. Now, for the first time she admitted it to herself. She was unhappy in her relationship.

"I'm tired," she said. "Can we go back to the hotel?"

FR DELUCCI was made aware of his sweaty and, most likely, smelly condition by the discreet but curious glances of Porriño's neatly dressed citizens who were out in force for their customary evening stroll to harvest the last sunshine of the day. He, in turn, glanced at his companion and it dawned on him that they cut a rather incongruous pair. Rod's weathered, leathered face, untidy hair, worn clothes and battered bag contrasted sharply to his expensive walking shoes. He himself, in his sombre tailored shorts and short sleeved shirt

– now dirtied from his futile searching for a staff in the undergrowth and hours of walking under the heat of the Spanish sun – didn't even have a backpack to mark him as a *peregrino*. His sole possession was the bulky leather satchel that he clung to under one arm.

Getting Rod to accompany him had not taken much persuasion, and the priest took this as a further sign that he was on the right track. Back at the clearing of the stone cross, his new traveling companion had quickly shown signs that he realised what Fr Delucci was planning when he saw the bread, water and wine being prepared on the make–shift stone altar. He had fallen into the supportive role with a readiness that suggested a youthful history in the role of an altar boy. Together, they had celebrated an unusual but completely orthodox Mass in the forest clearing. A few *peregrinos* had passed during the ceremony and he was delighted when a middle aged man and woman stopped to form a tiny congregation. At one side of the clearing there were a number of small square stumps that had been placed there as crude seats. The couple sat on those, partaking in the Mass with the appropriate responses and gestures. At communion they had come forward and received the bread and wine. For Fr Delucci that simple, tiny Mass was of vast significance. He had asked for a second sign and he had received it. His soul–searching trip had become, he felt, a genuine pilgrimage.

Only say the word and my soul shall be healed.

Afterwards, as he and Rod walked on together, they had struck up a form of communication that consisted of each one speaking loudly and slowly in his own language. While it proved generally unintelligible to the other, they accompanied the words with mimes and gestures that sometimes succeeded in getting the message across. More often than not, the priest grew weary of trying to understand, so he smiled and nodded in agreement as if he had comprehended. He suspected that Rod was employing the same tactics. They had stopped, some time later, to polish off the remainder of the bread. Fearing dehydration, the priest had refused to partake further in the wine, much, he suspected, to the relief of Rod.

The bread was welcome, but *man does not live by bread alone*, thought the priest and, as they had arrived at the outskirts of Porriño, the question of what to eat and where to sleep had loomed in his mind. He had tried to make his plight clear to Rod by miming the actions of someone eating, shaking his head in the negative and then raising his hands and eyebrows in a gesture of appeal. He repeated a variation of the process for sleep and was rewarded with a comforting reaction from his new travelling companion.

"*No hay problema*," said Rod, and the words 'no' and '*problema*' in proximity to each other were close enough to the English to somewhat allay the anxiety of the priest.

It struck him as quite bizarre that Rod didn't question his lack of possessions or money. Perhaps a seasoned walker like Rod had encountered many eccentrics on the way, he thought. Then a revelation struck him with something that bordered on absolute certainty.

Rod is not surprised because he knows he is fulfilling a role in a divine mission.

Buoyed up with this knowledge he mentally chastised himself.

Oh you of little faith.

He was reminding himself of this now as the *albergue* came to view further along the riverside path upon which they were walking. Outside, young people were drinking and eating, and from somewhere there was the distinctive smell of fried onions.

Jehovah–Jireh – The Lord will provide.

"*Albergue, no*," said his companion authoritatively as the priest looked longingly through the large windows behind which a number of *peregrinos* were resting after their long days walk.

Rod strode purposefully past the building, gesturing for the priest to do the same. Fr Delucci's attention was drawn, however, to a line of small blue writing on a plinth at the base of the *albergue*.

"Wait, wait!"

Rod watched in bemusement as the priest frantically

pulled out his bible, thumbed through its pages and found the passage.

Mark 16.17 – And these signs will accompany those who believe: in my name they will cast out demons; they will speak in new tongues

When the priest looked up it was with a sense of joyful wonder in his eyes.

"Rod, you must teach me Spanish," he said, then shook his head at the other's blank look. He spoke again, loudly and slowly.

"Me learn *talko Spañolo. Capito?*"

"*Si. Soy Español. Eres Americano, no?*"

The priest had a brainwave. He accosted a young couple who were sitting nearby, sharing a bottle of the local *Albariño* white wine in the evening sun.

"Excuse me. Do you speak English and Spanish?"

"Yes," said the woman, "not so good the English, though."

"Oh great. Perhaps you could translate for me."

"Of course."

"Thank you. Could you please tell my friend that I want him to teach me Spanish?"

Words were exchanged and Rod turned, beaming, to the priest.

"*Sí. Vamos a hablar Español si lo prefieres.*"

"He says that you can both begin to speak in Spanish if you wish," explained the woman.

The priest seized upon the opportunity of the translator.

"Could you please tell him that I am Fr Joe Delucci, an American priest. Can you ask him if he is going to Santiago and, if so, will he accompany me. Also, you should probably tell him that I have no money. I am trusting in the Lord to provide."

The woman looked a little taken aback but she relayed the information and Rod responded.

"He says that he knows all of this," she said. "He says he will help you."

The priest felt a lump of emotion rise in his throat.

"Thank you," he beamed at the woman, then he turned and clasped Rod's arm.

"And thank you, my friend. My *amigo. Gracias.*"

Rod smiled back, a little embarrassed, then gestured to the road ahead.

"*Vamos.*"

"He says you must go," said the woman.

As the priest turned to accompany the *vagabundo* the woman placed a hand lightly on his arm.

"*Padre*, are you okay? Perhaps you need help finding somewhere to stay tonight?"

The priest felt a warm flush as he basked in this benevolence.

So must it have been for the disciples as they set about the Lord's work with a sense of trepidation, but buoyed up by their faith.

"No my child, I am in safe hands. This man is my Rod and my staff. Where he goes I follow."

The woman looked doubtfully at Rod's retreating figure then turned and said something rapidly to her companion while taking a purse out of her handbag. He began to retort but she cut him off with some brusque words. He shrugged, reached into his pocket and drew out some notes. The woman selected a twenty and added it to one of her own.

"Here Padre. Please take this and pray for us when you reach Santiago."

The labourer is worthy of his reward.

He took the money, then, raising his hand, solemnly bestowed a blessing on the couple and strode after Rod, who had reached the main road and was crossing a bridge that carried it across the river. The stainless steel rails of the structure gleaming in the day's last burst of sunlight.

"*Ahora, vamos a comer,*" said the *vagabundo*, illustrating the meaning of the words with an elaborate mime of eating.

"Food? Oh yes!" said the Fr Delucci, nodding enthusiastically holding up the forty euro.

"*No lo necesitamos,*" said the *vagabundo*, shaking his head and gesturing for the priest to put his money away. He turned on his heel and marched on with his bewildered companion close behind.

Moments later they found themselves in the town centre, surrounded by a noisy mix of locals and *peregrinos* who were strolling down the bustling street or eating and drinking at outdoor tables. The priest's attention was drawn to one individual who stood out amid the other diners. He was a young man, and, at that moment, he was launching himself into a large plate of lasagna and chips that a waitress had just set down before him. Aside from the baggy tee–shirt and knee length khaki combat shorts that marked him as a tourist, he was extremely larger than those around him. In fact, he was, decided Fr Delucci, bordering on obese. Not for the first time it struck the priest that obesity was so much more rare in Europe than his native USA. Back home he wouldn't have looked twice at the young man.

The *vagabundo* took off his battered pack, lay it on the ground and took out a plastic lunchbox.

"*Espera aquí,*" he demanded, motioning for the priest to stay with the bags. Waiting until the waitress had disappeared into the café, he made a quick tour of the several recently vacated tables that had not yet been cleared. He selected untouched pieces of food from plates and whatever bread remained in the breadbaskets, scooping the lot into the lunchbox. The priest watched, torn between admiration and embarrassment. A short time later, however, as the pair enjoyed a somewhat varied but, nevertheless, delicious feast – washed down with a bottle of cheap but decent red wine that Rod had stopped to purchase in a mini–market – any misgivings were overcome. As a matter of fact, he recalled, the Pope had spoken out against wasting food.

Throwing away food is like stealing from the table of those who are poor and hungry.

For the first time in days his thoughts went back to his parish in Boston. It had its fair share of poor and hungry yet, he realised with a pang of guilt, he had spent most of his time indulging the more affluent members of his congregation and leaving the problem of the poor and homeless to the various charities. He had convinced himself that letting them use the Church hall for their fund raising activities was playing his part. Here, however, in an alien community – not knowing where he would sleep nor where his next meal would come from – he was getting a real taste of what life was like for those living on the cold edges of his cosy society.

If… when I return, things will change.

Rod belched contentedly and reached for the half empty wine bottle. The priest put a restraining hand on his arm.

"Can we keep this for Mass tomorrow?" he said.

Rod looked puzzled.

"Mass," said the priest, slowly and loudly. He took up a piece of bread and the bottle.

"Mass. Tomorrow."

Rod nodded in comprehension.

"Okay. *Entiendo. La Misa. Mañana.*"

He picked up the bottle's cap and handed it to the priest who screwed it into place and gave it, with the bread, to the *vagabundo* to pack away.

"Thank you, Rod. *Gracias.*"

"*De nada*," replied his companion, clambering to his feet. "*Ahora, vamos.*"

As they navigated a major roundabout intersection on the edge of town, Fr Delucci kept his eyes peeled for new messages in blue chalk while continuing to reflect on the last one. The 'speaking in new tongues' bit was obvious – he must learn Spanish – but what did the message mean by 'casting out demons'?

DUBLIN, IRELAND

THE TRANSPORT COMPANY'S SERVICE included packing the house contents, but Helen Casey didn't like the idea of strangers going through her daughter's personal items. She had spent the day, therefore, carefully removing the contents of cupboards and drawers and sorting them into cardboard boxes. The task had left her physically and emotionally drained. In the boxes on the floor, tenderly packed, was an eclectic mix of objects with one thing in common – each one represented a milestone in Grace's life.

The first item that Helen had come across was an orange, plastic, clockwork dog with a black top hat. Frank had bought that for Grace's second birthday. She remembered clearly her daughter's reaction when her husband had put the dog on the floor and pressed firmly down on the hat. First the toy's eyes closed and Grace's shot open. Next a pink, lolling tongue dropped from its mouth and Grace's mouth fell wide with surprise. When the rubber wheels beneath the dog spun into action and sent the toy trundling across the carpet, however, Grace leapt as if she'd been stung, before bursting into tears. Her initial shock, though, had soon given way to endless hours of fun. The dog had been Grace's constant companion until about the age of five when school had introduced her to other children and other playthings.

There was a jeweller's watch box but, instead of a watch, it contained a small digital device, the purpose of which Helen didn't recall at first. Then it had come sweeping back to her. It was a 'Toma–something or other' – an electronic pet that Grace had agonised over keeping 'alive' by pressing buttons to feed it, wash it and generally look after its wellbeing. Neglecting any one of the device's demands led to its untimely death and the child had to start all over again. Helen had smiled as she remembered the weekend that Grace had forgotten the thing when she went to stay at her grandparents. There had been a panicked phone call from the child who refused to be calmed down until Frank had promised to keep the gadget 'alive' until Grace returned to resume her maternal duties. That night, they had been at a fancy restaurant when the device had started beeping. Under the bemused gazes from the other diners and the waiter, Frank had tended to the 'pet', dutifully, though she'd known that he was mortified.

In a large brown envelope she had found six diaries. They varied in size and colour. The years marked on the covers showed that they covered her daughter's teenage years. Helen had been tempted to open the books but she had fought the urge and replaced them into the envelope before packing them, ready for transport to the other side of the world.

There were various ticket stubs from concerts attended, birthday cards from Grace's 18th and assorted knick–knacks that were clearly of significance only to her daughter. Then, in one drawer, she had come across the wedding things. She felt herself welling up as she flicked through the wedding

album, seeing Grace and David so madly in love and day–
dreaming of the perfect future that lay before them. Looking at them together, Helen could see Angela in them both.
She had her father's thoughtful eyes but her mother's overall
features and, in that look, Helen saw Frank. There was so
much of Frank in Grace. One of the wedding photos was the
father–of–the–bride and daughter dancing. The photographer had captured a moment where Grace was looking up at
her Dad as though seeking approval while Frank gazed back
with a smile of pure happiness for his daughter on her big
day. Another picture showed Frank and David at the after–
party in the hotel. They were onstage with the band singing
raucously into a shared microphone, arms around each other's shoulders as if they were old friends. Now both of them
were dead. Helen thought about her husband, lying cold in
the little cemetery near their retirement home in Spain and a
she was struck, suddenly, with a revelation. Why hadn't she
seen it before? Why had she thought that Frank was in that
tiny plot of foreign soil. She realised now, as certainly as if he
was whispering it into her ear, that he wasn't there and never
had been. His soul was with his family. It was in the strength
that Grace had found to go on for Angela's sake. It was in
those early hours when, somewhere between dreams and reality, she felt his warmth beside her. Most of all, though, it
was in the quiet internal voice that she had only been aware
of subconsciously until now, telling her that, somehow, she
was the key to their granddaughter's recovery.

*You promised her that you were only minding 'Pablo the pin
cushion man'. It's time to return it in person.*

"I love you, Frank Casey," she said aloud.

And I adore you, Helen Elizabeth Josephine Casey.

She turned, half expecting to see him beside her, the reply had seemed so real. Instead she saw a room where, like
Frank's grave, the soul had fled, leaving behind some items
to be packed and sent on to where the family was waiting –
her family. Laying aside the album she checked the time and
did the calculations. It would be almost 7am in Australia.

The phone rang a few times before she heard her son's
voice. While he went to wake his sleeping sister Helen re–

examined her decision. She found that, rather than regret, she nursed a growing sense of excitement that had replaced a knot of anxiety she had been unaware of until now. Tony returned. Grace had been in the shower and was dressing. They chatted while they waited for her to come to the phone.

"For the first few days she was all over the place, Mum. She would be laughing one minute and in tears the next but she's started to settle in now. Don't worry. She's going to be fine."

"It's been a huge change for her" said Helen. "She's had to leave everything that she and David had together behind her. I know what that feels like. What about Angela?"

"We've got her a puppy. She loves it to bits but it's a bloody nuisance. She's called it Chewy and it's a good name for the little wretch. I don't have a pair of shoes left that it hasn't chewed. But Grace says she hasn't seen Angela as close to happiness since David died."

"She hasn't spoken yet, though?"

"No. Nothing yet, but there are some very good specialists over here. They might spot something that the guy in Ireland missed."

"Let's hope so."

"She really misses you, Mum. Grace does too."

The excitement grew stronger within Helen but she didn't tell her son. She wanted to tell Grace first. In fact, she decided, she'd then make Grace promise not to tell Angela. What a surprise her granddaughter would get.

SANTIAGO DE COMPOSTELA, SPAIN

THE LITTLE YELLOW CITROEN pulled up outside the house and stopped. Isabel toyed with the remote control for the garage door before putting it back in the dashboard cavity where it was habitually kept. The man from the *policía* had said that they had taken the body away. Still, she didn't want to enter the house alone. Her godfather had suggested that she stay with him for a few days but, not wanting to cause a fuss, she had declined. Now, as the horror of the night before came flooding back, she regretted her decision. Checking the time on her mobile phone, she found that she had ten minutes before her meeting with *Subinspector* Pedrosa. He had already taken a preliminary statement from her at the hospital but had arranged to meet her in the house at eight to go through everything again before she signed the final one.

"It's a formality, really," he'd said. "I just want you to talk me through what happened at the scene so I'm sure I have everything correct."

Isabel thought that there might be a more benevolent motive for the arrangement, however. The appointment had been made after she'd admitted her fear of returning to the house alone. She suspected that he was being chivalrous. Although it had seemed like an eternity, she realised that it must have been less than ten minutes before he'd arrived at the house on that terrible night. He'd been a tower of strength as the police and ambulance people had taken control of the situation. During the hours in the hospital he'd stayed nearby, bringing her coffee and sandwiches and using his influence to get constant updates from the harried emergency staff.

She flicked down the sun visor and assessed herself in the small vanity mirror. She looked as tired and anxious as she felt. Reaching into her handbag, she took out her small makeup case and set about improving her look. She wasn't quite finished when she caught sight of the car in the mirror with the distinctive checkered blue and white stripes of the *Policía Local*. She stuffed the makeup back into her bag, regarded herself once more in the mirror and then climbed out of the Citroen. *Subinspector* Pedrosa was alone.

"Señora de Medeiros," he said, offering his hand.

"I prefer Quintana," she replied, instantly regretted the correction as she accepted his handshake.

"I'm sorry. I'm being fussy. It's just that I always think it sounds as if I am my husband's possession rather than his wife."

"It's an understandable point," smiled Pedrosa. "A lot of our tradition is very patriarchal, but at least a woman is not expected to change her name and surrender her own when she marries like the English do. Our children have the names of both parents."

The mention of children reminded her of the little life that was starting to make itself known within her. She pushed the thought back down and forced a smile.

"That's true… Look, why don't you just call me Isabel?"

"Then you must call me Pedro."

"Pedro Pedrosa?"

"Yes, my parents, between them, had many gifts but, unfortunately, imagination wasn't one of them," laughed the *Subinspector*.

"Sorry, that was rude. I don't know what's wrong with me. Pedro Pedrosa has a lovely ring to it," said Isabel. "I'm so appreciate of all your support and I'm so glad that you are here to go into the house with me. With the hospital and everything I've managed not to think of what happened too much but now that I'm here… well I didn't even have the courage to drive into the garage."

"It has been a terrible day for you," said Pedrosa. "You are very brave to be holding up so well."

Isabel flushed.

"I'm not brave. I'm petrified."

"In my opinion, it's a common misconception to think that bravery means feeling no fear," said Pedrosa. "That's more often foolhardiness. Real bravery is feeling the fear and having the strength to do what has to be done regardless."

Isabel smiled and held out her bunch of keys to the policeman.

"Thanks, but I'd still prefer if you went in first."

The heavy lined curtains were drawn in the living room, effectively keeping the light out. Isabel crossed the room and threw them open. She stared through the patio doors at the cobbles where the man's body had lain, half expecting to see a white chalked outline. Instead, the only evidence of a tragedy was a discomfiting dark patch near the flower bed where the stranger's blood had ebbed away. She shuddered, stepped back and turned to see Pedrosa looking curiously at Anxo's makeshift bed on the sofa. The duvet was trailing from one end onto the parquet floor where he had cast it aside to dash upstairs the night before. In Isabel's statement she had said that Anxo was downstairs when the intruder had broken in. She had not, however, clarified that he was sleeping there and Pedrosa had refrained from questioning her beyond the essentials when he had arrived like a super-hero in the midst of her crisis.

"My husband and I had an argument," she said, picking out a point on the floor and staring at it.

"That's none of my business," replied the *Subinspector,* so long as we are treating this as misadventure by a perpetrator in the commission of a crime – which, is exactly what we are doing. Thank you for your honesty, though."

Isabel flashed him a smile and then stared, once more, out the window.

"Are you okay?"

Isabel was unsure if the policeman was referring to the trauma of the death or that of her marriage. She chose the former.

"I thought I'd see a white outline where the body was," she said.

Pedrosa smiled. "We don't do that anymore. We are in the age of digital photos and video."

"Of course," laughed Isabel, nervously. "I'm sorry. I'm be-ing a terrible hostess. Can I get you a coffee or perhaps a cold drink?"

"No thanks. What you might do is take me upstairs and show me where everything happened."

By the time *Subinspector* Pedrosa had taken her around the house and had her talk through the events of the previous night Isabel had begun to feel her confidence returning.

"The fact that a man lost his life is, of course, tragic," Pedrosa said, "but, to be horribly blunt, it does mean that you don't have to worry about him coming back. It was clear from an examination of the body that the man was a heroin addict. His arms were like pin cushions from where he ha-bitually injected himself. We haven't identified him yet but we expect to do so quite easily. Somebody usually comes forward sooner or later and, if not, he had a very recent tattoo that we should be able to trace."

Isabel felt the policeman regarding her closely before he spoke again.

"In fact, it's that tattoo that makes me ask the next question. There was also a sketch in the dead man's pocket. It was a drawing of a body with a very unusual and rather grim tattoo."

Again, he paused, as if deciding on how much to say or how to say it. When he resumed he spoke carefully.

"Isabel. I must stress that we are working on the theory that the man broke in to burgle the house. But I wouldn't be doing my job if I didn't explore every possibility. I must ask you to think carefully. Can you think of any reason why anybody would want to cause harm to you or your husband?"

GALICIA, SPAIN

MARK AND JOHANNA had landed on their feet. They had stumbled across a delightful restaurant at the end of a narrow laneway off the main pedestrian street. It had that rare, sought–after combination of antiquity and cleanliness. They were now "oohing" and "aahing" over an extensive menu that the waiter was patiently translating for them.

In the end, they decided to leave themselves in his hands and to share a selection of local delights that he enthusiastically recommended.

Mark was thrilled with the *Jamon de Bellota* – a cured ham that, because the animal had spent its life eating acorns, purportedly contained no cholesterol.

"I can't believe I can eat as much as I want of this and not worry about getting a heart attack," he laughed. "Then again, just because it has no cholesterol doesn't mean it's not full of calories."

"I never think about calories," said Johanna. "I just eat a little bit of whatever I want and make sure to get some sort of exercise in every day."

"I wish I could do that," said Mark. "but I just don't have the will power. I love my food and I love big quantities of it. The funny thing is that I can go all day without eating if I'm working on a project or busy with something. It's at night that I generally lose control and pig out. Also, I think that I'm just one of those people with a slow metabolism."

"I remember seeing a TV documentary," said Johanna, "and they said that all those theories about metabolisms were rubbish. In fact, they found that the people who were struggling with their weight usually had an emotional problem behind it."

Mark picked up his glass of *Albariño* and took a long sip in an attempt to mask his discomfort. It didn't work.

"I'm sorry. That was probably insensitive of me," said Johanna.

"No. It's grand. You're probably right. My dad died before I was old enough to remember him and my Mum took to drinking vodka and popping all sorts of pills to get over it. It wasn't the most stable childhood."

"That must have been tough."

"Well, when I look back it isn't any surprise that I ended up fat. She never cooked. It was always frozen pizzas or take-away Chinese when she remembered to feed us at all. Then, when I was twelve, she tried to kill herself. I came home from school and found her unconscious on the sofa. She'd swallowed a whole box of pills."

He gave a humourless laugh.

"I knew there was something wrong as soon as I came into the room 'cos there was a western on the TV. She hated westerns."

Johanna reached across the table and put a hand on his.

"God. I'm so sorry."

"Don't worry. I'm over it. After that it wasn't so bad. An aunt ended up taking me in while they put Mam into rehab. I was an absolute nightmare for my poor aunt. I can see that now. She hung in there, bless her, 'til I ran away the day after my seventeenth birthday. I managed to get a job and sent word I was okay so she could wipe her hands of me with a clear conscience. To be honest, I reckon it must have been a huge relief for her."

"What about your mother?"

"Oh, while I was living with my aunt they finally decided

that they'd cured her. They sent her home and she killed herself that night – slit her wrists."

Mark felt almost guilty at the horrified look that came to Johanna's face. He hastened to appease her.

"To be honest it didn't really affect me as much as it probably should have. I guess, in my mind, I'd lost her a long time before that."

Johanna gazed at him with a mixture of pity and fascination before picking up her glass and holding it aloft.

"Here's to you – an amazing survivor. To have come through all that and to end up the funny, kind, smart guy that you are. You should be so proud of yourself."

"It's hard to be proud of yourself when you look like this."

"But you're doing something about it, aren't you? I mean that's why you're here."

"I guess so, yeah. But I've tried so many things so many times that it's hard to believe that anything's ever going to work. They say you have to be ready."

"So, are you ready?"

Mark thought about it for a moment and then a smile spread across his face.

"You know, maybe I am. Yeah. I think I am."

Johanna lifted her glass again.

"Here's to new beginnings."

Mark raised his wine and the distinctive sound of two quality crystal glasses coming together rang clear and cheerful above the bright hubbub of the restaurant.

"You know, I've never told anybody all that," said Mark, suddenly. "It's weird. I hardly know you and it all just came out."

"That's not so weird really," said Johanna, smiling. "It's the *Camino*."

For a moment he considered telling her about Adelina and the doctored photographs but he decided against it. If tomorrow came without regrets for the information he'd already shared then there'd be time enough in the coming days on the way to share more of his inner conundrums.

8. Colossians

" And you, that were sometime alienated
and enemies in your mind by wicked works,
yet now hath he reconciled."

MARK WOKE with a start, leapt up and just came short of banging his head on the underside of the bunk above him. Something had prodded his leg. He looked and saw the lower end of a telescopic, aluminium walker's stick dangling suspiciously near to where his leg had been attacked. A man's bearded face appeared, upside–down, in the gloom between him and the rest of the sleeping dormitory.

"You were snoring," it said.

"Sorry," he mumbled as the head disappeared back to the upper bunk.

He was lying on his back. People were more likely to snore when they lay on their backs, he reminded himself. He wondered if Johanna, sleeping at the other end of the dormitory, had heard him. Even if she had, he reasoned, she couldn't be sure that it was him. Anyway, after the quantity of wine they had both downed he doubted that she was aware of anything.

He rolled onto his side and was alarmed at the amount of creaking and rocking this caused the bunk bed to make. For a while he remained motionless then, ever so carefully, he reached down to the floor and groped around for the old mobile phone. Locating it, he pulled it free of the charger cable and drew it into the sleeping bag with him so that the glow of the screen wouldn't light up the room. There were no new messages. He checked the time. It was just after three in the morning. The *peregrinos* would begin rising in two or three hours.

I can stay awake that long.

To keep his mind occupied he began to work out the number of calories he had burned with all of his walking the previous day and to balance that against the number of calories in the meals he had consumed. Seven hours of walking at, say, 300 calories per hour was 2,100. The lasagna and chips would come in at about 1,500, he reckoned. The meal with Johanna along with the wine… He gave an inward groan. He had conveniently forgotten the wine, tortilla and oil–soaked tomato that he'd lunched on in the stable outside Porriño and he'd eaten at least two bowls of nuts that came with the after–dinner drinks. Whatever way he worked the mathematics, one thing was certain. He was no closer to the weight loss that he needed to achieve before Adelina's arrival. At the thought, her picture arose in his mind and, with it, he became aware of a new complication. As he tried to focus on Adelina's face smiling statically at him from his favourite of her *Facebook* pictures, Johanna's face, laughing over dinner, broke in and pushed the image aside. He recalled Johanna's concern as he'd talked about his messed–up childhood. He recalled the laughter that had followed too many glasses of wine. He felt the closeness of her as she linked his arm on the way back to the *albergue* and the secret thrill that he'd felt when she'd said, jokingly, that they might have to share a hotel room for the night if they didn't make it back by the 10pm curfew. He took a deep breath and forced one part of his brain to detach itself and play devil's advocate.

Let's face it Mark. You're in danger of becoming infatuated with any half decent–looking woman who shows you attention. You haven't had attention from a female in years. At least not in real life.

He forced his thoughts to return to Adelina, but not to the images. Instead he focussed on the emails – months and months of daily conversation through which they had shared and explored each others hopes, fears, dreams and ambitions... He stopped at that thought. He wasn't being totally honest. Certainly she had shared such things with him but he had to admit that there was a good deal of fiction in the hopes, fears, dreams and ambitions that he'd shared with Adelina. His slim, fit alter ego had planned hikes up to the base camp of Everest and road trips in a VW combi to the centre of Australia and the Aboriginal holy mountain of Urulu. The fictitious fears that he'd stated to her belonged to the virtual Mark that he'd created for her benefit. The truth was that his plans involved losing a few stone and his fears were that he would be found out for the fraud that he was. Another realisation struck him. He had intended to find an internet café and to email Adelina but he'd been distracted by his evening with Johanna. The combination of physical weariness, mental anguish and inebriation had proven too much.

I'll figure it all out tomorrow.

Once more, he began to work out the calorie count for the day and to balance it with calories burned. Seven hours walking at 300 calories an hour was 2,100 but surely, with a heavy backpack, he could add another 100 calories per hour... The counting lulled him. Tomorrow he would do better, he swore, as sleep began to overtake him.

HE RODE *through the English countryside, the sunlight gleaming on his polished armour and his faithful pageboy jogging tirelessly alongside. Through sheer strength of will he ignored the stabbing pain from the wound in his back. He would not let it deter him from his quest. He glanced over his shoulder to where the other knights galloped en masse behind him, out–stripped by the...*

"Delucci. *Vamos.*"

The words, whispered urgently into his ear, snapped him out of his dream, and it all flooded back. They were just beyond a small village called Mos, four or five miles beyond Porriño. He and Rod had spent the night on the concrete floor at the back of a raised, square pool of water where, he was guessing, local women must have come to hand wash the laundry in the times before washing machines and coffee mornings. A sign over it proclaimed the spot to be the *Fonte dos Cabaleiros*. Unlike other such pools that they had passed the previous day, this one had a roof covering it and protective walls on all sides with the exception of that which faced the road. It had been enough to keep the dampness of the night off them and the constant sound of water pouring into the trough had served to lull the priest's aching body into a deep sleep. During the night he must have rolled off the clothes that Rod had laid on the floor as a makeshift mattress for him and, now, something was digging painfully into his back. He sat up and discovered that the offending item was one of his sandals.

Rod, satisfied that he was finally awake, grunted something and began to stuff a tightly rolled sleeping bag into his pack. Fr Delucci instantly regretted his own sleeping bag, now far behind at the Portuguese border. As soon as the priest staggered to his feet, Rod gathered the clothes that he had slept upon and packed them neatly into his bag.

"*Tenemos que irnos,*" he said as he finished tightening the strap to secure his load, stood and hoisted his pack onto his shoulder. "*Vamos.*"

"*Vamos, vamos.* Always *vamos*! First we have coffee," said the priest. "I have some money now. I buy us coffee then you can *vamos* all you like."

"Okay. *Sí. Café, si quieres,*" said Rod. "*Vamos.*"

The priest smiled and began to put on his sandals but stopped, wincing in pain as his right foot rubbed against the leather straps. He remembered that the foot had grown painful the previous evening but he had been too tired to do anything more than hobble on. He examined the angry, red patch where a blister had formed. Rod was quickly on his knees surveying the damage with an expert eye. He tut–tutted like a disapproving grandmother then, reaching into his bag pulled out a needle and thread. The priest began to protest but the *vagabundo* shut him up with a raised hand and a look that brooked no argument. Fr Delucci submitted himself, with a quick mental prayer, and watched, at first in trepidation and then in amazement, as Rod passed the needle and thread through one side of the blister and out the other.

The blister drained rapidly. Rod allowed the thread to slip off the needle so that it was left dangling through the skin. He then replaced the needle into its place in his backpack and rummaged for something else. When he turned he held out a pair of black, cotton socks.

"*Estará mejor con estos,*" he said, passing them over, and Fr Delucci was amazed to find that they were held together with a rubber band. It was a trick that he, himself, had picked up from a book entitled: "*Self Maintenance for the Single Man.*" It seemed that he and Rod had a lot more in common than might be expected at first glance.

"I read the same book," he said.

Rod simply looked uncomprehending and uncomfortable so the priest shrugged and smiled.

"Never mind. It's okay."

Fr Delucci moved awkwardly due to both his damaged foot and the stiffness that came from a night spent on a hard floor. They made their way slowly back downhill to Mos, which proved to be a small, pleasant village. It had been too dark and the priest had been too preoccupied to get a good sense of it the previous evening when they had arrived. Now, he found himself looking around with approval as they entered the empty, wide main street. On the right was a pilgrim *albergue* and, across the road from it, a small café with a terrace outside. It was there that they took their coffee, accompanied by large *crausans* that seemed much bigger than the French style *croissants* with which Fr Delucci was familiar. After a quick, impromptu Spanish lesson, where the priest learned the words for coffee, milk, sugar, salt, pepper, table and chair, they sat in companionable silence. Fr Delucci's €40 was reduced somewhat but, looking back at the series of events that had led him here since abandoning his possessions on the River Minho bridge, he found himself letting go of any remaining doubts and surrendering himself to his reburgeoning faith.

A short time later, as he trudged up the hill from Mos behind Rod, he held his breviary open in one hand, quietly praying his *Matins* and *Lauds*.

The way passed by their refuge of the previous night and

steeply upwards until, eventually, it flattened out somewhat. Shortly afterwards, they came upon a few scattered houses around a left hand turn in the road. Here sat a tall stone crucifix, mounted on a stepped, concrete plinth and surrounded by flowers and shrubbery. Two glass cases, one on either side of the crucifix, contained used candles that suggested that the place was utilised for religious ceremonies of some sort. There was an iron railing encasing the lot.

"Rod, here I say Mass. *Capito?* Mass."

SANTIAGO DE COMPOSTELA, SPAIN

IT HAD BEEN a troubled night for Isabel. In that twilight place, somewhere between consciousness and sleep, her mind had thrown up images of the horrors that had taken place only 24 hours before mere metres from where she now lay. She could see the twisted shape of the body on the cobbles but, in her dream, it morphed into Anxo's crippled form. She had rushed to his side and knelt to attend him but, looking into his face, had recoiled in alarm. Instead of the pain or anguish that she had expected to find there, she was confronted by that cold, unfathomable look again.

At about six in the morning she gave up on sleep. It was still dark. She stumbled her way into the bathroom and took a long shower. She stood for a while with her hand on the place where she had felt the faint flutter of the baby kicking but it seemed to be enjoying the sleep of which she was deprived. The sting of the hot water penetrated the fog of trauma and sleeplessness leaving her feeling somewhat better. In the kitchen she went through the comforting ritual of making her morning *cafe con leche,* using fresh beans crushed in the old hand grinder that had belonged to her parents. When the milky coffee was ready, she sat sipping it at the kitchen table and attempted to put her thoughts into some sort of order. So much had changed in such a short space of time. She was, she felt, totally adrift with nothing left to anchor herself to and the *Subinspector's* hints that the burglary might have been something more personal than a random crime disturbed her. The policeman had seemed to be suggesting something unthinkable.

I wonder what Subinspector Pedrosa made of Anxo sleeping on the sofa.

Why had that thought crossed her mind? A flush of guilt brought a knot to her throat. Anxo was in a horrible condition in hospital and she was carrying his child. With that thought, she became aware, again, of the dread that was hovering beneath the surface of her conscious thoughts. What if it had been her fault? She had prayed to *the saint*. Had he answered her prayer in a sudden, dramatic and terrible fashion? With the guilt came a growing sense of remorse. She had to admit that, from the moment that she had suspected her pregnancy, she had given up any pretence of interest in sex. Whatever intimacy they continued to have had been initiated by Anxo. She had performed her 'marital duty' in response and no more. Could she really blame him completely, then, for seeking physical fulfilment elsewhere?

I must take part of the responsibility. For the sake of our baby I must try to give our marriage every chance.

Prompted by that thought, she made her way into the living room and set about folding away the covers and pillows that had made up Anxo's temporary bed. It was as she stooped to pick up a pillow which had fallen to the floor that she saw the mobile phone, attached to the slender cable where Anxo had plugged it in to charge while he slept. She stared at it for a moment. Anxo never left his phone out of his sight. He was obsessively possessive of it. Almost reverently, she picked it up. As her hand made contact with the touch screen it lit up. The phone wasn't locked. A small envelope graphic with the number '5' beside it indicated that there were unread messages and, beneath that, a telephone symbol announced three missed calls. The phone calls were from her godfather, timed five minute apart. They had been made the previous morning shortly after Anxo was due to be in work. There was no doubting what those calls were about. He hadn't known that Anxo was in hospital and would certainly have been calling to berate him. Anxo had been right about that much at least. Her godfather had never liked her husband. Next, she clicked on the messages symbol. Five names came up. Four she recognised as Anxo's usual friends and colleagues. The fifth name, however, made her blood run cold. Vicki – the girl that Anxo claimed was besotted with him.

Isabel sunk into the sofa, holding the phone in both hands. Her thumb hovered over the message. One touch of the screen would reveal its contents and, perhaps, tell her the truth once and for all. At first she thought that the baby was kicking and then she realised that the thumping was her heart, beating wildly.

She had a natural abhorrence of invading her husband's privacy. What if he had been telling the truth?

If he was fighting off her advances, why would he give her his number?

Her mind was made up at this thought but another stayed her hand. Once she clicked the message it would be consigned to the 'read' rather than 'unread' message folder and Anxo would know she had looked at it. An idea occurred to her. She navigated the phone's menu until she had found the read messages. She paused with her thumb over the screen. Once she clicked open that folder there would be no going back.

It doesn't matter what I find. I have to give him a second chance. But I want to know...

She tapped the screen and a list appeared. She didn't have far to scroll down before she encountered Vicki's name. She tapped the message and, as simply as that, her husband's infidelity lay exposed before her on the small device. With the proof of Anxo's guilt, all reticence disappeared. She scrolled to the very start and began, painfully, to trace the course of the affair.

He had been seeing the girl for about three months. It coincided exactly with her realisation that she was pregnant. He had been fiendishly cunning and ruthless in seducing the girl. Not only had he admitted having a wife but had thrown in an imaginary daughter for good measure. Isabel felt almost sick with grief and anger at the irony as, through the text messages, she saw patches of the tale that he had carefully woven. It was a story that told of a devoted father, bound in a loveless marriage for the sake of his little girl. She fumed at the fictitious picture he painted of his wealth and status. She tried to feel anger towards the girl who was sleeping with her husband but she had to admit that Vicki had stood no chance. In fact, at one point in the text messages the girl had raised the question of Anxo's wife and had expressed uneasiness. Anxo had swept such considerations aside, saying that he and Isabel had 'an arrangement'. She now turned to the pictures folder and had no difficulty in identifying Vicki. There she was – a young, beautiful girl of about 20 years, pouting seductively in numerous 'selfies' with Anxo or striking provocative poses for him while, presumably, he took the photograph. One picture made the knot in Isabel's stomach rise to her throat and threaten to choke her. It showed Anxo with his young mistress in the very restaurant where he had proposed to her almost a decade before.

Casting the phone down on the sofa, she grabbed her coat and, without having any idea where she was going, fled from the house.

Forty minutes or more had passed before she returned. She felt raw with a tumultuous mix of emotions but she could control it now. She had a plan. Returning to the living room she sat and picked up Anxo's phone again. She created a new blank text message and selected Vicki's name from the contacts.

Guapa, sorry I haven't been in touch. Something has happened. Meet me at 8pm at...

Isabel hesitated as she tried to think of a suitable meeting place. Somewhere with lots of people where she could wait unnoticed.

... the front of the Catedral at the main steps. Please don't let me down. It's important.

She signed it with the three 'x's that had marked each one of her husband's more recent texts to his mistress. She read it over once and then quickly, before she had a chance to change her mind, pressed 'send'. It was all very well to give Anxo a second chance but if he decided to blow it she was going to make sure that she was the first to know.

BENDIGO, AUSTRALIA

GRACE WAS AWAKE instantly. The bloody dog. It was barking, furiously, in its sharp, puppy voice. She glanced at the alarm clock on the bedside locker and cursed. She'd only just fallen asleep. She and Angela had been going to bed early as their bodies continued to recover from the jet lag.

A huntsman she thought. The huge spiders that were so common around Tony's ranch were harmless but they terrified her and drove Chewy mad. Angela would be alarmed.

"Angela, it's all right, honey. I'm coming."

She slipped out of bed, armed herself with the first weapon that came to hand – a wooden clothes hanger – and went into the landing. She bumped into Tony coming from the living room where he'd been indulging in late night TV. Chewy was standing on his hind legs against Angela's door that, thanks to a strip of rubber placed by Tony along its edge, was now too stiff to give way to the puppy's efforts. The dog, still barking, was in a frenzy to get into the room.

"Bold dog," said Grace as it became apparent that the puppy's outburst was as a result of his inability to get to his beloved Angela. Then a feeling of disquiet arose within her. There was no way that her daughter could have slept through that racket and she was a softie when it came to giving Chewy his way. Why hadn't she come out of her room? The feeling became an intuitive dread.

"Angela..."

She covered the distance to the bedroom door in a few paces and flung it wide.

IT WAS CHEWY that had awakened Angela with his barking and scraping, but she'd instantly become aware of a presence in the room. She loved waking with the sunrise so she slept with the curtains open. The full moon was streaming in through the window, lighting everything with its bright bluish hue. A movement at the end of her bed made her heart leap and she snatched her feet up to her chest. One of the soft toys she had made with Granny was a draft excluder in the shape of a snake. What she was looking at now she recognised immediately as the real thing. It was dark with light diamond shapes all over. The lower part of it disappeared over the end of the bed so she could not guess its size, but the head and its upper body seemed the length of her leg. The serpent's unblinking eyes stared at her. Transfixed with terror, she opened her mouth to scream but nothing came out. She could hear her puppy's frenzied efforts to force open the door but Uncle Tony had fixed it. Then the snake began to move slowly, silently and smoothly across the foot of the bed and this motion snapped her out of her paralysis. She scrambled to her feet, almost falling forward as her legs became momentarily entangled in the pillows. Again her mouth fell open in a silent scream that the blackness would not give voice to.

Then she heard her name being called and the door flew open. Mammy provided the scream that she had failed to and leapt forward. Her face was a picture of fear but her arm swung, what appeared to be, Uncle Tony's toy boomerang at the object on the bed. A part of Angela's mind, strangely detached from the terror that she was experiencing, was noting that the object was not a boomerang but a wooden coat hanger when there was a blur of movement and Chewy was on the bed, launching himself at the serpent. As Uncle Tony entered, the snake recoiled and both animals fell to the floor, hopelessly tangled in each other.

"It's okay. It's harmless," she heard Uncle Tony say as Mammy grabbed her and buried her in a fiercely protective hug. "Carpet python. They don't normally wander into houses so it might be a pet that's escaped."

"Oh darling," said Mammy. "It's okay. It's okay."

She peered out in time to see Uncle Tony carrying the snake from the room, holding it out of the puppy's reach. The serpent's body was coiled around his arm, as Chewy launched himself into the air again and again in an effort to reach it. Her heart was still racing but the terror was giving way to a rising jubilation. She was surrounded by heroes. Chewy had known something was wrong and had taken on the snake. So had Mammy. Okay, so it wasn't dangerous, but Mammy didn't know that. And there was Uncle Tony – a real bushman like in the stories, holding the snake by the neck and chucking it out as if it was nothing more than a troublesome fly. Mammy was watching her with a worried look so she smiled reassuringly. She saw relief wash over her mother's face.

"Come on, love. You're sleeping in with me tonight."

Angela wished, so much, that she could say something, but, like the scream, the words were locked somewhere inside her. A line from one of the nursery rhymes that Daddy used to read to her at bedtime came to mind.

All the king's horses and all the king's men couldn't put Humpty together again.

GALICIA, SPAIN

MARK WOULD HAVE missed Johanna had it not been for the message from Shay jolting him awake with it's harsh, vintage, digital alert tone. He took a groggy look around the dormitory and saw that it was already a hive of activity as *peregrinos* busied themselves for the day ahead. He picked up the phone and opened the text message.

"Today you walk to Redondela. In addition to your own, carry the backpack of a fellow pilgrim. Don't forget to write your name and the exact time when you have completed this task."

Mark's heart sank. This, he decided, was contrived, ridiculous and more likely to give him a heart attack than make much of a difference to his weight. He was struggling enough with his own backpack without having to take on the burden of somebody else's bag. In addition to all of that, there was the difficulty of finding someone who was willing to let him carry their pack.

Excuse me. Do you need a hand with that?

He could guess what any self–respecting pilgrim would say. The message was also annoyingly vague. If he found somebody who let him shoulder their pack for five minutes would that count?

Noticing that he was one of the last people in the dormitory, he decided to get going and worry about it on the road. When he bent to get fresh clothes from his backpack he groaned. He was momentarily dizzy and his head felt tender from the excesses of the previous evening. On top of it all, he was experiencing the feeling of gloom that always seemed to follow a wine soaked night.

Fifteen minutes later he descended from the dormitory just in time to see Johanna making for the door. He called to her and she stopped.

"I thought you might have left already," she said.

"Are you joking?" he laughed. "After all that wine I'm lucky to be up at all. And, while we're on the subject – how come you look as fresh as a daisy and I look like this?"

She gave a half smile.

"Trust me, I'm looking pretty bad from the inside."

They set off at a slow pace. Despite the overnight rest, Johanna's foot was clearly continuing to cause her discomfort. Mark looked at her large backpack. While this was an opportunity to fulfil his task for Shay, he'd look like a complete idiot if he offered to carry Johanna's bag and then couldn't manage to do so. He had half decided to wait until they had covered most of the distance to Redondela but the same stubborn voice that had seen him abandon the bread at the San Telmo monument berated him for his faintheartedness. He took a deep breath.

"Hey, why don't you let me carry your pack for you?"

Johanna looked surprised.

"No, thanks. I'll manage."

"Are you sure? Your foot looks like it's still giving you problems..."

"It's not great but I'd feel that I was cheating if I didn't carry my own backpack. Thanks anyway."

Mark nodded.

"Okay. But if you change your mind..."

They walked on a few paces before Johanna spoke again.

"Look. If you want to walk faster, go ahead. I don't want to slow you down."

"Not at all. This pace suits me."

The way led across the train track and back to the main road but, instead of turning right to the cafés and restaurants, the *Camino* ran to the left and out of town past a large, busy roundabout. Here Mark's journey almost came to an abrupt and unpleasant end.

Since his offer to carry her pack, Johanna had cut off any further attempts to make conversation. At first he thought that she was simply tired, struggling with her foot or nursing a hangover from the wine of the previous evening. The more he dwelled upon it, though, the more he became convinced that, earlier, she had been trying to slip away from the *albergue* without him. There was something about the look she had given him when he came downstairs that hadn't registered at the time but that had lingered in his subconscious. He had still not gotten used to the traffic driving on the right instead of the left as it did back home in the UK. Caught up in his brown study, therefore, he looked right, saw nothing coming and would have stepped under a truck approaching from the opposite direction had it not been for Johanna's lightning reflexes.

"Thank God I had you with me," he laughed as the truck thundered past with a deafening blast of its horn. But the laugh came out hollow and Johanna's face was white.

They walked on in silence again and Mark, found himself ever more oppressed by the gloom that seemed to subdue them both. It was almost a relief, therefore, when Johanna came clean.

"Mark, I hope that you don't take this the wrong way but, if you don't mind, I think I'd prefer to walk alone."

"Oh, absolutely. No problem," he stumbled, feeling himself flush under the weight of his embarrassment. "I hope you don't think I... Well, last night, I hope I didn't do anything that..."

As he ran out of words Johanna hurriedly stepped in.

"No, of course not. I really enjoyed last night. It's just that I came on this walk to get my head sorted out and I need time alone to think. We only have a few days left before we reach Santiago. The time seems to be going so fast."

"Of course. I totally understand," said Mark.

He stopped walking and so did Johanna.

"How will we do this?" he said. "I guess with your dodgy foot I should walk ahead."

She gave him a weak smile and nodded.

"If you don't mind."

"Right. Well, I might see you later, then."

As he covered the fifty metres or so to the next bend on the trail he imagined her scrutinising him from this unflattering position. He tried to walk tall and confident but he was burning inside with a mix of negative emotions. He forced himself to push them aside and concentrate, instead, on each step. When he reached the bend he summoned a smile to his face and turned to wave her goodbye but the road behind him was empty. Where she had disappeared to he didn't know, but he reminded himself, somewhat bitterly, that it was no longer his concern. He marched on, determined to put as much distance as possible between them.

Shortly afterwards, the trail crossed the busy, main road and entered lush farmlands. The steady tread of his footsteps began to beat a rhythm. It was soothing. He let his mind wander freely over the enigma of Johanna. Had he done something under the influence of the wine that he couldn't recall? No. There were no blank spots in his memory of the evening. Perhaps it was the revelation of his past that she had given more thought to and now found distasteful. That theory didn't ring true either. She had seemed genuinely concerned. Maybe she had needed to go to toilet in the bushes and was too embarrassed to say – that would account for her disappearance. Or perhaps she was afraid that he was entertaining hopes that there might be something between them… It was as though the tumblers of a lock had fallen into place and the door of a safe had swung open to reveal what lay behind. That was it. She thought he fancied her. Indignation rose at the thought of her presumption until a small voice reminded him that she was right. He recalled his nighttime struggle to remain faithful, in his mind, to Adelina. It also struck him that offering to carry her bag might have been misconstrued as a sign of growing possessiveness. Damn Shay. He found that he was distinctly dissatisfied with himself and his thoughts, inevitably, swung to food. He hadn't had any breakfast and, thankfully, Shay hadn't said he couldn't do so. He found himself confronting the same problem as the previous day, however. He was surrounded by farmland with just the occasional house. There was no sign of a café nor even a shop.

A road sign informed him that he was in a district called Mos. This is where the Spanish girls had been making for the previous day. Given the uncomfortable situation that had developed with Johanna, he deeply regretted not having walked on with them.

Perhaps they decided to start late today. If I hurry and don't stop I might catch up with them.

It was highly unlikely but the thought of that possibility saw him picking up his pace.

After a while he came across a drinking fountain, set back from the road beside a concrete table with benches either side. It had clearly been provided so that pilgrims could re-fill their water bottles and rest before tackling the trail again. There was a curious little statue of a shrunken woman wearing a headscarf on a granite plinth. He drank the cold, refreshing water and walked on, revived and, to his pleasant surprise, no longer occupied with the thought of food. When he arrived in the quaint village of Mos, therefore, he marched determinedly past first the small restaurant and then the café bar across from the *albergue* with barely a glance. The way beyond climbed steeply and saw him huffing and puffing before long. He began zigzagging across the road. In this way the gradient was not as steep. The downside, of course, was that it resulted in him having to walk a lot further.

To add to his discomfort, the sun was starting to make its presence felt. By the time the road finally flattened out, therefore, he was bathed in sweat and gasping so it took him a few moments to notice the small crowd gathered ahead of him at an intersection to the left. There was some sort of ceremony going on. The first thing that struck Mark was the realisation that the proceedings were in English rather than Spanish. He was walking very slowly so he had plenty of time to observe as he approached. There were about ten people gathered on grass verges around a railed monument which proved to be a tall crucifix. Some were standing beside backpacks that clearly marked them as *peregrinos* whilst others had the appearance of locals. At the foot of the crucifix a man in dark clothing was addressing the gathering. Beside him, kneeling, was a second, bedraggled looking, man of indeterminate age.

In an instant Mark knew what was happening. He had stumbled upon a priest saying Mass at the roadside. His aunt had been a Roman Catholic and a Mass–goer and Mark had accompanied her each Sunday. Apart from this, religion was not something that had figured in Mark's life yet there was a part of him that had enjoyed the sense of community that he had felt at those Sunday morning occasions. The priest had been a kindly old soul who would dash from the altar as the choir played out the final hymn so that he could be at the front door of the church where he'd be sure to shake each and every parishioner by hand as they left.

He's probably dead by now or, after all the scandals in the church, wishing he was.

On top of the weariness from the long climb and his disquiet over the situation with Johanna, Mark felt a flood of nostalgia sweep over him.

I wonder how Aunt Lilly is? I haven't seen her in so long.

He let his backpack slip from his shoulders to the ground and dragged it over to where the little crowd was gathered.

OUT OF THE CORNER of his eye, Rod saw yet another pilgrim – a fat one – join the impromptu congregation. He tried to concentrate on Delucci, reading aloud from the Bible, but his mind was racing. Alone on the *Camino* he had honed survival down to a fine art. However, he was finding that there was a lot that one person could do which simply didn't work so well for two. The *vagabundo* also had a suspicion that his new companion, being a religious man, might frown upon some of the survival tactics he was accustomed to employing. To further complicate matters, Delucci was clearly not used to walking. Their progress was painfully slow and, as a result, Rod was loath to detour from the road – a necessity in foraging from his usual haunts but one that, in the current circumstances, would slow them down even more.

A movement caught his attention. Behind the young, fat man who had just arrived, a party of four more *peregrinos* were taking off their backpacks to join the congregation. An idea began to form in his mind and quickly took hold.

El obrero es digno de su salario.

As inconspicuously as he could, Rod unhooked a cooking tin from his backpack and got slowly to his feet. With his head bowed down in a show of reverence, he crossed the short distance to the nearest person – a middle aged woman who had come out of one of the neighboring houses – and held out the tin. Without hesitation, she dipped into her pocket, pulled out a handful of coins and dropped them in. Rod, nodded his appreciation, shoved the tin into her hands and signed for her to pass it on. As he slipped back to his place near the makeshift altar, the clinking of coins on metal signaled the tin can's fruitful journey around the gathering.

FR DELUCCI was vaguely aware that a collection was going on among the members of his motley congregation.

The labourer is worth of his hire.

He focused his complete attention, again, on the Eucharistic Prayer. He savoured the familiar words with a new delight for they were no longer simply words to him. He realised that, for the first time since those first few enthusiastic years after his ordination, he was truly immersed in the Mass – lost in this great mystery of pure faith. A memory stirred of long hours knelt in prayer before the statue of St James in his childhood parish church in Boston.

Suffer little children to come to me, and forbid them not: for of such is the kingdom of God.

Earlier, as he went about preparing a makeshift altar for the service, he had felt somewhat apprehensive. He was, after all, in a foreign country on a back road in the middle of nowhere. He had no frame of reference to gauge the attitude of the people who lived in the few houses scattered around the intersection. While he had hoped that the presence of candles at the stone cross meant that the locals would not object to his saying Mass, they could have been put there by one small cohort of believers. His studies had included the Spanish tragedy that devastated the land at the end of the 1930s. One of the first blows in that civil war had been the burning of convents in Madrid. The people followed priests in Spain, he had once heard, with either a candle or with a cudgel.

However, the neighbours, when they had emerged, had done so to stand in reverent participation. What's more, as the service had progressed they were joined by pilgrims who appeared in a slow, steady trickle up the hill from the direction of Mos. Fr Delucci had flicked open the Bible at a random place to choose the reading. The page had fallen open at the story of the Baptism of Jesus by John. With a start, he'd recognised it as the tale that marked the beginning of Jesus' ministry.

Now, as he started the 'Our Father' a chorus of voices joined in – some following him in English, others joining Rod in the Spanish version of the prayer.

When it came time for him to say; *May the peace of the Lord be with you all*, he gazed, fondly around the attentive faces of his motley congregation.

"Let us offer each other a sign of that peace."

In his Boston parish, Fr Delucci had, on more than one occasion, addressed his congregation from the pulpit in an attempt to promote a greater level of restraint when it came to sharing the sign of peace. Hugs, kisses and 'high–fives' were, he had lectured, excessive. A simple handshake with one's immediate neighbour on each side was sufficient, he had said. It was as much to his own surprise as Rod's, therefore, that he found himself approaching his new companion and embracing him like a long–lost brother. A flood of joy welled up inside him and expressed itself in tears which began to stream, unchecked, down his cheeks. Releasing Rod, he bound across to the woman from the neighbouring house and clasped her hand warmly.

"Peace be with you."

"*Y con su espiritu, Padre,*" she answered, smiling broadly.

MARK WATCHED the priest move steadily, person by person, towards him, lighting each one with his infectious exuberance like a bush fire spreading from tree to tree. Mark felt like a fraud amid this celebration of a faith that, to him, was associated with no more than a sense of vague nostalgia. He considered slipping away but the thought came too late. The priest stood before him. Mark looked up, apologetically and, to his great surprise, found himself swept away in the moment. The priest's unshaven, tear–streaked face seemed to glow with an other–worldly aura. His eyes met Mark's with a look of recognition. It was a look that seemed to lay bare his petty concerns and strip them away to reach in and touch his very soul.

Peace be with you.

The fact that the accent was American lent a Hollywood–like undertone to the experience. Mark felt that he should do or say something but the occasion, he discovered, was beyond him. His quandary was resolved by the action of the cleric. He found himself caught in a strong, brief embrace and then the priest had moved on to the next member of the congregation, leaving Mark glowing every bit as much as those who had gone before him. When the tin can had come past, aware that nobody was paying any attention to whether he contributed or not, he had refrained from doing so. On an impulse, now, he crossed to where the can lay on the ground beside the priest's dishevelled companion and dropped €5 into the mixed coins and notes that lay within.

Some short time later, after the priest had placed a broken piece of consecrated bread on his tongue, he found himself, in his mind, forming the first sincere prayer that he had ever attempted.

Dear God...

He stopped. Talking directly to a God he had ignored all of his life seemed to be reaching a bit high. He began again.

San Tiago. You are the one that this Camino is dedicated to. If you can hear me, please let this bread fix whatever it is that's broken in me. Make this the beginning of a new relationship with food. I know what I need to do. I have the theory. Give me the strength to actually do it.

The part of his brain that took delight in ridiculing his attempts to overcome his eating disorder fed greedily off this new, rich source of fuel.

You idiot. You're here in a hopeless attempt to walk half your body weight off and now you're clutching at religious mumbo jumbo.

The service came to its conclusion. The priest, smiling, slowly gazed around at them all.

"Our Mass is over. Go in peace to love and serve the Lord."

As Mark hoisted his backpack into place and set off on the way once more, the scene he left behind reminded him of small gigs where the musician hangs about after at the end of the show to accept the praise of his fans. The priest was deep in conversation with a young woman while his dishevelled companion played security man – keeping others in check until their turn came. Mark's inner critic continued to berate him but he pushed it aside as he became slowly aware of something else. A tiny but stubborn flicker of hope had just made its home in a heretofore dark corner of his mind. An old joke popped into his mind and he smiled.

How many psychologists does it take to change a light bulb? Just one, but the light bulb has to want to change.

THE YOUNG MAN stepped out of his boxer shorts and stuffed them on top of the other clothes in the small gym bag. Naked, but for his socks and sneakers, he stood for a moment, faced the sun and closed his eyes, letting the afternoon heat soak into his skin. His mind turned to thoughts of what he was about to do and, despite the autumn warmth, he shivered in tingling anticipation. He picked up the three–quarter length coat from the rock upon which he had placed it and put it on, zipping the front up tightly. Slinging the bag over one shoulder, he moved to where he could peer out from the bracken–rich undergrowth at the trail. It was empty but would not, he knew from experience, remain so for long. A steady stream of *peregrinos* was guaranteed at this time of year. He just had to wait for the right victim.

Not ten minutes had passed when he heard the distinctive, rhythmic clump of a walker's stick on the dirt track. He slipped a hand into the pocket of his long coat and, reaching through the cut he had made in the lining, he began to arouse himself in preparation. He could feel his heart rate rise as he stared at the bend in the trail. Into view came two young men, the one on the further side of the path keeping rhythm with a walking stick fashioned from a tree branch. They chatted as they walked, their accents sounding Scandinavian to the man. He remained very still until they had passed his hiding place and disappeared around the bend in the trail ahead.

A further five or ten minutes went by before, in a flash of colour, a young woman came into view. She was striding purposefully, her eyes fixed on the ground ahead as if lost in thought. She wore tight, lycra knee–length shorts and a green vest top that showed a wet patch of sweat at her stomach. Her hair was tied back with a cloth of some sort but, even from a distance, the man could see that it wasn't keeping the perspiration from running down her forehead. He could feel his heart pumping more vigorously than normal in his chest as his adrenaline surged. He had hung the bag containing his clothes over the short branch that he always used. With deliberation, he slipped off his coat and draped that over the same branch. Then, naked and fully aroused, he waited. There was a tree on the far side of the track that he used as a marker. When she crossed the line between his position and that tree he would make his move. She drew closer, oblivious to his presence. He drew deep breaths to control his excitement. She approached the imaginary line and then, just as she was about to cross it, she stopped and gazed back in the direction from which she had come.

Is she waiting for someone else?

Before he had a chance to make up his mind on the point, she turned and continued walking. He stared past her at the bend. There was no sign of anybody but now she had passed his mark and come too close to his place of concealment.

I'll wait for her to pass. That will give me more time to see if she is with someone else.

As she passed his place of concealment he stared, hungrily, at her features and at the side profile of her slim body. She was five metres away and getting further when he stepped out onto the track.

"*Hola, señora.*"

He began masturbating even before she turned. When

she did she let out an involuntary shriek and brought a hand up to cover her mouth, staring wide–eyed in a way that thrilled him.

"Bad, bad," she yelled at him and it heightened his pleasure. One of the reasons that exposing himself to *peregrinas* gave him so much satisfaction was the sense that they were 'holy'. Her innocent protestations turned him on and drove him to a rapid climax. She shouted louder and, in the wave of self loathing that inevitably washed over him, he became aware of two things simultaneously. Firstly, that she seemed to be looking past him rather than at him. Secondly, there was an 'r' in the word she was yelling. Not 'bad', then, but 'Brad'. He spun around and was confronted with a sight that filled him with abject terror. A man, muscles rippling from beneath his vest top, was just metres from him and closing fast, his face a picture of fury. The newcomer's backpack lay on the trail behind where he had obviously dropped it so that he could run faster. The flasher turned heel and fled as if running for his life. He crashed into the undergrowth near to where his coat and bag lay but he was out of his usual position with the woman's 'Brad' breathing down his neck. He abandoned any thought of retrieving his things and concentrated, instead, on trying to make good his escape. Bushes tore at his naked skin as he ran but he felt nothing, struck numb, as he was, from fear.

The first sign he got that the pursuit had ended was a bellow from the big man, coming from some distance behind. He risked a glance over his shoulder and saw that his pursuer was sitting on the ground, clasping one of his legs in agony. The flasher's relief was short lived, though. Behind the man, the woman was rushing to his aid. To the flasher's dismay, she was carrying his coat and bag. The injured man shook his fist at him as the woman arrived and dropped to her knees beside him. The man snatched the coat and bag from her and held them aloft, shouting in English. The flasher didn't understand the words but the meaning was clear enough. The articles were being seized as trophies of war. Dismayed, he had little option but to turn and make good his escape into the depths of the undergrowth. The immediate threat past, his heartbeat slowed and he became acutely aware of the bushes tearing at his skin.

Joder. What will I do now?

THE WAY TURNED left, off the roadway, and across some cobblestones before hitting a dirt track. Although the surface was uneven and he had to keep his eyes on the ground to avoid stepping on stones that might twist an ankle, Mark preferred this to the black, hot surface of the main road. The track swept to the right, past a house on the left hand side of the bend. A man was cleaning his car on the driveway. He paused from his labours to nod a greeting.

"Buen Camino."

"Gracias," replied Mark and trudged on. He was in a wooded area. On either side of the trail the landscape boasted a rich palette of greens, golds, reds and browns as fonds of bracken and trees put on their autumn display. The trees cast a welcome shade from the increasingly hot sun. With nobody on the path ahead nor behind, Mark was lost in a world of his own when he was startled from it by an unexpected sight. There was a backpack lying in the centre of the track. Before he could come up with a reasonable explanation for such an anomaly, a female voice called out to him from somewhere ahead in the undergrowth.

"Excuse me. I wonder if you could help us?"

It took a moment for Mark to locate the source. When he did he was surprised to see that it was Brad's girlfriend. Brad, himself, was beside her, one arm round her shoulder as she supported him. He held his right leg bent with the foot barely resting on the ground and it was obvious that he was in real distress. Mark hurried, as quickly as he could manage, to where they were standing. The young woman flashed him a grateful smile.

"I was afraid that he might fall if we try to get down this bit. Maybe with one of us on each side…"

They they were standing at the top of a clearing that might once have been a path but was now steep and overgrown.

"Of course," responded Mark, struggling out of his backpack and scrambling up the slope. Even in the drama of the moment a part of his brain registered that her accent was English rather than American like that of her boyfriend.

He took up his position on the other side of the injured man and they painstakingly made their way onto the level surface of the trail.

"He's twisted his ankle," explained the girl. There was a guy in the bushes exposing his..."

She nodded downwards.

"Good God. Unbelievable," said Mark, grimacing suitably.

"...Brad tried to catch him."

"I'd have had the bastard too," exclaimed Brad vehemently. "But at least I have his bag and his clothes. Let's see how far the sick son of a bitch gets in his birthday suit."

He brandished the flasher's belongings.

"I'm Tanya," said the young woman, reaching out her hand.

Mark involuntarily wiped his own on his shorts before shaking hers.

"Mark."

"I know," she said. "You were talking with Brad in the restaurant back in Porriño."

"Yes," said Mark. "He was kind enough to give me his chair."

An awkward silence followed broken, shortly, by Brad.

"I need to sit down."

"Well, let me return that favour," said Mark. "I've nothing breakable in my rucksack. Sit on that."

"Cheers."

Brad collapsed onto the haversack and began to take off his walking boot.

"Damn. It's swelling already."

"What do you want to do," asked Tanya.

"My options are a bit fucking limited. I won't be doing any more walking on this sucker. I guess I'll have to see if there's a bus from that last little village we passed through but how I'm going to get down the hill in this state I have no idea."

In the end they adopted the same system as they had used

to get Brad onto the trail. After much protestation from Tanya and to Brad's obvious embarrassment, Mark carried his own backpack in its normal place and Brad's much smaller one strapped to his front. Then, one either side of the injured man, they slowly made their way back down the hill to Mos. Mark begrudged every downward step that undid his hard labour of that morning's uphill climb but, he reminded himself, that he was, at least, fulfilling Shay's instructions and carrying the backpack of a fellow pilgrim. They walked in silence. It seemed inappropriate to make idle conversation in light of Brad's condition and he was clearly in no mood to talk.

They passed a number of pilgrims who Mark recognised from the impromptu Mass congregation and received various utterances of concern and advice along with well–meaning but impotent offers of help. Shortly afterwards they passed the site of the Mass where the priest and his assistant were still in conversation with two pilgrims.

When they finally reached the café in Mos the owner proved to be very sympathetic. He soon had the injured man ensconced in a corner with his leg elevated on a chair. Meanwhile, Mark wearily slid Brad's backpack from his body and was mortified to see that it was soaked with his sweat. He swiftly lay it, unmarked side out, against the wall, praying that it would dry before Brad got around to moving it.

Despite the usual language difficulties, the man from the café was able to inform them that there was a bus at 16.45 that was bound for Vigo from where a train could be taken for Santiago.

WHEN THE VAGABUNDO AND THE PRIEST were, at last, left alone, Fr Delucci turned to Rod and smiled.

"Rod, my friend," he said, "there is something that I want you to do for me."

It took a lot of gesturing and miming before the priest made his intention known but, finally, Rod understood. He was already aware that the priest was undergoing some sort of emotional catharsis so he determined to play along. They trooped downhill towards Moss for the third time. At the font where they had spent the night the priest stripped to his underwear. He folded his clothes carefully and lay them across the metal rail at the top of the steps leading down to the subterranean trough.

"Come Rod. Baptise me."

The cold water took his breath away but, as his body recovered from the shock he felt fabulously refreshed. Rod held the bible in one hand then, with rather more exuberance than strictly necessary, he plunged the priest's head into the water, holding it there while he said the words:

Yo te bautizo en el nombre del Padre, del Hijo y del Espiritu Santo.

Fr Delucci rose, spluttering but beaming with happiness. Rod smiled also as he helped the priest out of the font where he stood, shivering in the shade.

Rod moved towards the steps and gestured for the other to follow.

"*Venga fuera al sol.*"

They emerged into the scorching daylight and, in unison, stopped aghast. The clothes were gone.

"*Oi! Cabron!*" yelled the vagabundo and began to run up the hill. Fr Delucci looked beyond him and was just in time to see a skinny, naked man disappear around the bend – naked, that is, but for a pair of ankle socks and sneakers. He had the priest's clothes, in a bundle, clutched tightly under one arm.

BRAD HAD INSISTED that Mark join himself and Tanya for a beer.

"You're soaking wet, man. That was some work out for you."

The glasses were now empty and Brad called for another round but Mark struggled to his feet..

"Thanks but I've some walking to do and I've been staggering enough with the weight of my bag without having a skinful of beer onboard too," he laughed. "If you're sure you're all right I'd better head off."

Brad held up a hand.

"Just a minute, man, okay?"

He turned to Tanya.

"Look, babe. I've been thinking. This leg is going to need a few days of elevation and compression so I'm out. But that doesn't mean that your walk has to be ruined too. This was about getting you toned up and, anyway, it'd cost a fortune to change the flights. I'm as comfortable as I'm going to get here. I just have to wait for the bus. How about this for a plan? You keep walking with Mark here and we'll hook up in Santiago in a few days."

Tanya looked stunned for a split second and then she recovered herself. Mark was just as stunned.

She wasn't expecting that. I wonder would he trust her with me if I wasn't just the harmless chubby guy?

But his resentment was academic rather than heartfelt. He realised he was hoping, desperately, that Tanya would agree. He watched closely as she seemed to reach a resolve.

"I wouldn't dream of presuming on Mark but I'm sure I'll be absolutely fine on my own. You just get that leg seen to and I'll see you in Santiago."

It appeared that Brad had been expecting resistance. He seemed rather taken aback at his girlfriend's easy compliance.

"Are you sure, babe? I can text you the details of the hotel and we can stay in touch by SMS – though I don't know if I'm comfortable with you doing it alone with that nutter somewhere on the road up there."

He turned to Mark.

"You don't mind walking with her, do you, big fella?"

Tanya responded before Mark had the chance.

"I'll be fine. I'm a big girl. I doubt that guy will still be hanging around now that he has lost his clothes but if he is I'm sure I'm quite capable of handling it. I just got a shock the last time."

Mark interjected.

"I'm happy to tag along as far as you want... That's if you don't mind the company."

"Of course you are," said Brad. "See, babe, Mark's the regular gentleman."

It was said with a laugh so Mark didn't know which way to take this but Tanya seemed to. She stood up.

"Well then. That's settled. Thanks Mark. We'll leave you to arrange things from here, Brad. We have a lot of time to make up so I think we should get going."

She bent suddenly and gave her boyfriend a peck on the forehead. His arms came up to embrace her but she had backed off too quickly.

"I'll see you in a few days."

She set off up the steep path away from the café and away from Mos. Mark shrugged at Brad.

"Chicks," muttered the latter. "She'll be like that for an hour or so and then she'll get over it."

Mark smiled weakly.

"Well, good luck with the leg."

He hurried after Tanya. She was marching at a pace that Mark couldn't hope to match and he was soon drenched in sweat again. He had all but despaired of catching her when, abruptly, she stopped. She looked back and seemed relieved to see him following. She waited until, huffing and puffing, he came up to where she was standing.

"Don't look now but I think that might be the pervert guy sitting over by those railings."

Mark looked discreetly to the place, further along the road, where Tanya had indicated. A man was sitting against a metal railing at the side of the road. He was leaning back with his eyes closed and a pleasant, dreamy expression on his face. He was wearing nothing but a pair of white boxer shorts.

"No," said Mark. "He's an American priest. We passed him when we were coming down the hill with Brad. I saw him saying mass earlier a little bit further up the way. There was another guy with him."

"Oh yes, I remember," said Tanya. "Are you sure that's him?

"Yes. But he had his clothes on then."

They walked past, by tacit agreement, giving the priest a wide berth. He didn't open his eyes and was soon left behind. They were now approaching the place where the flasher had caused all the drama. Mark noted the exact place by the mark left by his backpack on the track. The memory struck him with a realisation. Having carried Brad's bag he had completed Shay's task and, once more, had forgotten to leave a message noting the time of completion as instructed. They were approaching a large, prominent rock at the road-side. Mark extracted the stick of blue chalk from his pocket.

"Just a minute," he said, approaching the boulder. He checked his wristwatch and began to write his name and the time.

"What are you doing?"

"Oh it's a silly thing really. Someone I know is walking the *Camino* too. They're somewhere behind. They asked me to leave messages now and then so that they'd know how far ahead I was."

"That's a nice idea," said Tanya. Mark stepped back to admire his handiwork. The message was sufficiently large that anyone looking for it couldn't miss it.

"Right," he said. "Let's go."

As he walked he realised that he had written the time as he had read it from his watch, not in the 24 hour clock digits that he normally used as displayed on the phone. Consider-ing it for a moment, he decided that it should make no dif-ference to Shay.

WHEN ROD RETURNED after a futile pursuit of the naked thief, he found Fr Delucci, quite dry now, relaxing in the sun with his eyes closed and his back propped against the rail-ing that surrounded the font. His precious leather satchel lay across his knees. He opened his eyes at the *vagabundo's* approach and looked inquisitively. Rod held out the priest's sandals and a blanket. The naked man, already suitably shod, had ditched the footwear but had, for the second time in as many hours, made good his escape, along with the clothing. Rod had resorted to stealing from a farmer's scarecrow. The straw–stuffed figure was less in need of the blanket, he had felt, than his friend, the priest.

"*Lo siento. Tu ropa es...*"

He made an apologetic dismissive gesture.

It appeared that the blanket had once been a deep brown. It now had lighter patches where wind, rain and sunshine had been at work over a long period of time. There was a hole in the middle through which the scarecrow's head had emerged. It functioned just as well on the priest. Rod stepped back and appraised the makeshift poncho on Fr Delucci. He pursed his lips and clucked as a fashion designer might having eyed up his creation on a model and found it wanting in some small but important detail. In a sudden flurry of activity, the *vagabundo* took a piece of rope from his backpack and used it to secure the blanket around the priest's waist.

"Mucho mejor," he said, stepping back and admiring his handiwork. *"Ahora se parece a Jesus."*

The priest didn't seem so sure about his new Messiah look. He tugged and twisted, turning and bending to exam himself. Finally he sighed.

"I suppose I should be thankful that I have the sandals. I'll have to get some proper clothes at the next town."

He turned to his companion and smiled.

"Thank you Rod."

They began to slowly retrace their steps up the hill. They were still some way from a large rock by the roadside when the priest gave an involuntary start, stopped dead in his tracks for a moment, and then hurried, eagerly towards the boulder where a message in blue writing could clearly be seen. As he jogged he fumbled with his satchel to extract the bible.

Mark 4.25.

"This wasn't here when we passed earlier," he called to Rod as the latter joined him.

Whether or not the *vagabundo* understood the words, he was looking at the blue chalk in a puzzled manner that suggested he was thinking the same thing.

The priest found the page and a look of wonder spread across his face as he read the text.

For to him who has will more be given; and from him who has not, even what he has will be taken away.

He leaned against the rock, deep in thought. Rod watched him patiently. Finally the priest spoke.

"I think it means that I am supposed to remain dressed in this..." He looked down at himself, somewhat dubiously.

"...in this 'robe' that you found for me until I have redeemed myself for my lack of faith."

Another thought struck him.

"And it comes from the parable that tells us not to hide our light under a bushel. I think it's telling us that we have to keep preaching to the people along the way like we did earlier with the Mass."

As he heard his own words aloud they rang, to his mind, with a sense of truth.

"Yes, that's it," he said, his face lighting up with a smile of conviction. "Rod, we are on the right road. There is a journey ahead, but we are on the right road."

Rod understood little or nothing of what his companion had said but he saw that something fundamental was changing in the priest.

Either he is truly a holy man... or he is crazy.

Delucci had clasped his satchel shut and was striding on up the hill, a new spring in his step. The *vagabundo* stared after him for a moment, shrugged and began to follow.

SANTIAGO DE COMPOSTELA, SPAIN

ANXO HAD ONCE found a menu on his computer that changed the monitor's colour settings from 'millions of colours' to '256 colours'. The result had pleased him. Photographs appeared with a poster–like quality onscreen, all the subtlety bled from them. He was remembering this because it was exactly how he felt that his world had become. Most of the time, the drugs managed to reduce the pain to a dull, constant throb. However, just as they subdued and clouded the pain, they subdued and clouded his thoughts. Topics entered his mind and flitted past like a slideshow. He tried to engage but he felt like an observer in his own mind – as though somebody else had the TV remote and was flicking through the channels. The sterile, alien surroundings of the hospital disoriented him further and the impersonal efficiency of the nurses frightened him. He stared at the ceiling and watched, helplessly, as his thoughts passed by.

Helio. Helio is dead. What had..? Vicki. Where..? Food. I'm

hungry. What time is it? Isabel. Does she know? Pain. Damn.
Pain. Helio. Did he… Helio is dead.

He closed his eyes, tensing. When he opened them Isabel was standing by his bed, staring at him with a look of concern that was a welcome contrast to the businesslike attitudes of the staff. It lasted just for a moment, though. A cold mask dropped like a shutter across his wife's face and he remembered. With the memory came an overpowering sense of guilt.

"Bela. I'm so sorry."

With a physical effort, he reached out to her. For a moment she simply stared at his offered hand but then, as tears welled up in his eyes, hers softened and she took it.

DUBLIN, IRELAND

NOW THAT she had made up her mind to join her son, daughter and granddaughter in Australia, Helen was impatient to get going. She had spent the day organising flights and making calls to Spain – explaining to friends and neighbours there that she was moving, indefinitely, to the antipodes. The support she received was all that she could have hoped for. A friend had promised to make sure that her affairs were kept in order until she got a chance to travel back to Malaga and tie up any loose ends, while a neighbour had said that he would keep an eye on the house.

"It is a good idea to see how Australia suits you before you make any permanent decisions," the neighbour had suggested, "and it's summer there now, isn't it? You'll have plenty of time to come back and sort things out here when the weather picks up again in Europe. And, in the meantime, you could always get some income by renting your place on one of those websites."

Adding to her sense of impatience was the fact that her daughter's house now resembled a storage facility more than a home. Everything was packed away, awaiting the removal people – apart from the bare necessities and a few items of clothing that Helen had singled out for repair before they were packed. Anxious to keep herself occupied, she took up a dress belonging to Angela. It was a favourite of the child but had grown too tight. Grace had suggested that the pair could make soft toys from the fabric but Helen offered to have a go at letting out the seams first, if possible.

She took up the dress now and, opening her sewing box, made herself comfortable in the accustomed spot where she and Angela used to work together. Carefully, she clipped the stitches with a small scissors and was pleased to see that the double seam would give her a centimetre to work with. There were three seams around the waist of the dress – one on either side and one at the back – so she could add an extra three centimetres to the waistline. When she had unpicked the seams, she took 'Pablo the pin cushion' from the sewing box. Holding the material together in its new position, she began plucking pins from the pin cushion and using them to tack the new seam in place.

SANTIAGO DE COMPOSTELA, SPAIN

AT THE TOUCH of Isabel's hand, Anxo felt a change. At first he couldn't identify it but, as it spread throughout him, he felt a thrill of hope. The constant, throbbing pain that attacked every part of his body was easing.

"What is it, Anxo? Are you okay?" asked Isabel, noting his startled look.

For a moment he didn't reply as he performed further self assessments to ensure that it was really happening.

"Oh Bela, it's feeling better. The pain – it's not as bad."

"Really?"

"Help me."

She supported him as he pulled himself into a sitting position.

"It's still there but it's so much better."

He looked at her in wonder.

"It was when you touched me."

Isabel felt conflicted. The pain of his betrayal felt raw but, as he gazed at her, she thought that she could identify real gratitude, hope and remorse in his look. She allowed herself to smile.

"That's wonderful, Anxo."

She released his hand and busied herself rearranging the pillows to support him.

"I'll let the nurse know."

"I want to go home, Bela," said Anxo. "All they do here is give me drugs and treat me like a guinea pig. I know that I'd be much better at home."

He saw the hesitation in his wife's eyes.

"Look, I know things have been difficult with us but this has changed me. I promise."

"I don't know, Anxo…"

"Please, Bela. Please don't leave me here."

"Are you still feeling better?"

"So much better. It was when you touched my hand. I think it's a sign."

I have said that I will give him a second chance and perhaps the saint is doing the same.

"I can't promise anything, Anxo, but I'll talk to Dr Velasco and see what he says."

"Can you do it now? Please. I want to get out of here while I can."

Not before I talk to your mistress.

"He's gone for the day," she lied. "I'll come first thing in the morning and speak to him then."

DUBLIN, IRELAND

HELEN REALISED that she was hungry. With so much going on in her mind she kept forgetting to eat. She continued sewing until she came to the end of the line of stitching then she made a loop with the thread, pushed the needle through it twice and pulled tight, forming a knot near to the cloth. She severed the thread with her teeth and held up the dress to assess her handiwork. The neat stitches were practically invisible. She had only one of the seams done but she had plenty of time to finish it over the next few days before leaving for Australia.

She rapidly withdrew the pins from around the hem that was now sewn, leaving those that were holding the unfinished pieces in place. She folded the dress and picked up the little pin cushion. For a moment she admired Pablo again before beginning to stick the redundant pins back into him.

SANTIAGO DE COMPOSTELA, SPAIN

ANXO had just pulled himself into a sitting position on the side of his bed when the attack hit. Isabel had gone home a short time before, leaving him alternating between feelings of anxiety and hope. His mind had still been fuzzy from the drugs but he had been clear about certain things. He had been punished for what he had tried to do to his wife and then, with the touch of her hand, he had been shown where his redemption lay. Somehow, he now realised, he needed to win back her trust. If she would agree to bring him home and tend to him he would make a full recovery. He had felt it with a certainty that he couldn't explain.

I was crazy to think that getting rid of her was the only way out. There's bound to be a way to keep her and to keep Vicki...

It was with this thought that a stabbing pain offered him a precursor to the attack that was to follow. The nurse, coming to examine him in light of Isabel's news that there was an improvement, entered the room just in time to see him collapse from the side of the bed and onto the floor where he writhed in agony as each new piercing bolt of pain hit him. The intravenous needle had been wrenched from his arm in the fall. Her voice seemed disembodied to him as she yelled for help and then there was somebody holding him still while she found a vein into which to sink the needle that would send him to a temporary, welcome oblivion.

GALICIA, SPAIN

THEY HAD WALKED mostly in silence since Mark had chalked the note, apart from his laboured breathing as he tried to keep pace. It was obvious that Tanya had a lot on her mind and Mark hadn't wanted to intrude with the usual mundane chatter. At first, the way climbed steadily uphill and, to Mark's embarrassment, they had been overtaken by a steady stream of pilgrims ranging from youngsters to walkers old enough to be Mark's grandparents. His humiliation had grown until Tanya turned, at one point, and said:

"I don't know why everyone seems to be in such a hurry. It's a walk, not a race."

He spent the next hour wondering if that was really how she felt or if she was being extraordinarily sensitive to his situation.

Finally, to his huge relief, the trail flattened out. The level terrain, however, proved to be a temporary reprieve. They came to a vantage point where they could see Redondela, the next major town, below at the far end of a wide valley. Here the trail began to drop steeply down to meet a main road that ran along the valley bottom. With the weight of his pack, it was all that Mark could do to prevent himself from breaking into an uncontrollable jog. Finally, however, the road was reached and they found themselves passing through farmland and past occasional houses on the infinitely more gentle section that led into the town.

Tanya suddenly broke the silence.

"So, what's your reason for doing this?"

"The *Camino*?" replied Mark, the unnecessary clarification aimed at buying himself a few moments to decide on his response.

"Yes, the *Camino*."

"It's a long story, really."

At that moment music erupted from Tanya's pocket and Edith Piaf launched into *La Vie En Rose*. Tanya pulled out her mobile phone and glanced at the screen.

"Sorry Mark."

She cut off the singer in mid sentence, and held the phone to her ear.

"Hi Brad. How is the leg?"

She listened.

"Oh, that's good."

Whatever Brad said next caused a frown of annoyance to flicker across her face. She involuntarily glanced at Mark and slowed down so that he moved further ahead.

"Mark and I are doing fine. We're nearly at Redondela, I think."

He said something insulting or nasty about me.

He knew it as though he had overheard. Partly annoyed

and partly embarrassed he walked on a bit before glancing
back. Tanya had stopped. She was listening to Brad talking
on the phone but her eyes were on Mark. When she saw him
looking she put on an apologetic face and raised a finger
to indicate that she would be with him in a moment. Mark
mouthed the words "no problem" and moved to a wall at
the edge of the trail where he leaned, waiting out of earshot.
To show Tanya that he was happily occupied, he reached
into his shirt front pocket to check his own phone. In fact, he
thought, he had heard nothing from Shay. Perhaps he had
missed hearing a message alert. When he took out the mobile
he noted, immediately, that it was wet.

That's sweat from carrying Brad's bag in front of me.

Worried, he looked at the screen and his anxiety turned
to alarm. Even though he had fully charged it overnight, the
phone was off.

Maybe the battery has worked itself loose.

He hit the power button. Nothing happened. Turning
the phone over he clipped off the plastic back. The inside
was soaked. Panicked, now, as the implications of losing the
phone began to hit him, he slid off his backpack, reached inside and pulled out a clean tee–shirt. Removing the battery
and the SIM, he meticulously wiped them and then the interior of the phone as dry as he could. For good measure, he
blew into any small holes that he could find in the plastic ap-
paratus. Reassembling everything, he hit the power switch
again. Still, nothing happened. He reopened the phone and
was repeating his desperate attempts to resuscitate it when
he heard Tanya approach.

"Problems?"

She must have seen the expression on his face because her
tone became more serious.

"What is it Mark? What's wrong?"

"It got wet. It's wrecked."

"How," she asked sympathetically. "Did you drop it."

"It's sweat. I had it in a pocket between me and the backpack. I should have had it in my bag."

"Maybe it'll be okay when it dries."

"It's not just the phone. It's..."

Without warning, he felt himself suddenly well up with emotion and he turned sharply away. However, he was not quick enough. Tanya placed a hand on his shoulder. The touch acted as if triggering a switch. The tears burst out. A part of his brain began to observe with a sort of detached, academic interest and attempted to puzzle out what had caused the sudden breakdown. The other part of his brain sank beneath an overwhelming sense of loss and sadness. He felt, rather than saw, Tanya stepping around to face him and then he felt her arms around him.

"It's okay, Mark. Just let it out."

He sank his head onto her shoulder and sobbed like a baby. She murmured soothing words that might be used to calm a troubled child and patted the back of his head. Finally, after what seemed like an eternity, he felt the emotion recede and the rational part of his brain began to wonder what he was going to say to Tanya in explanation of his outburst. His sobs subsided and he stood upright, bringing a hand up to wipe his tear streaked face and, perhaps more importantly, to hide it and his embarrassment.

"I'm sorry," he sniffled. "I feel like an idiot."

"Don't be silly. I think that one of the problems with men is that they find it hard to connect to their feelings. Letting them show is a good thing."

He stepped back and she let him go. He still clasped the tee–shirt with which he had been trying to dry the phone and he used this, now, to wipe away the tears properly and then to blow his nose.

"I never understand why your nose runs when you cry," he said with an attempt at levity. Tanya smiled briefly.

"Let's sit for a while."

They sat on the wall.

"It's obviously not just the phone, is it?" said Tanya. "Do you want to tell me?"

At first, he expressed himself unwilling to burden her but Tanya was persuasive and, before long, he found himself telling her everything. She sat, listening sympathetically. He picked a spot on the ground near his feet and stared at it as he spoke. He began with his online relationship and the news that Adelina was coming to see him. He explained about Shay and the text message instructions that – due to the loss of the phone – he would not, now, be able to receive. He even found himself telling her about Finnish Johanna and her rejection of him on the road that morning. That, in turn, led him to open up, for the second time in as many days, about his childhood.

"Wow," Tanya said, when he finally fell silent. He sat staring at his feet more intensely than ever. He had found that a lot of things which had seemed to make sense in his head took on a different complexion when voiced aloud.

"You really do have a lot on your mind. Let me start with this girl, Johanna, because that's an easy one. She said that she wanted to walk alone. That's perfectly normal on the *Camino*. Lots of people that Brad and I met are doing this because there is something in their lives that they need to think about and they want to be alone with those thoughts. Also, from what you've told me she was probably hung over from all the wine that you guys drank and didn't feel like talking anyway."

"I suppose that's possible," said Mark, begrudgingly.

"The rest... Well, let's walk while we're talking. That's all a little more complicated, I think."

They set off on the last few kilometres into Redondela.

"First of all, I think it might be helpful for you to know that I was very overweight until a couple of years ago so I know what I'm talking about. Trust me, Mark, at least in that area, I know what you've been going through."

Mark stopped and stared, looking her up and down in frank astonishment.

"What? You, overweight?"

She smiled.

"Yeah."

She fumbled in a pocket, took out a wallet and, from an inside compartment took out a small photograph.

"I keep it to remind myself whenever I think I'm getting off track."

Mark stared at the person in the picture and then at Tanya.

"Holy shit."

He gazed again at the photograph for a while then, slowly, handed it back.

"So how did you lose the weight? Diet and exercise?"

"It was more than just that. It was a complete lifestyle change. The main breakthrough, though, was that I met Brad."

"So love is the answer," laughed Mark.

"That's a whole different story," replied Tanya. "No, he took me on as my personal trainer. He's incredible at motivation."

"It seems to be a gift that Americans have," said Mark.

"Oh Brad's not American. He spent some time there and that's where he got into health and fitness but he's actually from Albania."

"God. I'd have sworn he was American," said Mark. "I'd have said he was the complete American stereotype – confident, sporty..."

"That's just it," replied Tanya. "He *is* the all–American stereotype. He's modelled himself on it but, to be honest, I'd be surprised if such people exist at all outside of movies and motivational YouTube videos."

They walked on in silence for a moment before Tanya spoke again.

"Anyway, he put me on a food and exercise regime and that started working immediately but the most important thing that he did was give me back my confidence. It's all emotional, you see. I was a shy kid and I was bullied in school so I'd eat to make myself feel better and that made me put on weight so I'd be bullied about that. I'd do some more comfort eating, put on more weight – you get the picture. It was a vicious circle."

She looked at Mark and smiled.

"Not unlike your story in some ways, huh?"

He nodded and she continued.

"Here's what I think. Your weight problem started because of that terrible situation you found yourself in as a kid. But you're an adult now, Mark. You're a smart, kind and funny guy. Your confidence is low because of your weight and from what you've told me that has stopped you from socialising so that's going to make you lonely and that's another reason that we comfort ourselves with food."

Mark was nodding vigorously.

"That makes so much sense. I can go all day without eating a thing and then, at night, I end up undoing all the good work by going into the kitchen and pigging out."

"I was exactly the same," said Tanya. "But trust me, Mark. Once you get going and start to see the kilos tumbling off everything will fall into place. You can start throwing out your old clothes because you'll never need big sizes again. Your confidence will grow. It'll be life–changing. I can tell you what you should be eating – exercise is important, of course, but really weight loss doesn't happen in the gym. It happens in the kitchen."

Tanya went on to explain the basics of the food regime that she found successful. It was nothing new to Mark but hearing from someone who had made it work gave it a new significance.

"The key," said Tanya, "is to give yourself time. It needs to be slow and steady if you're going to really make it sustainable."

Mark's face fell.

"I don't have time, though. Adelina is coming in less than four weeks."

"Look. Sorry to disappoint you but as far as that's concerned I think that this Shay guy is a complete fraud. I hate to say it but the amount of weight you're trying to lose is certainly possible but not in such a short time. He's a total con–artist, as far as I can see."

Mark sighed.

"I know. I was clutching at straws, I guess. But if I could lose even some of weight..."

"You can, but to be honest I don't think that it is your weight that is the big problem here when it comes to Adelina."

"What do you mean?"

"Think about it, Mark. You've been completely dishonest with her from the start. We can put up with a lot from guys but dishonesty's a deal–breaker for every girl I know."

Mark looked miserable.

"I guess it was a stupid thing to do but let's face it – do you really think that she would have had anything to do with me if she knew I looked like this?"

"Well, you'll never know because you never gave her that chance. We aren't as shallow as you guys. I'm not saying it doesn't help if you find a guy attractive to begin with but you're an interesting, intelligent guy. You could have started as pen pals and then, who knows, she might have fallen in love with your personality and your mind. Now she's just going to feel betrayed."

They walked on in silence for a moment before Tanya spoke again.

"How does that work, anyway – dating online without having met. Do you change your Facebook status to 'in a relationship' or something?"

Mark looked uncomfortable.

"No. My relationship status is private so that wouldn't matter..."

"Is hers on private too?"

"Actually, she has hers on single but I reckon it's because she doesn't want to change it until we've met. We've never really talked about it."

"So it's just for the cybersex, really, then," joked Tanya but Mark didn't laugh. He looked ever more uncomfortable.

"It's not that kind of relationship. She's far too nice for that kind of thing."

"So if there's no cybersex and both your statuses are on 'single' then what makes it a relationship?"

"We write every day. Sometimes even more than that."

"But how is that different from a pen pal?"

The smile suddenly dropped from her face. She stopped and put a hand on his arm so that he turned to face her.

"Wait a minute. Seriously. Have you had a discussion where you agreed that you were in a relationship?"

Mark flushed red.

"Well, we haven't officially talked about it but we've sent each other gifts and we're totally monogamous..."

"Mark. I don't mean to be rude or hurtful but it sounds

like you have a really good friend who cares for you a lot and is coming to visit you but what makes you think that she feels she's in a relationship?"

"That's something, isn't it? She's coming to visit."

Tanya put a hand on his shoulder.

"Look. She obviously likes you a lot…"

Tanya ran out of words as she saw the misery on Mark's face.

"Well, the good news is that, if you're not actually in an official relationship, she's not going to be as mad that you lied about your weight. I mean, it's not like you slept with her and then told her you were married."

They were now walking alongside a main road and into the town of Redondela.

"Don't look so miserable, Mark. Let's make this a turning point. Maybe that phone getting wet will turn out to be the best thing that ever happened to you. We're going to be walking together for the next few days so I can show you what you need to do to shake off that 'cocoon', as Brad would say."

"Okay," said Mark passionately. "This is it. It starts right now…"

"Woah," laughed Tanya. "How about we start tomorrow. After the day I've had I could do with a glass of wine."

9. Thessalonians

*"Let no man deceive you by any means: for that day
shall not come, except there come a falling away first,
and that man of sin be revealed,
the son of perdition"*

SANTIAGO DE COMPOSTELA, SPAIN

VICKI HAD DECIDED that things were over between her and Anxo. She had felt empowered when she left him at the petrol station. She had been curious to see if he would bombard her with texts pleading with her not to contact his wife or if he would sweat it out and wait to see if she would say anything before contacting her. What she had not been prepared for was silence. Two days passed and there was nothing. Vicki was frequently made aware of her youth and beauty in the reactions of the opposite sex – ranging from hopeless, youthful adoration to the predatory efforts of men old enough to be her father. She had learned to navigate her way through them all. This, however, was new. That a guy should ignore her was a situation outside of her experience and she discovered that she didn't like it in the least.

Her golden rule was to let the boy be the one to text first. Now, however, she found her resolve wavering. She had, after all, been particularly provocative. She had spent an entire lunch break at work composing and recomposing a text message that would illicit a response without, at the same time, making her sound desperate or needy. After much agonising she settled on a single line:

I had you worried, didn't I :)

When hours and then days passed without a reply her confusion turned to the kind of annoyance that is born in disappointment.

To hell with him. Even if he calls now I will tell him that it's over.

When the text message did finally come, though, she felt nothing but relief. There was obviously a good reason why Anxo had not been in touch and he wanted to meet her so that he could explain. Perhaps her taunting had made him realise that, despite saying that she didn't care, she did actually resent the fact that Anxo was putting the wife of his loveless marriage before her. Maybe he had confronted Isabel and told her that he had fallen in love with someone else. On the other hand, perhaps he had spoken to his wife and this meeting was to say that he was giving his marriage another chance.

In the end, the result of weighing up the various scenarios had an unforeseen outcome. Vicki found herself confronting her feelings about Anxo. After careful consideration, she found, to her surprise, that the thought of being in a relationship with him, if it involved marital complications, didn't appeal to her at all.

It has been fun but I can do without him. Él no es mi media naranja.

The wailing of a *gaita* playing Galician music signalled her arrival at the cathedral end of *Rúa de San Francisco*. She stopped and checked her makeup in the front camera of her smartphone before entering *Praza do Obradoiro* at the front of the towering church. The square was relatively quiet. As she approached the twin steps leading up to the main entrance she could hear the muffled music and voices from within as evening Mass was celebrated. The inevitable group of newly arrived pilgrims stood before the building. Some stared, others whooped and high–fived, a number seemed rather bewildered as the realisation hit them that their long–sought for destination had been reached and a return to their fast–paced and ultra–connected lives was imminent. Vicki pushed past and stopped, looking equally lost. Anxo wasn't there. Before she could gather her thoughts one of two young women approached her with a camera.

"Excuse me. Could you take a photo of us, please?"

Vicki grasped at the opportunity of having a reason to stand there as she decided whether to leave or to wait and see if Anxo showed up. The camera's owner indicated the correct button to press and joined her friend to pose in front of the cathedral. Vicki crouched to get as much of the building into the background of the shot as possible, the *peregrinas* beamed big, fixed, fake, toothy smiles and the shutter clicked. The young woman stepped over to retrieve the camera and pressed the appropriate button to display the picture on the small screen.

"Oh thanks. That's great," she said, showing the image to Vicki.

Vicki glanced, politely, and then stared more closely. She had been concentrating on framing the two *peregrinas* properly so she hadn't noticed it while taking the photograph. On the steps of the cathedral, behind the pair, a woman was staring intently, directly into the lens.

"We need to talk."

Vicki, turned to find herself confronted by the woman from the photograph. It seemed to Vicki that an array of conflicting emotions were fighting for dominance under the surface of her gaze. It took just a moment for the epiphany.

Anxo's wife.

"Look," she stammered, caught completely off guard, "If this is about Anxo…"

What else could it possibly be about?

She continued:

"Whatever is going on between you two is your business. I really don't want anything to do with it."

The two pilgrims for whom Vicki had taken the picture were staring. Isabel glanced at them before looking almost pleadingly back to Vicki. She lowered her voice.

"I've read his messages to you. I know what he told you

about us so I'm not blaming you," she said. "but I need to speak with you for just five or ten minutes. I need to know the whole picture – but not here. Can we go to a bar?"

Vicki hesitated and Isabel played her trump card.

"Anxo is in hospital. It's pretty serious."

They sat outside a nearby bar on the *Rúa da Raiña* end of *Praza de Fonseca*. The waiter appeared immediately and, as Isabel enquired about what herbal teas were available, Vicki had the chance to study her properly. The woman before her was about 30, she decided, and was unquestionably beautiful. There was a tension about her mouth and eyes, however, that hinted at opportunities lost and happiness denied.

"And you, *señora*?"

Vicki turned to answer the waiter and felt the weight of Isabel's scrutiny upon her in turn.

"*Un agua con gas,*" she rushed and turned to meet Isabel's gaze.

"Anxo and I have no child," Isabel began.

"Cold?" enquired the waiter, oblivious to the situation, as Vicki's head spun. She used the distraction to scramble for something to say but drew blank.

"*Sí, fría,*" she replied and turned her attention back to Isabel who continued to speak as if there had been no interruption.

"I've read all of the text messages so I know what he told you. I know he said that we had a daughter and I know he told you that we had an 'arrangement' when it came to seeing other people."

The way she said "arrangement" gave an indication of the hurt she was labouring under.

"The truth is that I had no idea that Anxo was cheating on me until a few days ago."

Vicki found her voice.

"I am so sorry. I feel like such an idiot. I totally believed him."

Isabel laughed scornfully. "

"You feel like an idiot? I have invested nearly ten years of my life in this man…"

Emotion rose and she couldn't continue. Vicki reached a hand across the table and put it on her arm.

"I'm so sorry. Really, I am."

There was a small, red, plastic tissue dispenser on the table and Isabel reached for a tissue with the arm upon which Vicki's hand rested, diplomatically but effectively shaking it off.

"Look. I know in my heart and soul that this thing with you and my husband was his doing but, even so, I can't help feeling angry with you about it also. I'm not here to make a friend. I'm here to find out if it is just a fling or if you are in love with each other. I need to know what you intend to do now that you know the truth."

"I understand," replied Vicki. "I can tell you honestly that there is nothing in it. He brought me places in those fancy cars..."

"Fancy cars

"Yes. He had a big BMW and the last time a Jaguar."

Isabel looked puzzled for a moment and then the penny dropped.

"They must have been from work. He works cleaning cars in a car hire place."

Vicki couldn't hide her surprise.

"I feel even more stupid now."

"Don't. He can be pretty convincing."

"Well, you needn't figure me into whatever you decide to do," said Vicki. "We had some laughs and it was fun but there was nothing else. Nothing real. I'd already planned to tell him I wouldn't be seeing him again."

Isabel's shoulders slumped a little as though she had been holding herself rigid.

"I'm sorry," Vicki continued. "I really didn't think anyone was being hurt."

The waiter arrived and gave them both time to recollect their thoughts as he busied around the table with the drinks. When he left Vicki spoke again.

"You said he is seriously ill..."

"We had a break–in at the house. The guy who was trying to rob us fell from the balcony and was killed. When Anxo saw it he had some sort of nervous fit or breakdown. It must have been from the shock. He collapsed and I had to get the ambulance. He's been in hospital ever since. He's pretty much paralysed and the doctors seem at a total loss to understand what it is that's wrong with him. He's in constant pain."

"Oh. How awful for you both."

Isabel flashed her a dutiful smile of appreciation.

"He's showing some signs of improvement so there's a chance that he could be looked after at home…"

She looked frankly at Vicki.

"I had to know where things stood with him and you. I have to decide if I should give our marriage a second chance."

"Well whatever you decide you can be sure that I'll have nothing more to do with him," Vicki said. "Whatever stupid thing we had is over as far as I'm concerned. *No lo quiero ni regalado.*"

Isabel looked at her bitterly and Vicki instantly regretted the last phrase.

"You're wondering why I'd even consider taking him back," Isabel said.

"No, I didn't…"

Isabel cut across her.

"I'm pregnant with his child."

GALICIA, SPAIN

THE GENEROUS DONATIONS collected by Rod from the congregation at Fr Delucci's impromptu Mass that morning had improved their lot immensely. Their lack of pilgrim *credenciales,* however, meant that they couldn't avail of the cheap official *albergues* to spend the night. Indeed, while the priest was determined to follow the signs that he had been receiving with blind faith, the strange glances that their arrival in town prompted made him doubtful of their welcome wherever they might try to stay. He caught their reflection in a shop window as they made their way slowly into the town centre and had to admit that they cut a rather unsavoury sight. Rod was unabashed however. Accustomed to hostility and rejection, the acquisition of an American priest as a travelling companion – however *loco* he might prove to be – was an elevation in his status. Each step he took was also accompanied by the rare, musical jingle of coins in his pocket. He had no intention of spending any of their new found wealth on a crowded, noisy hostel. He led Fr Delucci to a café bar on a side street. A young woman was cleaning one of the umbrella–shaded plastic tables outside.

"*Oi, guapa,*" called Rod as he approached.

The woman looked up and the priest noted the ready smile that came to her face when she saw the *vagabundo*. Then her gaze moved to him and he felt a flush of self consciousness as her look changed to one of cautious curiosity. Although he didn't understand the Spanish he was aware that Rod was introducing him.

"Maria," he said.

The young woman extended her hand

"Rodrigo says that you are a holy man," she said in heavily accented English.

"I am a priest, yes."

Maria smiled.

"Welcome."

She conversed with Rod for a moment and the Fr Delucci gathered that they were talking about accommodation. She then popped her head through the open doorway, called something to someone inside and led them to a neighbouring door which she opened with a key.

"*Venga,*" said Rod, following her up the stairs that lay behind and beckoning for the priest to follow.

They found themselves in a neat little room with two single beds and an *en suite*. Rod nodded his approval. Maria said something and to which he objected, patting his pocket and making the change there jingle. She turned to Fr Delucci.

"I hope that this is okay."

"It is perfect. Thank you."

"I have told Rodrigo that there is no problem for money but he has said that he wants that you will pay something."

"Oh yes. You are very kind but we must pay."

"It is okay, Padre. This room is for when musicians are

coming to play music in the bar. It is not, how do you say? Commercial?"

"Yes, commercial. Well, you are very kind, Maria, but Rod is in charge of the money so it is him that you'll have to convince."

She smiled and spoke in Spanish with Rod. There followed an amicably heated exchange which ended by the pair leaving the room.

"*Venga Delucci. Café.*"

"How do you know Rod?" enquired the priest as they came back into the sunlight.

"He has been walking past this way since I have been working here five or maybe six years ago. It is not an easy life that he has."

The priest smiled at the young woman and was suddenly filled with a sense of her goodness.

"Well, if you will not accept our money, perhaps you will accept a blessing."

Maria smiled.

"I would like that very much."

Rod, having heard his name mentioned, was watching the pair as they turned to face each other. He also noticed that a group of pilgrims from the Mass that morning were observing them from where they were enjoying cool drinks at the tables outside the café. Delucci placed a hand on Maria's head and her eyes met his.

Maria. Our Lady's name.

Suddenly, his mind was cast back to the childhood hours spent gazing into the eyes of the Madonna in the recess of his parish church in Boston. A well of joy, long suppressed, rose from somewhere deep within him and he felt his face glow. Maria's eyes seemed to shine in reflection.

"I bless you in the name of the Father and of the Son and of the Holy Spirit."

To his utter astonishment, she dropped like a stone and was only saved from a nasty impact with the pavement by the quick reflexes of Rod.

"*Estoy bien,*" she told the concerned *vagabundo* as she got clumsily to her feet and, without looking at the priest, half stumbled into the café. As he helped her inside, Rod caught sight of the bewildered look on the priest's face as he stared at the hand with which he had performed the blessing.

Inside, Maria's work colleague was already halfway to the door with her handbag which he pushed into her hands before guiding her to the nearest chair. She fumbled inside the bag until she found the packet of pills. She swallowed two, washed down with a glass of water that her co–worker had ready.

"She'll be fine in a few minutes," he said in answer to Rod's concerned look. "The medication works very quickly."

Indeed, already the colour was returning to the young woman's face and she managed a weak smile.

"You had me worried," said the *vagabundo*, sinking into a seat beside her. As she drank again from the glass he looked out the window. The priest was standing where he had left him but he now had several *peregrinos* gathered around. A rather large man was kneeling in front of him, his head bowed for a blessing. His companions, taking no chances, flanked him on either side to prevent injury should he, too, fall.

SANTIAGO DE COMPOSTELA, SPAIN
"BUENOS TARDES."

Isabel, who was in the process of deleting the message she had sent to Vicki on Anxo's phone, as well as the girl's reply, looked up guiltily. She found herself confronted by the kindly eyes of her neighbour, Señora Nieves.

"*Buenos tardes,*" she replied. "How is your husband?"

"Still alive, worse luck," cackled the old woman, "but we live in hope."

The elderly lady shuffled on, still chuckling and Isabel fumbled for her house keys, her mind whirling with implications. It seemed that Señora Nieves was unaware of the drama that had been taking place in Isabel's life. And if Señora Nieves didn't know then nobody in the neighbourhood did. Was that possible with all the comings and goings of police cars on the morning of the death? Improbable as is it seemed it was even more improbable that the old lady would have

missed an opportunity to pry had she been aware of the attempted burglary, the subsequent tragedy and Anxo's illness.
When she got Anxo home, then, it was just possible that life
could go on without the pitying looks of nosey neighbours.
As she put the key in the door the implication of the thought
struck her. Somewhere between leaving Anxo's mistress near
the cathedral and arriving home she had subconsciously decided to give Anxo a second chance.

*Before I forget I must put his phone back where I found it, under
the sofa.*

The door closed behind Isabel. From a corner across the street
Vicki stared at the lifeless house until, shortly afterwards, a
light leapt out from the semi–shuttered window of a downstairs room. The shadow of Anxo's pregnant wife passed
back and forth a couple of times and then disappeared. A second light came on in an adjacent room. Isabel's silhouette appeared at the window and then heavy curtains slid into place
bringing the drama to an end. Vicki didn't know why she
had felt compelled to follow the woman home. Maybe she
had expected to find evidence that Isabel's story was the desperate fabrication of a jealous wife but, confronted with the
bricks and mortar reality of Anxo's family home, Vicki was
left feeling rather sickened by the whole affair. She was about
to turn and retrace her steps away when a police car, coming along the road, slowed and stopped outside the house.
Vicki watched, curious. After the passage of a few minutes
the driver's door opened and a man in plain clothes got out.
He strode purposefully to the front door and raised the large
knocker. Then he paused for what seemed like an eternity.
Even from a distance Vicki could see his shoulders slump
suddenly. He gently lowered the knocker, turned heel and
walked slowly toward his car. About midway he stopped,
turned, took a step towards the house, stopped again and
then, his mind made up, walked briskly to the car, slid in and
pulled slowly away.

Vicki began her thoughtful walk home.

Get over it girl.

She was approaching a rubbish skip outside a building

site. From her pocket she pulled out the piece of paper upon which Isabel had written her telephone number.

If he gets in touch with you you'll call me, won't you?

Vicki scrunched the paper into an angry ball and flung it into the skip. At that precise moment a van thundered past, travelling too fast on the narrow street. The gust of wind that it generated caught the paper and whisked it neatly back at Vicki, whose hand opened instinctively to catch it. She gazed at the paper in bemusement. She opened it and looked once more at the name and number.

If I was superstitious...

She took the two paces between her and the rubbish skip, scrunching the note up again as she moved. Seeking out a gap between some twisted metal and a long, wooden plank she dropped the ball of paper into the recesses of the bin.

One number gone. Now for the other.

She strode away feeling control returning to her life. Taking out her phone she opened the contacts *app* and scrolled down to Anxo's name, near the top of the list. She hit series of clicks and a message popped up on the screen.

Are you sure you want to delete?

She pressed "*Sí*». Anxo, his wife, his fictitious daughter and his unborn baby were banished from her life in a blink of binary code.

GALICIA, SPAIN

THE MUFFLED SOUNDS of early rising *peregrinos* penetrated Mark's slumber and his eyes blinked open. Tanya's bunk, opposite his own, was already vacated. He had a moment of disappointed panic at the though that she had abandoned him like the Finnish girl Johanna, then he saw her unpacked rucksack at the foot of the bed.

She must be in the showers.

He reached for his mobile phone to check the time and realised, again, that he no longer had one. With the activity in the *albergue* dormitory it was clearly "peregrin–o'clock", as he and Tanya had laughingly coined it the previous morning – the period between 5.30 and 6am when the dormitory became a hive of activity with pilgrims rolling up sleeping bags, packing rucksacks and getting ready for the day's walk ahead. He swung out of his bunk and realised, for the second day in a row, that he felt good. In keeping with Tanya's new rules they had refrained from eating after 8pm the previous evening and, in place of the bloated feeling that he associated with mornings, he recognised a genuine, healthy hunger for breakfast. This was just the third day of walking with Tanya but, already, he was beginning to feel like a changed man. When he pulled on his trousers he was overjoyed to find that the belt slipped easily onto a new notch. He was struck by the exciting realisation that something had switched in his mind. He had embraced the new health–conscious regime with open arms and was loving it. It wasn't about denial or diets. The fresh, natural, tasty food that Tanya was choosing to cook with him was delicious. In addition, his friendship with Tanya was blossoming. The more that he got to know her the more he liked her. And he had been particularly delighted when she chose to confide in him. The previous evening they had sat outside the *albergue* in Briallos sharing a bag of plump, ripe cherries. They talked about their lives back home.

"I don't even particularly like modelling. There can be a lot of bitchiness. I think I got into it because I'd been so un-happy with my body before so it was almost like celebrating the new me. Brad had connections in the agency so he got me in."

"I'm sure they'd have snapped you up with or without Brad," said Mark.

"Aw, you're so sweet."

He returned her smile.

"What would you do if you gave up modelling?"

Tanya picked up a cherry and stared at it for a moment as if it were a crystal ball.

"Maybe I'd go back to education. I had such a bad time in school that I couldn't wait to get out of there but I can't help feeling that I've missed out by not going to uni."

"What would you study?"

"I think something to do with languages. I love travelling

but it always feels like you're only getting part of the picture when you don't speak the language."

Mark nodded vigorously.

"It'd be dead handy on this trip."

"What about you?" asked Tanya, after a while.

Mark had just begun to tell her about his work in graphic design when he was interrupted by the muffled but unmistakable tones of Edith Piaf from Tanya's pocket. She gave him an apologetic glance, took out her phone and looked at the screen. It rang on and she didn't answer.

"Brad?"

"Yes."

Decisively she pressed a button and, although the screen continued to flash, *La Vie En Rose* was muted mid–chorus.

"I can't talk to him now."

Mark tried to think of something appropriate to say but couldn't so he remained silent. Tanya stared at the phone until the light stopped flashing then she returned it to her pocket.

"I don't know what to do."

"Do you love him," asked Mark, hesitantly. "I'm sorry. That's very personal."

"No, it's okay."

She thought about it.

"I used to think I did but, to be honest, I'm not even sure that I like him now."

"Then why are you with him?"

"I know. That's what I've been thinking."

"Well leave him."

Tanya picked another cherry from the bag and ate it while Mark watched her. She chewed it as if chewing on her thoughts.

"You know, it was that day in the restaurant – the first time that we saw you – that I realised how horrible he can be. I was so embarrassed at the way he behaved."

"It wasn't your fault."

"Yeah, but it said something about me because I'm with him, didn't it? And I didn't like what it said."

"I think you're being a bit hard on yourself."

"You know, he's like that with me all the time but I've just considered it his way of keeping me motivated."

Mark snorted derisively.

"You deserve so much better than that."

Tanya looked at him and laughed.

"You really are such the gentleman, aren't you? But don't go getting all romantic on me, Mark. You're not my type and I very much doubt that I'm yours."

He laughed with her but her words stung and it must have shown because she felt the need to qualify her point.

"Let's face it. Girlfriends and boyfriends come and go but it's really hard to find good friends. I think we could be really good friends, don't you?"

"Yeah. Great. I'd like that."

A heavily moustached Dutch *peregrino* who they had seen at the hostel the evening before passed at that moment and they exchanged greetings. When he had gone inside Tanya stood up and started picking up the bag with the remaining few cherries and the jacket she had been sitting on.

"Caldas de Reis tomorrow," she said. "Apparently they have thermal spa waters for pilgrims to bathe their feet."

Mark got slowly up.

"So, what are you going to do?"

"Bathe my feet, of course."

"No, I mean about Brad."

Tanya shook her head.

"I honestly don't know. What are you going to do about Adelina?"

"Yeah. I've been thinking about what you said. I need to write and be honest with her."

"Good man. When?"

"When I get somewhere with an internet café."

Tanya pulled out her smartphone and offered it.

"No need to wait."

Mark stared at the phone in her hand for a moment.

"Fuck it," he said, taking the device. "I don't suppose you fancy helping me to write it?"

Tanya smiled.

"What are friends for?"

10. Corinthians

"If any man among you seemeth to be wise in this world, let him become a fool, that he may be wise."

THE YOUNG MAN had counted thirty seven *peregrinos* passing by his self–appointed lookout during the long period that he had been waiting. Each time walkers appeared around the distant bend his hopes rose, and whenever the walkers turned out to be two men, they rose further. He had eagerly scrutinised the faces, as they drew nearer but, so far, he had been convinced that none of them were those that he sought. When the priest and his companion finally did come into sight there was no mistaking them. They were the first of a large group to appear around the bend. They were closely followed by eight or ten *peregrinos*. As reported by those who had seen the holy man and his companion on the way, the smaller of the two figures at the head of the group had the appearance of a wiry, weathered *vagabundo*.

That one is the compañero.

He turned his attention to the other of the pair, hungrily taking in the details as the walkers drew closer. The priest cut a strange figure – even on the *Camino de Santiago* where people of all sorts were quite commonplace. The youth could see, clearly, how comparisons with *Juan el Bautista* had come about. On a school trip to Toledo as a boy he had been fascinated by *El Greco's* painting of the Baptist when the teacher had explained to the class that John had been beheaded at the whim of Herod's daughter and had his head served to her on a plate. The holy man certainly looked like someone who had stepped from the pages of the Bible. He wore a long, crude robe of some indistinct dark colour, tied at the waist. His shaggy, black hair fell to his shoulders and blended with the unkempt beard and moustache that masked his lower face. While he walked with the slow, deliberate, limping steps that one might associate with an invalid, the young man felt an aura of power emanating from the priest even from the considerable distance that still separated them.

The murmur of voices began to reach him.

¡Oh clemente! ¡Oh piadosa! ¡Oh dulce Virgen María! Ruega por nosotros, santa Madre de Dios para que seamos dignos de alcanzar las promesas de nuestro Señor Jesucristo.

He recognised the Holy Rosary and silently joined in as the walkers drew slowly closer. The bedraggled *compañero* was leading the prayer while the rest of the group supplied the chorus of response. The priest, meanwhile, remained silent, his face cast down as though in deep contemplation of the dusty trail before his feet.

To the youth's relief, the recital came to its conclusion before the group of *peregrinos* drew level with him. He slid from the wall upon which he had been sitting and approached the holy man, tentatively. The latter stopped, facing him, at first, with a penetrating look before his face softened to an encouraging smile. The young man began to deliver his mother's message but faltered as the priest's companion pushed his way to the front.

"*Sí? Dime,*" the *compañero* demanded.

Uncertain, the young man continued to deliver the message. The self–appointed inquisitor waited until he was finished before stepping aside, apparently satisfied.

"*El Padré no habla Español,*" he said, as he did so.

"Oh, *perdón*, Father," said the youth, addressing the priest, now, in English. "My mother – we live here in this village – has told me to ask you if you would like to stay tonight in our house. She has prepared a room and food for you and your companion. We would be very honoured."

Fr Delucci beamed at him.

"What is your name, my son?"

"Álvaro."

"Well, Álvaro. A blessing on this village and especially on you, your mother and your family. We will be very glad to accept her kind offer."

Álvaro felt a thrill of pride as he led the group, triumphantly, into his village. The holy man had been the talk of the region for the past few days. He and his *compañero* had been travelling slowly on the *Camino* and word of his doings had spread rapidly ahead of him. It was said that his teachings went back beyond the corrupt Popes, the paedophile priests and the seemingly endless other controversies of the church to the simple, pure message of Jesus Christ. It was said that many had been *slain in the spirit* – falling to the ground in religious ecstasy – at his touch. Miracles had also been reported. A farmer near *Arcade* had returned from attending a Mass said by the priest at a roadside crucifix to find that a fresh water spring on his land that had been dry since the time of his grandfather was flowing again. A couple from a village near *Pontevedra*, on their way to the doctor with their firstborn had stopped to obtain a blessing for the child from the priest. When the child had later been examined in the surgery, the angry, red rash that had covered its back had all but disappeared.

Álvaro's family home lay just beyond the ancient village fountain and its stone benches which were located in a small plaza. There were several villagers sitting out in the late sun. They stared with unconcealed curiosity.

The priest turned to his companion and nodded.

"*Mañana*, Mass, Rod."

In his coarse Spanish, the *vagabundo* addressed Álvaro.

"Let the people know that tomorrow morning Fr Delucci will say Mass here for all who wish to attend. We will need water, bread and wine."

Álvaro's mother couldn't contain her delight at the coup she had pulled off in getting the priest to spend the night under her roof. Raised a Catholic, Señora Lopez had gone through most of her life contentedly acting out the role that was expected of a good Christian in her small parish. She was, at least technically, a virgin when she married Álvaro's father, she had been one of the volunteers who took turns to clean the church or arrange the altar flowers each weekend and she had baked cakes for the fund–raisers to pay for bad-ly needed repairs to the church roof. It was her son, in the end, who had opened her eyes to certain aspects of the her religious upbringing that didn't sit easily with her personal sense of social conscience.

"*Mamá*," he had said one evening, standing before her, clutching in his small hands the big family bible that had been passed down through at least three generations. "Why does the Bible say that slaves should be obedient to their masters? Isn't slavery an evil thing?"

"Sometimes things don't mean what they seem to mean in the Bible, *miho*," she had replied. "Let me see."

Taking the book, she had sat at the kitchen table and start-ed to read. She was so engrossed in what she found that she didn't notice Álvaro grow bored and slip away to his room. She spent the next couple of hours lost in the letters of the New Testament. To her chagrin, the conclusion she eventu-ally arrived at was that the Good Book had, in her opinion, some serious flaws. Furthermore, she identified the writings of St Paul's as the source of much of her discontent. From what she could make out, not only did he expect slaves to take it on the chin but he was pretty adamant that women should stay quiet and let their menfolk do the talking for them. She had no first–hand knowledge of slavery but the thought of her slow–witted husband Manuel speaking on her behalf while she sat back and played the dutiful wife was a nonsense. She had been in no doubt that they would still be living in that awful one–roomed apartment of his uncle's rather on a property that they could call their own, if that had been the case.

She had sought out Álvaro and admitted, gravely, that – so far as she could determine – he had raised a valid point. Furthermore, she had promised him that she'd get to the bot-tom of it. The following day, after she had packed him off to school, she had taken a lift with Manuel to Caldas de Reis where she had paid her first ever visit to the *Biblioteca Mu-*

nicipal. There, with the assistance of the librarian, she found a book on the saints that contained a comprehensive chapter on Paul. When Álvaro returned from school that day she was prepared.

"Son. I must thank you. You have opened my eyes."

Over dinner she had given Manuel and Álvaro the benefit of her findings.

"Most of the New Testament in the Bible is the word of men that were considered to be holy and wise – but, at the end of the day, they were just men. It is only in the Gospels of Matthew, Mark, Luke and John where they talk about what Jesus said that you are hearing his word. Paul – you know Paul?"

Her menfolk had nodded obediently.

"He didn't even know Jesus. He didn't become an apostle until long after Jesus was dead and buried," she announced triumphantly.

"So," she continued, in the silence that greeted her news. "From now on I follow only the actual teachings of Jesus. And…"

She glanced at them both to ensure their full attention.

"… the eleven commandments."

She picked up an empty dish from the table and carried to the sink while she waited for the penny to drop. It was Álvaro who spoke.

"Eleven? I thought there were ten commandments."

My clever boy.

"Originally there were but in John 13:34 Jesus said to the apostles:

A new commandment I give unto you, That ye love one another; as I have loved you, that ye also love one another.

It's lovely, isn't it?"

Álvaro nodded, smiling. Manuel, however, had looked both uncomfortable and perplexed.

"Manuel. I'm happy to have a discussion about this if you want. I've written down many things that will show you the truth of what I am saying."

"No Mirella. That is not necessary. I was just wondering.

Does this mean that you will not be going to church on Sundays?"

She was somewhat taken aback.

"I hadn't thought about it."

"Well, I would be very grateful if, for the sake of my mother, we could continue to go to church. You know how miserable she would make my life if we didn't."

She began to retort but the words stuck in her throat as the veracity of his statement hit her. She turned to her son instead.

"Álvaro. Your father is right. For the sake of your grandmother we should continue to go to church but it doesn't mean that we need to believe everything that the priest says – especially if he is reading from Paul."

That had marked the beginning of a new understanding between mother and son. At Sunday morning Mass knowing looks would pass between them as the priest read from the pulpit. As their appreciation of religion waned, the depth of their spirituality blossomed.

When word had reached them, therefore, of the American priest who was approaching Santiago with nothing but the Good Book and the «grass–roots» words of Jesus, their excitement had been akin to 60's teenagers anticipating the arrival of The Beatles.

Dinner was a lavish affair with enough food to satisfy the biblical multitudes, all washed down with a most superior *Albariño* from the vineyard of a family friend. Mirella seated the priest at one end of table and Rod at the other, relegating her husband from his usual spot, much to his simmering discontent. He sat, sullenly, as his wife, using Álvaro as a language intermediary, bombarded the holy man with questions about himself, about life in America and about his teachings. He was only half listening to the questions and responses because his attention was focused on the last piece of *Chorizo al Vino Blanco*. He needed to spear it when Mirella wasn't looking but she had seen him contemplating it up and was keeping one eye on the priest and one eye on him. Then all thought of the food was forgotten as Mirella finally popped the big question.

"Father. Is there a name for someone who does not believe in the teachings of the Bible that were written by people other than Jesus – people like St Paul, for example."

The priest considered the question.

"Do you mean people who follow only what Jesus himself said?"

"Yes. Exactly."

Fr Delucci considered again and then a smile slowly lit up his face.

"Well, Señora Lopez. I had never considered that question until now but I guess that – although it has been hijacked to mean something else in our modern society – the word for a true follower of Christ's is a Christian."

Álvaro smiled as he translated for his mother.

"*Ah sí!*" she exclaimed, beaming. "*Un Cristiano!*"

That night, Fr Delucci lay awake despite his tiredness and the comfort of the soft sheets. Álvaro's mother had shown them to a large, pleasant room with two matching beds and a door opening to a generous sized *en suite*. When Álvaro had finally convinced her to stop fussing over them and they were alone, Rod, as had become his habit when sleeping indoors, had dragged the mattress off the bed closest to the open window, stripped off the bed clothes and replaced them with his mummy sleeping bag. With a grunt of satisfaction he had curled up and was now breathing gently and evenly. The priest had not been so fortunate. After taking a long, luxurious shower and climbing, naked, under the bed covers he had sighed in blissful contentment as his body sank into the mattress. However, after a half hour of trying to drift into unconsciousness, sleep continued to elude him. Two things were occupying his mind and his thoughts drifted back and forth between them. His answer to the question of Álvaro's mother had come to him on the spot. Indeed, it had seemed obvious and simple. However, the implications, he now realised, were enormous. Señora Lopez had said that she was drawn to him by his reputation for returning to the basics of the faith, yet this had not been a conscious decision on his part. The fact that he was drawing ever closer to the bones of

St James – one of the disciples who had walked shoulder to shoulder with Jesus – had prompted him to select readings that came directly from Christ's time on earth but there was something more. He realised that he, like Álvaro's mother, could trace his uneasiness with his church to the parts of the Bible that were attributed to those other than Jesus.

I am a follower of Christ – a Christian. Perhaps my mission is to reclaim the true meaning of that word.

The other thought that kept him from sleeping was the last blue chalk message that he had received on the wall of the *albergue* in Porriño: *"And these signs will accompany those who believe: In my name they will cast out demons; they will speak in new tongues"*. He was more perplexed than ever about this. He had no idea what demons he was supposed to cast out and, as for the "speaking new tongues", his attempts to learn Spanish from Rod had started poorly and gone downhill from there. He was beginning to think that he had misinterpreted the message.

What am I missing?

Rod was aware of the priest's insomnia because he, too, was having difficulty sleeping. As a *vagabundo* living on the cold fringes of society his emotional world had become greatly simplified. The range of his feelings ran, generally, on a scale that had cold and hunger at one end and warmth and contentment at the other. The bulk of his time was taken up in trying to avoid the former and seek the latter. Usually he found himself somewhere in between. Whenever his thoughts threatened to dwell on the demons of his past he plunged them into a fog of cheap alcohol to drown. It didn't make him forget but it made the edges grow fuzzy and turned sharp pains into a dull aches. Since meeting Delucci, however, things had changed. Without any conscious decision on his part he had fallen into a role that was giving him a real sense of purpose. For the first time in very many years he felt useful. In the bank balance of life he could feel his worth moving from the red into the black. However, this evening, the appearance of Álvaro had tipped the fragile balance. The boy spoke English and had sat, at dinner, beside

Delucci, translating the many questions of the mother and the few words of the father before explaining the priest's responses. More annoyingly, he had conversed privately with Delucci in English and Rod had experienced that paranoid but understandable thought: *They're talking about me.*

Well, tomorrow they would leave both this village and the boy behind. They would pass through Caldas De Reis, Padrón and then arrive at Santiago. It was two easy days of walking but with Delucci's growing popularity and his wounded feet their progress was slow.

Three days, probably. Three days and then what?

MORNING MASS in the little village plaza was a grueling experience for Rod. By a prearrangement of which he had been unaware, Álvaro stood at Delucci's right hand side and translated as he spoke a homily calling for the thirty or forty strong congregation to sweep aside the centuries of corruption and return to the simple message of Jesus. The priest had raised his game to a new level of charisma and the *vagabundo* had to admit that the boy, swept up in his fervour, spoke well.

When the ceremony was over, Álvaro stood by the priest, translating, as the latter patiently greeted each of the many people who wanted to speak personally with him or obtain his blessing. As Rod sat, alone, in a corner of the plaza, patiently waiting with the backpacks, he counted the proceeds of the collection. Over the past few days their income had been rising with their congregations and, thanks to the hospitality of the local people along the way, their expenditure was little or nothing. There was €78.42 in the cooking tin. Added to what they already had they could now boast a nest egg of just over €300. He tucked the money into the inner pocket of his backpack and, as he did so, caught sight of the small, plastic rectangle that resided there. The €300 was, most likely, a pittance compared with the money available on Joe Delucci's credit card – the card that the *vagabundo* had retrieved from the priest's backpack all those days and kilometres before. His musings were disturbed by the familiar deep laugh of the priest. He looked up to see Delucci facing the boy with a hand on either arm. The beaming smile on each face portended something sinister. The priest glanced over and, seeing him observing, walked over.

"Rod…"

The priest, turned laughing to Álvaro and said something in English. The youth addressed the *vagabundo*.

"He says that he won't have to struggle to speak with you now. I have offered to walk with the Padre on his pilgrimage and he has kindly accepted my company."

"*Perfecto,*" said Rod, turning abruptly to hide his displeasure. "*Vamos.*"

He marched back to collect the bags, his mind swirling in dark distress. As he picked up his own backpack his thoughts focused on the cash and credit card that lay in the inner pocket.

The labourer is worthy of his hire.

SANTIAGO DE COMPOSTELA, SPAIN

ANXO WAS HAVING his daily battle with the large yellow pill that almost choked him each morning. As had become his custom, he had left it until last and, as always, Isabel was supporting him, propped up on the sofa. She fed him sips of water while she watched, with grave concern, his attempts to swallow it.

"I must ask Dr Velasco if it is possible to have this one in two smaller pills."

Anxo gulped once more, grimaced and then sighed with weary relief as the medicine went down.

"Thank you, Bela. That would actually help a lot."

"Can I get you anything?"

"No. I'm okay, thanks."

She helped him to settle back onto the sofa and made sure that the TV remote control was within reach.

"I'll be in the kitchen if you need anything."

She was halfway there when the ponderous knocker on the front door startled her with its thunderous crash. Subinspector Pedrosa, a white A4 envelope in his hand, was waiting on the step.

"*Buenos días, Señora de Medeiros,*" he said and, while glad that he had used her married name in case Anxo could hear from the living room, his use of it stung nonetheless. She acknowledged the reassertion of formalities by replying in kind.

"*Buenos días, Subinspector*. Please come in."

"Thank you. I went to the hospital to ask some questions of your husband and they told me that you had decided to look after him at home."

"Yes."

His eyes seemed to search hers for something beyond the words and she had an overwhelming sense that she had disappointed him. Flustered, she turned away and took a pace towards the living room.

"Anxo is in here."

She pushed open the door.

"Anxo, it's Subinspector Pedrosa. He was looking for you at the hospital."

The television was showing one of its mindless daytime gameshows and Anxo, engrossed, had heard nothing. He pressed the mute button and looked at her inquisitively. Then the policeman entered behind his wife and Isabel was struck by the sudden caged, wary look that came to her husband's face.

"*Buenos días Señor de Medeiros*," said Pedrosa. "I am glad to see that you are out of hospital. How are you feeling?"

"I'm still in a lot of pain, unfortunately, Subinspector, but I am fortunate enough to have my wife to help me here at home. What can I do for you? Do you have news?"

Pedrosa indicated a chair.

"May I?"

"Of course," said Isabel. "Can I get you something to drink?"

"No, thank you. I won't stay long."

Anxo looked decidedly uncomfortable.

"Perhaps you could bring some cold drinks anyway, Bela. The subinspector might want to talk to me alone."

"On the contrary," said Pedrosa, quickly. "I'd prefer if you stayed. Two heads, after all, are better than one."

Isabel sank into a seat, aware of a tension in the atmosphere that she didn't understand.

"Well, Subinspector, what is it?" asked Anxo.

"Helio Pereira."

It was microscopic but it was there. Isabel had seen Anxo flinch at the name. Doubtlessly, she thought, Pedro had seen it too.

"Who's that?" said her husband, a little too casually. "Should I know?"

"That is the name of the dead man who tried to break into your home."

"Pereira," said Anxo, thoughtfully. "Actually, that name does ring a bell for some reason."

Pedrosa said nothing but regarded him closely. Isabel watched both men.

"No," said her husband, after a moment. "It's not coming to me."

"I believe you come from the same neighbourhood," prompted the policeman.

"Ah. Yes. Helio Pereira. There was a kid in school by that name."

Anxo stared at the ceiling as if searching his memory.

"As far as I remember he was expelled for something – trying to sell drugs to the other kids, I think."

"That's the one," said the subinspector. "It was all downhill from there. Petty crime to support his habit..."

"Where are the parents of children like this?" said Isabel as her thoughts turned to the child growing within her.

Pedrosa nodded to her in acknowledgment but turned back to Anxo to pursue his line.

"He was not known for house burglary though, strangely enough. He was known to snatch a bag or break into a tourist's car but he had no track record of breaking into homes."

"You'd know more about drug crime than I, of course," replied Anxo, "but I'm guessing that it must be progressive. As the habit grows I would imagine that the addict needs more money so he takes bigger risks."

"That was another interesting thing, actually," returned the policeman. "According to some neighbours and acquaintances, this guy had come into some money just days before he arrived at your house with that great big butcher's knife. He stole the knife from a local *carnicería*, by the way. We also found a significant personal stash of heroin hidden at his mother's home. He was by no means desperate for a fix. Also, there was this...

As Pedrosa spoke he pulled out the contents of the envelope that he had been holding – a single A4 sheet, torn from a notebook – and tossed it onto the sofa where Anxo reclined. Anxo looked down at where the page had fallen, unmoving. Isabel crossed, quickly to his side.

"Anxo can move very little," she explained as she picked up the paper and held it where both she and her husband could view it. Involuntarily she gave a shudder. The page contained a rough drawing. Although badly executed, it was, unmistakable, a naked female body with the torso covered in a massive, dark tattoo of the grim reaper that stretched from the crotch to where the blade of the sickle disappeared over one shoulder. Across the middle, just below the breasts, were the words: *Soy el ángel de la muerte*. What was further disturbing was the expression on the face of the crude image. The staring eyes and open mouth were fixed in a look of sheer terror.

Isabel glanced up at the policeman and saw that he was watching her husband intensely. A thought struck her with the conviction of fact.

He suspects Anxo.

"Pretty intense," the latter said.

"As you can appreciate, when we have an attempted burglary by a junkie who has no form in house breaking and that junkie is carrying a weapon as well as a rather sick image of a naked woman tattooed with an angel of death picture, we can't help wondering if it is something more than a simple attempted break–in."

"You think that maybe I pissed him off as a kid in school and that he was coming to get his revenge?" quizzed her husband, with a note of ridicule.

The policeman shrugged.

"Well, did you?"

Anxo gave a dry laugh.

"Why don't you tell us what you think, Subinspector?"

"The other thing that bothers me is the balcony," said Pedrosa, ignoring the question. "Your wife tells me that it was used frequently by her when hanging the washing to dry."

"Yes," said Anxo. "That is the only thing good about this Helio guy situation. I can't bear to think what might have happened if he had not been the one on the balcony when it fell."

"But why did it fall?" rejoined the policeman. "It had sat there solidly for God knows how many years..."

"Actually, Subinspector, it was anything but solid. For as long as I remember it would shake when you stepped on it," said Isabel, relieved to deflect from where the policeman's line of thought seemed to be going. "I realise now that it's ridiculous, but I thought that it was normal. It never dawned on me that it was an accident waiting to happen."

"I see," said Pedrosa, seeming to deflate somewhat.

Anxo grimaced.

"Are you okay?" asked Isabel.

"As okay as I ever am these days," replied her husband with a weak smile. "Don't worry, the pain killers will kick in soon."

The policeman took his cue and got slowly to his feet. He reached for the drawing and Isabel gave it to him."

"Well, thank you both for your time," he said as he made his way to the door, stuffing the sketch back into the envelope as he went. "If we come up with anything else I'll let you know. And I do hope you'll be back on your feet soon, Señor de Medeiros.

Anxo nodded then closed his eyes and lay back. Isabel saw the policeman to the front door.

"Thank you Señora de Medeiros," he said then, once more, he held her gaze somewhat too long. "Take care of yourself."

The words were casual but there was an intent behind them. He turned and strode briskly towards his car, climbed in and drove away without looking back.

In the living room Anxo heard the door close and a long

pause before his wife's footsteps approached. The cocktail of pills that he was on was the result of a lot of trial and error at the hospital. Between the mysterious malady and the toxic drug combination Anxo was weak to the point of semi paralysis, but the pain was now manageable and, most importantly, he could think clearly. He was thinking furiously now.

Pedrosa suspects.

An overwhelming desperation gripped him. His life had been built on his good looks, charm and resourcefulness. He had risen from nothing to a situation where he had a desirable wife, a respectable home and the promise of enough wealth that, with a little careful management, would ensure that he never needed to work another day in his life. He had risked all of that for a mere "piece of ass" and had been crushed like a fly for his stupidity. But, behind it all, Anxo was a survivor and his survival now rested upon Isabel. She had unwittingly taken the sting out of the policeman's probing questions about the balcony. Without her, in his present state, he would be at the mercy of the efficient but impassive medical staff at *Hospital Privado Virgen del Cielo*. The wife he had plotted to kill was now crucial to his survival.

She entered the room and her look warned him that Pedrosa's insinuations had not been lost on her.

"Bela, whether it's because I've been so caught up in my own problems or whether, subconsciously, I just didn't want to face it. What he said about the balcony..."

He trailed off, choked with an emotion that he fuelled with his recent thoughts of self preservation. He watched, with concealed satisfaction as his wife's face softened into a look of relief and she crossed to kneel beside him.

"If anything had happened to you I don't know what I would have done," he gushed.

Isabel took his hand and he held her gaze, marvelling at his own ability to bring tears to his eyes.

"Anxo. I've been meaning to tell you something."

His heart plummeted but he managed to keep the fear from his one word response. "What?"

"We're having a baby."

"Oh Bela."

The joy was real as he beamed and held out his arms.

She sank into them, shaking with sobs of relief as she let the floodgates of her pent up emotions burst open.

Anxo held her tight and with her head on his shoulder she couldn't see his look of calculated triumph.

Gotcha!

GALICIA, SPAIN

IT TOOK SOME TIME before Fr Delucci grew aware that all was not well between Rod and Álvaro. He was so swept up in the joy of having someone with whom he could communicate that he talked, *ad nauseam*, as they walked through the pleasant, sun–drenched countryside. Álvaro told him of the growing sense of hope that was spreading like wildfire along the way at the news of a holy man who was bridging the gap between the people's disillusionment with an outdated church and their need to fill the void left by Godlessness.

"We started to hear about you from the *peregrinos* who had listened to you preaching along the way. I think that such people come to the *Camino* looking for something. Their minds and hearts are open and when they listened to your words about following the simple life of Jesus it gave them what they were looking for."

"I, too, came here looking for something," said the priest, "and the Lord, in his goodness, has shown me the way: *For this my son was dead, and is alive again; he was lost, and is found.*"

He thought of the message about driving out demons.

"A lot has been made clear, Álvaro, but I have also been given signs that I don't, yet, understand."

A contemplative silence followed. The priest gazed fondly at the back of Rod as he trod along some way ahead. It dawned on him, suddenly, that Rod had been marching ahead all day rather than occupying his normal place by his side. He called to the *vagabundo* who stopped and waited for them to catch up.

"Álvaro, there are many things that I've wanted to ask Rod. Could you translate for us?"

"Of course."

The young man spoke to Rod. Fr Delucci did not understand the response but, even without the language, he detected hostility. With a scornful: *"La curiosidad mató al gato"*, Rod marched on ahead once more, leaving Álvaro and the priest staring at each other in surprise.

"He says that we should save our breath for walking and that curiosity killed the cat."

BENDIGO, AUSTRALIA

IT WAS his own fault, really, and he'd been quick to admit it. He had insisted on taking off his Sperry deck shoes at the hall doorway, much to Grace's bemusement.

"I know," said Tony, noting his sister's suppressed smile. "He always does it. It's not like my carpet is worth protecting. He says it's a habit left over from an overly pedantic ex–wife."

Tony's friend Nick had the decency to look suitable abashed.

"That's probably why the marriage hit the rocks," he laughed. "I was whipped."

"All the more reason to rebel," said Grace. "Go on. Put the shoes back on. Live a little."

"Well, I was considering it. But now that you've told me to I can't. I've made a vow never to blindly obey a woman again just because she's attractive."

Angela watched as Mammy flushed red and pushed Nick's arm the way she used to do when Daddy teased her.

"I bet you say that to all the girls."

Laughing, the adults went into the dining room where Mammy and Uncle Tony had set four places at the big table. Chewy, excited by the new smell of a stranger, jumped all over Uncle Tony's friend as soon as he sat down.

"Get him off, Angela," said Mammy.

"No, it's fine. He's a little beaut."

Angela watched and decided that Nick really did like dogs. That was a big part of the test. Mammy had told her that Uncle Tony's friend was coming to dinner in a very casual way but she'd spent the day trying on different dresses and she'd been over an hour in her room getting ready while Angela helped Uncle Tony to set the table downstairs.

"Are you okay Angie," he'd asked her and when she nodded that she was it was not just to make him feel good. If this was part of Mammy getting happier then it was a good thing. If Mammy could be fixed then maybe she could be fixed too. For a while, now, the blackness inside hadn't seemed so close to the surface.

"Don't worry. It's my own fault," Nick had said when, after a meal with lots of laughter, they'd all walked to the door to say goodbye. One of the shoes was only chewed a little. The other one, though, was ripped so badly that it wouldn't stay on his foot.

"I'm so, so sorry," said Mammy. "Tony, do you have something that Nick can borrow."

"No, honestly. I can drive in my socks. It's fine."

He caught Angela's worried look.

"Puppies will be puppies and he's such a beautiful little fella. It's my own silly fault for taking them off in the first place. Your ma did tell me to put them back on."

Later, when Mammy tucked her in and Chewy jumped up on the end of her bed where he had been allowed to sleep ever since the night with the snake, she told him off but, while she was telling him what a bad dog he was, she was stroking his fur and speaking in such a nice voice that Chewy was wagging his tail. Mammy was happy and Angela was glad. She thought of Daddy and, in the picture that came to her mind, he was smiling too.

11. Galatians

"I am afraid of you, lest I have bestowed upon you labour in vain."

SANTIAGO DE COMPOSTELA, SPAIN

IT WAS THE LOW MURMUR of a male voice that woke her. The moon was flooding her bedroom with a brightness as clear as daylight but lacking its warmth. Slipping silently from the bed, Isabel glided noiselessly out of the room and onto the landing. She glanced towards the balcony doors where the drama of that traumatic night had been enacted although she could tell, already, that the murmuring was coming from the other direction. In fact, she realised, it was rising through the still night from downstairs. It struck her as odd that she could hear the sound from this distance. Without being conscious that she had descended the stairs, she found herself at the door to the living room where Anxo now spent his tormented days and nights on the divan. The makeshift bed was empty, the covers thrown back as if recently vacated. The same cold moonlight beamed in at the glass French doors that led to the cobblestoned courtyard where the burglar's body had lain. She didn't see anything out of place at first and then, as her ear tuned in to the source of the murmuring voice she saw it – a hunched silhouetted form to one side of the doors. As her eyes grew accustomed to the light she could make out the bent figure of her husband. He was kneeling with his head close to the ground,

203

concentrating his attention on a hole in the skirting board that Isabel had never noticed before. His open hand lay on the wooden floor in front of the tiny opening and his indistinct, murmured words were just beginning to have an effect. A small black mouse was peering out of the gloomy recess, its whiskers twitching nervously as it sniffed the proffered hand. Isabel watched, repulsed but transfixed, as it emerged tentatively and climbed onto Anxo's palm. He cupped his hand like a tiny nest and rose to his feet, the little creature held close to his face as he continued to speak gently to it. Isabel was not aware that he had noticed her arrival until he turned and addressed her.

"It's stuffy in here. Come outside."

As they stepped into the courtyard Isabel's eyes were drawn to the place on the ground where the burglar had fallen to his death and she shuddered at the sight that greeted her. The moonlight seemed to reveal what daylight had failed to show – a phosphorescent glow where the body had lain, broken by an ugly dark trail where the dead man's blood had ebbed towards the flower bed. Isabel shuddered and turned to Anxo. He smiled at her before turning his attention to the mouse. He whispered something to the tiny animal and then, with a sudden, violent movement flung it down, dashing its body upon the stones. Isabel's horrified scream drew a dismissive glance from Anxo glanced.

"It's okay. Watch."

He returned his attention to the broken clump of fur and blood amidst the phosphorescent glow and Isabel's gaze followed his in unwilling compulsion. Her eyes widened. The mouse's body was swelling and spreading.

"He's okay," said Anxo. "He had the Extreme Unction."

Isabel stared at him, uncomprehendingly and then back at the thing on the ground. It had grown to the size and shape of a human body and was rising, awkwardly, into a sitting position. The chilling grin took shape before its face had fully materialised and she stared, transfixed.

"See, I told you" she heard Anxo say from somewhere afar.

Isabel found herself confronted by the cold, mocking eyes of Helio Pereira, the dead burglar.

Bolting upright in bed, she was unsure if her nightmare scream had emerged in reality as she woke. She listened. There was no sound of Anxo stirring downstairs. Her heart still pounding from the night terror, Isabel slipped from her bed and made her way to the stairway. She descended noiselessly and peered into the living room. Anxo's huddled shape lay covered upon the sofa. From where she stood she could see that the skirting by the French windows was unblemished by any sign of a mouse hole and the courtyard outside was empty.

As she carefully returned to her bedroom an idea was beginning to take hold. Picking up her smartphone from where it was charging on the bedside locker she activated the screen and typed "*Sacramento de la unción de los enfermos*". The Wikipedia entry that came up made her heart give a little jump. The Sacrament of Extreme Unction for the sick had been introduced to Christianity by none other than San Tiago:

Are any among you sick? They should call for the elders of the Church and have them pray over them, anointing them with oil in the name of the Lord. And their prayer offered in faith will heal the sick, and the Lord will make them well. And if they have committed sins, these will be forgiven.

THE BELLS had chimed 9am when the woman, took up her position outside the premises on Santiago's narrow, busy *Rúa do Franco*. Unlike the more popular French Way route into the city, here, where the Portuguese Way entered, the steady stream of *peregrinos* would not start in earnest until later in the morning as they arrived for the special midday pilgrim's mass at the cathedral. But there were some tourists stirring and there was always the chance of early arrivals from amongst those pilgrims who had spent the last night at the tiny *albergue* in Teo, just 8km from the city. She cast a glance down the flagstoned street and saw, what appeared to be, two such arrivals. An unlikely pair of *peregrinos* – one a fat young man and one a beautiful, slim young woman – were approaching slowly. She was striding easily, taking in the shop fronts on either side as she walked. He was struggling after the long incline from the city outskirts into the old town. His tee shirt was soaked with sweat and it ran in droplets from his forehead. As they drew level the woman offered the plate she had been holding with it's neat samples of *Torta de Santiago*, each one pierced with a cocktail stick.

"No thanks," said young *peregrina*.

The man, panting too heavily to speak, flashed the woman a smile and shook his head in the negative, sending a spray of sweaty droplets everywhere. The woman looked down in dismay at the white icing sugar on the almond cake which was now speckled with darker wet spots of perspiration.

"Oh. Sorry," Mark said, hastening after Tanya. The confectioner gave a snort of disgust and tipped the contents of the plate into a bin by the shop door. Then she disappeared inside to cut up a replacement.

Further up the street Tanya had stopped and was pointing excitedly to Mark.

"Look. The cathedral."

The towering steeples could be seen above and beyond the buildings ahead. Mark found his strength renewed at the proximity of the destination he had been striving to reach for a long, gruelling week. *Rúa do Franco* brought them to the side of the massive structure. They made their way around to the front of the building, passing a semi naked, wiry beggar who knelt with his forehead touching the ground in front of him and his outstretched hands cupped in supplication.

Mark reached into his shorts pocket. Among the coins that he drew out, he saw a small piece of blue chalk. It prompted him to wonder whether Shay had, somehow, continued to keep an eye on his progress, even after the destruction of the mobile phone and the subsequent cessation of his chalked messages. He shrugged off the thought, dropped the coins into the beggar's outstretched hands and hurried on after Tanya.

They entered the vast square at the front of the cathedral and found themselves in the full blare of the dazzling early morning sunshine. They made their way to the centre of the plaza, turned and stared up, suitably impressed, at the massive, ornate building.

"Well. Congratulations Mark. You did it. Mission accomplished."

He beamed.

"Come on," said Tanya, taking out her phone. "Selfie."

They posed in front of the building and Tanya, hand outstretched to get as much of the vast facade in as possible, took a snap.

"I guess we might as well go in and have a look," she said. "After all, we've walked over a hundred kilometres to get here."

They made their way wearily, but happily, to where the stone steps rose symmetrically on either side of the cathedral entrance and, with a sense of occasion, climbed slowly to the great door. There they were stopped by a security guard who pointed to a sign which stated that they could not enter with their backpacks.

"There is a place nearby that you can leave them for a fee," he explained.

"That's a bit of an anticlimax after walking for a week," grumbled Tanya as they made their way back down the steps to the square below.

"Yeah. It doesn't seem very spiritual, does it?"

"How about we get something to eat and come back later," she suggested. "I'm starved."

"What about Brad," asked Mark, voicing the topic that had been on his mind all morning.

"Brad can wait," returned Tanya, simply.

They walked down one of the side streets near the cathedral, looking for somewhere where they could sit outside. All of a sudden there was a loud, female screech and Mark heard his name being called excitedly. Jumping up from where they had been sitting outside a café were Maria and Berta, the two Spanish *peregrinas,* and with them, smiling just as excitedly, was Johanna, the Finn.

"I won't hug you because I'm dripping wet but it's so cool to see you guys," he smiled as the three greeted them. "Oh, and this is Tanya."

Soon they were swapping tales of the road over a jug of ice–cold *sangria*. The Spaniards had arrived the previous day and had found Johanna already there.

"I had to call it quits and get the bus," she explained, ruefully, to Mark. "That day I told you to go on I was really suffering but I didn't want to admit it. They say that the *Camino* teaches everybody something. Well, I've learned that I have a stupid stubborn streak. I went into a pharmacist at that next town to see if I could get something to support my leg and she told me that I was in danger of being permanently crippled if I tried to keep going. It was so frustrating but she was deadly serious so I ended up getting the bus."

"Well, the *Camino*'s been here for hundreds of years," said Mark. "so I'm sure it'll still be here waiting for you when you are ready to come back."

Johanna smiled.

"Absolutely."

They ordered food and, despite the early hour, another jug of *sangria*. The three girls were staying in a private hostel on the outskirts of town and felt sure that there were plenty of spare beds. Tanya made no mention of contacting Brad and Mark was content not to remind her. Since writing to Adelina to confess the truth, he had been using Tanya's phone to check his *Facebook* account two or three times a day for a response but, although he could see that she had been online and read his message, there had been none.

"It's a lot for her to take in," Tanya had said. "Give her time to figure out her feelings. I think that, for now, no news is definitely good news."

After he had sent the message he had agonised all night. When, the next day, no response came he had felt devastated and Tanya had been a pillar of support. However, as the days had passed with no word, he had begun to see his virtual relationship from Tanya's point of view. How much of his feeling for Adelina was real and how much was the result of too much time spent alone?

The morning slipped pleasantly away. The café filled up with the lunchtime crowd and then emptied again as locals returned to their offices and schools. Still the five chatted on.

"What's next for you guys?" asked Mark.

"We're leaving tomorrow morning for Finisterre," said Maria.

"Where's that?"

"It's just about four days walk away. It was known as the end of the earth in pagan times. It's the north east tip of Spain and meant to be very beautiful."

"Yeah," added Berta. "We're not ready to go home yet."

"I know the feeling," said Mark, warmly.

"Why don't you come?" suggested Berta, brightly.

Mark was about to make an excuse but stopped himself.

Why not?

He smiled.

"Why not? Count me in."

"Great," beamed Berta.

"I'd love to go," said Johanna, "but this stupid leg..."

"What about you," asked Berta to Tanya.

"Yeah," said Mark. "What about you."

Tanya scowled.

"You know damned well why I can't."

She looked at her phone. Actually, I should be going.

She smiled wanly at Mark.

"Three missed calls and a bunch of texts. Brad's starting to fret."

There was a silence. Tanya made no move to leave.

"Did you go to the *catedral* to hug the saint and did you get your *compostelas* yet?" asked Berta, sensing an awkwardness and seeking to change the subject.

"The *compostela* is the certificate thingy, right? But what's all this about hugging the saint?" asked Mark

"That's part of the whole ritual when you get here," said Berta incredulously. "Did nobody tell you? Did you not read anything about it?"

Mark gave a blank look. She turned to Tanya.

"I was just walking it because my boyfriend said it'd be good for shaping up, to be honest," she said. "I didn't read about it at all."

"Infidels!" laughed Maria.

"You have to hug San Tiago for giving you a *buen Camino*.

Also, whether you are religious or not, there's something amazing about the crypt below the altar where his body is. When you think that you are standing in front of the bones of somebody who you learned about in school. Somebody who was a friend with Jesus. It's... well, it's pretty cool," added Berta.

"We did try to go in but they wouldn't let us with the backpacks," said Mark.

Berta turned to Maria and Johanna.

"I'll tell you what. How about if I take them to the *catedral* and to get their *compostelas* and you wait for us here with the rest of the *sangria* and the bags?"

Mark turned to Tanya.

"Do you think you can hold off on Brad for another hour or so?

Tanya smiled.

"I've an idea he'll survive."

THE GIRL was used to seeing *peregrinos* of every kind at the café where she worked in Milladoiro's cultural centre. Some stopped for refreshments and to get a last *sello* stamped into their *credenciales* before the forest descent and the long, steep climb through the outskirts and into the historic centre of Santiago. Others hurried on, anxious to arrive before the midday pilgrim mass at the cathedral. The three men that were approaching now, as she looked up from where she was cleaning one of the outside tables, were among the motliest pilgrims she had yet seen. Striding ahead was a weatherbeaten, middle–aged man with worn–out clothes and an ancient, faded backpack. A few paces behind was a bearded man with shoulder–length dark hair. He carried a plastic bag in one hand and a leather satchel in the other. But what was particularly striking about him was the long, discoloured robe that came over his head like a Mexican poncho and was tied, with a cord, around the middle. Beside him, deep in conversation, was a young man whose only unusual feature appeared to be the company he was keeping. The girl disappeared into the café ahead of their arrival. She observed from inside as the first man took a chair and sat, gazing into the distance.

His two companions joined him a few moments later. The bearded one with the robe put his leather satchel on the table and the younger one took off his small backpack, leaving it on an empty chair. They asked the seated man something and he shook his head brusquely. The two entered, the robed man sighing in relief as the chill of the air conditioning greeted him. As they looked at the *bocadillos* and *tortas* in the glass cabinet the girl glanced through the window at the one who had stayed outside. He had pulled his companion's satchel towards him and his hand was rummaging inside it. The girl watched him glance, nervously, towards the door then snap the clasps of the satchel shut and slide it back into its original position.

They ordered coffee and water, drank it in the air conditioned interior, used the toilet and asked for the bill. All the while the third man stayed outside, staring into the distance. For a moment the girl considered saying something about what had looked like a theft, but two things dissuaded her. The pair were speaking English and, when they paid, they left no tip. She watched as all three made their way back to the paved footpath and past the commercial buildings and apartments until they disappeared into the trees at the top of the road.

"Think of a drop of rain," Fr Delucci was saying to Álvaro. "It has everything within it to sustain life. It falls alone but it gains power when it joins other drops. You've seen raindrops trickle down a window, getting faster and stronger as they merge until they flow and pour onto the ground. There they become streams. The streams become rivers. The raindrop is now part of a huge flow of water but everywhere – whether a mighty river or a tiny stream – the desire is the same. To reach the ocean and become one with it. That is what we are like. Drops of rain making our way to the ocean that is God's vast love."

Álvaro was smiling and nodding and the priest savoured the moment. His mind had been racing with new interpretations of his faith and, in the young man he found a willing audience upon whom he could try his ideas out.

They rounded a bend and found Rod seated at the side of the trail, waiting for them.

«Santiago,» he said, gesturing ahead across a valley to where the myriad buildings of their long sought for destination lay clustered across a hilltop.

Fr Delucci broke into a beaming smile, his eyes devouring the cityscape for a view of the famous cathedral.

"*Y ahora tengo que decir adiós,*" said Rod, blotting out the priest's view and offering a handshake.

"What?"

He turned to Álvaro.

"What did he say?"

The young man looked equally confused. He spoke rapidly to Rod.

"*Yo voy,*" replied the *vagabundo*.

There followed a conversation in which Álvaro became increasingly agitated while Rod remained passive but firm.

"What's going on?" asked the priest.

"He's leaving us."

"What?"

"He's going back."

"But... I don't understand..."

The priest turned to his old companion who was now removing something from his pocket.

"Rod. What's happening?"

Rod turned to Álvaro and nodded towards the priest.

"*Explica.*"

The priest looked desperately at the young man.

"He says that he will not be coming with us to Santiago. He says that while he walks on the way he is a pilgrim with respect, but that, as soon as he enters Santiago, he becomes just a *vagabundo* – that the people look down at him. He will walk back to Porto and start the *Camino* again."

"Tell him... No. He can't do that. Tell him... "

The priest appeared suddenly close to tears. He addressed the *vagabundo* directly.

"Rod. Don't leave. I need you."

Rod shook his head, smiling sadly.

"*No, Delucci. Es mejor así.*"

He caught the stunned priest in a rough embrace, pressed something into his hands and marched rapidly back along the way they had just come, leaving the two others standing in mute bewilderment staring after him.

He turned at the top of the trail.

"*Id!*" he called. "Go!", and he disappeared around the bend.

The priest took some steps to follow and then stopped. He looked down at the small bag that the *vagabundo* had pressed into his hands. Opening it, mechanically, he found a neat bundle of bank notes and a quantity of coins. As his spinning thoughts settled he found himself left with two predominant emotions. A deep sense of loss and a sudden, strong conviction. He turned to Álvaro who was stood, looking rather stunned, staring at the bend around which Rod had disappeared.

"Álvaro. I need you to do something for me."

The youth looked blankly then managed to focus.

"Of course. Anything, Father."

The priest held out the bag.

"Go after him. Bring him this and make sure he takes it."

Everything seemed to be happening too quickly for Álvaro. The blank look re–appeared on his face and he made no attempt to take the money.

"Álvaro. I know that this is sudden and that you will be disappointed not to finish the *Camino* with me, but this has happened for a reason. I started this journey alone and it seems that I am destined to end it alone. I'll be okay but I owe it to Rod to make sure that he will be also."

The young man nodded, hesitantly, and took the bag.

"It has been a great honour to walk with you, Padre."

He held out his hand but the priest ignored it and moved in to embrace him instead.

"Go with God."

Álvaro flashed him a solemn smile and then, filled with the urgency of his mission, he turned heel and began to jog back along the track. Fr Delucci waited until he had disappeared around the bend before turning back to gaze across the valley at Santiago.

«Almost there,» he said aloud to himself. An unspoken thought followed immediately.

Then what?

REFRESHED AND WITHOUT the burden of their heavy backpacks, Mark and Tanya followed Berta into the solemn, majestic vastness of the cathedral. She stopped them just inside the entrance and pointed out a thick stone column that was roped off beyond the public's touch.

"See those holes in the stone?"

She pointed to a number of indents about a metre from the base of the column which were clustered together, each one about the size of a large grape.

"Those holes were made by thousands and thousands of pilgrims touching the column when they arrived. It was part of the ritual."

"Why have they roped it off?

"Probably for the same reason that you can't bring your bags into the church."

"And why's that?"

"I've no idea."

Mark glanced around furtively, and then reached over the security ribbon. At a stretch, he managed to slot his fingers into the holes. The stone was cold to his touch and he couldn't help feeling a thrill as he thought of the generations upon generations of other fingers that had touched that very spot.

"You rebel," laughed Tanya as Berta led them up one of the side aisles towards the massive gilted altar with the huge statue of San Tiago at the back. Skirting to the right they joined a rather long queue outside a doorway.

"Most of these people are just visitors here for the day," whispered Berta. "But you can spot the real *peregrinos*."

Sure enough, among the well dressed, largely middle aged, people in the line, those with worn walking shoes, deep tans and the serene, patient look of someone who has grown used to taking all day to walk 20 or 30 kilometres stood out as the genuine pilgrims. Mark felt an inner glow to be able to count himself among that group.

When it came their turn they mounted the stone steps, worn in the middle from the passage of so many feet over the centuries, and found themselves entering a narrow, raised area at the back of the altar. Half way along on the left was the top of San Tiago's statue – the broad shoulders and over-sized head. Mark watched the person in front of him throw her arms around the neck and whisper some words before descending a matching set of steps on the far side.

"Go on," whispered Tanya, giving him a shove.

He approached the statue, embraced it and whispered his thanks for a *buen Camino*. Berta had skirted the altar was waiting at the bottom of the further steps when they came down. She led them to a similar door. This time the steps descended below the altar. Here they found three people in the small, subterranean chamber. There was a rail with a padded *prie dieu* in front of a gate to one side. Two of those there were standing in contemplation and the third was kneeling at the rail, gazing through the bars of the gate. The subject of her gaze was a silver cask – about the size of a seaman's chest – which was covered in intricate engraving.

"The bones of the saint and his two disciples," whispered Berta, and Mark was enveloped, for a moment, in a sense of genuine awe.

Aunt Lily would love this.

Back in the main body of the church Berta showed them the enormous *botafumeiro* – according to her, the largest in the world.

"They need about six or eight guys to lift that thing," she explained, "and when they get it going it swings from one side of the church to the other, nearly hitting the ceiling. Apparently, in the old days, they needed it to spread the scent of burning incense through the building because the smell of the pilgrims was so awful."

"When can you get to see it?" asked Tanya.

"Sometimes they swing it at the 12 o'clock pilgrim Mass but you've missed that today."

They spent another ten or fifteen minutes examining the various alcoves, statues and paintings before emerging into the afternoon sun again.

"What did you think?" asked Berta as she led them to the pilgrim office where they would receive their *compostelas*.

"I have to admit, I really did feel moved," said Mark.

"What strikes me as strange," said Tanya, "is that there's hardly any queue to see the actual bones of the saint but a huge line waiting to hug the statue of him."

"Yeah," laughed Berta. "Good point."

The pilgrim office was a large building a short walk from the cathedral. A security man was restricting entry to those with *credenciales* so Berta had to wait outside.

"They'll ask if you did it for spiritual or for other reasons. The *compostela* you get for spiritual reasons is a lot nicer than the other one. I'm just letting you know," she laughed.

They entered the building and stood in line, waiting to be called to one of several counters.

"Are you going to go 'spiritual' or 'other'," asked Tanya.

"I was just thinking about that. I started this walk as part of a crazy weight loss thing but I really feel that, somewhere along the way, it became spiritual," said Mark.

"And I'm not just saying that to get a nicer certificate," he added, laughing.

"Yeah, that's fair enough. Go for it," said Tanya.

"What about you?"

"Nah. I'd feel like I was cheating. I'd better go with the crap one."

"So you haven't done any 'soul searching' in all these days?"

Tanya looked at him and gave a wry smile.

"You certainly know how to push a person's buttons, don't you?"

"Sorry."

At the counter Mark handed over his pilgrim passport to the young woman seated there. She glanced at the various stamps that he'd collected at the stops along the way, each one a memory to him now. After a few questions, the answers of which she entered into a computer, she spread out his certificate and took up a pen to fill it in.

"Is there any possibility that I could dedicate the walk to someone else?" he asked, with a sudden flash of inspiration.

"Certainly. Just write the name here."

He watched with a sense of quiet achievement as she filled out his name, using the Latin 'Marcus' for 'Mark' and then added, "on behalf of Lillian McGill". Aunt Lilly would like that, he was sure. It would make the perfect peace offering when he got home.

"Let's see the one that soulless people get," he teased as he and Tanya left the building to rejoin Berta.

"No. It's none of your business."

He looked at her.

"You got the good one, didn't you."

"Of course not. Do you honestly think I'd be so hypocritical?"

"Actually, I do."

Tanya laughed.

"Okay then. Maybe I did do a bit of soul searching."

As they crossed in front of the cathedral on their way back to join Maria and Johanna, Mark glanced at the steps of the towering building. He stopped.

"Wait guys. I just have to do something."

He held up the blue chalk to Tanya.

"As you said, 'mission accomplished' so I might as well do a check–in for Shay one last time."

Tanya smiled.

"Go for it."

Mark hurried over to a spot at one side of the steps, glanced around and then, bending, wrote his name discretely at the base of the wall. He consulted his watch and added the precise time.

When he returned to the two others he was grinning.

"What was that about," asked Berta, curiously.

"Oh, just a game."

"I DON'T KNOW, Bela. I don't have..."

Anxo considered what he was about to say and decided that it was inoffensive enough to proceed.

"I don't have your faith."

He was slumped on the sofa, supported by a pile of pillows. His face was pale and bathed in sweat. The attacks were no more frequent nor intense than they had been in the hospital, but Isabel felt helpless and unsupported as she witnessed them, especially now that she was so hopeful about making the marriage work and the child they were going to raise together. She had met with resistance when she had mentioned the idea to Anxo that morning but had raised the issue again over lunch.

"I have enough faith for the two of us, Anxo. I just need you to cooperate.

She saw him wavering and pressed home the advantage.

"Think about it. You have nothing to lose."

"Okay. If it makes you happy. But not Fr Santos. He hates me."

Isabel smiled and gave his hand a squeeze.

"Okay. I'll find someone else. I'm sure it won't be a problem. The cathedral is full of visiting priests at this time of the year."

FR DELUCCI had reached the bottom of the valley that rose on the other side to take him into Santiago de Compostela and the end of his *Camino*. He was weary, lonely and full of doubt. Having relied upon Rod to lead the way he was unused to seeking out the yellow arrows that marked the right path. Between his uncertainty, his still–tender foot and the heat of the day his progress had been slow. Now, he was brought up abruptly at a fork on trail. Arrows went both left, up a tarmacadamed, wide path, to where he could hear a busy road above, and right, along a wooded path. Loathe to use his last resources of energy on pursuing the wrong road, he looked for further clues as to which way was the correct one. He drew a blank. He looked behind but there was no sign of any other *peregrino* on the way. It was already early evening and most pilgrims had arrived hours ago in time for the midday Mass that Álvaro had told him about.

Do I take the busy route or do I take the quiet way?

The internal question struck him, forcefully, as a metaphor for where he had arrived at in his life. With all that he had learned and all that he had thought through in the past days his faith had changed radically. It had been a personal journey, but he had seen his truth echoed in the faces of those who had attended his roadside Masses. He had seen the trust and hope in the eyes of those who had sought his blessing. He thought of his congregation in Boston for the first time in days. Those he had met upon the *Camino* were already expressing their faith. In many ways he had been preaching to the converted.

And these signs will accompany those who believe: in my name they will cast out demons; they will speak in new tongues.

The last chalked message came back to him like a revelation. New tongues – the simple Christian message that he had come to preach. And the demons were, of course, the age old demons of greed, envy, materialism and selfishness that were the curse of modern society.

I must return to my people.

He began walking up the tarmacadamed roadway to the left.

But how do I get home? I have no money.

As he climbed the long, weary route into town, he was formulating a plan to have money wired to him. He had no phone numbers with him so he would have to make an international reverse charge call to the diocesan house. In these days of the internet did people still make reverse charge calls? Would the operator be able to look up the number? Would the operator understand English? Where would he get them to send the money? Where would he stay that night? He began to feel a growing desperation which was uncomfortably at odds with his newly rekindled faith.

Get thee behind me Satan.

His ponderings had, at least, distracted him from the tedious walk through the newer part of the city. Now he crossed a large park with nicely dressed people sitting along a central path under the shade of neatly planted trees. A boy was taking a photograph of his parents posing beside a bright, modern sculpture of two caricature–like women at the far end of the park. The boy stared and then swung the camera to photograph the priest instead. The parents turned to see what had caught their son's attention. Fr Delucci glanced down at his shoddy, disreputable robe and flushed with embarrassment. His attire had seemed somehow acceptable on the *Camino*. Here, amid the sophistication of a city, it felt suddenly ridiculous. An overwhelming desire to reach the cathedral swept over him and he hurried his pace.

In the old town the narrow streets provided some shade and the sense of antiquity made him feel less conspicuous. The heat of the day and his long uphill walk had left him desperately thirsty but he had no money to buy so much as a small bottle of water. Every last coin had been in the bag that he'd given to Álvaro to return to Rod. He kept his head down, and hurried up the flagstoned street towards where the towering steeples of the cathedral could be seen through gaps in the buildings. As he neared the top of the road, a small leafy square opened out on the right. There was a fountain in the middle and he hurried across to it. Water poured from four spouts set around a bulb–like column in the middle. His thirst was severe but he had no way of knowing whether or not the water was safe to drink. He glanced around. On a stone bench nearby an elderly woman sat watching him. She shook her head slowly and looked away.

That was a close call. The cathedral. Once I get there I'll be okay.

Leaving the square he continued to the end of the street where the massive church rose ahead of him. Turning left, he made his way towards the front of the building. At the corner, a beggar was pitching his story of woe to each passer-by. He glanced at the priest in his shabby robe and, ignoring him, moved directly on to whomever was following behind.

The plaza in front of the cathedral was huge so the crowd there looked less numerous than it actually was. The priest joined the queue filing up the old stone steps to the main doors. His mind was beginning to calm as he glimpsed the solemn interior of the building but, just as he was about to enter, a hand blocked his way. A security guard pointed to a sign.

"No backpacks."

The priest raised his precious leather satchel and the plastic bag containing the few possessions that he had found necessary for his personal hygiene.

"These are not backpacks."

"No bulky bags," the guard clarified. "There is a place where you can leave them."

At the bottom of the steps the priest stopped and looked around. He didn't even have the couple of euro required to leave his belongings in the baggage office. He felt suddenly overwhelmed. Overcome with mental, emotional and physical weariness as well as a desperate thirst, he moved to one side, out of the flow of pedestrian traffic, and sank down, his back against the wall. Dismissing Álvaro and leaving himself penniless seemed an act of madness now.

What was I thinking?

The hard truth nudged at the edges of his mind. Lulled by the warm reception from the *peregrinos* and local people along the way he had expected to arrive, triumphantly, into Santiago to a fanfare of welcome. The reality was that Santiago was a modern, vast, impersonal city where the pilgrims represented a tiny number among the population of students, business people, workers and such who went about their daily lives oblivious to rumours from the country villages about holy men and *vagabundos*.

My God, my God. Why hast thou forsaken me?

DUBLIN, IRELAND

THE TAXI DRIVER was piling the last piece of luggage into the boot when Helen was hit by the familiar feeling that she had forgotten something.

"I'll just be a minute," she said and hurried back towards the house.

"Take your time. The meter's running," called the man after her as she let herself in. She went from room to room, rechecking what she had checked numerous times already that morning. Again, she was struck by the sterile atmosphere now that all traces of Grace, David and Angela had been removed by antibacterial cleansing liquid and the men with the removal truck. Upstairs she opened the hot press and confirmed that the boiler had been switched off. In the bedroom she found the only reminder that a family had once been happy here. On the door frame of the small bedroom there were pencil marks at various heights, each labelled with a number indicating the age that Angela had been at that point in time.

The taxi driver was engrossed in something on his smartphone when she slipped into the back seat.

"All sorted?"

"Yes," she replied. "All sorted."

She experienced another moment of customary panic.

"Wait!"

She opened her shoulder bag and rummaged through the pockets until, with a sigh of relief, she located her passport and ticket.

"Sorry. You can go on."

She caught a glimpse of the taxi driver's disparaging look in the rear view mirror but it didn't bother her. A surge of joy had filled her as the taxi pulled away to commence her journey. Just 24 hours or so and she'd be with her family in Australia. What a surprise Angela was going to get.

SANTIAGO DE COMPOSTELA, SPAIN

AN ANGRY VOICE made Fr Delucci raise his head. The beggar who had ignored him on his way into the square was standing in front of him, berating him loudly in rapid Spanish.

"I'm sorry. I don't speak Spanish," the priest said, wearily.

"This is my place," said the beggar, switching to English. "The front and the side of the cathedral are my place. You need to go somewhere else. If there is more than one of us the police will make us both leave."

"Oh, I'm not a b... I'm not asking anyone for money," he stammered, surprised at the mistake but realising, with a quick glance down, that he should not have been. If anything the beggar looked better groomed than he. "Don't worry. I'll go."

The beggar eyed him suspiciously but the edge was gone off his anger.

"You are a *peregrino*?"

"Yes, I have just arrived."

"Are you okay?"

The priest smiled wearily.

"I think I'm just dehydrated. I've left my friends behind and they were carrying the water."

The beggar reached into a sack he was carrying and pulled out a paper bag.

"Here. Have this," he said, holding it out.

The universal symbol of the snake wound around the chalice identified the bag as having come from a pharmacy.

"Thanks, but I don't need anything like that. I just need water," said Fr Delucci.

"It is water."

"Oh," said the priest, embarrassed.

"If the sun gets on the bottle then the plastic melts into the water," explained the beggar. "It's bad for you so I keep it covered up."

The priest took the bag, unscrewed the cap from the water inside, and, in doing so, noted that it was not a new, unopened bottle. He hesitated for a moment about whether it would be impolite to wipe the neck, decided that it would be and raised the water to his lips instead. He drank deeply and gratefully. The small bottle was almost empty when he handed back the bag.

"Thank you," he said. "I'm afraid I've drank most of it. I would buy you another but I don't have any money."

"It's no problem," said the beggar. "I just fill it up from the fountain."

"Oh," said the priest, the snake and chalice motif on the bag looking rather more ominous now.

"Well I have to get back to work," said beggar. He turned to walk away then paused and looked back over his shoulder.

"Maybe you would sit somewhere else. The police will get confused."

"Yes. No problem," said Fr Delucci, rising slowly as the beggar hurried off. He started walking wearily towards the middle of the square and then stopped. He had no idea what to do or where to go. In addition, no matter how irrational he told himself he was being, he couldn't shake the fear that he might have been poisoned by the beggar in a mistaken case of professional jealousy. In his thirst he hadn't noticed it at the time but now the aftertaste of the water was decidedly unusual.

"Excuse me. Did you see a camera?"

He was being addressed in perfect but accented English by a tall Scandinavian looking man beside a tall Scandinavian looking woman.

"Sorry?"

"I think it might have fallen from my wife's bag in the place where you were sitting a moment ago. I was minding our backpacks there earlier while she went into the cathedral."

"No. I'm sorry. There wasn't anything there when I sat down."

The man was obviously not convinced. He stared down at the priest's plastic bag.

"You don't believe me," said Fr Delucci. He held the bag out. "Do you want to check?"

"No. That's fine," said the man, embarrassed. "Sorry to bother you."

The pair turned away.

"Are you sure that's were you were standing," Fr Delucci could hear the woman say.

"Yes. I remember because it was right where the blue writing was on the wall."

The priest froze. He spun around and stared through the milling crowd at the spot where he had been sitting. Sure enough, even from here he could glimpse the neat chalked message at the bottom of the wall.

AS SHE APPROACHED the steps of the cathedral Isabel was reminded of her recent meeting here with Anxo's young mistress. For a moment she had a sense of foreboding about what she was about to do. She truly believed that her dream had been a message. Prayer could restore her husband's health.

But if he is cured will he return to his mistress? Maybe it is better to leave him as he is. This way he depends on me.

She felt instantly ashamed at the thought.

San Tiago. Forgive me. The spirit is willing but the flesh is weak. Help me to find the one who can make Anxo well again.

At that moment the swell of *peregrinos* making their way towards the steps of the cathedral parted for a moment and her attention was drawn to a man who appeared to be reading some chalked graffiti at the wall to one side. Amongst the multifarious throng he stood out. His dark hair fell, rich but unkempt, to shoulder length. He was dressed in, what seemed to be, a monk's tunic but it lacked the pristine costume–like aspect of those she was used to seeing on the many religious who flocked to Santiago. This looked like the genuine article – as might have graced the back of St Francis of Assisi in his tiny forest church 800 years ago. As she watched, the man stood, snapped open a leather satchel and began thumbing through the pages of a tome within. She noted the abundant beard and moustache that intermingled with his wild hair. It crossed her mind that John the Baptist might have looked like this. The gilt edging on the heavy book suggested, to Isabel, that it was a bible and she was struck by a sudden certainty.

This is the man I need.

She approached the stranger and waited politely until he had completed his intense examination of the text that he had eventually settled upon. She didn't have to wait long. He read rapidly, stared for a moment and then glanced around him as though looking for something. Isabel took a step towards him and caught his attention.

"Excuse me. You are a priest, no?" she asked.

"I'm sorry. I don't speak Spanish," the man replied. Isabel switched to her halting school English.

"Ah. My English is not so good. I'm sorry. I was asking if you are priest."

He seemed to consider the question as if it were a new idea. Then he smiled.

"Yes. I am."

"Father, my husband needs you. He is sick and the doctors do not know why. I had a dream and when I woke up I knew that Anxo, my husband, needs the *unción de los enfermos* – I do not know how is called in English..." She trailed off. The priest was staring at her with growing intensity as she spoke.

"The anointing of the sick," he said, his voice full of won-der. "It seems that you were meant to find me. Look."

He turned the bible to Isabel and pointed.

"Mark 14.18," he clarified.

She looked at where his finger was indicating and read:

They shall take up serpents; and if they drink any deadly thing, it shall not hurt them; they shall lay hands on the sick, and they shall recover.

"Bring me to your husband," Fr Delucci said.

12. Philemon

*"For perhaps he therefore departed
for a season, that thou shouldest
receive him for ever."*

THEY WERE SITTING on the low wall of the fountain in Plaza do Toural. The hostel where Johanna, Maria and Berta were staying lay in one direction and the hotel where Brad was waiting in another. The three young woman were in a chocolate shop, leaving Mark and Tanya to say their good-byes.

"Are you sure you don't want me to walk you to the hotel."

"Nah. I can find it. Unlike you, I have a phone with *Google Maps*."

"Yeah. Rub it in."

Tanya held the phone out.

"Speaking of which, do you want to check your messages one more time?"

"Sure. Thanks."

He signed into his account.

"Nah. Nothing, though she was online this morning."

"How do you feel about it?"

Mark thought.

"To be honest, it's probably better to be going through this now rather than having her arrive and then being faced with it. There was no way I was ever going to look anything like those photographs that she thought was me."

"I have to say, it's only been a few days but you're certainly looking more trim. You've been doing great with the food. I'm proud of you."

Mark beamed.

"Thanks. I'm definitely feeling it in how much looser my clothes feel."

"You'll be down to the size you want in no time," said Tanya.

"Well, not in a month," laughed Mark, "but, yeah. I'm feeling good about it. Maybe this time next year."

Tanya got up and began to pick up her haversack.

"Well. I'd better get going."

"Are you going to be okay?"

"Yeah. I'll be fine."

They walked, together towards the chocolate shop where the other three were emerging.

"Stay in touch," said Tanya.

"Of course."

She kissed both cheeks of the three *peregrinas* and then turned to Mark.

"Come here big boy."

As they hugged Mark felt a real sense of sadness.

I'm going to miss her.

DUBLIN, IRELAND

CHECK–IN had been a nightmare for Helen. She was used to the convenience of travelling with no more than a carry–on cabin bag on Europe's low–cost airlines. The long queue of people with piles of long–haul luggage moved painfully slowly. To make matters worse, there was a couple with a young boy behind her. The father had seated the child on top of the cases and the boy was taking great delight in kicking Helen whenever she came within range. Annoyingly, as the line stumbled and stuttered forward, this was all too often. When she did finally reach the check–in desk she was decidedly peeved. With some difficulty she hoisted her two suitcases onto the short conveyor belt that was a tributary to the main rolling rubber pathway that fed the baggage out to the awaiting handlers for loading onto the aircraft.

"Hmmm. I'm afraid you're overweight on this one," said the young woman, tapping the first of the two cases with the business end of her pen.

"But they're less than 46kg," protested Helen. "I weighed them before I came out."

"Together they are but no individual bag can weigh more than 23kg, I'm afraid. Do you want me to calculate the excess baggage charge?"

"I do not! Give me a minute."

She dragged the two cases back off the belt and opened them, side by side on the floor. The one that was most bulky was, in fact, less heavy. All she needed to do was make room in that case to accommodate some of the heavier items from the other. Opening her shoulder bag she deposited into it the box of 320 teabags – Grace's favourite brand – and her sewing kit. In doing so she caught sight of Pablo, the little pin cushion man that Angela had made for her. Her granddaughter would be delighted to know that she'd treasured him faithfully and had fulfilled her promise to return him. Her ill humour vanished as she thought of the evenings ahead of her, sewing happily with the child.

SANTIAGO DE COMPOSTELA, SPAIN

FR DELUCCI was rather taken aback by the apparent hostility in the sick man's attitude towards him. Anxo had regarded him incredulously from head to toe and had then, turning to Isabel, launched into, what seemed to be, an animated rant. Despite his lack of Spanish comprehension, the priest could tell that she had leapt to his defence. Embarrassed to be the subject of a domestic argument he looked away and, in doing so, caught his reflection in the polished glass of a large china cabinet. He took in the unkempt hair, the worn sandals and the dirty, untidy robe. He waited for a lull in the heated exchange between husband and wife and then spoke to Isabel.

"If you could tell your husband that I understand his doubt but point out that he may as well let me do what I can. He has nothing to lose and everything to gain. As he spoke

Fr Delucci could see Anxo gathering himself. When he nodded his head in acquiescence the priest suspected that it was
more to do with his own internal reasoning than the argument Isabel had presented on his behalf.

"Do you have holy water?" he asked when Isabel had
confirmed Anxo's cooperation.

"Yes, I'm pretty sure that I do. I'll get it."

"The other thing I'll need is some oil. Normally we use
sacramental oil that has been blessed by the bishop but I can
bless something like olive oil in a situation like this."

When everything had been gathered the priest knelt
beside the stricken man. He opened his bible and glanced
around for somewhere to put it where he could consult it
while his hands were otherwise occupied. Anxo spoke
brusquely to Isabel.

"He says to put it on top of him if you want," she explained. "He says that he won't be able to feel it anyway."

"Thank you," said the priest, laying the open book on the
sick man's upper legs.

Husband and wife watched as Fr Delucci began to perform a blessing over the olive oil.

DUBLIN, IRELAND

HELEN STOOD on the far side of the security check and
watched the two plastic trays that contained her belongs
emerge from the screening tunnel before trundling along
the steel conveyor belt towards where she was waiting. She
glanced at her arm to check the time and found her wrist
empty. Of course, her watch was at the bottom of the first
tray with her rings, necklace, coins, mobile phone and plastic bag of liquids that she would need to freshen up on the
day–long journey ahead. She turned and squinted to make
out the time on the screens at the back of the security area
that showed the departing flights, their gate numbers and
their departure status. In the top, right corner the time was
displayed. Despite the long queue through security screening, she should have enough time to do a bit of shopping and
to avail of the duty free offers for those, like her, travelling
beyond the boundaries of the European Union. She turned

back to the conveyor belt and gave an inward groan. Only one of the two trays was arriving beside her. The other, containing her carry–on bag, had been diverted onto a secondary belt where a sombre looking security woman had caught it and was looking, inquisitively at all the waiting passengers to identify it's owner.

"That's mine," said Helen.

"I need to take a look inside. Is that okay?"

"Yes, of course."

The security guard lifted the tray across to a stainless steel examination table and Helen made her way to the far side of it. The woman began transferring the contents of the bag, one by one, into an empty tray. She didn't have to look far to find the objectionable item.

"I'm sorry. You can't take this onboard," she said, holding up Angela's little pin cushion man with it's embedded collection of assorted pins and needles.

Helen's face showed her dismay.

"Why not?"

"Well, there are quite a lot of sharp objects."

"If I take those out?"

"Sure. The little doll's no problem."

"Fine," said Helen, relieved.

The woman passed the pin cushion over."

"His name's Pablo," smiled Helen, as she grasped the pins and needles to yank them out. "My granddaughter made him for me. I promised her I'd keep him safe."

SANTIAGO DE COMPOSTELA, SPAIN

"THROUGH THIS HOLY ANOINTING may the Lord, in his love and mercy, help you with the grace of the Holy Spirit", said Fr Delucci, anointing Anxo's forehead with the olive oil. He then took the sick man's hand and read from the Bible.

"May the Lord who frees you from sin save you and raise you up".

He had barely spoken the words when he felt a shudder run through Anxo's body and the sick man's eyes shot open wide. The priest recoiled, startled as if he had broken something, and, in doing so, collided with Isabel who had leaned forward in alarm.

"Anxo. Are you okay?"

He suddenly sat bolt upright on the sofa, knocking the leather satchel from his legs and onto the floor where its contents spilled across the wooden parquet. Fr Delucci backed further away as Anxo rose to his feet, a look of pure joy and wonderment spreading across his face.

"It's gone! Holy fuck. It's gone!"

Isabel's mouth fell open and she gazed in delight, first at her husband and then at the priest who was staring at his hands. Anxo caught his wife up and swung her around with a whoop.

"It's fucking gone. I can't believe it!"

He put Isabel down and faced Fr Delucci who didn't understand a word of the Spanish exclamations. Anxo beamed at the priest and then caught him in an embrace before planting a kiss on his nose. Then, shouting excitedly in Spanish, he spanked his wife on the backside and rushed from the room, still shouting triumphantly.

Before Fr Delucci had time to control his spinning thoughts he found himself wrapped up in the arms of Anxo's wife. Then, to his further discomfort, she began weeping, loudly, on his shoulder. Awkwardly, he patted her head and let her cry. His mind was racing with sheer elation. There had been several telling signs on the way but now God had used him to heal – just as Jesus had healed. The man had been all but paralysed and now he could be heard laughing and whooping as he ran about the house. He felt Isabel's sobs subside and she drew away from him.

"Are you okay?"

Her face, when she looked up at him, was beaming with happiness.

"Thank you so much. I..."

Her voice trailed off. She used her shirt to wipe her eyes.

"I don't know how to thank you. It's a miracle."

A quote from scripture came to the priests mind.

There is no man which shall do a miracle in my name, that can lightly speak evil of me.

"No. Thank *you*," he said earnestly as the ramifications of what had happened began to sink in. "Through this miracle my faith is fully restored. The Lord has given me the sign I asked for. I am ready to return to my flock. I'm ready to go home."

Isabel smiled. Then, the ecstasy of the moment over, she began to grow aware of their surroundings. Her eyes fell to the mess on the floor.

"Oh, your bible. I'm so sorry."

She moved towards the contents of the leather satchel that were scattered at the foot of the sofa.

"No, let me," said the priest bending quickly.

He reached for the breviary and then froze. There, among the items that had spilled from the satchel, was a small, plastic card with a shimmering hologram and his own name written in raised letters upon its surface. In somewhat of a daze, he picked up the credit card that he had last seen on the bridge between Portugal and Spain what seemed like an age ago.

"What is it *padre*?" asked Isabel, noting the look of shock on the priest's face. He turned, beaming, towards her and held up the card.

"Another miracle," he laughed. "Another miracle."

THE HOSTEL WAS large, clean and bright. It had a range of thoughtful facilities for the pilgrims. The dormitories each had eight beds at the most. There was a well equipped kitchen and a small, enclosed garden at the back of the building with tables and chairs so that guests had the choice to eat outside rather than in the communal dining room. Perhaps one of the most useful provisions for *peregrinos* – who had spent days, weeks or even months on the road – was a laundry with coin operated washers and dryers. In the lobby, vending machines offered snacks and beverages. The bathrooms had powerful showers with steaming hot water in plentiful supply and, in a small room off the lobby, a desktop computer, connected to the internet, had been provided for general use. While Mark's dirty laundry had been sent spinning behind the glass porthole of a washing machine, he had queued patiently until the computer had become available. As he typed his username and password into the login page on *Facebook*, Berta popped her head through the doorway.

"We're going to sit outside with a bottle of wine."

"Cool. I'll be there in a minute."

He pressed enter. He had new mail. He paused a moment.

What do I want her to say? What's the best I can hope for? What's the worst?

He could feel his heart beating louder than usual as he positioned the mouse over the message icon and clicked. With a feeling of anticlimax he read the name. The message was from a gaming community friend back in Ireland. He clicked, halfheartedly onto his timeline and glanced down the screen of inspirational quotes, mundane moments, advertisements and images of updated profile pictures boasting pursed lips and 'beauty face' filters that made the features look like they were wrapped in cellophane. He felt too deflated even to massage their egos with a 'like'.

He was about to log out of his account when a thought struck him.

What if she messaged me and it somehow appeared as 'read' so I didn't see it?

He clicked back onto the message icon and scanned down the list of recent mails. He spied the first line of the message that he had sent her.

So she hasn't replied.

He was about to click off when he noticed that her name was gone. In its place it simply read 'Facebook User'. He clicked on the message thread. All of the messages were there but, in each case, Adelina's name had been changed to 'Facebook User' and her profile picture had been replaced with a generic icon of a white silhouetted face on a grey background. The suspicion hit him like a physical punch in the gut. He typed 'Hi. Just wanted to say how sorry I am again. Hope you're okay.' into the message box and pressed 'send'. A notification popped up.

Message Not Sent This person isn't receiving messages from you right now.

He clicked into the search tab at the top of the page and

typed in 'Adelina'. He held his breath as he clicked the magnifying glass symbol to initiate the search. A list of strangers bearing her name, and variations of it, appeared. Her profile wasn't among them. Adelina had blocked him.

He sat for a moment staring blankly at the screen, trying to assess his feelings. He was, of course, hurt. But he was also aware of other emotions finding their way to the forefront of his mind. A shadow suddenly blocked some of the light streaming in from the brighter lobby.

"Did she write?"

Mark stared over the computer monitor to the door where Tanya stood grinning.

"What are you doing here?" he beamed, jumping to his feet and meeting her halfway across the floor with a big bear hug.

"Well, you know. Thought I'd swing by and see if you were sticking to the regime or if you'd started eating pizzas the minute my back was turned."

He laughed.

"The girls are outside drinking wine. They'll be delighted to see you."

"Well, did she write?" asked Tanya again as they crossed the lobby.

"She sent me a message, alright."

Tanya stopped and caught his arm, making him stop too. "What did she say?"

Mark gave a mirthless grin.

"Well, it wasn't that kind of message. It was the kind that says everything without words."

"What do you mean?"

"She blocked me."

Tanya's face was the picture of genuine sympathy.

"Oh Mark. I'm so sorry. Are you okay?"

Before he had a chance to answer she led him to some chairs at a coffee table to one side of the lobby and they sat.

"Well, I'm hurt, of course," he said. "But I understand. It's like you said. I was totally dishonest with her so it put a question mark over everything I'd said. How could she trust me? How could she know what was real and what wasn't."

Tanya nodded sadly.

"And how are you feeling?"

"Actually, the biggest thing I feel is relief. Can you imagine what it would have been like if I'd showed up at the airport without telling her?"

"Yeah," nodded Tanya. "You had to tell her. I'm just really disappointed that she didn't give you a chance."

"Look,' said Mark, smiling. "If none of this had happened I'd be stuffing my face at home in my little fantasy online relationship. Now, I have some cool new friends and, thanks to you, I'm really on a road towards being healthy. It's like the *Camino* — it's a long way and it's really slow. But it's steady, and if I keep putting one foot in front of the other then I'll reach my Santiago in the end as sure as night follows day."

Tanya smiled.

"I'm proud of you, Mark."

He grinned and then changed the subject.

"What about you? How's Brad?"

Tanya laughed.

"Well, I kind of blocked him as well – though in the real world, not online."

"What? You..."

"It's over. I told him what I thought of him. He got pretty angry and then said we'd talk about it when we got home. I told him that I wasn't going home. That I was walking to Finisterre with some friends."

Mark gave a whoop.

"You're coming with us?"

"If you don't mind the company."

Mark held out his arms for another hug.

"Now don't be getting any ideas," laughed Tanya. "Remember, you're not my type."

"That's fine by me. You're much too important as a friend to risk having as a girlfriend."

13. John

"Raging waves of the sea, foaming out their own shame; wandering stars, to whom is reserved the blackness of darkness for ever."

GALICIA, SPAIN

A LIGHT APPEARED in an upstairs window of the farmhouse and Rod knew it was time to move on. The sun was threatening to make an appearance in the east and was notifying the world with a pre–dawn glow across the landscape that turned the darkness to grey. Backpack in place, Rod slipped out of the wooden shed where he had slept and joined the trail again. He would wash in the warm public thermal font in Caldas De Reis. In the one day since leaving Delucci he had covered the same distance as he, the boy and the priest had walked in three. The gruelling pace had helped to numb his mind but, as he made his way into the sleeping town, the lonely streets seemed to echo a loneliness that had been growing on the *vagabundo*. He missed the priest and, even more, he missed the sense of purpose that he had discovered by the preacher's side.

Half an hour later, washed and refreshed, he left the Roman spa town by the bridge over the river Umia and, gratefully abandoning the hard tarmac of the N550, made his way along the dirt trail of the *Camino* as it passed through farmlands and vineyards. The sun was beginning it's climb into

237

the blue sky when he approached the hamlet where they had encountered Álvaro – the place where Delucci had no longer needed him. A figure by the roadside ahead caught his eye from a distance. It was at a place where the road curved to the east so the rising sun made it impossible to make out more than a silhouette. Years of fending for himself on the fringes of an often hostile society had left him with a tendency to err on the side of caution – especially now that he was alone again. He slowed his pace and assessed the risk. The man – for he could tell that it was a man – was leaning back on a wall with his head drooped forward. He appeared to be deep in thought and was paying no heed to Rod's approach. There was something unnaturally still about his behaviour.

Perhaps he's dead.

The vagabundo's first instinct was to slip by and continue on his way.

Al perro que duerme, no lo despiertes.

But, as he passed in front of the man, walking on the balls of his feet to minimise the sound of his sneakers on the dirt track, he found that his conscience wouldn't let him. Stopping, he stared at the figure. His heart leapt.

"Álvaro?"

The young man shot to attention, startled.

"Oh, thank God. I thought I had missed you."

The *vagabundo* was completely confused.

"What are you doing here? Where is Delucci?"

"He went on to Santiago. He sent me after you. He said that he had started the journey alone and felt that he should finish it the same way. I couldn't catch up with you. I walked through the night and then I figured – well I hoped – that you'd stopped somewhere so I've been waiting here ever since. I knew you'd have to pass this way."

He suddenly flushed embarrassedly.

"I must have fallen asleep."

"You're crazy," said Rod, scornfully, but he felt a glow of warmth.

"Here," said Álvaro," holding out the bag of money. "Padre Delucci insisted that you should have this."

"What for?"

"We didn't have time to talk because he wanted to make sure that I caught you but I've been thinking and I believe that he wants you to continue his work."

"Me? I'm no priest."

"You are his assistant. You have been the one that he relied on to do his work. He told me this."

Rod stared at the younger man.

"This is what he said?"

"Yes. When we were walking on the road together he talked a lot about you. The words that he used in English were his 'rod and his staff' which means *vada y cayado* in Spanish."

Rod paused a moment while this revelation sank in. In spite of himself he smiled. He took the bag of money.

"Thank you, Álvaro," he said. "Thank you for making such a big effort to bring this to me. You must be tired."

The young man smiled.

"You're welcome."

He stretched and yawned.

"Come. My mother is expecting us."

Somewhat dazed, the *vagabundo* followed the young man into the village. As they passed one of the first houses the door flew open and a woman emerged half dragging a young girl behind her.

"This is him, no?" she enquired of Álvaro. He nodded.

"My daughter is suffering from anxiety about going into senior school," she said to Rod. "Will you give her your blessing?"

He stared blankly at her and then at Álvaro. The young man simply took the girl by the hand and brought her to stand in front of the *vagabundo*.

Rod stared for a moment at the top of the girl's bowed head, then at the mother's expectant face. He placed his hand on her crown as he had seen the priest do so many times.

"May the Lord comfort and protect you in the name of the Father and of the Son and of the Holy Spirit."

A chorus of response came from the girl, her mother and Álvaro.

"Amen."

"*Gracias Señor,*" said the woman, beaming as she led the

child away. The girl glanced back and gave a shy smile of appreciation that warmed Rod's heart.

He was trying, with great difficulty, to remember the last time that he had been called *'señor'* when they arrived at Álvaro's house.

"Mamá," he called as he let them in at the front door. «I have brought the apostle with me.»

A well of emotion that had been bubbling below the surface since encountering Álvaro on the road surged up at the words.

'Apóstol' was a much more pleasant word than 'vagabundo'.

SANTIAGO DE COMPOSTELA, SPAIN

LUCÍA NEVER PAID attention to the passengers waiting in line to check in at her desk. She had learned, early on, that a simple accident of eye contact could result in a smile and that tenuous relationship could then lead to all sorts of additional problems if the same passenger happened to present with overweight luggage, an out–of–date passport or any one of the other various issues that she faced on a daily basis. She was, therefore, surprised and somewhat annoyed to find herself returning the smile of the man in the dark suit. She had glanced up while the woman she was checking in was fumbling in her handbag for her misplaced passport. His shoulder length dark hair, tied neatly in a small ponytail, and well groomed beard and moustache on his tanned features were certainly striking, but it was more than his aesthetic appearance. There was a sense of charisma emanating from him that made him stand out in an intangible way. As her mind skipped through this line of thought he looked, sharply, in her direction and caught her regarding him. He smiled readily and she found herself reciprocating.

When his turn came he strode forward with his passport in hand. The nails were beautifully manicured.

"Good afternoon," he said. The accent was American.

"Good afternoon, sir," she responded, taking the passport and keying the pertinent information into the computer to bring up his ticketing details.

Joseph Delucci.

"Your final destination is Boston, sir?"

"Yes."

"Are you travelling alone today?"

"I am."

"Do you have any luggage to check in?" she asked, having already noted that he was carrying nothing more than a brown leather satchel.

"No."

"Okay. Have you any seating preference."

"Window please."

"Certainly, sir," she said as she typed.

She pressed 'return' and the printer spit out two boarding passes.

"Boarding is from gate three. This is your boarding pass for the Madrid flight and the second one is for your Madrid to Boston."

"Thank you."

He smiled, turned and strode away leaving her with an unspoken 'have a good flight' on her lips and a desire to know his story on her mind.

What an interesting man.

ISABEL OPENED the kitchen door and listened. There was no sound of movement from the bedroom above.

I'll leave it open. Perhaps the smell of the onions will bring him down.

It was little wonder that he was sleeping still. In the exuberance of his recovered health he had finished a bottle of *Godello* and made a significant dent in a second.

She crossed over to the stove and stirred the onions.

And then he took me to our bed and made love to me.

She brought a smile to her face at the thought but it was mechanical and failed miserably.

No. He fucked me.

Her mind recoiled from the vulgarity of the unspoken phrase but it rang true. There had been a selfishness and violence about the act. It was a demonstration of his returned virility, not of his love for her. She put her hand on her stomach and waited. The baby, on cue, gave a reassuring movement

– gentle but unmistakable. Anxo had made no allowance for her condition in his passion. She had read that sex during pregnancy posed no danger to the foetus but his forcefulness had worried her nonetheless.

She picked up a fork and impaled a piece of potato from the heavy pot. They were ready to be drained and added to the onions. As she reached for a tea towel footsteps on the stairs signalled Anxo's descent. She smiled.

Nobody can resist the smell of onions.

He popped his head in at the kitchen door.

"I'm off, Bela."

Her face reflected her dismay.

"Jesus, Isabel. Don't look at me like that. I've been on the flat of my back, doped up and in agony for weeks. I just want to get out, drive up to the mountains, stretch the legs, think... You know, feel alive again."

"Of course, I understand. I suppose I just thought that we might do that together. Actually, I thought it might be an idea to visit my Godfather and tell him about the baby. There was money available when you were ill that we hadn't known about. Perhaps there is provision in the will in the case of pregnancy."

This struck a chord with Anxo.

"God. You could be right."

He came into the kitchen, crossed to the stove and lifted the lid on the potatoes. It provided a culinary reminder for his wife.

"Oh. They were ready a few minutes ago. They'll go mushy."

She busied herself with draining them.

"Paella?" he asked.

"Yes. I thought you'd like it."

"Lovely."

He watched her transfer the potato pieces into the pan with the onions.

"Listen Bela. Do me a favour. Don't say anything to Cardosa or anybody about me being cured just yet, okay? I'll be under pressure to go back to work and I don't feel up to that just yet. And there's something else to consider. At the moment we're getting an income from the inheritance. If we tell your Godfather then that'll stop. We might be better off saying nothing until we see what the story is with money for the kid."

Isabel's heart, already at a low ebb, sank further.

"We were managing fine before you got sick, Anxo. It's only two more years before we have all the money. Can we not just be honest and get our lives back? Otherwise we're going to be creeping around, looking over our shoulders..."

"Look, let's talk about it tomorrow," he interrupted, meeting her worried look with a reassuring smile. "Just give me today to celebrate being well again and to think it all over. You could be right but do me a favour. Don't tell anyone until we've had a proper chat, okay?"

Isabel forced herself to return his smile.

"Okay."

He gave her a peck on the forehead and squeezed her backside.

"Great night last night."

As he left the kitchen he called back.

"Don't wait up, Bela. I'm just going to drive until I feel like stopping. I've no idea how far I'll go."

"Okay," she said weakly after a pause but the word clashed with the sound of the door that led to the garage closing behind him. She heard the garage gate rise and the little Citroen start up. Isabel felt sick in the pit of her stomach. The miracle had happened less than 24 hours before and, already, the picture–perfect second chance that she'd dreamed of for her marriage was crumbling. And a further worry refused to be silenced.

What if he's gone to her?

THE FOUR COMPANIONS decided to wait until after lunch to set off on their walk to Finisterre. Mark and Tanya hadn't had a chance to explore the old town and, although they had to vacate the hostel early, it was raining and the others were content to wait for them with the backpacks in a vast café that they had discovered. It boasted big, comfy armchairs, lofty ceilings, fascinating paintings and, most importantly –

according to Berta and Maria – the best *churros* with chocolate that they had ever tasted.

"I'm proud of you," said Tanya to Mark as they left the
others and strolled along the footpath under a long portico
that sheltered them from the light, persistent drizzle that had
been falling all morning.

"Why?"

"You literally had a tiny taste of Maria's *churro* and
stopped there. That's will power."

"I thought you'd be frowning at me for having any."

"No. It's important not to feel like you're denying yourself. There's absolutely no harm in a sample of something
that's a treat as long your main diet is healthy."

"To be honest, I found it too sweet. I think my taste buds
have grown used to less salt and sugar."

"Perfect," smiled Tanya. "That's what you want."

They stopped outside the first of the souvenir shops that
they came to and stood looking at the window display of
tee–shirts, tea–towels, pens, jewellery, mugs, statues and ce-
ramic tiles – all sporting the yellow arrow symbol or the shell
of San Tiago.

"Look," said Tanya, pointing. "There's one of those little
hut things on stilts that you see all along the way."

"*Hórreos*," said Mark, surprised with himself that he'd
remembered the word. "They're for keeping corn. The first
time I saw one I thought it was for burying the dead."

"I want to get a necklace or a bracelet or something," said
Tanya. "I want something to remind me of all this."

"Yeah. Me too. Whatever happens I'll never forget this
trip. I know that to say that something's life–changing is so
clichéd but there's no other way to put it. This has been life–
changing for me."

Tanya smiled at him.

"Do you think you'll come back?"

"Definitely. I'd love to do the French way or even the
Portuguese way again but starting further back. What about
you?"

"Yeah. It has a way of getting under your skin, doesn't
it?"

Mark glanced at her. His face grew serious as he looked into her eyes and tried to frame what he suddenly felt the urge to say.

"Oh–oh. I see something deep and meaningful coming on," said Tanya, hurriedly. "Down boy."

She turned, grabbed his arm, and moved towards the shop door.

"Come on. Let's go buy some tacky souvenirs."

Mark laughed and followed.

"Actually, what I was thinking was that I might drop an email to Shay on that weight loss website and thank him," he lied. "He might have been a complete fruitcake but in a roundabout way it all kind of worked."

Tanya, her attention caught by a display stand of leather bracelets, took her phone from her pocket and handed it to him.

"Go for it."

Mark typed in the website URL. Sending a message via the contact form would save him from having to go through the cumbersome effort of logging in to his email account from somebody else's phone. A rectangular icon with an unhappy face popped up. Perplexed, he read the message beneath it.

This site can't be reached.

igottalosemyfatass.com's server DNS address could not be found.

"Looks like he's gone out of business," he said to Tanya, handing back her phone.

"I'm not surprised," she grinned.

She held out a brown leather band with a silver shell motif in the middle.

"What do you think of this one?"

ANXO WAS FRUSTRATED, irritated and well on his way to being drunk. He had arrived at the hairdresser's a half hour before Vicki's normal lunch time in case she left early. From the bar across the street he had strained to catch sight of her in the gloomy interior through the darkened glass of the shop front. At various times he caught a glimpse of her work colleagues but, of Vicki, there was no sign.

Fuck. Probably her day off.

He had downed three beers over the two hour period that it took for all of the employees to come and go on their lunch breaks in two shifts. When the second batch emerged Vicki was not among them.

Fuck.

He had returned to the car and driven to her apartment. He rang the doorbell and waited. Nobody came and, through the glass panel in the front door, he could see no sign of movement within. He rang the bell again, put his ear to the glass and listened. As far as he could tell, there was absolute silence inside.

Fuck.

Back in the car he had sat and pondered for a moment. He had wanted to surprise her but he was running out of time. He needed to see her today. Isabel would kick up if he left her home alone two days in a row.

Fucking Isabel.

Taking out his phone he'd sent Vicki a message on the communications *app* that they both used.

Hey babe. Sorry I've been out of touch. I've been in hospital. Total nightmare. Only got your message today. Really want to see you and explain. Are you around?

He pressed send. A notification popped up onscreen.

Message not sent.

He pressed 'send' again with the same result.

Fuck.

Starting the engine, he had driven, angrily, to an impersonal bar on the N550 that was frequented by passing motorists. He selected a corner table and sat, leaving his sunglasses on against the chance that someone he knew would happen by. Insulated by the noise and bustle of the bar, he made his way through several more beers as he tried to organise his thoughts. Whatever had been wrong with him was gone. Physically, he felt on top of the world. There was no trace of the pain that had crippled him since the night of Helio's burglary fiasco. After all, the doctors had said that his condition might well disappear just as mysteriously as it had come.

How weird that the priest had been doing that bible mumbo–jumbo when it happened.

Maybe, he thought, there was something in what the specialists said about the illness being in his mind. Maybe he was not as tough as he'd thought he was. Perhaps, when it came down to delivering the simple push that would have sent Isabel falling to her death, something inside him – some weakness – had kicked in. Maybe that weakness had caused his mind to be tormented with some sort of self–inflicted phantom pain. And then it was possible that having the priest praying for him resulted in that fucked–up part of his brain feeling that everything was okay again.

Yeah. That's probably it. I'm too fucking soft underneath it all.

He drained his beer glass, checked the time on the plastic wall clock and signalled for another. He still had half an hour to kill. He turned his thoughts to the child growing inside his wife and scowled.

It was going to complicate matters. In two years the inheritance money would come through and there would be a kid to complicate the picture. He tried to remember the provisions of the will in relation to offspring. Isabel's crafty bastard of a father was sure to have tied up at least a chunk of the money to provide for his grandchildren. How much would that effect the amount Anxo could walk away with after the divorce?

If Helio had done the fucking business when he was supposed to...

The distant sound of Angelus bells finally signalled six o'clock. Anxo got up and took a step towards the bar to settle his tab. To his annoyance, his feet became entangled in each other and he had to grip the table to stop himself from falling. He found, suddenly, that he was decidedly light-headed.

Not surprising after all that time on the flat of my back.

He waited until the wave passed and then made his way out to the toilets where he splashed water onto his face.

Better.

He paid the bill, left the bar and slid into the Citroen. He was aware that he was well above the drink–driving limit but, having recently come through such suffering and back into the bloom of full health, he felt invincible.

The gods owe me big time.

Twenty five minutes later he was back at Vicki's house. No lights showed through the glass panel in the front door. He pressed the bell and waited. Nothing stirred.

Fuck.

He put his finger on the button and held it there for a minute or two. He could hear the persistent chime within but it seemed that, once more, nobody was home to respond.

Maybe she's gone away somewhere. That might explain why the message didn't go through on her phone.

He turned and made his way back to the car. There seemed to be a problem with the lock. The key didn't slide in the way that it was supposed to.

Fuck.

The concentration made his head spin so he looked up to clear it. The sight that greeted him drove all thoughts of locks and keys from his mind. A couple was approaching at a leisurely pace on the opposite side of the street. The man, somewhere in his early twenties, had the look that people referred to as 'hipster'. His black jeans were tight and tapered. He had a herringbone jacket over a waistcoat and starched white shirt. His hair was shaved around the sides and carefully teased, voluminously, to one side on top. He sported a meticulously trimmed beard and moustache, the sides of which were lifting as he laughed at something the stunning young woman, whose shoulders he had his arm around, had just said. The woman was Vicki.

For a moment Anxo's rage propelled him forward but a cold, sober part of his brain broke through almost immediately and brought him to a halt.

Don't show your hand. Wait and see how far the bitch has gone with this pompous fuck.

He watched, seething, as the two came to a stop outside Vicki's apartment. They faced each other, Vicki looking up with that sexy, coy smirk that had driven him wild on the first night that she and Anxo had met. With her habitual micro miniskirt, and stiletto heels, her tanned legs looked impossibly long and sexy. Her hair was hanging loose and wild. The combination of his anger and desire almost choked him.

Fuck.

The hipster said something and Vicki laughed. She put the key in the door and opened it. She took a step inside and switched on the hall light before turning back to face the young man. There was an awkward moment and then they came slowly together, mouth crushing mouth hungrily. Anxo's blood boiled.

Fuck.

Breaking contact suddenly, Vicki backstepped into the hallway of her apartment. The man made a move to follow but she stopped him with a restraining hand on his chest. She said something, flashed him a seductive smile, moved back further and closed the door slowly but decisively in his face. The hipster stood for a moment gazing through the glass panel until the hall light snapped off. Then he turned, smirking, and strode jauntily away in the direction that he and Vicki had come from.

Adrenalin pumping, Anxo stormed across the road and pressed the doorbell. After a moment the hall light came on, throwing a bright glow through the glass. He sank into the shadows to one side of the door. Then, as it began to open, he stepped forward and gave it a shove. Vicki's hand was in the process of slipping the chain off the retainer and behind it he saw her face switch from smiling anticipation to stunned shock. The door gave for a few inches and then jolted to an abrupt halt as the chain, having snapped from her grasp, stretched taut.

"You're some fucking girlfriend," Anxo growled. "I've been lying half dead in hospital while you've been off mooning over that smarmy, faggot–haired bastard."

Vicki, recovering from her initial shock, stared at him contemptuously. Her face was flushed and her eyes flared with an anger to match his own.

"Oh that's rich, Anxo. How's your daughter? The daughter that you invented so you could screw around on your pregnant wife."

It was Anxo's turn to look stunned.

"Yes," sneered Vicki, seeing her thrust find its mark. "I know all about it, Anxo. Your wife and I had a good long chat about what a complete *coño* you are."

Anxo stared through the gap between door frame and door where Vicki's taunting face mocked him. He felt his blood boil. With a curse he threw himself at the door. Vicki recoiled in alarm but the chain held and Anxo stumbled back. Before he had a chance to recover his balance Vicki had slammed the door shut.

"Open the fucking door, you bitch," he roared, taking a kick at the glass panel.

"Fuck off, Anxo," yelled Vicki. "Fuck off or I'll call the police."

The implications penetrated Anxo's fog of alcohol and anger. He forced himself to laugh drily.

"Okay, Vicki. I'll go – for now. But you've been a heartless, interfering bitch and you're going to pay for that. You and that bitch wife of mine and maybe that prick in the suit too."

He pressed his face up against the glass until he could see Vicki. She met his stare defiantly.

"I know you think I'm just mouthing off but you'll see."

Without breaking eye contact he slammed the door suddenly with the palm of his hand and smiled sadistically as Vicki jumped in fright. He turned and made his way back to the Citroen. The cold anger had sobered him somewhat and he had no difficulty with the key this time. He climbed in, started the engine and gunned the accelerator.

At the sound of the car pulling away, Vicki opened the door and watched the little yellow Citroen reach the end of the road before turning in the direction of the old town.

In the living room she sat down, picked up the TV remote and then began to shake uncontrollably. Five minutes later the TV screen was still blank. She hadn't moved. Horror scenarios were racing through her mind. What if the chain hadn't held? What if he came back in the night? How could she make sure she would be safe in the future? Should she tell someone?

He's drunk. He'll feel like an idiot in the morning.

Then another thought struck her.

What about his wife?

She felt a surge of pity but there was little she could do. She had her own worries.

He's just drunk. He wouldn't really do anything.

The words rang hollow. There had been a look on his face as he stared through the glass at her. A look she hadn't seen before. A look that frightened her more than anything he'd said or done in his drunken anger.

Still. It's none of my business.

She clicked a channel at random on the remote and the room was filled with the canned laughter of a cheap, South American TV serial. She flicked through a few channels and then, with a curse, clicked off the set, got up and went into the kitchen. She opened the door of the fridge and stood there.

I promised. I told her I'd tell her if he got in touch.

With a shrug she opened the freezer compartment and took out the bottle of vodka that she kept there.

There's not much I can do. I threw her bloody number away.

MELBOURNE, AUSTRALIA

AS THE FLIGHT ATTENDANT began to pass through the cabin with an aerosol can firing from each hand to dowse the passengers with a fine, chemical mist of pesticide, Helen hurriedly rummaged through her bag. Pablo, the pin cushion, came to hand and she used him to cover her mouth against the fumes. She was exhausted from over 24 hours of travelling across a number of time zones but Angela's beautiful piece of work revived her as she thought of being reunited with her granddaughter before long. She turned her attention back to the mustard coloured 'Incoming Passenger Card' before her. At the part where it asked 'Do you have any criminal conviction/s?' she was momentarily tempted to put 'I didn't know you still needed one' – but thought the better of it. Customs officials, in her experience, weren't noted for their sense of humour.

The wait on the tarmac at Tullamarine Airport seemed painfully long with all onboard anxious to escape the confines of the plane. Then came the long, weary queue at the entry control point where her passenger card and passport were checked. It was at some predawn hour of the morning and, between the tired passengers and weary staff, there were few smiles apparent on faces. She got a pleasant boost when her luggage was among the first to pop out onto the carousel. Loading it onto a trolley, she wrestled it to customs and quarantine where she presented her Incoming Passenger Card again and declared that she had nothing to declare.

At last, she broke through the last barrier of the arrivals system and found herself confronted by a sea of expectant people, all awaiting friends, business associates, clients or loved ones. Some held small signs with the names of the passengers they had come to meet. The tech–savvy ones had the names displayed on tablets. Helen stifled a laugh as she saw one man whose attempt at bored nonchalance was somewhat ruined by the fact that the tablet upon which he had presumably been displaying a name had somehow been flicked into camera mode and was, instead, displaying a preview of his crotch as seen by the device's front camera. To make matters worse, his zipper was at half mast.

Someone should tell him.

Then her eye caught her own name written boldly and neatly on a sheet of A4 card just beside the unfortunate with the tablet. She looked at the bearer and found herself appraising a young man somewhere in his 30s. He had a healthy, smart look about him and features that seemed as if they smiled readily. He saw her looking and raised his eyebrows in query. She made her way towards him and his face broke out into that promised smile.

"Helen?"

"Yes."

"I'm Nick, Tony's mate. They're dying to see you but they knew how much you wanted to surprise Angela so I said I'd swing by and pick you up. I hope that's okay."

"Oh great. You're very good."

"No worries," he smiled as he took over control of the trolley and led her towards the exit.

"Welcome to Australia. We should hit Bendigo in about

an hour and a half. There's little or no traffic at this ungodly hour of the morning."

SANTIAGO DE COMPOSTELA, SPAIN

VICKI WAITED until the taxi had pulled away before approaching the house. There was a light on in a downstairs room. Cautiously, she peered through the window. Inside, Isabel was kneeling, very still, at the far end of the room. In front of her, on a dresser, a candle was burning in front of a small, religious statue.

She's praying.

Vicki, until then consumed by anxiety, felt a pang of pity. She waited, observing, until Isabel crossed herself, stood and left the room. Then she made her way, cautiously, to the front door. She raised the heavy knocker, took a deep breath, and let it fall. A moment later the door opened. Isabel stared at her.

"Is Anxo here?" whispered Vicki urgently.

"You want to see my husband?"

"God no, Isabel. I came to... Look, I'm so sorry but he came to my apartment looking for me. He's drunk. He was really aggressive."

A distraught look flashed across the older woman's face but she recovered her composure quickly.

"You'd better come in."

Isabel began to lead her into the living room then thought better of it.

"Actually, let's go into the kitchen."

As Vicki followed her she glanced through the open doorway and saw the candle still burning in front of the statue. As it happened, the kitchen proved to be even more poignant. The table was set out for two, complete with wine glasses, and food simmered on the stove, filling the room with an appetising smell. Vicki's heart sank further as the broader consequences of the news she bore struck her.

It took her just a few minutes to fill Isabel in on the events of the evening. Vicki watched the other's face grow pale.

"I'm so sorry but I was worried. I would have phoned but I lost your number."

She didn't realise that she had glanced at Isabel's swollen stomach until Anxo's wife put a self conscious hand on it. Vicki looked away, disconcerted.

"I thought I should let you know."

"Thanks."

There was an awkward silence.

"Look, if you need somewhere to stay..."

Isabel, stared at her blankly and then the significance of Vicki's words seemed to hit her and she choked back a sob.

"Oh God."

She stood up, embarrassed, turned and stumbled over to the stove where she raised the lid on whatever was cooking there, picked up a utensil and stirred the food.

"Look," she said, without turning around. "I really appreciate you coming to let me know and I don't mean to be rude but I think I need to be alone now."

"Of course."

Vicki turned at the front door.

"What are you going to do?"

Isabel, dry eyed but tear streaked, looked frail, broken and ever so vulnerable.

"I don't know."

"Really, I think you should come with me, Isabel."

"I know you mean well, but this is my husband that we're talking about. I think I can deal with my own husband."

She began to close the door, brooking no argument. As the lock clicked home with a sense of finality Vicki was overcome with a foreboding of disaster.

If she had seen what he was like... I should have convinced her.

She hesitated, staring at the forbidding, old wooden door. At that moment she was startled by a noise behind her. She spun around in alarm. The scream that rose as she found herself staring into Anxo's face was choked off before it could escape. His features contorted in rage as his hands dug, agonisingly, into her neck, cutting off the oxygen and filling her head with blind panic. She grasped his wrists and wrestled but her efforts seemed feeble against his grip of steel. She stared with horrified pleading into the eyes of her former lover and saw only cold, merciless rage there. Her chest was burning agonisingly and her head was pounding.

I'm going to die.

It was over quickly. One moment Vicki's bulging eyes were staring into his as she twisted and struggled and then he almost lost his balance as her body went limp in his hands and she sank, unresistingly to the ground. Kneeling as she fell, Anxo maintained the pressure on her slender neck for a few moments more. There was no reaction. Panting he let go and she fell like a discarded rag doll. For a moment he felt breathless at the enormity of what he had done and then a feeling of elation welled up, charging him with a sense of his power.

I warned the bitch.

Glancing around to ensure that he continued to be unobserved he grabbed the body by its long, smooth legs and dragged it towards an area of the garden that lay in shadow. The hair trailed behind like seaweed and the miniskirt slowly rose up over the hips, exposing tiny underwear. In the low light Anxo couldn't decide if it was white or some pastel colour.

What a fucking waste.

His hands were encased in thin, rubber surgical gloves from the box of 100 that Isabel kept in the glovebox of the car for cleaning. He checked that they were still securely in place before he opened the small handbag that hung from Vicki's damaged neck. He removed her phone. To his relief, there was no password lock. He found the message that he had sent her and deleted it before replacing the handset. Leaving the body in the shadows, he walked briskly around the house, peering in through the lit windows one by one until he found Isabel. She was in the living room, kneeling in front of her homemade altar to San Tiago. He took out a cigarette. To his annoyance, his hand was shaking violently as he tried to light it.

She's dead. I did it.

He took a deep, steadying breath and lit the cigarette at the second attempt.

And now it's Isabel's turn.

As he drew on the cigarette, he stared at the figure of his wife through the window. When he'd arrived at the house there had been nothing more than vague violence on his mind but seeing Vicki and Isabel together had stirred the embers of an idea. Now, the first part of that plan had been carried out. It was time to go through with part two. No weakness. But the story had to hold together. No mistakes.

I couldn't stop her, officer. Vicki must have come looking for me when she hadn't heard in so long. Isabel went crazy. She said some terrible things. Of course I don't blame her. She didn't know that I'd been having an affair. It was all my fault. They fought. I tried so hard to move but I couldn't. If only the doctors could have done something... If only I wasn't paralysed I could have stopped it.

He wondered how long he'd have to pretend to remain bed bound before he could safely stage his miraculous recovery. In fact, it might be better to make a slow return to health.

Baby steps. Nobody believes in miracles.

As he took a last drag on his cigarette, his eyes fixed on his wife whose gaze, in turn, was fixed on the statue, he thought about the strange, wandering priest. By this time he'd be safely back in the USA where they were too caught up in the fall out from their own gun crime society to pay any attention to murders and suicides in obscure Spanish cities.

Then it all went quiet, officer. When Isabel came in I knew something was terribly wrong. I can't remember the exact words but she told me that she'd killed Vicki. "I've strangled your bitch", is what she said, I think. The way she looked at me... For a moment I thought she was going to kill me too. There was nothing I could have done to protect myself... Maybe it would have been better if she had.

Ooh, he liked that. He would falter there and, if possible, shed a few tears. With his looks he would have made a superb actor. People had always said so. Yes, tears, and he'd mention the baby.

Did you know? She was carrying my baby. That's why I ended things with Vicki. I really wanted to give my marriage a chance. I've been selfish and stupid but I loved my wife. I think, deep down, she knew that. I think that might be why she didn't kill me – why she killed herself and our baby. She knew that would be the worst possible punishment for me.

He checked that the gloves were intact and properly in place again. He had been lucky with Vicki. He had overpowered her so quickly that she had hardly fought back at all. He couldn't afford to get so much as a scratch. Any sign of injury on him and his story was fucked. He would need to take Isabel by surprise and restrain her so that she couldn't fight him.

I'll have to use something soft. Struggle marks are okay because she could have got them in the fight with Vicki, but not rope marks.

As he made his way to the patio door he was weighing up the possibilities presented by nylon tights.

"ANYTHING STRANGE?" asked Subinspector Pedrosa of the duty officer as he crossed the reception area and tapped in the code that would grant him access to the offices that lay behind the 'staff only' door.

"Nah. Usual stuff."

Pedrosa made his way to the open–plan office he shared with the other members of his unit. It was empty as he'd known it would be this late in the evening. He'd been at a meeting with a group who worked with *peregrinos* on the *Camino*. A number of women had been confronted by a flasher at a certain spot on the trail over recent weeks and the group wanted reassurances that the police had a plan to apprehend the pervert. Pedrosa had expected the meeting to take about an hour. As it happened it had dragged on for several. Now, the subinspector needed just to grab his jacket and clock out for the day.

He was about to leave when he noticed an official buff coloured envelope in the tray on his desk. He picked it up and tore it open. Inside were the set of bank statements he'd been granted permission to examine as part of his investigation into the circumstances surrounding the death of Helio Pereira.

Anxo De Medeiros's expenditure was consistent. He topped up at the same petrol station every few days and always with just €10 worth of petrol. The little Citroen was clearly fuel efficient. There was a direct debit coming out of the account each month for his mobile phone bill – Pedrosa was still awaiting clearance to look at that. There were some internet purchases... And then he saw it. Several days before the burglary took place at his home, De Medeiros had withdrawn €500 from a *Cajero*. The date coincided with the anecdotal accounts of Helio Pereira's sudden financial windfall.

Pedrosa sank into his leather office chair and clicked the mouse to bring the computer out of sleep mode. Opening the web browser, he typed in the location details of the transaction from the statement and clicked on 'search'. A map appeared in a pop–up screen.

Bingo.

The cash machine was within two blocks of the dead burglar's house.

My God. I was right. The bastard paid to have his wife killed.

He wasn't aware of exactly when the suspicion had begun to grow on him. His attraction for Isabel had doubtlessly complicated matters. It had been difficult for him to know if he was acting on professional instinct or base jealousy. Now, however, his suspicions were supported with evidence and a warm glow of vindication spread over him like a balm.

He sent the page, showing the cash machine's location, to print. He'd need more than circumstantial evidence to nail the bastard but now he knew what he was looking for. *Cajeros* had cameras. Perhaps Pereira had been with De Medeiros when he made the withdrawal. He had a lot of work to do to ensure that the case he built was rock solid. For now, he felt, Isabel was safe. De Medeiros wouldn't be stupid enough to try anything so soon after the death of Pereira and, what's more, he was all but paralysed. The latter point assured him both that Isabel was safe and that her husband wouldn't be going anywhere any time soon.

The subinspector slipped the printout into the envelop with the bank statements, locked the envelope into the drawer in his desk and strode out of the police station. He felt warmed by his glow of satisfaction. Tomorrow he'd approach his boss with what he'd discovered and request some additional staff to secure the footage from the cash machine as well as any surveillance cameras in the surrounding area.

I'm coming for you. Just you wait, cabrón.

IN THE END it proved pathetically easy. Almost ten minutes had passed by the time Anxo had let himself in, crept upstairs and helped himself to three of Isabel's winter scarves from her wardrobe along with a pillowcase from the hot press in the landing. When he descended, he found his wife still knelt, trancelike, in front of the statue of the saint where he had left her.

He approached patiently, stealthily. If she heard him and confronted him he had no doubt that he could overpower her but he couldn't afford to risk injury to himself. He had tied the scarves loosely but securely around his waist. He held the pillowcase, scrunched, accordion–like, in both hands and raised, ready, before him. The room was dim, lit only by the glow of the streetlights and the candle that burned a steady, tall flame. He had covered more than half the distance between the door and the prone figure of his wife when the strangest thought crossed his mind.

She knows.

The thought stopped him in his tracks.

Don't be ridiculous.

The same thought crossed his mind again, however, when he brought the pillowcase suddenly over her head and shoulders, pinning her arms to her sides. Instead of the scream that he was ready to stifle as quickly as possible with one of the scarves, Isabel's body convulsed and she gasped out just one word.

"Anxo."

She hadn't seen his face but she knew that it was him. There was no question in her voice. It was a statement. He was glad that the pillowcase hid her from him. It made it all easier.

It's a painless death. It'll be over soon.

As he began to tie her, Isabel started to shake with heartbroken sobs, like a little girl whose pet kitten is lost. For just a moment his resolve weakened. But it was just a moment. He remembered the dead girl outside. Once, as a young boy, he'd brought a pigeon tumbling out of the sky with a freak shot from his air rifle. His first thrill of exhilaration had turned to disconcertment when, on approaching the fallen bird, it became obvious that it was badly injured but still alive. He had agonised between trying to nurse it back to health and putting it out of its misery for a minute or two before calculating that it was more humane to end the animal's suffering. However, the rock that he had thrown down upon the small, struggling bird was badly aimed and only succeeded in shattering a wing in an explosion of feathers without killing the creature. Now, however, it was too badly mutilated for him to do anything other than proceed with his efforts to end its life. It took two further attempts before the pigeon's crushed corpse stopped moving. The guilt had come back periodically to haunt him for several years thereafter.

A mixed sense of nausea and inevitability had begun to replace the initial high that had followed Vicki's death. It reminded him of the incident with the bird.

There's no going back now. Isabel has to die. There's no other way out.

Leaving the pillowcase in place he used the smallest of the scarves as a gag to muffle the sobs, that were more disturbing to him than screams. Then, with the others, he secured her arms and legs. His anger was gone. It had been replaced with a grim, adrenalin–fueled determination.

I've only one chance to get this right. Pedrosa suspects me already. No mistakes.

Lifting Isabel's dead weight, he carried her to the door that communicated with the garage. Her body was warm in his hands. The last time that he had held her in this position was eight years before when he had carried her across the threshold in her wedding dress – the dress that she had donated to the charity shop.

No weakness.

He set her down where he would be able to keep an eye on her through the open door as he prepared her 'suicide'. He raised the garage door so that he would be able to drive straight in then left the house by the patio to minimise the chances of being seen. He glanced at the shadows where the body of his former mistress lay concealed as he made his way towards where he had parked the car, half expecting to see her ghostly form emerging to haunt him with his deed. But all was deadly quiet. It took him a cautious five minutes to reach the car. When he had parked it safely in the garage, closed the door behind it and checked that his wife lay where he had left her, he breathed a sigh of relief.

He almost burned himself as he went to attach the spare hose from the washing machine outlet onto the still–hot exhaust but was saved by a rag he decided to use to avoid getting his gloved hands dirty.

Close call. That would have been hard to explain.

He had been fortunate that the car was so old. According to the suicide assistance website, the low carbon emissions in newer cars would have foiled his plan. As he applied gaffer tape to seal the gap between the larger exhaust pipe and the rubber hose a thought struck him.

Fingerprints.

The surgical gloves would take care that his prints were not on the hose but the absence of Isabel's would be equally damning. He glanced through the open doorway to where she lay, her body shaking slightly as she continued to sob. He would have to keep track of any item she was supposed to have touched and press them into her dead hands afterwards. There were so many things to think of, so many ways to go wrong. Murder was turning out to be a complex affair. His huge advantage was that his story relied on him being paralysed on the sofa while Isabel, having killed Vicki, took her own life. That meant that he would have extra time. He could not, after all, be expected to call the emergency services immediately.

It was horrible, officer. I heard the engine start up and thought she was leaving but when the garage door didn't open and the car continued to run I realised what she was doing. I dragged myself onto the floor. I think it must have been over an hour before I managed to wriggle over to the table where the phone was and knock it over so I could call 112.

Yes. An hour should give him time to make sure that Isabel was dead and all the boxes ticked. He'd have to shower and change to get rid of the smell of exhaust fumes...

No. By that time they'll probably be leaking into the house.

He fed the loose end of the hose through the back window of the Citroen and then sat into the drivers seat. As he put the key in the ignition he made a mental note that Isabel's fingerprints would have to be found on that also. The engine, hot from having been used recently, started on the first turn.

BENDIGO, AUSTRALIA

ANGELA HAD HEARD the gentle knock on the front door and the footsteps of somebody passing down the hallway to answer it with the detached curiosity of semi sleep. Chewy, however, had been wide awake at the first noise and was watching the door. He stood on the end of the bed with his ears twitching forward and his little tail – which wagged slightly from side to side – sticking out behind. He gave a bark and jumped onto the floor when Mammy's voice called out.

"Angela. Come here, darling."

This might have something to do with the surprise they've been talking about.

She was wide awake now. She swung out from beneath the covers. Chewy wagged his tail furiously and ran to the door, pushing his nose into the crack in a futile attempt to open it with his snout. He glanced back at Angela, who was putting her feet into her slippers, and barked impatiently. She dashed out of the room and down the stairs overtaking the puppy who was still small enough to treat the steps with a degree of caution. She entered the living room and stopped dead, her mouth falling open in absolute delight. Mammy, Uncle Tony and his friend Nick were all there, grinning in anticipation, but she barely noticed them. Sitting on a low armchair, was Granny, her face beaming with pleasure. She held out the little pin cushion man that Angela had made for her.

"This little fella has been missing you," she said. "I told you I'd bring him back."

Angela dashed to embrace her. But a yapping bundle of

fur proved faster. Chewy, back on level ground after the challenge of the stairs, hurtled past and launched himself at the waving toy in Granny's outstretched hand.

"Chewy! No!"

Angela knew that the voice was too young to belong to anyone else in the room but it took her a moment to realise that it was her own.

SANTIAGO DE COMPOSTELA, SPAIN

ANXO WATCHED as light bluish smoke began to pour out of the hose pipe and into the car.

The engine's hot so it shouldn't be smoking. Must be burning oil.

The smell of the fumes reached him.

Time to get my wife.

The thought had scarcely entered his mind when the most agonising pain seized his entire body. He screamed and slumped sidewise, the handbrake pushed up into his stomach. But he couldn't feel it. He was totally paralysed.

BENDIGO, AUSTRALIA

THERE WAS A MOMENT of stunned silence during which the puppy chewed happily on the pin cushion man and everyone stared, delightedly, at Angela. Then everybody began to talk at once and Mammy had her enveloped in a huge hug.

"Oh my baby."

Angela tested her newfound voice.

"I love you Mammy."

SANTIAGO DE COMPOSTELA, SPAIN

ANXO'S SCREAM HAD penetrated the cloud of despair that was filling Isabel's mind. She could hear the uneven rhythm of the Citroen's engine but all other sounds had ceased. Whatever Anxo had used to gag her was covering one ear but the other was free. She lay motionless, listening intently for a while. Nothing. She began to test the bindings that held her, but Anxo had secured her tightly. She couldn't work anything loose. Once more, she began her prayer to the saint.

San Tiago. Please come to my aid for my sake and the sake of my baby.

Perhaps ten minutes had passed before the exhaust fumes reached her and cut off her mantra with a chilling thought.

The car has been running so the garage will be filling with fumes. He is killing me with the car fumes.

She wondered about the scream. She wondered if he was nearby, watching her die. The coughing began and, with her body tied in such an unnatural position, the restriction on her lungs made it more painful. She fought down the panic as her instinct for survival kicked in.

Panic won't help.

She tried, desperately, to wriggle to safety away from the source of the fumes. In the semi darkness of the house, she could make very little out through the fabric of the pillowcase, but she was guided by the direction of the engine noise. Her attempts to move away from it, though, had little success and the exertion had the effect of exacerbating the coughing. Her head was pounding and she was beginning to feel nauseous. She tried to return to her prayer to San Tiago but, instead, a vision of Subinspector Pedro Pedrosa bursting through the front door to save her in a scene like a Hollywood movie popped into her mind.

Why did I think of him?

The nausea worsened and, with her mouth gagged, she fought down the urge to vomit. A bout of coughing wracked her body and her head burned.

San Tiago...

Then all went black. In that blackness, she saw the vision of an old man with flowing hair that seemed to merge with a long, indeterminate cloak or robe. He was smiling gently at her and, suddenly a joyful sense of calm washed away her pain, her despair and her panic. He held out his hand and, despite the ties that bound her, she clasped it as she slipped into oblivion.

14. Revelation

*One woe is past; and, behold,
there come two woes more hereafter.*

SANTIAGO DE COMPOSTELA, SPAIN

DESPITE HIS CONSIDERABLE AGE, the man moved with a sense of urgency. A glance at the digital numbers displayed above the stainless steel doors of two elevators revealed that they were occupied several levels above, so he bypassed them and took the stairs instead. In answer to his query, a nurse on the third floor pointed to a door further down the corridor. When he entered the room he found Isabel lying motionless, a respiratory mask covering her lower face and an assortment of wires running from beneath the sheet to a machine that was displaying information on her vital signs. A man was sitting by the bedside. He had been gazing at her but turned and rose to his feet when the other entered.

"Señor Cardosa?" asked the younger man.

He spoke in a low voice and Isabel's Godfather matched the tone.

"Yes."

"I'm Subinspector Pedrosa."

"How is she?" asked Cardosa as they shook hands. "What happened?"

"She's okay. She had a pretty bad headache when she woke and she was very traumatised so they've given her something to help her sleep."

Pedrosa glanced at the pale, strained face on the pillow then at Cardosa.

"Shall we step outside so that we don't disturb her?"

They found a quiet corner in sight of Isabel's room and sat.

"Señor Cardosa, we have official policies when it comes to what we can reveal in cases like this but I'm going to be completely frank with you and trust that you'll be discreet."

Cardosa nodded.

"Isabel was still in shock so we were only able to get the bare bones of the story from her. We're still piecing what happened together. We've got some of the details from another source and, until your Goddaughter is in a position to fill in the blanks, we're guessing the rest."

Pedrosa glancing at the passersby in the busy corridor, leaned closer to the older man and lowered his tone.

"Since the burglary at the house I've been working on the theory that we were dealing with something more than a straightforward robbery that went wrong. In fact, to put it simply, I suspected that your Goddaughter's husband knew more than he let on. Yesterday evening I found evidence that not only supported that view but suggested that the so–called burglar, Helio Pereira, was hired by Isabel's husband to kill her."

Cardosa's face went first pale and then bright red.

"Where's the fucking bastard."

"Dead."

Cardosa blinked.

"What?"

"De Medeiros died of carbon monoxide poisoning in his car last night."

He hurriedly corrected himself.

"Well, in the interests of accuracy, we haven't had the autopsy report to confirm it but the hose pipe from the exhaust in through the back window of the car suggests that that's what they'll find."

Cardosa looked stunned.

"Suicide?"

"I don't believe so. Of course, it *is* possible that he was engaged in some sort of murder suicide attempt... but I'm pretty sure that he was trying to kill Isabel and make it look like she had committed suicide. My guess is that, somehow, something went wrong and he ended up killing himself instead."

Cardosa's face was ashen. He said nothing but was clearly clinging to the policeman's every word.

"De Medeiros had been having an affair with a young woman before all this happened," continued Pedrosa. "Isabel found out about it and confronted her while De Medeiros was in hospital. The young woman – Vicki – told her that it was all over and she agreed to let Isabel know if Anxo made contact with her again.

"I can't believe that Isabel gave the bastard a second chance," said Cordosa, his voice quivering with anger.

"I imagine that she wanted to give her marriage every possible chance because of the baby."

Cordosa stared.

"What? Baby?"

The confused look on his face cleared to one of wonder as the penny dropped.

"Are you telling me that Isabel is pregnant?"

Pedrosa reddened.

"I... I thought you knew."

"No."

Cardosa glanced at the door of the room in which his Goddaughter lay, his features clearly showing the fight that he was engaged in to bring his emotions under control.

"I'm sorry. I wouldn't have said..." began Pedrosa, flustered. He ran a hand absentmindedly through his hair.

"It seems that I've breached a confidence."

The older man paused and then brushed the policeman's concerns aside with a wave of his hand.

"I've seen my Goddaughter quite frequently through all this mess and I'm observant enough to have noticed if she were more than two or three months gone. I'm sure she would have told me soon enough. Just tell me all you know about what happened to her."

Pedrosa nodded.

"It seems that Anxo's paralysis was fake or that he made a sudden recovery. Either way, he showed up at Vicki's apartment drunk and aggressive yesterday evening. When she told him she wanted nothing to do with him he left in a pretty violent mood. She was concerned about Isabel's safety so she went over to her home to tell her what had happened in the hope that she'd get out of there before Anxo showed up but Isabel insisted on staying. As Vicki left she was attacked by De Medeiros and throttled to within an inch of her life. She blacked out. When she came too she went straight to the nearest neighbour and they called us. I was already in the car on my way home when the call came in so I was on the scene within minutes. I found Isabel tied and gagged on the floor unconscious from exhaust fumes that had been leaking into the house from the garage. De Medeiros was dead in the driver's seat of the car."

He paused and watched the older man struggle to take it all in.

"So if you hadn't arrived..."

"Actually, much as I'd love to be the hero, my arrival had nothing to do with it. I noticed from his bank statements that De Medeiros never put more than €10 of petrol into the car at a time. I reckon that's what saved your Goddaughter. The car ran out of gas."

The old man's face was ashen and he slumped in the chair.

"I realise that this is all very unnerving but the worse of it is over," said Pedrosa. "They say that both mother and baby should be fine."

Cardosa shook his head.

"Maybe Isabel will be fine physically but who knows what effect this will have on her. She's bound to be badly traumatised. I never took to that husband of hers and neither did her father but this... I don't think either of us would have believed that even he could..."

Lost for words, he sighed deeply, and glanced at the door of Isabel's room. When he spoke again his voice was more controlled.

"It was the money that he was after. Her father didn't trust him an inch. His will put a hold on her inheritance until her marriage had lasted ten years. Anxo only had two to go before he got his hands on a fortune."

"And with her dead?"

"As I said, I don't think anybody dreamed that he would kill for the money. I'd have to check but, as far as I know, there was no provision for denying Anxo the inheritance if Isabel died before the ten years were up."

"Money brings out the worst in people," said the policeman. "They kill for a lot less than a fortune."

The two men felt silent for a moment before Pedrosa spoke again.

"I'll have someone from victim support with her as soon she comes around."

"It's going to be tough but she's young and she's her father's daughter," said the older man. "And I'll be there every step of the way. She'll come through."

The policeman nodded.

"I've no doubt about it."

ROD WAS weighed down by a burden of doubt. He had risen early with the idea of setting off alone but had found Álvaro downstairs putting some final items into a backpack. The *vagabundo* made a feeble protest about taking on his new apostolic role.

"I don't know what I should be doing," he complained. "I'm not a priest like Delucci. I don't even have a bible."

Álvaro smiled patiently.

"I'm sure you'll know what to do when it is time to do it."

Rod snorted in annoyance and sipped his coffee. Later, he protested again when Álvaro presented him with a neat, leather–bound bible just before they left.

"I can't take this."

"Oh, I insist," said Álvaro's mother who was fussing over them both. "It would be an honour to know that my bible was being used on your mission."

Rod raised his eyes.

"Now I am on a mission. Fantastic."

He turned to Álvaro and grunted.

"*Vamos, chico.*"

They set off, following the blue arrows that marked the way for those pilgrims who were returning from Santiago rather than the yellow ones that led to the city. Rod walked quickly and Álvaro, sensing that the *vagabundo* needed time with his thoughts, followed a couple of paces behind. Before long they began encountering back–packing *peregrinos* who inevitably greeted them with a nod of respect.

You guys are returning from Santiago. You've have achieved what we're trying to achieve.

Álvaro returned each nod with a *buen Camino*. Rod scarcely noticed them. It was towards evening when he did, however, take note of one particularly large pilgrim who was labouring in the heat of the sun. It was on an onerous section where the way took to the hard tarmac of the N550. The young man managed a nod of acknowledgement but was too out of breath to accompany it with words.

"*Buen Camino*," grunted Rod, somewhat begrudgingly.

They had marched all day without stopping to eat. In the shade of a large barn Rod halted to take some water and Álvaro overtook him.

"I got a message from my mother. She has contacted some friends of hers. We can stay there tonight if you want. They had heard about you and the *Padre* so they're quite keen to meet you."

Rod gave an exasperated sigh.

"Look *chico*. It's not me that they're keen to meet. It's Delucci. It was all Delucci. I'm just a *vagabundo*. I'm a drunk. A drunk who hasn't had a drink for too long."

He faltered.

"That's it. I need a drink."

Álvaro looked pleadingly.

"Rod. What you decide to do is up to you but the *Padre* believed in you."

The *vagabundo* shook his head.

"Delucci wouldn't be the first to believe in me and he wouldn't be the first to be wrong."

Álvaro tried again.

"He started something here. Something important. And for some reason he believed that you could continue it. I know you doubt yourself but while we were walking he told me that his path had been full of doubt too. It was doubt that brought him here in the first place."

"You can't compare," snapped Rod. "Delucci is a priest. He is an actual preacher. You know – he could say Mass. He could give blessings. He got bloody signs from God, for God's sake. There's no comparison!"

He stormed a few paces back along the way that they had just come and then stopped.

"What am I going back for? You go back. I'm going to get a drink."

He turned again and marched back to where the chastened young man was standing. He slipped his backpack off as he walked. He fumbled with the clasp, reached in and withdrew the bible.

"Give this back to your mother," he said pushing the book into Álvaro's hands. Unprepared, the young man fumbled and dropped the leather–bound volume onto ground. Rod's anger evaporated instantly. The two men stared for a moment at the holy book lying open and face down in the dust, then they both bent to pick it up. Their heads collided painfully. Álvaro fell backwards against the wall of the barn.

"Are you okay," Rod asked, rubbing his head and looking with concern.

"Yeah. I'll be fine."

Rod scurried over to him.

"Honestly, I'm fine."

But Rod wasn't looking at him. His eyes were fixed on a spot at the base of the wall behind.

"*Chico*. Look."

Together they gazed at the neat writing in blue chalk.
Juan 15:27

Álvaro snatched up the bible. He made as if to turn the page and then froze. Open mouthed he held the book for Rod›s attention. The facing pages were dirtied where they had lain in the dirt, open at that point. Álvaro›s finger pointed to the heading on the page.

John

He then pointed midway down the second column on the right hand page.

15:27.

He read out loud.

"Y vosotros daréis testimonio también, porque habéis estado conmigo desde el principio."

And you also shall bear witness, because you have been with me from the beginning.

Reverently, Rod took the bible, closed it and put his lips to the cover. As he replaced it securely into his backpack, he returned the younger man's beaming smile. He swung the pack onto its accustomed place over his shoulder.

"Vamos, chico. I don't have a clue what it is we're supposed to do – but let's get going and do it."

THE NURSE finished noting down the readings from the monitor and dropped the clipboard back into the mesh tray at the foot of the bed.

"That's all fine," she said with a brief smile before hurrying out of the room. Alone once more, Isabel's gaze fell back to her swollen stomach and the thought returned.

Part of him is still alive in this tiny person that's growing inside me. How do I feel about that?

She placed a hand where she knew the feet were but the child failed to kick on cue. She stared up at the ceiling – a vast, white expanse broken only by a single light bulb in the centre.

"Isabel?"

She looked up to see Vicki, poised uncertainly at the doorway. It was on the tip of her tongue to dismiss Anxo's lover but her eyes were drawn to the ugly purple marks around the young woman's neck and the dark rings around her eyes. She too had put her trust in him and she too had suffered for it.

"I hear that you were the one who got the police. Thanks."

Vicki crossed the room and sat on the plastic visitors' chair the end of the bed.

"I should have come looking for you to see if you were okay."

"No, you did the right thing. I should have left when you suggested it... But I guess I had to find out for myself."

She glanced at the younger woman's face and Vicki smiled.

"That's totally understandable. How were you to know?"

There was an awkward silence.

"So, baby and you. You're both okay?"

"We're fine. They're only keeping me in as a precaution. What about you?"

"I've just been discharged. I thought I'd drop by to see how you were before I headed off."

She held out a small paper bag.

"Cherries," she said. "A friend brought them but I don't eat fruit."

Isabel forced a smile but didn't move to take them. Vicki stood and put the bag on the locker at the bedside.

"Well, I'd better get going. Take care of yourself."

"Thanks. You too."

Vicki hadn't quite left the room before Isabel felt the tear on her cheek. She blinked it away angrily but the seal had been broken. At first they trickled softly. Then, as she surrendered to all that she'd been holding inside, the tears gathered force and the emotions began to empty themselves in torrents down her face. She wept for wasted time and misspent love. She sobbed for the naive young girl of that distant sunny day in Alameda Park and the friends she'd lost in the twists and turns of the years. She cried for her unborn child and its uncertain future.

San Tiago. I need your help.

For those who may be thinking of walking the Camino...

First of all, if you're here because you've just read Pins and Needles, thanks for doing so. I hope you enjoyed it.

In researching the book I walked the last stage of the Portuguese Way – the stretch from Valença where the stories of Fr Delucci, the *vagabundo* and Mark are played out – over ten times. I wanted to make the background to the story as credible as possible and, while the *Camino Portugués* dates back to the middle ages, it does change from time to time with such things as minor re-routes to improve the experience for the growing number of people walking it each year.

Some have the time, dedication and motivation to take on the 800km length of the French way or to undertake similarly lengthy trips on one of the other, lesser known routes. To get your certificate or *compostela*, however, you must complete just 100 kilometres on foot. This makes an ideal one week trip, averaging 20 kilometres a day for five days with a couple of days left over for enjoying the historic city of Santiago de Compostela. For such an adventure, the two best options are the final 100 kilometres of either the French or Portuguese way. For me, especially in high season, the Portuguese route is the better choice.

Many of those that I met on the final leg of the French way who had completed the earlier sections of that route, complained about the increased numbers of walkers and sense of commercialism that they found on this stretch. Indeed, I found that even the metal plates in the stone distance-markers that tell you how far you have still to walk before reaching Santiago had been stolen, presumably by souvenir collectors. Instead, the last stage of the Portuguese way, upon which Pins and Needles is set, remains pretty much unspoiled. You get a real taste of the *Camino*.

I've written a guide to this 'one week trip on the road less travelled' that you can have as a free download from my website, **www.declancasidy.com**. I also keep a blog there if you want to stay in touch with what I'm up to. Thanks again for reading!

- Declan

Coming soon...

Sticks and
Stones

Declan J Cassidy's sequel to
Pins and Needles

Follow the author's blog on

www.declancassidy.com

or drop us an email on
mail@screenpublications.com
to receive publication updates

A Kindle© version of *Pins and Needles*
is available online through Amazon©